HOOK, LINE, AND SINKER

Tessa Bailey

HOOK, LINE, AND SINKER

a novel

AVON

An Imprint of HarperCollinsPublishers

This is a work of fiction. Names, characters, places, and incidents are products of the author's imagination or are used fictitiously and are not to be construed as real. Any resemblance to actual events, locales, organizations, or persons, living or dead, is entirely coincidental.

FIRST EDITION

Designed by Diahann Sturge
Woman-dancing emoji © streptococcus / Adobe Stock
Other emojis throughout © Giuseppe_R; Valentina Vectors; weberjake; TMvectorart / Shutterstock

Library of Congress Cataloging-in-Publication Data has been applied for.

ISBN 978-0-06-304569-9 (paperback)
ISBN 978-0-06-321274-9 (hardcover library edition)

23 24 25 26 27 LBC 44 43 42 41 40

To the nurses and doctors of NYU Langone Health—
particularly 15 West, Tisch Building, Manhattan

Acknowledgments

I really don't know where to begin thanking people for this book! This one was delayed, writing-wise, because my husband had the absolute nerve to get sick and spend three months in the ICU. If we hadn't received a miracle and gotten him back home, I'm not sure this book would have ever gotten written, let alone any others. So I truly have modern medicine, doctors, nurses, science, friends, and faith to thank for boosting me back to this place where I can write a madly touching love story and escape back into Westport with my beloved Hannah and Fox.

Thank you to Floral Park, Long Island, for rallying around me in my time of need. I didn't know the meaning of friendship until I was huddled out in my backyard in ten-degree weather, surrounded by frozen-solid friends in masks determined to give me moral support no matter their discomfort. For *months*. They went above and beyond. I'll be forever grateful.

Thank you to the romance community, authors and readers alike, for sending me love and support and gifts meant to comfort. Thank you to my (thankfully alive!) husband for making me love so many different kinds of music (even, maybe especially, Meat Loaf), as well as fostering my appreciation for record collecting. It really helped when writing Hannah to understand how particular one can be about vinyl. I'll never set my drink on one of your sleeves—especially the Floyd. Promise.

Thank you to my editor, Nicole Fischer, for really understanding the vibe and vision of the Bellinger Sisters series and for helping to give it so much life. This marks eleven books together, and I've loved every single finished product we've worked on. Thank you to everyone at Avon Books, including cover designers, publicists, and marketing gurus. You make all this possible!

Lastly, thank you to everyone who fell in love with this series. This one was straight from the heart, and I'm honored you came with me on the journey! Here's to many more.

HOOK, LINE, AND SINKER

Prologue

September 15

HANNAH (6:00 PM): Hey. Fox?

FOX (10:20 PM): Yeah.

H (10:22 PM): It's Hannah. Bellinger? I got your number from Brendan.

F (10:22 PM): Hannah. Shit. Sorry, I would have answered sooner.

H (10:23 PM): No, it's fine. Is it weird of me to text you?

F (10:23 PM): Not weird at all, Freckles. You make it back to LA safely?

H (10:26 PM): Not a scratch on me. Missing that signature Westport fish aroma already (only half kidding). Anyway, I just wanted to say thank you for the Fleetwood Mac record you left on my sister's doorstep. You really didn't have to do that.

F (10:27 PM): No big deal. I could tell you wanted it.

H (10:29 PM): How could you tell? Was it me openly sobbing when I left it behind at the expo? 😞

F (10:30 PM): Kind of tipped me off. 😉

H (10:38 PM): Ah. Well. I wish you could hear it play in person. It's magic.

F (10:42 PM): Maybe someday.

H (10:43 PM): Maybe. Thanks again.

F (11:01 PM): You didn't have to tell me your last name. There's only one Hannah.

H (11:02 PM): Sorry, can't say the same. I know several Fox's. 🎷

October 3

FOX (4:03 PM): Hey Hannah

HANNAH (4:15 PM): Hey! What's up?

F (4:16 PM): Just pulled back into the harbor after 3 days out.

F (4:18 PM): This is stupid, but you're okay, right?

H (4:19 PM): I mean, my therapist would probably say that's debatable. Physically I'm in one piece tho. Why?

F (4:20 PM): Just a weird dream. IDK . . . I dreamed you were missing. Or lost?

H (4:25 PM): That wasn't a dream. Send a chopper.

F (4:25 PM): 😒

F (4:26 PM): Fishermen don't ignore the dreams they have on water. Sometimes they're nothing, other times they're a premonition.

H (4:30 PM): If anyone worries in this friendship, it should be me. I've seen the Perfect Storm.

F (4:32 PM): That makes me Wahlberg in this scenario?

H (4:33 PM): Depends. Can you pull off white boxer briefs?

F (4:34 PM): And then some, babe.

F (4:40 PM): So this is a friendship?

H (4:45 PM): Yeah. Are you on board?
(fishing puns, they are happening) 🎣

F (4:48 PM): I'm . . . yeah. So I can
just text you whenever?

H (4:50 PM): Yeah.

F (4:55 PM): Okay then.

H (4:56 PM): Okay then.

October 22

FOX (10:30 PM): Hey, Freckles. What are you up to?

HANNAH (10:33 PM): Hey. Not much. How
can you tell if you have a "flat" tire?

F (10:33 PM): Why what's going on??

H (10:35 PM): My car was making a weird noise, so I
pulled over. I'm going to go check if it popped.

F (10:35 PM): Hannah it's past ten o'clock at night. Stay in the car. LOCK THE DOORS and call a tow truck.

H (10:36 PM): Yeah . . . I won't know how to describe where I am to them. One of the makeup artists at work had a séance. I think I'm in Los Feliz?

F (10:37 PM): You don't know where you are?

F (10:38 PM): This is my dream. It's happening. Premonition.

H (10:39 PM): Come on. No way.

F (10:40 PM): You were just at a séance and don't get to be skeptical.

H (10:41 PM): You know what? That's fair.

F (10:42 PM): Map your location on your phone and call a tow truck.

F (10:43 PM): Please?

H (10:45 PM): Are you this protective of all your female friends?

F (10:48 PM): You're the only one I've got.

H (10:49 PM): Fine. I'm calling a tow truck.

F (10:49 PM): 🙏

November 22

HANNAH (12:36 AM): Are you awake?

FOX (12:37 AM): Wide.

H (12:38 AM): Are you alone?

F (12:38 AM): Yes, Hannah. I'm alone.

H (12:40 AM): Let's start "Leaving on a Jet Plane" at the exact same time and listen to it together.

F (12:41 AM): Hang on. I have to download it.

H (12:42 AM): You're killing me.

F (12:42 AM): Sry my phone isn't a music encyclopedia like yours. Why this song?

H (12:44 AM): IDK. I miss my sister. A little in my feelings about it. Have you seen her around town?

F (12:45 AM): I've seen her lipstick on Brendan's collar. That count?

H (12:47 AM): That's why I'm bugging you, instead of her. I don't want to burst their bliss bubble.

F (12:48 AM): You're not bugging me, Freckles. Ok ready?

H (12:48 AM): Yup. Go.

F (12:51 AM): It's crazy how much better this song is than I remember. Why am I not listening to this all the time?

H (12:52 AM): Now you can. Isn't it amazing?

F (12:53 AM): Uh-huh. Do I get to pick next?

H (12:55 AM): Oooh. Okay. Whatcha got for me, Peacock?

F (12:57 AM): Something to cheer you up. You have the Scissor Sisters in that encyclopedia phone?

H (12:58 AM): Studio albums or live? Yes to both.

F (12:59 AM): Jesus, should have known. Start "I Don't Feel Like Dancin'" in 3 . . . 2 . . . 1 . . .

January 1

FOX (12:01 AM): Happy New Year.

HANNAH (12:02 AM): Same to you!
May it bring you crabs.

F (12:03 AM): 🙁 Any resolutions?

H (12:07 AM): Normally I would say no. But I want
to take more risks this year. Put myself out there
a little more workwise, you know? Don't copy
me. You are AT CAPACITY on workplace risks.

F (12:09 AM): How else am I going to get crabs?

H (12:10 AM): At a restaurant, like a normal person.

F (12:10 AM): I always order the steak.

H (12:11 AM): That's irony for you.

February 5

FOX (9:10 AM): It's raining here. Give me
something moody to listen to.

HANNAH (9:12 AM): Hmm. The National.
Start with "Fake Empire."

F (9:14 AM): On it. Got any plans for this weekend?

H (9:17 AM): Not really. My parents are in Aspen, so I have the house to myself. I have it to myself a lot lately. I keep expecting Piper to walk around the corner in a charcoal mask.

F (9:18 AM): Women put charcoal on their faces?

H (9:20 AM): That's tame. There is such a thing as a snail facial.

F (9:21 AM): Jesus. I'm just going to pretend I never heard that.

H (9:28 AM): Do you have plans this weekend? Heading to Seattle?

F (9:35 AM): That's always a possibility.

F (9:36 AM): But it's my mother's birthday. Might just run her over some flowers and say hey.

H (9:38 AM): You're a good son. Does she ever come see you in Westport?

F (9:45 AM): No. She doesn't.

F (9:46 AM): Thanks for the music rec, Freckles. Text you later.

February 14

HANNAH (6:03 PM): Happy Valentine's Day! Doing anything special?

FOX (6:05 PM): God no. I'd rather light myself on

F (6:09 PM): Are you? Doing something special?

H (6:11 PM): Yes, sir. I'm on a date.

F (6:11 PM): With who??

H (6:15 PM): Myself. Very charming. Might be the one.

F (6:16 PM): Lock that girl down. She's the kind you bring home to mom.

F (6:20 PM): Do you want to be on a date? With someone besides yourself?

H (6:23 PM): IDK. It wouldn't suck? Unfortunately, my type would probably define this whole holiday as a commercial gimmick. Or he'd buy me dead roses to represent the evils of consumerism. 😕

F (6:26 PM): That's a pretty specific type. Are we talking about your director crush? Sergei, right?

H (6:28 PM): Yes. My sister likes to tease me about pining for starving artists.

F (6:29 PM): You like them dark and dramatic, huh?

H (6:30 PM): Careful! You're going to give me an orgasm.

F (6:30 PM): If that was the plan, babe, you'd have had two already.

F (6:33 PM): Shit, Hannah. Sorry. I shouldn't have gone there.

H (6:34 PM): No, I went there first. Blame it on the single glass of wine I've had. #lightweight 😊

F (6:40 PM): Apart from being dark and dramatic . . . what makes a man your type? What is eventually going to make a man The One?

H (6:43 PM): I think . . . if they can find a reason to laugh with me on the worst day.

F (6:44 PM): That sounds like the opposite of your type.

H (6:45 PM): It does, doesn't it? Must be the wine.

H (6:48 PM): He'll need to have a cabinet full of records and something to play them on, of course.

F (6:51 PM): Well obviously.

February 28

FOX (7:15 PM): How was your day?

HANNAH (7:17 PM): It had sort of a "Fast Car" by Tracy Chapman feeling to it.

F (7:18 PM): Like . . . nostalgic?

H (7:20 PM): Yeah. A little blue. I think I miss Westport?

F (7:20 PM): Come here.

F (7:23 PM): If you want.

H (7:25 PM): I wish! We just started casting a new movie. Not a great time.

F (7:27 PM): Have you kept your resolution? To take more risks at work?

H (7:28 PM): Not yet. I'm working up to it, tho.

H (7:29 PM): Seriously. Aaaany minute now. (crickets)

F (7:32 PM): This is where I remind you that the first time we met, you were facing off with a boat captain twice your size, ready to tear his limbs off for shouting at your sister. You're a badass. 💪

H (7:35 PM): Thanks for the reminder. I'll get there. It's just . . . imposter syndrome, I guess. Like, what makes me think I'm qualified to make movie soundtracks?

F (7:37 PM): I get imposter syndrome.

H (7:37 PM): You do?

F (7:38 PM): If you could only hear me laughing.

H (7:39 PM): I . . . wish I could. Hear you laughing.

F (7:40 PM): Yeah. Wouldn't mind hearing your laugh, either.

H (7:45 PM): How was your day, Peacock?

F (7:47 PM): Worked on the boat with Sanders, so a shit ton of Springsteen.

H (7:49 PM): Blue collar boys. Making money! Sweating in jeans! Bandanas in pockets! 😎

F (7:50 PM): It's like you were right there with us.

March 8

HANNAH (8:45 AM): Hey. I think you're out on the boat.

H (8:46 AM): Hope you're being safe.

H (9:02 AM): When you're out on the water and can't text back, I really notice it.

H (9:03 AM): The lack of you.

H (9:10 AM): So I'm glad we're friends. That's all I'm awkwardly trying to say.

H (9:18 AM): If you dream of me this time, try dreaming I can fly or turn invisible. Or that my best friend is Cher. That's way cooler than a flat tire.

H (9:19 AM): Not that I'm assuming you regularly dream of me.

H (9:26 AM): I don't dream of you that often, of course. So.

H (9:39 AM): Anyway. Talk soon!

Chapter One

Hannah Bellinger had always been more of a supporting actress than a leading lady. The hype girl. If she'd lived in Regency England, she would be the second at every duel, but never wield the pistol. That distinction was never more obvious than now, as she sat in the dark audition room watching a girl with pure leading-lady material emote like her life depended on it.

Hannah's hands disappeared into the sleeves of her sweatshirt like twin turtles ducking into their shells, her hidden fingers curling around the clipboard in her lap. Here it came. The big finale. Across the Storm Born production studio, their lead actor ran through a scene with their final actress hopeful of the day. Since eight A.M., the studio had been a revolving door of wide-eyed ingénues, and didn't it figure that not a single one of them would click with Christian until Hannah was past the point of starving, her mouth tasting like stale coffee?

Such was the life of a production assistant.

"You forgot to trust me," the redhead whispered brokenly, tears creating trails of mascara down her cheeks. Dang, this girl was fire. Even Sergei, the writer and director of the project, was held in a rare thrall, the tip of his glasses inserted between his full, dreamy lips, that ankle crossed over the opposite knee, jiggling, jiggling. That was his *I'm impressed* posture. After two years of working as his production assistant—and nursing a long-unrequited crush on the man—Hannah knew all his tells. And this redhead could bet the rent on getting cast in *Glory Daze.*

Sergei turned to Hannah where she huddled in the corner of the freezing conference room and raised an excited black eyebrow. The shared moment of triumph was so unexpected, the clipboard slid off her lap and clattered to the ground. Flustered, she reached for it but didn't want to lose the moment with the director, so she jackknifed and gave Sergei a thumbs-up. Only to remember her thumb was trapped inside the sleeve of her sweatshirt, creating a weird, starfish-looking gesture that he missed, anyway, because he'd turned back around.

You absolute turnip, you.

Hannah replaced the clipboard in her lap and pretended to write Very Serious notes. Thank God it was dark in the rear of the studio. No one could see the tomato-colored tidal wave surging up her neck.

"End scene!" Sergei crowed, standing up from the table of producers that faced the audition area to deliver a slow clap. "Extraordinary. Simply extraordinary."

The redhead, Maxine, beamed while simultaneously trying to wipe away her dripping mascara with the hem of her black T-shirt. "Oh wow. Thank you."

"That felt fine." Christian sighed, signaling Hannah for his cold brew.

I have been summoned.

She rose from her chair and set the clipboard down, retrieving the actor's beverage from inside the mini-fridge along the wall and bringing it to him. When she held out the metal travel tumbler and he made no move to take it, she gritted her teeth and held the straw to his lips. When he had the nerve to look her in the eye while sucking noisily, she stared back stone-faced.

This is what you wanted.

A regular job that would allow her to earn money—and not rely on the many millions her stepfather had in the bank. If she dropped her last name, slurpy ol' Christian would spit out his cold brew. But apart from Sergei, no one knew that Hannah was the legendary producer's daughter, and that's how she chose to keep it.

Stepdaughter, she mentally corrected herself.

A distinction she never would have bothered to make before last summer.

Had that trip to Westport six months ago really happened? The weeks she'd lived above the Pacific Northwest bar, restoring it lovingly with her sister in tribute to their birth father, seemed like a hazy dream. One she couldn't seem to shake. It rode her consciousness like dolphins outlined in a barrel wave, making her wistful at the oddest times. Like now, when Christian was bugging his heartthrob eyes out, letting her know he was ready for straw removal.

"Thanks," he huffed. "Now I'm going to have to pee."

"Look at the bright side," Hannah murmured, so as not to interrupt an effusive Sergei. "There are mirrors in the bathroom. Your favorite."

Christian snorted, allowing a grudging uptick to one side of his mouth. "God, you're such a bitch. I love you."

". . . is what you say into the mirrors?"

They traded a lip-twitching glare.

"I think I speak for the production team when I say we've found our Lark," Sergei said, coming around the table to kiss both cheeks of the bouncing actress. "Are you available to begin shooting in late March?" Without waiting for the girl to answer, Sergei pressed a row of knuckles to his forehead. "I am seeing an entirely different location for the shoot now. The energy Christian and Maxine create together does not work against the backdrop of Los Angeles. I'm certain. It's so earthy. So original. They sanded the edges off each other. We need a softer location. The sharp corners of LA will only snag them, hold them back."

Hannah stilled, watched the table of producers trade nervous glances. The artistic temperament was real—and Sergei's tended to be more volatile than most. He'd once made the entire crew wear blindfolds on set so they wouldn't dilute the magic of a scene by viewing it. *Every set of eyes strips another layer of mystery!* But that temperament was one of the main reasons Hannah gravitated toward the director. He operated on chaos, bowing to the whims of creativity. He believed his choices and didn't have time for naysayers.

Real leading-man material.

What was that like? To be the star in the movie of your life?

Hannah had been playing second fiddle so long, she was getting arthritis in her fingers. Her sister, Piper, had demanded the spotlight since childhood, and Hannah was always comfortable waiting in the wings, anticipating her cue to walk on as best supporting actress, even providing bail money on more than one occasion. That was where she shined. Bolstering the heroine at her lowest point, stepping in to defend the leading lady when necessary, saying the right thing in a pivotal heart-to-heart.

Supporting actresses didn't want or need the glory. They were content to prop up the main character and be instrumental in their mission. And Hannah was content in that role, too. Wasn't she?

A memory trickled in without her consent.

A memory that made her jumpy for some reason.

That one afternoon six months ago at a vinyl convention in Seattle when she'd felt like the main character. Browsing through records with Fox Thornton, king crab fisherman and a lady-killer of the highest caliber. When they'd stood shoulder to shoulder and shared a pair of AirPods, listening to "Silver Springs," the world just kind of fading out around them.

Just an anomaly.

Just a fluke.

Restless, probably because of the nine cups of black coffee she'd drunk throughout the day, Hannah returned Christian's cold brew to the fridge and waited on the periphery to see what kind of curveball Sergei was about to throw the team. Honestly, she loved his left turns, even if no one else did. The tempest of his imagination could not be stopped. It was enviable. It was hot.

This guy was her type.

She just wasn't his, if the last two years were any indication.

"What do you mean you no longer see Los Angeles as the backdrop?" one of the producers asked. "We already have the permits."

"Am I the only one who saw the rain falling in this scene? The quiet melancholia unfolding around them?" Who didn't want to date a man who dropped that kind of terminology without batting an eyelash? "We cannot pit the raw volume of Los Angeles against them. It'll drown them out. We need to let the nuance thrive. We need to give it oxygen and space and sunlight."

"You just said you wanted to give it rain," the producer pointed out drily.

Sergei laughed in that way artists do when someone is too dense to grasp their vision. "A plant needs sunlight *and* water to grow, does it not?" His frustration was causing his normally light Russian accent to thicken. "We need a more subtle location for the shoot. A place that will lend focus to the actors."

Latrice, the new location scout, raised her hand slowly. "Like . . . Toluca Lake?"

"No! Outside of Los Angeles. Picture—"

"I know a place." Hannah said it without thinking. Her mouth was moving, and then the words were hanging in the air like a comic-strip quote bubble, too late to pop. Everyone turned to look at her at once. A very un–supporting actress position to be in, even if it was refreshing to have Sergei's eyes on her longer than the usual fleeting handful of seconds. It reminded Hannah, rather inconveniently, of the way someone else gave her his undivided attention, sometimes picking up on her moods simply via text message.

So she blurted the next part in an attempt to block out that useless thought. "Last summer, I spent some time in Washington. A small fishing town called Westport." She was only suggesting this for two reasons. One, she wanted to support Sergei's idea and possibly earn herself one of those fleeting smiles. And two, what if she could sneak a trip to see her sister in the name of work? Counting their brief visit at Christmas, she'd only seen Piper and her fiancé, Brendan, once in six months. Missing them was a constant ache in her stomach.

"Fishing village," Sergei mused, rubbing his chin and starting to pace, mentally rewriting the screenplay. "Tell me more about it."

"Well." Hannah unwrapped her hands from inside her sleeves. One did not pitch a genius director, a location scout, and a panel of producers with her fists balled in a UCLA sweatshirt. Already she was cursing her decision to pile her straw-colored hair into a baseball cap this morning. *Let us not add to the kid-sister vibe.* "It's moody and misty, set right on the water. Most residents have lived there since they were born, and they're very, um"—*set in their ways, unwelcoming, wonderful, protective*—"routine-oriented. Fishing is their livelihood, and I guess you could say there's an element of melancholy there. For the fishermen who've been lost."

Like her father, Henry Cross.

Hannah had to push past the lump in her throat to continue. "It's quaint. Has kind of a weathered feel. It's like"—she closed her eyes and searched through her mental catalogue of music—"you know that band Skinny Lister that does kind of a modern take on sea shanties?"

They stared back at her blankly.

"Never mind. You know what sea shanties sound like, don't you? Imagine a packed bar full of courageous men who fear and respect the sea. Imagine them singing odes to the water. The ocean is their mother. Their lover. She provides for them. And everything in this town reflects that love of the sea. The salt mist in the air. The scent of brine and storm clouds. The knowledge in the eyes of the residents when they look up at the sky to judge the oncoming weather. In fear. In reverence. Everywhere you go there's the sound of lapping water against the docks, cawing seagulls, the hum of danger . . ." Hannah trailed off when she realized Christian was staring at her like she'd swapped his cold brew for kitty litter.

"Anyway, that's Westport," she finished. "That's how it feels."

Sergei said nothing for long moments, and she forced herself not to fidget in the rare glow of his attention. "That's the place. That's where we need to go."

The producers were shooting flamethrowers at Hannah from their eyes. "We don't have it in the budget, Sergei. We'll have to apply for new permits. Travel expenses for an entire cast and crew. Lodging."

Latrice tapped her clipboard, seeming kind of eager for the challenge. "We could drive. It's a trek, but not out of the question . . . and skipping the plane would save on funds."

"Let me worry about the money," Sergei said, waving a hand. "I'll crowdsource. Put my own cash toward it. Whatever is necessary. Hannah and Latrice, you'll work out the permits and travel details?"

"Of course," she said, agreeing to a slew of sleepless nights.

Latrice nodded, shooting Hannah a wink.

More flamethrowers from the men who'd been silly enough to think they were in charge. "We haven't even scouted locations—"

"Hannah will take care of it. She obviously knows this place like the back of her hand. Did you hear that description?" Sergei gave her a once-over, as if seeing her for the first time, and her toes curled inside her red Converse. "Impressive."

Don't blush.

Too late.

She was a cherry tomato.

"Thank you." Sergei nodded and started collecting his things, draping a worn leather satchel over his slim shoulder, messing up his dark boyish locks in the process. "We'll be in touch," he called to Maxine, sailing out of the studio.

And that, as they say in the business, was a wrap.

Hannah escaped the collective glare of the producers and jogged from the room, already drawing the phone from her back pocket to call Piper. She ducked into the ladies' lounge for privacy, but before she could hit the call button, Latrice popped her head in through the door.

"Hey," she said, sticking a thumbs-up through the opening. "Good job in there. I've been dying to stretch my legs a little. Between us, we've got this."

Thank God they'd hired Latrice to take location-scout duties off Hannah's plate. She was a dynamo. "We've so got this. I'm starting an email to you as soon as I make this call."

"You better."

Latrice dipped out again, and, bolstered by the vote of confidence, Hannah dialed Piper. Her sister answered on the third ring sounding out of breath.

Followed by the very distinct groan of bedsprings.

"I don't even want to know what you were doing," Hannah drawled. "But say hi to Brendan for me."

"Hannah says hi," Piper purred to her sea captain fiancé, who'd obviously just rung her bell, which was a constant event in their household. A fact Hannah unfortunately knew all too well after living with them for a couple of weeks over the summer. "What's up, sis?"

Hannah hopped up onto the counter beside the end sink. "Is your guest room free?"

A rustle of sheets in the background. "Why? Oh my God. Why?" Hannah could almost see the wild flutter of her sister's hands in the vicinity of her throat. "Are you coming here? When?"

"Soon." Then she qualified: "If we can get permits to film."

A beat passed. "Permits to film in Westport?"

"Pretty sure I just convinced Sergei it's the only place on earth that will work for his vision." Hannah sniffed. "My powers of persuasion often go unrecognized."

"Like hell a film crew is coming here," Brendan said in the background.

Hannah's chest squeezed at the familiarity of her sister's ebullient nature set alongside her fiancé's growly, no-bullshit personality. She missed them so much.

"Tell the captain it will only be for a couple of weeks. I'll make sure to scrub the Hollywood stink off every precious cobblestone before we leave."

"Let me worry about him," Piper said playfully. "He's forgetting what a good mood I'll be in having my sister in town. And of course you can stay here, Hanns. Of course. Just . . . I hope you're not planning for *this* month? Brendan's parents are coming to visit soon. They'll be using the guest room."

"Ooh." Hannah winced. "If we get a fast enough turnaround on the permits, it could be late March. Sergei is on a mission." Hannah turned on the counter to check her reflection, wincing at the hair sticking out of the sides of her ball cap. "But don't stress, I can just stay wherever they put up the crew. Getting to see you will be more than enough."

"Can't you stall Sergei? Maybe tell him Westport is extra moody in April?"

"How did you know he was going for a moody vibe?"

"His last film was called *Fragmented Joy*, wasn't it?"

"Valid point." Hannah laughed, pressing the phone tighter to her ear, trying to feel her sister's warmth over the phone. "Seriously, though. Don't worry about the guest-room thing. It's no big—"

"You know, there is one poss . . ." Piper trailed off. "Never mind."

Hannah's head tilted at her sister's hasty retreat. "What?"

"No, really. It was a bad idea."

"Then tell me. I want to pooh-pooh it, too."

Piper humphed. "I was going to say that Fox has that empty bedroom at his place. And as you know, he's out on the boat with Brendan for long stretches. But, like, he's also home for stretches, which is why it's a bad idea. Forget I said it."

Stupid, really. The way Hannah sprang off the counter at the mention of the devilish charmer's name and started shoving pieces of her hair back under the brim of her hat. "It's not a bad idea," she said, automatically defending Fox, even though they hadn't seen each other in six months.

There had only been the daily texts.

That she definitely wouldn't be mentioning to Piper.

"We're friendly." *Lower your voice.* "We're friends."

"I know that, Hanns," Piper said indulgently.

"And you know"—she dropped her volume even more—"I still have that thing for a certain someone." Why Hannah suddenly felt the need to prove to Piper—and possibly herself—that she was, indeed, only friends with a man who went through women like nickels in a slot machine, she had no idea. But there it was. "Staying with Fox isn't a terrible idea. Like you said, he'll only be there half the time. I'll be able to keep food in the fridge, which I won't in a hotel room. It will slice a little off the production's expenditures and earn me points with Sergei."

"Speaking of Sergei, are you finally going to ask him?"

Hannah took a deep breath, glancing toward the door of the bathroom. "Yeah, I think this might be my moment, since I just proved my worth in there. There is already a music coordinator on the payroll, but I'm going to ask to assist. It's a step in the right direction, at least, right?"

"Damn right," Piper said, clapping at the rate of a hummingbird's wings in the background. "You got this, bish."

Maybe.

Maybe not.

Hannah cleared her throat. "Will you talk to Fox for me about using the guest room? He might feel pressured if I ask him directly. It's just to put the idea out there, in case it's March for sure and the guest room will be taken."

Piper hesitated briefly. "Okay, Hanns. Love you."

"Love you, too. Hugs to the mean one."

Hannah hung up the phone on a giggle from Piper and tapped the device against her mouth. Why was her pulse racing? Surely not because there was a possibility she could occupy a room in Fox's apartment. There might have been an inescapable attraction toward the relief skipper the first time they met, but after his phone pinged for the thousandth time with blatant booty calls, it became woefully obvious that his incredible looks were used to his advantage with the opposite sex.

Fox Thornton has not her type. He was bad boyfriend material. But he *was* her friend.

Her thumb hovered over the screen of her phone momentarily before tapping on their text thread, reading the one he'd sent last night just before she drifted off to sleep.

FOX (11:32 PM): Today was a Hozier vibe for me.

HANNAH (11:33 PM): My day was so very Amy Winehouse.

There was nothing friendlier than sharing what kind of music defined their day. It didn't matter how much she looked forward to those nightly texts. Staying with Fox imposed no risk whatsoever. It was possible to be just friends with a man who exuded sex—and she would have no problem proving it.

Satisfied with her logic, Hannah got on the phone and started organizing.

Chapter Two

$\mathcal{F}$ox settled back into his couch cushions and tipped a beer to his lips, taking a long sip to disguise the urge to laugh at the serious expression of the man sitting across from him. "What is this, Cap? An intervention?"

It wasn't that he'd never seen Brendan looking disgruntled before. God knows he had. Fox just hadn't seen the *Della Ray*'s captain anything but blissful for the last six months since meeting his fiancée, Piper. It was almost enough to make a man want to reevaluate his position on relationships.

Yeah. Right.

"No, it's not an intervention," Brendan said, adjusting the beanie on his head. Then taking it off altogether and resting it on his knee. "But if you keep putting off the conversation about taking over as captain, I might have to stage one."

This marked the eighth time Brendan had asked him to step up and lead the crew. At first, he'd been nothing short of baffled. Had he given the impression he could be responsible for the lives of five men? If so, it must have been an accident. He was content to take orders, do his job well, and skedaddle with his cut of the haul, whether his earnings came from crabs in the fall or fishing the rest of the year.

Thriving under pressure was in a king crab fisherman's blood. He'd stood beside Brendan on the *Della Ray* and stared death in the eye. More than once. But battling nature wasn't the same as taking charge of a crew. Making decisions. Owning up to the mistakes he would inevitably make. That was a different kind of pressure entirely—and he wasn't sure he was built for that. More specifically, he wasn't sure the crew *believed* he was built to lead them. Speaking from a lot of experience, a fishing vessel's team needed to have total trust in their captain. Any hesitation could cost a man his life. Those assholes barely took him seriously as a human being, let alone as the one giving orders.

Yeah. All he needed was a place to sleep and watch baseball, a couple of beers at the end of a hard day, and a willing, lush body in the dark.

Although the need for that last one hadn't been all that pressing lately.

Hadn't been pressing at all, really.

Fox popped his jaw and focused. "An intervention won't be necessary." He shrugged. "Told you, I'm honored you'd think of me, man. But I'm not interested." He wedged the beer bottle between his thighs and reached down to stroke the braided leather wrapped around his wrist. "I'm happy to relieve you when you're belowdecks, but I'm not looking for permanent."

"Yeah." Brendan eyed Fox's barren apartment pointedly. "No kidding."

That was fair enough. Anyone who walked into the two-bedroom overlooking Grays Harbor would assume Fox was in the process of moving in, when in reality he'd just passed his six-year anniversary in the place.

At thirty-one, he was back in Westport, with no plans to leave. Once upon a time, he'd purposely attended college in Minnesota, but that didn't turn out so well. Served him right for thinking this place wouldn't suck him back in. It always did eventually. Leaving the first time had cost him most of the ingenuity he possessed, and now? He channeled what was left into fishing.

And women. Or he used to, anyway.

"Have you considered asking Sanders?" Fox forced himself to stop messing with his bracelet. "He could use the extra cut with the baby on the way."

"He belongs on deck. Your place is in the wheelhouse— that's a gut feeling." Brendan didn't blink. "The second boat is almost finished. I'll be forming a new crew, expanding. I want to leave the *Della Ray* in good hands. Hands I trust."

"Jesus, you don't let up," Fox said on a laugh, pushing to his feet and crossing to the fridge for another beer, even though he'd only drunk half of the first. Just for something to do with his hands. "Part of me is almost enjoying this. Not every day I get to tell the captain no."

Brendan grunted. "I'm going to wear you down, you stubborn bastard."

Fox gave him a tight smile over his shoulder. "You won't. And you're one to call someone stubborn, dude who wore his wedding ring seven extra years."

"Well," Brendan rumbled. "I found a good reason to take it off."

There he went, looking blissful again.

Fox chuckled, uncapped his second beer with his teeth, and spat the cap into the sink. "Speaking of your reason for ending your self-imposed celibacy, shouldn't you be home having dinner with her?"

"She's keeping my spaghetti warm for me." Brendan shifted in his seat, pinned him with a laser look that was famous among the crew. It translated to *Sit down and shut the hell up.* "I had another reason for coming over here to talk."

"Do you need advice on women again? Because you're way out of my depth now. If you're here to ask me what your fiancée wants, ask me to recite the periodic table, instead. There's a better chance of me getting that right."

"I don't need advice." Brendan looked at him hard. Closely. On the hunt for bullshit. "Hannah is coming to town."

Fox's throat closed up. He was halfway to sitting down when Brendan said those five words, so he twisted at the last second, staying half turned, stuffing an unnecessary pillow behind his back so he wouldn't have to look his oldest friend in the eye. And, God, how absolutely pitiful was that? "Oh yeah? What for?"

Brendan sighed. Crossed his arms. "You know she's still working for that production company. Somehow she convinced them Westport would be a good place to film."

Fox's laughter cracked in the sparse living room. "You must be thrilled."

The captain was the unofficial mayor of Westport. He was notoriously a man of few words, but when he gave his opinion on something, everyone damn well listened. In some towns, football stars were revered. In this place, it was the fishermen—and that went double for the man behind the wheel. "I don't care what they do as long as they stay out of my hair."

"People from LA staying out of your hair," Fox mused, forcing himself to delay the conversation about Hannah. Like some kind of weird, self-inflicted punishment. "How did that work out last time?"

"That's different. It was Piper." *Well, I'll be damned.* The tips of the man's ears were red. "Anyway, my parents will be here visiting while this whole filming business is going on. That's why Hannah can't use our guest room."

He feigned annoyance. "So you offered mine."

It was hard to tell if Brendan was buying his act. "Piper had kind of nixed the idea, but Hannah seemed interested."

Fox's thumbnail dug into the beer label and ripped a clean strip down the side. "Really. Hannah wants to stay here?" Why were his palms turning damp? "How long are they going to be filming? How long would she stay?"

"Two weeks or so. Figured she'd have the place to herself half the time, when we're out on the boat."

"Right."

But the other half of the time, they would be there together.

How the hell was Fox supposed to feel about that?

More importantly—and this was a question he asked himself way too often—how the hell was he supposed to feel about Hannah? He'd never, not once, had a girl for a friend. Last summer, Hannah and her sister had crash-landed in Westport, two rich girls from LA who'd been stripped of their allowances by Daddy. Fox had only been trying to help Brendan nurse his crush on Piper by distracting the younger sibling with a walk to the record store.

Then they'd gone to the vinyl convention together. Spent the last six months texting each other about everything under the sun . . . and she'd had the nerve to crawl up under his skin in a way that made absolutely no sense to him.

Sex was a non-possibility between them.

That had been established early on, for a host of reasons.

Number one being that he didn't fish local waters.

If he needed the company of a woman—and he should really get back to doing that kind of thing sometime—he went to Seattle. No chance of accidentally sleeping with someone's sister or wife or cousin's cousin, and he could wash his hands of the whole encounter afterward. Return to Westport with no chance of bumping into a hookup. Easy. No muss, no fuss.

The second reason he couldn't sleep with Hannah was the very man sitting in his living room. Fox was read the riot act last summer. It was seared into his memory. Sleeping with Piper's little sister would spell disaster, because if she got attached, Fox would undoubtedly hurt her feelings. And that would make his captain and best friend's life hell, because the Bellinger sisters stuck together.

But Fox had a third, and most important, reason for keeping his hands off Hannah. She was his friend. She was a woman who genuinely liked him for something other than his dick. And it made him feel terrifyingly good to be around her. To talk to her.

They had fun. Made each other laugh.

The way she translated song lyrics out loud made him think. In the six months that she'd been gone, he'd noticed the sunrise more. He'd started paying attention to strangers, their actions. Listening to music. Even his job seemed to have more gravity to it. Hannah did that somehow. Made him look around and consider.

Brendan was staring at him, brows drawn. Uncomfortable.

"Of course Hannah can stay here. But are you sure it's a good idea?" His stomach drew in on itself. "People might notice she's staying here. With me."

The captain hedged. "I think certain speculation might be par for the course. As long as what folks are speculating on isn't really happening."

"Say it plainly." Fox made an impatient sound, growing increasingly aware of what was coming. "Tell me not to fuck her."

The captain rubbed the center of his forehead. "Look, I hate having to say this to you more than once. Feels like overkill and . . . Jesus, your sex life is your own business, but it could be different with her staying here. Close quarters and all that."

Fox refused to make the conversation easy for his friend. And he suspected Brendan had known that coming here. They were men who regularly took responsibility for each other's lives. They didn't lecture each other. It *was* overkill. Maybe that was why the conversation hit below the belt this time, when before it felt more like a minor slap.

When the silence extended without Fox saying anything, Brendan sighed. "She's my future sister-in-law. She's not temporary in any way, okay? Hands off." He made a decisive gesture. "That's the last time I'll bring it up."

"Are you sure? I can pencil you in for tomorrow—"

"Don't be a jackass." They both visibly shook off their irritation, adjusting shirt collars and pretending to be interested in the television. "We probably didn't even need to have this conversation, considering she's still got a crush on this director guy. Sergei." Brendan tapped his knee. "Am I supposed to do something about that situation, too? Go threaten to break his jaw if he takes advantage of Hannah?"

"No. Christ, it's not the guy's fault she likes him." Fox said the words in a burst to relieve the pressing weight on his chest. He'd known about this crush of Hannah's since summer and she'd still been pining for him in February, so it had probably been stupid of him to hope the infatuation had run its course. It wasn't his favorite subject to discuss. On account of any mention of the director making him want to kick a hole through his drywall. "You're going to be busy with your parents while Hannah is here. I'll keep an eye on it, if you want. This thing with the director."

Why on God's green earth did he offer to do that?

Not a damn clue.

But he'd be lying if Brendan's immediate gratitude didn't ease the sting of their prior conversation. Fox might be a man-whore, but he could be trusted to protect someone's back. He'd made a career out of it. "Yeah?"

Fox jerked a shoulder, took a sip of his beer. "Sure. If I think something is developing there, I'll . . ." Sabotage came to mind. "Make sure she's safe." He didn't even want to explore why those words spread like warm honey on his agitated nerve endings. Protecting Hannah. What a responsibility that would be. "Not that she isn't capable of that herself," he added quickly.

"Right, sure," Brendan said. Also quickly. "Even so . . ."

"Uh-huh. Watch him like a hawk."

Brendan filled up his barrel chest and let out a gusting exhale, slapping the arm of his chair. "Well. Thank God this is over."

Fox pointed his beer straight ahead. "Door's that way."

The captain grunted and took his leave. Fox didn't even pretend to be interested in his beer after that. Instead, he got up and crossed the room, stopping in front of the cabinet he'd picked up at a rummage sale. Buying furniture went against his grain, but he'd needed somewhere to store the vinyl records he'd started collecting. He'd bought his first on their trip to Seattle. The Rolling Stones. *Exile on Main St.* Even Hannah had approved when he'd picked it out at the record convention.

Anyway, the damn thing had started looking lonely, just sitting there all by itself, so he'd walked over to Disc N Dat and purchased a few more. Hendrix, Bowie, the Cranberries. Classics. The stack had grown so much, it felt almost accusatory in its silence, so—after trying to talk himself out of it for a couple of weeks—he'd ordered a record player.

Fox reached back behind the cabinet where he kept the key, sliding it out of the leather pouch. He unlocked the door and looked at the vertical rainbow of albums, only hesitating for a second before pulling out Madness. Dropping the needle on "Our House." After listening to it all the way through, he pulled out his phone and started the song again, recording an audio clip and firing it Hannah's way.

A few minutes later, she sent him back a clip of the *Golden Girls* theme song.

Through music, they'd just acknowledged she'd be staying in his guest room—and this was how it had been since she left. Fox waiting for the messages to stop, holding his breath at the end of every day, only releasing it when the text came.

Swallowing, he turned and looked at the guest room. Hannah was in LA. This was a friendship based on something more . . . pure than he was accustomed to. And it was safe. Texting was safe. A way of offering more to someone without giving up everything.

Would he be able to keep that up with her living in the same apartment?

Chapter Three

For two weeks, Hannah and Latrice had worked overtime to make the location swap from LA to Westport happen in the name of artistic vision. Westport business owners had been finessed, the chamber of commerce fluffed. Permits sealed and housing nailed down. Now they were T-minus ten minutes until the chartered bus reached the small Washington fishing village.

If Hannah was going to make professional strides during the filming of *Glory Daze*, it was now or never. She finally had to woman up and ask Sergei for the opportunity, because as soon as the bus pulled to a stop, he'd hit the ground running and she'd miss her chance.

Stalling shamefully, Hannah sunk down in the pleather seat and scrubbed her hands over her face. She yanked out her AirPods, cutting off Dylan's greatest hits, and shoved the devices into her pockets. Reaching up, she removed her ball cap, running nervous fingers through her hair several times, struggling to see her reflection in the window. Her movements stilled when she realized the impromptu primp session wasn't working. She still looked like a PA. The lowest woman on the food chain.

Definitely not someone Sergei would trust with an entire film soundtrack.

She flopped back in the seat, knee jiggling, and let the raucous sounds of the bus drown out her sigh. Over the top of the seat in front of her, she watched Sergei and Brinley, the music co-ordinator, lean their heads together to converse and then break apart laughing.

Now, Brinley?

She was leading-lady material. A tailored, tasteful, bobbed-brunette transplant from New York who had a different statement necklace for every outfit. A woman who walked into a room and got the job she applied for, because she dressed for it. Because she exuded confidence and expected her due.

And Brinley had Hannah's dream job.

Two years ago, Hannah had purposefully asked her stepfather to find her a low-level position at a production company, and he'd tapped Sergei at Storm Born. At Hannah's request, her step-father had asked his casual acquaintance to be discreet about their connection, so she could be just Hannah, as opposed to famed producer Daniel Bellinger's stepkid. She had a bachelor's in music history from UCLA, but she knew nothing about film. If she'd leaned harder on her stepfather's name, she probably could have landed a producer position, but where was the fair-ness in that when she didn't know the industry? It had been a choice to learn from the sidelines.

And she had. Being in charge of boatloads of paperwork and record keeping meant she'd had a lot of opportunities to study Brinley's cue sheets, synchronization contracts, and notes. No one technically knew she'd taken a quiet interest in that side of the production company. Hannah still lacked hands-on training, but two years later, she was ready to move up the ranks.

She observed Sergei and Brinley with a hole in her stomach. They were behind-the-scenes talent, but approaching them was just like walking up to the lead actors. Still, she was growing weary of holding Christian's straw and getting slurped on.

A salt-air breeze filtered in through the cracked bus window. While it jolted her with nostalgia, kissing her skin with welcome wherever it touched, it also told Hannah they were really close to Westport. If she wanted to make the slightest step toward progress, she needed to act now.

Hannah rolled her shoulders back and shoved the baseball cap into her tote bag, ignoring the curious looks from cast and crew as she picked her way up to the front of the bus. Her pulse ticked in the base of her neck, moisture fleeing from her mouth. When she drew even with Sergei and Brinley, they smiled expectantly. Kindly. As in, *Kindly explain why you're interrupting our conversation.*

Not for the first time, she wondered if Brinley and Sergei were secretly seeing each other, but the gap of pleather seat between them—and the rock on Brinley's finger from someone else—spoke to them being just friends.

Fact was, the two of them had to work closely. Coordinating music for movies was an intricate process, the score often crafted in postproduction. But Storm Born had their own way of compiling the track list that would play beneath the dialogue or during montages. They created it *while* the filming process took place, relying heavily on the mood of the moment (read:

Sergei's whims). And they tended to use music that already existed and trimmed it down accordingly, rather than creating music to fit the film.

Hannah couldn't dream of anything better than summing up a distinct moment with the right song. To help weave together the atmosphere. Music was the backbone of movies. Of everything. One line from a song could help Hannah define her own feelings, and the opportunity to put that passion to art was something she spent every day wanting.

Ask them. The bus is almost there.

"Um . . ."

Oh, good opener. A filler word.

Hannah dug deep for the girl who'd been brave enough to pitch Westport to a room full of producers and talent. She was starting to think her nostalgia for this place had spoken on her behalf. "Brinley. Sergei," Hannah said, making herself look them both in the eyes. "I was wondering if—"

Of course the bus chose that moment to stop.

And of course Hannah was too busy adjusting her clothing and twisting her rings and generally fidgeting to catch hold of anything that might prevent her from sprawling sideways down the center of the row. She landed hard on her shoulder and hip, her temple connecting with the floor. A truly humiliating *oof* launched from her mouth, followed by the most deafening silence that had ever occurred on planet Earth.

No one moved. Hannah debated the merits of crawling under one of the seats until the world had the decency to end, but thoughts of hiding vanished when Sergei hopped across Brinley and stepped over Hannah's legs, bending down to help her back to her feet.

"Hannah!" His eyes ran over her, top to bottom. "Are you okay?" Without waiting for an answer, Sergei directed an angry look toward the front of the bus where the driver sat watching them, unfazed. "Hey, man. How about making sure everyone is seated before hitting the brakes?"

Hannah didn't have a chance to rightfully claim the blame, because Sergei was already ushering her off the bus while everyone stared openmouthed at the PA with the growing knot on her head. Yup, she could already feel it forming. Good God. She'd finally mustered up the courage to ask if she could observe the soundtrack process. Now she might as well just quit and start looking for positions as a sandwich-board operator.

Although, there were worse consequences to stupidity than having the dreamy director's arm around her shoulders, helping her off the bus. This close, she could smell his aftershave, kind of an orangey clove scent. It was just like Sergei to pick something unique and unexpected. She looked up into his expressive face, at the black hair that met in the middle of his head in a subtle faux-hawk. His goatee was engineered to perfection.

If she wasn't careful, she'd read too much into his concern. She'd start to wonder if maybe Sergei could learn to love an accident-prone supporting actress instead of a leading lady, after all?

Realizing she was staring, Hannah tore her wistful eyes off the man she'd been crushing on for two years—and saw Fox crossing the parking lot in their direction, his striking face a mask of alarm. "Hannah?"

Her mind made a scratchy humming sound, like the one a record makes in between songs. Probably because she'd communicated with this man every day for six—no, nearly seven—months now but never heard his voice. Perhaps because his identity had been whittled down to words on a screen, she'd forgotten that he commanded attention like a grand finale of fireworks in the night sky.

Without turning around, she knew every straight woman had her face pressed up against the windows of the bus, watching the maestro of feminine wetness cross the road, his dark blond hair blowing around in the wind, the lower half of his face covered in unruly, unshaped stubble, darker than the hair on his head.

With that pretty-boy face, he really should have been soft. Used to getting his way. Maybe, possibly even short. *God, if you're listening?* But instead he looked like a troublemaker angel that got booted out of heaven, all tall and well-built and resilient and capable-looking. On top of everything else, he had to have the most dangerous job in the United States, the knowledge of fear and nature and consequences in his sea-blue eyes.

The relief of seeing Fox practically bowled her over, and she started to call out a greeting, until she realized the fisherman's gravitational-pull eyes were homing in on Sergei, setting off a tectonic shift of plates in his cheeks.

"What happened to her?" Fox barked, bringing everything back to regular speed. Wait. When did her surroundings go into slow motion to begin with?

"I just fell on the bus," Hannah explained, prodding her bumped head and wincing. Great, she'd split her skin slightly as well. "I'm fine."

"Come on," Fox said, still bird-dogging Sergei. "I'll patch you up."

She was about to raise a skeptical brow and ask to see his medical degree, but then she remembered a story Piper had told her. Fox had once given Brendan makeshift stitches for a bleeding forehead wound. All while keeping his balance during a hurricane.

Such was the life of a king crab fisherman.

Couldn't he just be super short? Was that so much to ask?

"I'm fine," she said, patting Sergei's arm, letting him know she was okay to stand on her own. "Unless you have a cure for pride in your first-aid kit?"

Fox licked the seam of his lips, brows still drawn, and his attention slid back toward the director. "We'll take a closer look when we get home. You have a bag I can carry or something?"

"I . . ." Sergei started, looking at Hannah as if there was something new about her and he wanted to figure out what it was. "I didn't realize you were . . . so close to anyone in town."

Close? To Fox? Seven months ago, she would have thought that a stretch. Now? It wasn't exactly a lie. Lately, she'd been talking to him more often than Piper. "Well—"

Fox cut her off. "We should get that bump looked at, Freckles."

"Freckles," Sergei echoed, checking her nose for spots.

Was something afoot here?

Both men were inching toward her subtly, like she was the last slice of pizza.

"Um. My bag is in the luggage compartment of the bus."

"I'll get it," they said at the same time.

Was her head wound releasing some kind of alpha pheromone?

Fox and Sergei sized each other up, clearly ready to argue about who was going to get her bag. The way her day was going, it would probably ensue in a tug-of-war, the zipper would break, and her underpants would rain down like confetti. "I'll grab it," Hannah said, before either one of them could speak, hotfooting it away from the masculinity maelstrom before it affected her brain.

She turned for the bus just as Brinley glided down the stairs, giving Fox a curious look that Hannah was amazed to see, thanks to the window's reflection, he didn't return. Those sea-blues were fastened on her bump, instead. Probably trying to decide which needle to use to mutilate her.

"Sergei," Brinley called, twisting her earring. "Is everything okay?"

"Yes, totally fine," Hannah answered, beelining for the luggage compartment and attempting to open it. Everyone watched as she jerked on the handle, laughed, yanked more forcefully. Laughed again, then slammed her hip into it. No luck.

Before she could try a third time, Fox reached past her and opened it with a flick of his tan wrist. "You're having a shit day, aren't you?" he said for her ears alone.

She exhaled. "Yeah."

He made a humming sound, tilted his head sympathetically. "Tell me which bag is yours and I'll bring you back to my place." Gently, he tugged on a strand of her hair. "Make it all better."

It was totally possible she'd hit her head and ended up in an erotic sex dream with Fox Thornton. It wouldn't be the first time—not that she would admit to that in a court of law. Or even to her sister. There was simply no way to combat the subtle transmissions he gave off that screamed, *I'm good at sex.*

Like, really, really good. She was powerless against it. Thing was, that went for every other woman he came into contact with, too. And she had no interest in being one of thousands. That's why they were friends. Hadn't that been established? Why was he hitting on her?

"How . . . ? What do you mean by that? That you'll make my day better. How are you going to do that?"

"I was thinking ice cream." He gave her a smile that could only belong to an irreverent rascal—and, Lord, she'd forgotten about the dimples. Dimples, for crying out loud. "Why? What were you thinking?"

Hannah had no idea what her reply was going to be. She started to stammer something, but the view of Sergei and Brinley strolling toward the harbor together made the words catch in her throat. He didn't glance back once. Obviously she'd imagined the new spark of interest she'd seen in the director's eyes. He was just being a good boss by making sure her head injury wasn't serious.

Tearing her attention off the pair, she found Fox watching her closely.

After falling and being escorted off the bus by Sergei, she must have been in a state of distraction. Now that it was just the two of them—although Angelenos were beginning to file off the bus—a bubble of gratitude and fondness rose up in her middle and burst. She'd missed this place. It held some of her most treasured memories. And Fox was a part of them. His text messages over the last seven months had allowed her to hold on to a piece of Westport without intruding on her sister's bliss. She appreciated him for that, so she didn't second-guess her decision to hug him. With a laugh, she simply walked into his arms and inhaled his ocean scent, smiling when he laughed as well, rubbing the crown of her head with his knuckles.

"Hey, Freckles."

She rubbed her cheek on the gray cotton of his long-sleeved shirt, stepped back, and shoved him playfully. "Hey, Peacock."

No one was hitting on anyone. Or pulling alpha moves.

Friends. That's what this relationship was.

She wasn't going to mess that up by objectifying him. There was more to Fox than a chiseled face, thick arms, and an air of danger. Just like there was a lot more to her than being a coffee holder and note taker.

Fox seemed to notice the glumness eclipse her joy, because he picked up the only black bag in the pile—correctly assuming it was hers—and threw his opposite arm around her shoulders, guiding her toward the apartment building where he lived, across from the docks. "You let me fix your noggin, I'll throw in a cookie with that ice cream."

She leaned into him and sighed. "Deal."

Chapter Four

You're off to a fine start, idiot.

After his intervention with Brendan, he'd had a few weeks to sit on the fact that Hannah was coming to stay with him. A lot of that time had been spent out on the water, the ultimate head clearer. It was going to be no problem. A girl would be sleeping in his guest room. He'd be in the other room. With no expectation of sex. Great.

Causal sex was easier than this.

Before Hannah, Fox had relied on his personality a grand total of once in his life when it came to a woman. His one and only serious relationship hadn't gone over well, mostly because it had only been serious to him. His college girlfriend's perspective had been entirely different. Yeah, Fox had learned the hard way that he couldn't escape the assumptions people made about him—that he was temporary entertainment. Growing up, he'd ached to escape this town and the role his face—and to be fair, his actions—had carved out for him. God, he'd tried. But those expectations followed him everywhere.

So he'd stopped trying.

If you're laughing with them, they can't laugh at you, right?

Looking down at the crown of Hannah's head, Fox swallowed hard. They were walking past Blow the Man Down, and he could practically hear every stool in the place swiveling to watch Fox escort Hannah toward his apartment. They would be making jokes. Chuckling into their beers. Speculating. And, shit, how could he even blame them? Most of the time, Fox was the one making jokes about himself.

How was Seattle? they would ask him, eager to be entertained by his exploits. Distracted from their fishing stories for a moment.

Filthy place, he'd say, winking at them. Filthy.

Now he had the nerve to put his arm around Hannah? Distractingly pretty, endlessly interesting, not-after-his-dick Hannah. They were the Big Bad Wolf and Little Red Riding Hood crossing the street in front of the docks, her no-nonsense bag dangling from his free hand. And when they stopped in front of his building so he could unlock the door, Fox was painfully aware of Hannah glancing back from where they'd come, hoping to catch a glimpse of her director.

He'd never been jealous over a girl in his life. Except for this one. When he'd caught sight of Sergei bundling Hannah down the stairs of the bus, his head ducked toward her in concern, that ugly green had splashed across his vision like a rogue wave across the deck, reminding him of the first time he'd heard the director's name. His first impulse had been to break the guy's nose—the opposite of what he should be doing. If Hannah was his friend, why would he want to mess up her budding romance?

Maybe he was jealous in a friendly way?

A total possibility.

People got jealous over their friends. Right? It stood to reason that Fox's first female friend would be the one to inspire the feeling. He did covet this relationship, even though it scared him. If he was a scale, hope would sit on one side, fear on the other. Hope that he could be more than a hookup to her. Fear that he'd fail at it and be exposed.

Again.

"Thank you for letting me crash," Hannah said, smiling up at him. "I hope you didn't take down all the *Baywatch* posters on my account."

"I hid them in my closet with my Farrah Fawcett centerfold." That got a laugh out of her, but Fox could see she was still distracted by something. It took him the entire walk up the stairs to convince himself he wouldn't make it worse by bringing it up. "So . . ." he said, opening his apartment door, tipping his head to indicate she should enter. The first girl he'd ever brought to his place. No big deal at all. "You want to tell me what's bothering you?"

She squinted an eye. "Did you miss the whole head-injury thing?"

"Definitely not." If he didn't get antiseptic on the cut soon, he was going to sweat through his shirt. "But that's not what's bugging you."

Hannah walked over his threshold, hesitated like she was going to come clean, then stopped. "I was promised ice cream and a cookie."

"And you'll get it. I wouldn't lie to you, Freckles." He set down her bag by his small, two-person kitchen table, searching her face for some indication of how she felt about his apartment. "Come on."

It was purely his nature to distract himself with something physical. One second Hannah's feet were planted on the ground, the next he'd plucked her up and settled her onto his kitchen counter. He'd performed the action without a thought. At least until her pretty lips popped open in surprise as her butt hit the surface of the counter. The feel of her waist lingered on his palms, and he was definitely thinking then about things he shouldn't.

Reeling his hands back, Fox cleared his throat hard. He stepped to the side to open a cabinet and removed his blue metal first-aid kit. "Talk."

She shook her head as if to clear it. Then opened her mouth, closed it again. "Remember how I told you I wanted to assert myself more at work?"

"Yeah. You want to make a shift to soundtracks."

She'd told Fox about her dreams of compiling song lists for films last summer, namely the day they'd gone to the record expo together. Fox remembered every single thing about that day. Everything she'd said and done. How good it felt to be with her.

Realizing he was staring into space, recalling the way her elegant fingers walked through a record stack, he wet a cotton ball with antiseptic and stepped close, hesitating only a second before pushing the hair back from her forehead. Their gazes met and danced away quickly. "Are you going to cry when this stings?"

"No."

"Good." He blotted the wound with cotton, his gut seizing up when she hissed a breath. "So? What happened with creating the soundtracks?" he blurted, to distract himself from the fact that he was causing her pain.

"Well . . ." She breathed a sigh of relief when he removed the soaked cotton ball. "I'm kind of a glorified serf at the production company. When a task arises and no one wants to do it, they summon me like Beetlejuice."

"I can't imagine you as anyone's serf, Hannah."

"It's by choice. I wanted to learn the industry, then work my way up on my own merit, you know?" She watched him sort through the bandage section of his kit. "We were almost to Westport. I thought this trip could be my chance to . . . flirt with a higher position. I was just about to ask Sergei and Brinley if I could observe the soundtrack process, and that's when Hannah went splat."

"Oh, Freckles."

"Yeah."

"So you didn't get to ask at all?"

"No. Maybe it was a sign that I'm not ready."

Fox snorted. "You were born ready for making soundtracks. I have seven months of text messages to prove it."

At the mention of the texts, their eyes clashed, splotches of pink waking up in her cheeks. Blushing. He had a friend's blushing little sister sitting on his kitchen counter. Jesus Christ. Before he could reach out and test the temperature of those splotches with his fingertips, he went back to sorting through bandages.

"All right," he said. "One missed opportunity. You'll have more, right?"

Hannah nodded but said nothing.

Kept right on saying nothing as he applied Neosporin to her cut and laid the small Band-Aid on top, smoothing it with his thumb.

Not leaning in to kiss her when they were inches away felt foreign. Had he ever gotten this close to a woman besides his mother without the intention of sealing their mouths together? Flipping through his memories, he couldn't pinpoint a single time. On the other hand, he couldn't recall all the times he *had* kissed women. Not with any clarity.

He'd remember kissing Hannah.

No the fuck you won't.

With grabby movements, Fox collected the Band-Aid wrapper and opened a lower cabinet so he could brush it into the trash. "Wanting to observe doesn't seem like a big ask, Hannah. I'm sure they'll say yes."

"Maybe." She chewed her lip a moment. "It's just . . . did you notice the woman who was walking with Sergei?"

"No," he answered honestly.

Hannah hummed, looking at him thoughtfully. "She's the music coordinator. Brinley." She picked up a hand and let it drop. "I can't see myself doing anything that woman does. She's . . ."

"What?"

"A leading lady," Hannah said on an exhale, looking almost relieved to have gotten that baffling statement off her chest.

Fox's confusion cleared. "You mean, she's one of the actresses?"

"No, I mean she's a leading lady in life. Like my sister."

Nope, still confused. "I'm lost, Hannah."

She fell forward slightly with a laugh. "Never mind."

Damn. She'd only been here for five minutes, and he already wasn't living up to the friend status. Did she not want to confide in him? It scared him how much he wanted to earn her trust.

Fox moved to the freezer and took out the ice cream. Chocolate-vanilla swirl had seemed like a surefire bet when he picked it out at the supermarket yesterday. Best of both worlds, right? Watching her reaction, he took a spoon out of the drawer and stabbed it into the top, handing her the entire pint. "Explain what you mean about Piper and this Betty chick being leading ladies."

"Brinley," she corrected him, laughing with her eyes.

Fox made a face. "An LA name if I've ever heard one."

"You sound like Brendan."

"Ouch," he complained, clutching his chest. Letting his hand drop away. "An explanation, please, Freckles."

She seemed to wrestle with her thoughts while taking a relishing bite of ice cream and drawing the spoon from between her lips slowly. Mesmerizingly.

Fox coughed and dragged his attention higher.

"I'm good at being . . . supportive. You know? Giving advice and doling out helpful suggestions. When it comes to my own stuff, though . . . not so much." She let that settle quietly in the kitchen before continuing. "Like I can pack up, put my job on hold, and move to Westport because Piper needs me. But I can't even ask my boss for a chance to observe? How crazy is that? I can't even"—she gave a dazed chuckle—"tell Sergei I've had this dumb crush on him for two years. I just kind of stand around waiting for things to happen, while other people seem to make them happen so easily. I can help others—I like doing that—but I'm a supporting actress, not a leading lady. That's what I meant by that."

Wow. Here she was. Confiding in him—in person. About her insecurities. About the guy she wanted to date. This was his first heart-to-heart with a girl. No flirting or pretense. Just honesty. Up until that moment, it was possible Fox hadn't fully grasped that Hannah really, actually, one hundred percent only thought of him as just a friend. That all those texts weren't a unique, platonic style of foreplay. After all, she had eyes. She'd seen him, right? But there was no unspoken interest on her part. This really *was* just friendship. She apparently liked whatever the hell Fox had lurking on the inside. And even though he felt like he'd been socked in the fucking stomach, he still wanted to meet her expectations. Although, he suspected his ego would be purple with bruises by the time this was over.

"Hey," he said, clearing the rust from his voice, putting another few inches of distance between them. "Look, I'll be honest, I've never heard such a load of bullshit in my life. You're supportive, yeah. The way you defended Piper to the captain? You are fierce and loyal. All those things, Hannah. But you're . . . Don't make me say it out loud."

"Say it," she whispered, lips twitching.

"You are leading-lady material."

Those twitching lips spread into a smile. "Thanks."

Fox could see he might have made Hannah smile, but the issues were far from solved. For one, she liked the director, and for some reason Fox couldn't fathom, the dumbass wasn't chasing after her with a bouquet of red roses. How could he help with that? Did he *want* to help her with that? It was a fisherman's nature to plug leaks, fix problems when they arose. For another, Hannah not feeling one hundred percent happy was a definite problem in his book. "The guy was jealous, you know. Back at the bus when I came to pick you up."

Her head came up, expression hopeful, but it faded just as quickly, unlike the knot tying tighter inside him. "No, he was just being nice," she said, digging back into the ice cream. Chocolate side only, he noted for next time.

Next time?

"Hannah, trust me. I know when I'm intimidating another guy."

She wrinkled her nose. "Is jealous the same thing as intimidated?"

"Yes. When men are intimidated by other men, especially ridiculously hot men like yours truly—"

She snort-laughed.

"—they assert themselves. Fight to get the upper hand back. It's a natural reaction. Law of the jungle. That's why he wanted to get your bag. That's why he kept his arm around you way too long." Fox grabbed at the sweaty, icy skin at the nape of his neck. "He didn't like that you were staying with me, and he especially didn't like me calling you Freckles. He was intimidated and, therefore, jealous."

Fox didn't add that he was speaking from experience.

Intimidated by some artsy goatee-sporting guy from LA. A Russian, no less. Russians were their main competition during crab season, as if he needed another reason to dislike the motherfucker.

God, he was jumpy. "Anyway, all I'm saying is . . . he's not *not* interested."

"This is all very fascinating," Hannah said around her spoon. "But if you're right, if Sergei was jealous, he'll eventually realize there is nothing happening between you and me, and he has no reason to . . . resort to jungle laws." Casually, she poked at the ice cream. "Unless we *let* him think we're sleeping together. Maybe he needs to be shaken up."

Alarm stole downward through Fox's fingertips. He'd walked straight into a trap. One he'd set himself. "You can't let him think that, Hannah."

"I was only brainstorming." Whatever she saw on Fox's face caused her to narrow her eyes. "But why are you *so* opposed?"

Trying to mask the panic, he let out a crack of laughter. "You don't . . . No. I'm not letting you associate your rep- utation with mine, all right? A couple of days in this town and he'll probably hear all about it. Trust me, if he's worth a damn, the fact that I got to bandage your bump will make him jealous enough."

Hannah blinked. "If he's worth a damn, he won't believe everything he hears. Especially about someone he doesn't know personally."

"Unless a lot of what he hears is true, right?" He smiled straight through that rhetorical question, trying to give the impression that the answer didn't bother him. When she only seemed to look deeper, curious, Fox said something he immediately regretted just to distract her. To bump her off the topic of his reputation. "Have you tried letting him know you're interested? You know, a little lip biting and arm squeezing . . ."

"Gross." She looked him up and down. "Does that do it for you?"

Nothing was doing it for him lately. Nothing but the three little dots popping up in their text thread. And now head wounds. How pathetic was that? "Don't worry about what does it for me. I'm talking about this guy. He's probably clueless, and a lot of men will remain that way without a little encouragement."

Visibly amused, she tilted her head. "Are you one of those men?"

Fox sighed, resisted the urge to scratch at the back of his neck. "Encouragement is kind of a given for me."

"Right," she said after a pause, something flickering in her eyes.

How did the conversation get here? First, he's giving her pointers on landing the director, and now he's inadvertently bragging about his luck with women? *Off to a great start, man.* "Look, I'm not in the relationship race and I never will be. Clearly you are. I was just trying to be helpful. Flirting with Sergei is one thing, but the bottom line is we're not letting anyone incorrectly assume"—he sawed a hand back and forth in between them—"this is happening. For your own good, okay?"

Hannah definitely wanted to discuss it further, pick it apart, but thankfully she let it drop. "You don't have to tell me you're not in the relationship race," she said, biting her lip. "I can see your apartment just fine."

Grateful for the subject change, he breathed a laugh. "What?" He chucked her chin. "You don't think women are into the waiting-room look?"

"No. Seriously, would an area rug and a scented candle kill you?"

Fox took the ice cream and spoon out of her hands and set them on the counter. "You're not getting that cookie now." He grabbed her by the waist and tossed her facedown over his shoulder, prompting a squeal as he stomped toward the spare room. "I'm not putting up with an ungrateful houseguest, Freckles."

"I'm grateful! I'm grateful!"

Her laughter cut off abruptly when they entered her room—as he'd already begun to think of it—no doubt noticing the row of scented candles, the folded towels, and the pink Himalayan salt lamp. He'd seen it in a tourist shop window and decided she definitely needed one, but at this juncture, the purchase made him feel utterly silly.

Shaking his head at himself, Fox eased Hannah off his shoulder and dropped her gently onto the queen-sized bed, his chest tugging at the way her hair flopped down to cover one eye. "Oh. Fox . . ." she murmured, scanning the row of supplies.

"It's no big deal," he said quickly, backing up to lean sideways against the doorjamb. Crossing his arms. Definitely not thinking about how easy it would be to prowl over her on that bed, tease her a little more, run his fingertips along that section of skin between her hip bones and waist, flirt until kissing turned into her idea, instead of his intention all along. He knew the dance moves well.

None of them were right for a friend.

"Listen." When his voice sounded gruff to his own ears, he forced some levity into it. "I'm heading down to the docks to load the *Della Ray*. We'll be on the water starting tomorrow. Coming back Friday. Don't burn the place down while I'm gone and make me regret my first candle purchase."

"I won't, Peacock," she said, lips lifting at the corners, her hand smoothing the bedspread he hoped she couldn't tell was new. "Thank you. For everything."

"Anytime, Freckles."

He started to leave but stopped when she said, "And just for the record, I would be honored to fake sleep with you. Sordid reputation and all."

With a stone blocking his windpipe, all he could do was nod, grabbing his keys on the way out of the apartment. "Cookies are in the cabinet," he called, walking out into the sunshine, welcoming the way it blinded him.

Chapter Five

Hannah came to a stop outside her grandmother's door and removed her AirPods, silencing her "Walking Through Westport" playlist. It mainly consisted of Modest Mouse, Creedence, and the Dropkick Murphys, all of which reminded her of the ocean, whether it be pirates or a hippie playing harmonica on the docks. As soon as the melody cut out, she knocked, pressing her lips together a moment later to stifle a laugh. Inside the apartment, Opal was muttering to herself about morons who let solicitors into the building, her footsteps ambling closer.

At what point would having a grandmother on her father's side begin to feel normal? Opal's existence had been kept from Hannah and Piper growing up, but they'd discovered her—by mistake—last summer. And the woman was a delight. Fierce and sweet and funny. Full of stories about Hannah and Piper's father, too. Was that the reason Hannah had taken four days to come for a visit?

Sure, she'd been kept very busy on the set of their first location. On top of Hannah's other duties, they'd needed her on set for the filming of the high school lovers' reunion scene between Christian and Maxine outside the lighthouse. Getting it right had taken the full four days—but during the night she'd gone home to Fox's empty apartment, instead of going to see Opal. Piper had been out of town those four days, having taken her in-laws for a side trip to Seattle, so Hannah decided she should just wait. That way they could all visit together. There was more to her stalling, though.

Hannah pressed a hand to her stomach to subdue the bubbles of guilt.

Now that her sister was back in town, she'd called and asked Piper to meet her at Opal's this afternoon. Where was she?

Hannah was still craning her neck to see the end of the hallway when Opal answered the door. The older woman blinked once, twice, her mouth falling open. "You're not selling magazine subscriptions at all. You're my granddaughter." Hannah leaned in, and Opal enveloped her in a back-patting hug. "When did you get into town? I don't believe this. All I can make you is a ham sandwich."

"Oh. No." Hannah drew back, shaking her head. "I already had lunch, I swear. I just came to see you!"

Her grandmother flushed with pleasure. "Well, then. Come in, come in."

The apartment had changed drastically since the last time Hannah was there. Gone was the outdated furniture, the combined scents of lemon cleaner and must that left a sense of solitude hanging in the air. Now it smelled fresh. Sunflowers sat in the center of a new dining-room table, and there was no longer a plastic protector on the couch. "Wow." Hannah set her tote bag on the floor and unzipped her Storm

Born windbreaker, shrugging it off to hang on the peg. "Let me guess. Piper had something to do with this?"

"You guessed it." Opal clasped her hands near her waist, her expression pleased and prideful as she scanned the new-and-improved living space. "I don't know what I'd do without her."

Affection for her sister wiggled its way in next to Hannah's guilt but did nothing to eclipse it. Over the last seven months, she'd spoken to Opal only a handful of times on the phone. She'd sent a card at Christmas. It wasn't that she didn't adore the woman. They got along very well. She'd made Opal a Woodstock-themed playlist last summer, and they'd totally bonded over it. Even now, the welcoming vibes of the apartment wrapped around Hannah and warmed her.

It was when the stories about her father—Opal's only son—inevitably started rolling that Hannah got uncomfortable.

Hannah flat out couldn't remember him. She'd been two years old when the king crab fisherman had been sucked to the bottom of the Bering Sea. Piper could remember his laugh, his energy, but Hannah's mind conjured nothing. No melancholia, no affection or nostalgia.

For Piper, restoring Henry's bar had been a journey of learning about herself and connecting with the memory of Henry.

For Hannah, it was about . . . supporting Piper on that journey.

Of course, seeing the finished product after weeks of manual labor had been satisfying, especially when they changed the name to Cross and Daughters, but the coming-full-circle feeling never happened for Hannah. So whenever she came to see Opal and her grandmother brought out pictures of Henry, or stories were told about him over the phone, Hannah started to wonder if her emotions were stunted. She could cry over a Heartless Bastards song, but her own father got nothing from her?

Hannah joined Opal on the new indigo-colored couch and cupped her knees through her jeans. "I'm actually in town because the production company I work for is shooting a short film. Kind of a heartbreaking art house piece."

"A movie?" Opal winced. "In Westport? I can't imagine people being too thrilled with the disruption."

"Oh, don't worry, I thought of that. We're giving as many background parts and walk-on roles as we can. Once the locals realized they might be in a movie, it was smooth sailing."

With a sound of delight, Opal slapped her thigh. "That was your idea?"

Hannah fluffed her ponytail. "Yes, ma'am. I made my director think it was his idea to add locals for authenticity. It's a good thing I don't use my powers for evil, or everyone would be in big trouble."

It would be fantastic if she could use her powers to move ahead in her career, too, wouldn't it? Greasing the production wheels was easy for her. There were no personal stakes. No risk. Applying herself to music coordinating was scarier. Because it mattered.

A great deal.

Opal laughed, reached over to squeeze Hannah's wrist. "Oh, sweetie, I've missed your spunk."

The sound of a key turning in the lock made Hannah whip around, and Opal clapped happily. Piper was only halfway through the door when Hannah launched herself over the back of the new couch and plowed into her sister, tension she'd hardly been aware of seeping from her pores. Hugging Piper was like walking into a room filled with your best memories. Her sheer-sleeved romper, impractical heels, and expensive perfume made Hannah feel like they were back in Bel-Air, sitting on the floor of Piper's room, sorting her jewelry collection.

They hopped in a happy circle, laughing, while Opal fumbled with her phone, trying and failing to open her camera app.

"You're here." Piper sniffed, squeezing Hannah tightly. "My perfect, beautiful, hippie-hearted little sister. How dare you make me miss you this much?"

"I could say the same to you," Hannah said, voice muffled by her sister's shoulder.

The sisters pulled back, wiping their faces in very different manners. Hannah swiped for efficiency, while Piper dragged a careful pinkie in a perfect U shape to repair her eyeliner. Arm in arm, they moved around the couch and sat down plastered up against each other. "So when are you moving here perma-nently?" Piper asked, her tone still slightly watery. "Like . . . tomorrow. Right?"

Hannah sighed, resting her head on the back of the couch. "Part of me doesn't hate that idea. Get my job back at Disc N Dat. Haunt the guest room at your house forever"—she poked at a sequin in Piper's bodice—"but LA is keeping me, I'm afraid. It's where my dream career awaits."

Piper stroked her hair. "Have you made any headway on that?"

"Imminently . . ." Hannah responded, chewing the inside of her cheek. "I think."

Opal leaned forward. "Dream career?"

"Yes." Hannah sat up straighter but kept her side pressed to Piper's. "Movie soundtracks. The making of them."

"Isn't that interesting." Opal beamed.

"Thank you." She moved some of her hair out of the way and performed a show-and-tell with the bandaged knot on her forehead. "Unfortunately, this is what happened the first time I tried to ask." Piper and Opal both looked at her wound with an appropriate level of concern. "It's fine. It doesn't hurt." She laughed lightly, letting her hair drop back into place. "Fox bandaged me up and gave me ice cream."

It was fleeting and subtle, but she felt Piper stiffen, giving off definite protective-older-sister vibes. "Oh, did he?"

Hannah rolled her eyes. "This is your one and only reminder that me staying with Fox was your idea."

"I took it back right away," Piper fretted. "Has he tried anything?"

"No!" Hannah squawked. Never mind that she could still feel the shape and exquisitely defined musculature of his shoulder on her midsection. "Stop talking about him like he's some kind of sexual predator. I'm adult enough to make these judgment calls by myself. And he's been a perfect gentleman."

"That's because he hasn't been in town," Piper grumbled, smoothing her romper.

"He decorated my room with a Himalayan salt lamp."

Piper sputtered, "He might as well be mauling you!"

"Someone explain to me what is going on here!" Opal scooted her chair closer. "I want to be involved in a conversation about men. It's been an age."

"There is no conversation to have," Hannah assured her grandmother. "I am friends with a man who happens to . . . appreciate women. Frequently. But it has been established that he won't be appreciating me."

"Tell her about the Fleetwood Mac album," Piper said, patting Hannah vigorously on the knee. "Go on and tell her."

Hannah released a gusting breath toward the ceiling. Mostly to hide the weird twist that happened inside her when she thought of the album and how she'd gotten it. "It's no big deal, really." *Liar.* "Last summer, we all went to Seattle. Me, Piper, Fox, Brendan. We broke off for a while, and Fox took me to this record convention. And I found an album that sang to me. Fleetwood Mac. *Rumours.*" A paltry description for a shock to the nervous system. "But it was expensive. At the time, me and Pipes were on a tight budget, so I didn't buy it . . ."

"And then the day Hannah left to return to LA, there it was. On my porch. Fox went back and bought it without her knowing."

Opal made an O shape with her lips. "Oh my. That is romantic."

"No. No, you have it all wrong, ladies. It was kind."

Piper and Opal traded a very superior look.

Part of her couldn't even blame them. Fox buying her that album was the one thing she couldn't seem to define as one hundred percent friendly. It sat in a place of honor back home, facing out on the hanging rack that displayed her albums. Every time she passed it, she replayed the moment at the convention when she'd gasped over the find, tracing the square edge of the album with her fingers. The warmth of his arm around her, the unsteady pound of his heart. How for the first time, she'd let someone into the music with her, instead of disappearing into it alone.

Hannah shook herself. "You're actually helping me prove my point, Pipes. If he wanted to . . . appreciate me, why would he wait until I was leaving to hand me his golden ticket like that?"

"She makes a good point."

"Thank you, Opal. Case closed."

Piper rearranged the perfectly curled ends of her hair, physically accepting the end of the subject. "So. How is LA? Does she miss me?"

"She does. The house feels even bigger without you in it. Too big."

Their mother, Maureen, had left Westport over two decades earlier in a cloud of grief after Henry Cross's death, relocating to Los Angeles where she'd worked as a seamstress for a movie studio. She'd met and married their stepfather at the pinnacle of his success as a producer. Seemingly overnight, the three of them had gone from residing in a tiny apartment to a Bel-Air mansion, where Hannah still lived to this day.

With Piper in residence, the mansion never failed to feel like home. But ever since Piper moved to Westport, Hannah felt more like a visitor. Out of place and disconnected in the gigantic palace. It had become obvious that their parents led a separate life, and lately, she'd started to feel like an observer of it. Instead of someone who was happily off living her own.

"I'm thinking of moving out," Hannah blurted. "I'm thinking of a lot of things."

Piper angled her body to face Hannah, head tilted. "Such as?"

Being the focus of the conversation was unusual, to say the least. It wasn't that it embarrassed her to be the center of attention. There was simply no use involving everyone in problems she could fix herself, right? Like finagling a trip to Westport because loneliness and a sense of missing something had started getting to her. "Never mind." She waved a hand. "How are things going with Brendan's parents?"

"She's changing the subject," Opal pointed out.

"Yeah. Don't do that." Piper poked her with the tip of a red fingernail. "You're going to move out of Bel-Air?"

Hannah shrugged a shoulder. "It's time. It's time for me to . . . grow up the whole way. I got stuck halfway through the process." She thought of Brinley. "No one is going to consider a promotion for a girl who lives with her parents. Or they'll consider me less, anyway. If I want adult responsibilities, I have to be one. I have to believe I am one first."

"Hanns, you're the most responsible person I know," Piper said, hedging. "Does your interest in Sergei have anything to do with this?"

"There's *another* man in the mix?" Opal split a glance between her two granddaughters and sighed. "Lordy, to be young again."

"He's my director. My boss—only. Nothing has changed on that front," Hannah explained. "What I want from a career and my love life are totally separate, but I'd be lying if I said I didn't want Sergei to look at me like I'm a woman, you know? Instead of the scruffy PA."

The guy was jealous, you know. Back at the bus when I came to pick you up.

Fox's voice filtered in through her thoughts. She'd been busy over the last four days, getting everyone settled in their temporary housing, unpacking supplies in the trailers, meeting with the local business owners. But she hadn't been so busy that she wasn't aware of Sergei. Of course she was always aware of him on set. With his passion on full display, he was a magnet for attention. But if the director had really been jealous of Fox, he'd forgotten all about it and gone back to treating Hannah with polite distractedness.

Trust me, if he's worth a damn, the fact that I got to bandage your bump will make him jealous enough. There went Fox's deep rasp in her head again, when she should be thinking of Sergei. Still . . . she couldn't stop replaying what the fisherman said to her in the kitchen. About his reputation. About how he wouldn't want people assuming they were an item, because he thought it would be a bad look for Hannah. He didn't really believe that nonsense, right?

"Well." Piper broke into her thoughts. "As someone who has only recently embarked on adulthood herself, I can tell you it's scary but rewarding. There's also lots of making my own meals and wearing jeans." She pretended to cry, and Hannah laughed. "But I couldn't have done it without you, Hannah. You made me consider possibilities I never dreamed of. That's how I know you're capable of anything. Don't let a head injury and feeling scruffy stop you. My sister is dependable and creative and doesn't take anyone's shit. If this studio doesn't give you the opportunity, another one will. Dammit." Piper smiled prettily. "And I'm sorry for cursing, Opal. I'm just trying to get my point across."

"I'm a fisherman's mother, dear. Cursing is part of the vocabulary."

Piper was being Hannah's supporting actress for once, and that fact wasn't lost on her. The role reversal, coupled with the warm pressure behind her eyes, probably accounted for Hannah doing something totally out of character. "Can you help me out with the scruffiness? Just for tonight." She poked a finger through the thumb hole of her sweatshirt. "There's a cast party at one of the houses we're renting."

Her sister slowly laid a hand on her arm, nails digging in lightly. "Are you asking me to dress you up?"

"Just for tonight. I need all the professional confidence."

"Oh my God," Piper breathed, teary-eyed. "I know just the dress."

"Nothing flashy—"

"Zip. Zip it. Not another word. You're going to trust me."

Hannah swallowed a smile and did as she was told. There might have been a speck of vanity inside her that wanted to catch Sergei's attention at the crew party tonight, and she wondered if a Piper-style dress might do it. But that definitely wasn't her reason for dressing up. If she wanted to move to the next level in this industry, people had to start taking her seriously. Plain and simple? In Hollywood, image mattered, whether it should or not. Sparkle got attention and forced people to listen. To consider. No one would ever ask Piper or Brinley to hold their straw or stir their coffee counterclockwise, would they? *I'm looking at you, Christian.*

Nor would they expect Brinley to do all the heavy lifting at the studio without paying her properly. For a long time, Hannah had reasoned that it didn't matter what her paycheck looked like. She lived with her parents in Bel-Air, for crying out loud. They had an Olympic-sized swimming pool in the backyard and a full-time staff. Since getting back in her stepfather's good graces, money was available to her again, if she ever needed funds beyond her paycheck. But her meager earnings were becoming a matter of principle. They wouldn't have managed this location shoot without her—and Latrice—pulling several all-nighters. The difference being, Latrice got paid what she was worth.

Dressing for success seemed almost too easy compared to the hard work she'd been doing lately, but giving it a try wouldn't hurt.

"All this movie-soundtrack and Fleetwood Mac talk reminded me of something," Opal said, pulling Hannah from her ruminations. "I have something to show you girls."

Their grandmother got to her feet and power walked to the other side of the living room, taking a slim blue folder off the top of her bookcase. Knowing whatever was in that folder would pertain to her father, Hannah's stomach started to drop. This was the part of catching up with her grandmother she always dreaded: when Piper and Opal would be moved to tears over some piece of Henry's history, and she would feel like a statue, trying to relate.

"One of Henry's old shipmates brought these into Blow the Man Down over the weekend. I was out with the girls." Their grandmother said the last part with pride, winking at Piper. For a long time, Opal's grief over the passing of her son had kept her inside the apartment. At least until Piper came along, gave her a sassy haircut and some new clothes, reintroducing her to the town she'd been missing. Hannah liked to think her playlists had helped motivate Opal to get social again, too. "These were written by your father," she said, opening the folder.

Both sisters leaned in and squinted down at the small handwriting that took up several pages of stained and age-worn paper.

"Are they letters?" Piper asked.

"They're songs," Opal murmured, running a fingertip over a few sentences. "Sea shanties, to be exact. He used to sing them around the house in the early days. I didn't even know he'd written them down."

Hannah felt a tug of almost reluctant interest. She'd gotten her hopes up a few times that a photograph or a token of her father's might bring on some tide of emotion, but it never happened, and it wouldn't now. "Was he a good singer?"

"He had a deep voice. Powerful. Rich. A lot like his laugh, it could pass right through you."

Piper made a pleasurable sound, picking up the folder and leafing through. "Hannah, you should take these."

"Me?" Mentally, she recoiled but tried to soften her tone for Opal's sake. "Why me?"

"Because they're songs," Piper said, as if she'd been crazy to ask the question. "This is what you love."

Opal reached over and rubbed Hannah's knee. "Maybe Henry is where you got your love of music."

Why did she want to deny that so badly?

What was wrong with her?

It was right there on the tip of her tongue to say no. *No, my love for so many kinds of music is mine. I don't share it with anyone. It's a coincidence.* But, instead, she nodded. "Sure, I'd . . . love to take them for a while and give them a read."

Opal lit up. "Fantastic."

Hannah accepted the folder from Piper and closed it, a familiar desperation to change the subject from Henry settling over her. "Okay, Pipes. We've been in suspense long enough. Tell us about Brendan's parents. How is the visit with your future in-laws going?"

Her sister settled back into the seat, crossing long legs that had been buffed to a shine. "Well. As you know, I brought them down to Seattle this week, since Brendan is out on the boat. I planned all our time there, down to the second."

"And then?" Opal prompted.

"And then I realized all the plans were . . . shopping-related." Her voice fell to a scandalized whisper. "Brendan's mother hates shopping."

Opal and Hannah fell back in their seats laughing.

"Who hates shopping?" Piper whined, covering her face.

Hannah raised her hand. Piper smacked it down.

"Thank God Brendan is coming home tonight. I am running out of ways to entertain them. We've been on so many walks, Hanns. So many walks to nowhere."

The spread of anticipation in Hannah's belly had nothing to do with Fox coming home tonight along with Brendan. She was simply excited to see her friend again and not be alone in his oddly barren apartment.

Piper split a look between Opal and Hannah. "Give me some ideas?"

Hannah thought for a second, slipping into her supporting role as easily as a second skin. "Ask her to teach you how to make Brendan's favorite childhood meal. It'll make her feel useful, and it's not terrible knowledge to have, like for birth-days and special occasions, right?"

"That's genius," Piper squealed, wrapping her arms around Hannah's neck and wrestling her down to the couch while Opal laughed. "I'm totally going to bond it up with my future mother-in-law. What would I do without you, Hanns?"

Hannah pressed her nose to her sister's skin and inhaled, absorbing the hug, the moment, "Time After Time" by Cyndi Lauper playing in the back of her mind. It was tempting to stay there, to bask in the comfortable feeling of being the one to prop others up. There was nothing wrong with it, and she loved that role. But being comfortable had kept her in the second-fiddle position so long . . . and tonight she was finally going to conduct the orchestra herself.

Chapter Six

$\mathcal{H}$annah walked extra slowly down the sidewalk, a bottle of wine in hand. Her snail's pace had a lot to do with the three-inch heels, but it was mainly the dress delaying her progress. As soon as Piper unzipped the garment bag, she'd started to shake her head. Red? *Red?* Her wardrobe had been compiled for comfort and functionality. Lots of grays, blues, blacks, and whites so she wouldn't have to worry about matching. The only red items she owned were a baseball hat and a pair of Chucks. It was a color you used for a pop. Not the whole ensemble.

Then she'd put it on—and she'd never been more annoyed to have someone be right. There was something kind of nineties about the dress, and that spoke to the grunge-headed old soul inside Hannah. It reminded her of the red minidress Cher wore to the Valley party in *Clueless*. Piper had agreed, making Hannah say, "I totally paused," at least forty-eight times while they straightened her hair.

In most lines of work, this outfit would have been considered inappropriate, but entertainment was its own animal. At the end of the night, it wouldn't be unusual to catch crew members making out in the hallways. Or right out in the open. Often there were drugs, and always alcohol. But really, as long as everyone showed up the next morning and got their job done, pretty much anything went. While judgments and gossip were inevitable, being unprofessional after hours made you one of the gang as opposed to a pariah.

A block away from the rented house, Hannah could see the silhouettes of cast and crew in the dimly lit windows and hear the low thunder of music. The raucous laughter. Well aware of how rowdy industry parties could get, even on this small a scale, she'd booked a place on the semi-outskirts of town to avoid noise complaints. And it was a good thing she had, because someone was already passed out on the front lawn and it wasn't even ten P.M.

Hannah stepped over the intern with a low whistle, hiked up the steps in her admittedly gorgeous shoes—who knew she'd feel so fancy with sparkly little bows on her toes?—and walked into the house without knocking, since no one was going to hear it, anyway. Before leaving Fox's apartment, she'd given herself a pep talk in the mirror of his bathroom, which smelled like the collision of a minty glacier and something more interesting . . . like a ginger-laced essential oil.

Did he use essential oils?

Why was she so tempted to go into his bedroom and check for a diffuser so she could inhale directly from the source?

With an impatient tongue click, Hannah stepped into the house and immediately had to check her urge to find the person in charge of the playlist. If she let herself, she'd sit in the corner all night searching for the perfect next song—probably some Bon Iver to chill everyone out after the crazy week—and that wasn't the mission tonight.

Resigning herself to a night of ambient techno, Hannah took off her coat and draped it over the closest chair, waving to a couple sound engineers on her way down the hallway to the living room where everyone seemed to be congregated.

The song ended right as she walked into the room. Or it might have been all in her head, because everyone—and she meant everyone—turned to stare. If this was what a leading lady felt like, she'd rather be an extra.

Only, she wasn't happy with that anymore, right? So even though her palms were clammy and she kind of felt like an asshole for wearing a designer cocktail dress to a casual hang, she had no choice but to brazen it out and proceed with the plan.

"Am I the only one who got the formal dress memo?" She fake-cringed over the jeans and T-shirts worn by a group of hair and makeup artists. "Sad."

There was some laughter, but then mostly everyone went back to their drinks and conversation, allowing Hannah to exhale. Some liquid courage would not go amiss. One drink, and then she'd make the professional move of a lifetime. Hopefully.

Hannah spotted the liquor and mixers station on a bar cart in the corner of the room and headed that direction, reminding herself she was a certified lightweight and not to overdo it. She was still recovering from her foray into day drinking with Piper at the local winery last summer.

"Hey," Christian said in a bored tone, coming up beside her. "What are you drinking? Poison, I hope."

She pursed her lips and perused the various liquor bottles. "What can I drink to give you a personality?"

Looking pointedly at her dress, Christian gave an appreciative snort. "So, what are you, like, trying now?"

"Could you do the same, please? It took you sixteen takes to nail four lines of dialogue this morning."

"Can't rush perfection." He made an impatient sound and snatched up a red Solo cup. "What are you drinking, PA? I'll make it."

Hannah's mouth dropped open. "You're going to make my drink?"

"Don't let it go to your head." While pouring vodka, he gave her a once-over. "Or your hips. That dress is a little snug."

"You wish you had the hips for this dress."

He added some grapefruit juice and ice to the cup, all but shoving the prepared drink into her hands. "I hate that I like you."

"I like that I hate you."

It cost them both a visible effort not to laugh.

"Hannah?" Christian and Hannah turned at the same time to find Sergei, Brinley, and an assortment of on-camera talent approaching, including Maxine and her fictional best friend. For once, Sergei seemed at a loss for words, the drink in his hand lowering to the side of his thigh. "You . . . dressed up," he said, his attention straying briefly to Hannah's hemline. "If I didn't see you sparring with Christian, I wouldn't have recognized you."

"I do get a certain look of horror on my face when she's around," Christian drawled, giving her a lazy elbow in the side.

"Yes. You look fantastic," Brinley said, though she was scrolling on her phone.

"Thank you." Being the center of attention made it necessary to take a gulp of her (hopefully not poisoned) drink, the abundance of vodka burning her throat on the way down.

It might have been the dress and the liquor rapidly dulling her nerves that encouraged her to speak up. Or it could have been Piper's supportive words earlier in the day. All Hannah knew was that if she didn't ask for what she wanted now, she never would. "Brinley," she blurted, grabbing her own wrist so the ice in her cup would stop rattling. "I was wondering if I could assist you in any way with the score. Not that you need assistance," she rushed to qualify. "I was more just hoping to learn from you. From the process."

Silence descended on the circle.

It was not unusual for people to use parties as a chance to industry climb. But it was unusual for a personal assistant to address someone so much further up the ladder—in mixed company, no less. Maybe she should have waited. Or asked to speak to Brinley and Sergei alone? She hoped Brinley might find the request more palatable since it was posed casually instead of officially. Hannah didn't want the woman thinking she was trying to steal her job.

"Oh . . ." Brinley blinked slowly, sizing her up with new interest. "Are musical scores something you're thinking of pursuing long-term?"

"I haven't really gotten that far yet," Hannah said in a release of breath. "But I'd love to learn more about the process. To see if maybe it could be a good fit down the road."

Brinley rocked on her heels a moment, then shrugged, eyes zipping back to her phone. "I don't have a problem with you observing—if Sergei can spare you?"

It struck Hannah how long Sergei had remained uncharacteristically silent, his forehead lined as he studied her. When Brinley prompted him, he jolted, as if becoming aware of his own silence. "You're vital to me on set, Hannah. You know that." There was no help for the flush that rose in her cheeks over Sergei saying those words. *You're vital to me.* She stopped just short of pressing her drink to her cheeks to cool them down. Meanwhile, the silence stretched, the director running a finger around the inside of his black ribbed turtleneck. "But if you can manage both, I won't object."

Heat prickled the backs of Hannah's eyes, an unexpected jab of pride catching her in the breastbone. Relief—and the distinct fear of failure—traveled so swiftly through her limbs, she almost dropped her cup. But she forced a smile, nodding her thanks to Sergei and Brinley.

"Who's going to bring me coffee between takes?" Christian complained.

A collective laugh/groan from everyone in the group broke the tension, thankfully, and the subject was changed to Sunday morning's agenda. They'd been waiting for a good-weather day to film a kissing scene between Christian and Maxine on the harbor, and the next few days called for sunshine.

While Sergei engaged the small gathering with his vision of a wide, sweeping shot of the kiss, she flipped through her mental music catalogue for the right song, the right feeling . . . and she was surprised to find nothing landed. Nothing.

Not a single song came to mind.

That was odd.

What if she'd finally been given this opportunity only to lose her knack for plugging in the right sound for any occasion? What if she forgot how to weave together atmosphere, something she'd been doing since she was old enough to operate a turntable?

The thought troubled Hannah so much that she didn't notice Christian refreshing her drink. Twice. The electronic music started to match the tempo of her pulse, and when she got the urge to dance, she knew that was her cue to stop drinking. Although . . . it was a little late for that. A pleasurable buzz tickled her blood, and she lost all self-awareness, talking to anyone who would listen about any topic that popped into her head, from the running of the bulls in Pamplona to the fact that people's ears never stopped growing. And her brain told her it was interesting. Maybe it was? Everyone seemed to be laughing, one of the actresses eventually pulling her out onto the makeshift dance floor, where she closed her eyes, kicked her shoes off, and fell into a rhythm.

At one point, her neck tingled, and she opened her eyes to find Sergei watching her from across the room, though his attention was quickly diverted when Christian asked him a question. Hannah went back to dancing, unwisely accepting another drink from a makeup artist.

Her movements slowed when the air in the room changed.

It kind of just . . . lit up.

Hannah looked around and noticed everyone's eyes were glued to the entrance of the living room. Because Fox was standing there, one forearm propped high on the doorjamb, watching her with amusement.

"Holy mother," Hannah muttered, stopping to stare along with everyone else.

There was no other way to herald his arrival but to be rendered mute and immobile. Fox swaggering into the party was like a shark swimming slowly through a school of fish. He was freshly windblown from the ocean, his tan skin slightly weathered from salt, sunshine, and hard work. He towered over everyone and everything. Cocky. So cocky and confident and stupidly hot. Outrageously hot.

"That's him," one of the girls nearby said. "That guy we saw from the bus."

"God, he is like a walking spank bank."

"Dibs."

"Screw that. I already called dibs."

A twitch in Fox's cheek indicated he heard what was being said, but he didn't take his eyes off Hannah, and she started to . . . get kind of pissed. Yeah, no, she *was* pissed. Who called dibs on a human being? Or referred to him as a spank bank? How dare they assume it would be that easy to just . . . appreciate her friend?

What if it was that easy, though?

What if he liked one of them back?

That wasn't any of her business. Was it?

She watched as more whispers reached Fox, and his smile lost power. Not for the first time over the last four days, she replayed what he'd said her first day in town. *I'm not letting you associate your reputation with mine, all right?*

Now his step hesitated on the way to Hannah. Was he second-guessing approaching her? Because all these people were watching?

Without another thought, she set down her drink on a nearby windowsill and walked toward the man with purpose. The fizzy pop of alcohol in her bloodstream might have been contributing to her actions in that moment, but it was more indignation than anything else. These girls didn't even *know* him. Nor did it sound as if they'd learned anything about his actual character while in town. Where were these assumptions coming from?

She'd made them, too. Hadn't she?

Day one. She'd called him a pretty-boy sidekick. Assumed he was a player.

There were all those times she'd texted, asking if he was alone. Tongue in cheek. Like there was a very good chance he'd be with a girl. Hooking up.

So maybe the sudden, crushing need to apologize drove her forward. No one else was going to judge Fox on her watch, and no way was she going to let him hesitate to approach her at a party. He was in the middle of a room being objectified, and she wanted to be the anchor for him.

She wanted to comfort him.

Okay, maybe she was jealous, too. At the possibility someone else was calling dibs, but she didn't want to think about that too hard. Instead, she licked her lips, picking a landing spot for her mouth.

Hannah was approximately five feet from Fox when his expression changed, and he read her intention. His creeping insecurity vanished, and he rocketed to inferno status on a dime. Those blue eyes darkened, and that square, bristled jaw flexed. Ready. A man well used to being wanted and knowing what to do about it.

He whispered her name right before she pushed up on her toes, locking their mouths together, right there in the entrance to the living room. She was immediately bowled over by the hunger of his masculine lips, and then he turned her, pressing her back to the inside of the arched doorway, opening his mouth on top of hers and licking into the kiss with a choked sound.

With her thoughts muddling and a languid heat rendering her arms limp, Hannah realized she'd made a huge mistake. She was Eve in the Garden of Eden, and she'd just taken a bite from the apple.

Chapter Seven

$\mathcal{B}$ig mistake.

Huge.

Unfortunately, trying to stop kissing Hannah was a laughable endeavor.

Fox shouldn't have come here in the first place. But he'd walked into his apartment after four nights on the water expecting her to be there, only to find a note that she'd gone to a party. His apartment had smelled like summer, a garment bag hanging on the back of the guest-room door. And he'd paced while staring at it, wondering what the hell she owned that needed a special bag.

He'd tried showering and drinking a beer but found himself out walking through town, searching for this party for which she'd obviously dressed up. Wasn't that hard to locate a house full of outsiders in a place like this. He'd seen a dude staggering down one of the blocks and asked where he'd come from, reasoning that he would just check on Hannah, make sure she got home all right. Hadn't he promised Brendan he'd keep an eye on her?

That little red dress, though.

He loved it—and he hated it with every fiber of his being.

Because she didn't wear it for him. She wasn't even kissing him for him.

Before Fox left for the trip, Hannah had mused about a way to make the director jealous. Letting the man think she and Fox were more than friends. Fox had spotted the son of a bitch the second he walked into the room, not twenty yards from where Hannah was dancing so adorably. He was watching them kiss right now. She'd obviously ignored Fox's warning about comingling their reputations, and now . . . *Damn.*

He couldn't stop for the life of him. They were already kissing, and selling his authentic enjoyment wasn't exactly difficult. Not at all.

Jesus Christ, she tasted incredible. Fruity and feminine and grounding.

Even though he'd stepped off the *Della Ray* earlier, he was only now back on solid ground.

Did he push her up against the entryway too forcefully? He'd never needed to get his tongue inside a woman's mouth so badly. He'd never been gripped by urgency or jealousy or a thousand other unnamed emotions that had him pulling down her chin with his thumb to get deeper. God. God.

She's not temporary in any way, okay? Hands off.

Brendan's voice in his head forced Fox's eyes open, only to find Hannah's shut tightly. So tightly. He traced his thumb down to her throat and felt the moan building there, would have died to taste it. He could probably keep this up—bring her home from this party and take her to bed, orgasm her into a stupor—because seducing women was an effortless skill.

Yeah, a little more of this and she'd spend the night underneath him, but did she truly want that? No. No, she had her cap set at another man. They were giving the impression that sex was definitely happening, but actually sleeping with Fox when she wanted Sergei? That wasn't Hannah's style. She was too loyal. Too principled. And he wouldn't take that away from her, no matter how insane she tasted. No matter how hard she was making his cock with those committed strokes of her tongue, her hands pulling at his shirt.

Bottom line was, Brendan was right.

Hannah was the furthest thing from temporary, and Fox only did short-term. Very short-term. That personal rule kept him from getting his hopes up, from thinking he could be one half of a relationship again. Women didn't bring Fox home to meet their parents. He was more of the side-piece type. He'd been told his whole life that he'd turn out exactly like his father, and he'd confirmed a long time ago that he shared more than a pretty face with the man. He was perfect for making Hannah's director envious.

Yeah. A ruse was all this could be. A friend helping a friend. Unfortunately, he knew enough about women to know Hannah wasn't faking her enjoyment. Those breathy whimpers were for his ears alone. It was on Fox to make sure they didn't take this too far. As in, all the way back to his bed.

Despite the effort it cost him, Fox broke the kiss, pressing their foreheads together as they both struggled to catch their breath. "All right, Freckles," he said. "I think we convinced him."

Her eyes met his in a daze. "What? Who?"

For the first time, Fox felt his heart speed up into a sprint while off the water. Had Hannah just kissed him . . . to kiss him? Because she wanted to? He thought of the way she'd stopped dancing when he walked in, the way she'd moved in his direction as if drawn by a magnet. Had he misread everything? Was this not about making the director jealous? "Hannah, I . . . thought you were trying to show Sergei what he's missing?"

She blinked at him several times. "Oh. *Oh.* Yeah, I know," she said in a rushed whisper, shaking her head a couple of times. "I knew what you meant. S-sorry." Why wouldn't she look at him? "Thank you for . . . being so convincing."

Fox couldn't account for the ripple of pain in his stomach when she glanced sideways at Sergei to see if he'd been watching.

Oh yeah, the guy was looking, all right.

This plan was already working.

He suddenly ached to bury his fist in the wall.

When Hannah shifted, Fox realized he still had her flattened against the entryway and backed off before she felt his erection.

"How, um"—she cupped the base of her throat, as if to hide the pink skin there—"how did you know I was here?"

"I followed the trail of drunk people." He remembered the red cup in her hand when he'd arrived and concern drew his brows together. "You're not one of them, are you? I didn't realize—"

"Stop, I haven't had enough to drink that you took advantage of me, Fox. Only enough to dance to electronica." She puffed a laugh. "Anyway, I kissed you, remember?"

"I remember, Hannah," he assured her in a low voice, unable to keep his gaze from dropping to her swollen lips. "Do you want to stay awhile?"

She shook her head. Stopped. A smile bloomed across her face, and all he could do was watch it happen, dazed. "I did it," she murmured. "I asked to assist with the musical score and they said yes. And I didn't fall and nearly crack my head open this time."

Dumb heart. Dumb, pointless heart, please stop turning over.

The problem was, Hannah was extra cute after a few drinks and happy with her good news. All Fox could think about was kissing her again, and he couldn't. He'd done his job; now he needed to move back into friend territory fast. She seemed to have no problem putting him back there, right? He treasured this friendship, so he needed to follow suit. Pronto.

"Congratulations," he said, returning her smile. "That's amazing. You're going to be great at it."

"Yeah . . ." A little line formed between her brows. "Yeah. I will. I'll wake up tomorrow and the songs will be back."

Songs were the way she communicated her moods and feelings. How she interpreted everything. He'd known it last summer, and that knowledge of her had only grown over seven months of text messages. Knowing exactly what she meant made him feel . . . special. "Where did the songs go?"

"I don't know." Her lips twitched. "Maybe some ice cream would help?"

"We'll have to stop on the way home. Only the vanilla side is left."

"The not-chocolate side, you mean?" She surveyed the room. "I guess I should say good-bye. Or . . ." An odd look crossed her face. Something like reluctance, but he couldn't be sure. "Or I could introduce you to, um . . . There were some interested parties . . ."

It took him a minute to realize what she was getting at. "You mean the girls who called dibs on me when I walked into the room?" He kissed her forehead so she wouldn't see how much that bothered him. It shouldn't. He'd embraced the way people saw him. "Hard pass, Freckles. Let's go get ice cream."

The first three times Hannah teetered in her heels, Fox started to worry that she was, in fact, shit-faced. Had she really wanted that kiss? At the very least, if he'd known she'd had a lot to drink, he wouldn't have let it go on so long.

The clear quality of her speech put most of his fears to rest—all except the one about Hannah breaking her neck in those heels. So on their way out of the convenience store, he stepped in front of her, gesturing impatiently so she wouldn't suspect that he wanted to carry her. "This is not the kind of ride I usually offer women." He bent his knees a little to accommodate their height difference. "But the ice cream is going to melt if we have to take a trip to the ER, so hop on."

He loved that she simply jumped. Not a second's hesitation to read his intentions or tell him a piggyback ride was crazy. She just shoved the pint of chocolate ice cream under her arm and leapt, looping her free arm loosely around his neck. "You noticed my lack of high-heel game, did you? Know what's crazy? I actually like them. Piper wouldn't tell me how much they cost—I highly suspect because she never checked the price tag—but the astronomical price means they're kind of like walking on cotton balls." She yawned into his neck. "I've been judging her for wearing uncomfortable shoes for the sake of fashion, but they are cozy and they really do elongate the leg, Fox. I think I just need some practice."

Okay, she wasn't drunk, but she'd had enough alcohol to ramble, and he couldn't stop grinning as they passed beneath a streetlight. "They look nice on you."

"Thank you."

What a gigantic understatement. They made her legs look delicate and strong at the same time, flexing her calves. Making him acknowledge how perfectly they would fit into the palm of his hand. Making him want to stroke the contour of them with his thumbs. Fox swallowed, tightening his grip on her bare knees. *Don't go any lower or higher, asshole.* "So you got the green light to assist on the musical score. What does that mean?" His throat flexed. "Will you be spending more time with Sergei?"

If she heard the slightly strangled note in his voice, she chose to ignore it. "No. Just Brinley. You know, the leading-lady type?"

Some of the pressure crowding his chest dissipated. "I'm not on board with you calling other women that. As if you're not in the same category."

She dropped her chin onto his shoulder. "I felt like I was tonight. Got my big, dramatic movie kiss and everything."

"Yeah." His voice sounded like it was coming from the bottom of a barrel. Now that his shock from the kiss was wearing off, he could only worry about people in town finding out about it. *Did you hear Fox put the moves on the younger sister? It was only a matter of time.* "Was there any forward movement on the Sergei front while I was gone?" he forced out.

"Oh . . . no. No yards gained."

The quiet disappointment in her tone had Fox turning sharply, stomping up the stairs to his apartment, the crowded sensation back in his chest, along with that foreign smack of jealousy that he really didn't want to get used to. "That'll teach you to outright dismiss my lip-biting and arm-squeezing advice," he forced himself to say.

"Oh, come on, that wasn't real, usable advice. What else you got, Peacock?"

What was he supposed to do here? Refuse to give her advice and make his pointless envy obvious? For a split second, he considered giving her terrible suggestions. Like telling her that men love to diagnose strange skin rashes. Or be the sole male attendee at drunk karaoke nights with the girls. Hannah was too smart for that, though. He'd just have to hope she ignored this advice like the last time.

Why was he hoping that again? Wasn't he supposed to be her friend?

"Huh." He attempted to swallow the guilt, but only about half of it went down. "Men like to feel useful. It stirs up our precious alpha male pride. Find something heavy and tell him you need it lifted. You will have emphasized your physical differences and thus, the fact that he's a man and you're a woman. Men need way less prompting to think of . . ."

"Sex?"

Jesus, it was like he'd eaten something spicy. He couldn't stop clearing his throat. Or thinking of her with the director. "Right," he practically growled.

"Note to self," she said, pretending to write a note in the air, "find boulder. Ask for assistance. Manipulate the male psyche. By Jove, I think I've got it."

Fox doubted Pencil Arms could lift a pebble, let alone a boulder, but he kept that to himself. "You're a fast learner."

"Thank you." She smirked at him over his shoulder. So adorable, he couldn't help but give her one back. "How was the fishing trip?"

He blew out a breath while retrieving the keys from his pocket, using the moonlight to decipher which was the one for his apartment. "Fine. A little strained."

Fox probably never would have admitted that out loud if he wasn't thrown off by his jealousy. Damn, this was *not* a good look for him.

It wasn't as if he wanted Hannah to be *his* girlfriend, instead.

God, no. A girlfriend? Him? He doused the ridiculous flicker of hope before it could grow any larger. It was bad enough he'd allowed that kiss to go so long tonight. No way he'd drag her all the way into the mud with him.

As soon as they cleared the threshold of his apartment, Fox kicked the door closed behind them and Hannah slid off his back. He couldn't stop himself from observing the way she tugged the skirt of her dress down. It had ridden high, torturously so, on her legs. And, God, the skin on the inside of her thighs looked smooth. Lickable.

"Why was the trip strained?" she asked, following him into the kitchen with her pint of ice cream.

Strained, indeed.

Fox shook his head while taking two spoons out of the drawer. "No reason. Forget I said anything."

Wide-eyed and flushed, she leaned against his kitchen island. "Is it Brendan's fault? Because I can't talk trash about my sister's fiancé. Unless you really want to." A beat passed. "Okay, you convinced me. What's his problem? He can be so mean. And, like, what is with the beanie? Is it glued on?"

A laugh snuck out before he could catch it.

How did she do this? How could she rip him free of the jaws of envy and bring him back to a place of comfort and belonging? The fact that they were in his kitchen, with no one else around, made it a lot easier to relax. It was just them. Just Hannah, now barefoot, working off the top of the ice cream, giving him her undivided attention. He wanted to sink into it, into her. He was . . . selfish when it came to Hannah. Yeah. He wanted his friend all to himself. No directors allowed.

"I guess you could say it was tense because of Brendan," Fox said slowly, handing Hannah a spoon across the island. "But I'm equally to blame."

"Are you guys having a fight?"

He shook his head. "Not a fight. Just a difference of opinion." That was putting it mildly, considering he and his best friend had been like oil and water all week. Brendan continued to broach the uncomfortable subject of his intentions with Hannah, leading to Fox avoiding him, which was not easy to do in the middle of the ocean. They'd stormed off the boat in opposite directions as soon as it reached the dock in Grays. "You know Brendan is adding a second crabbing boat to the company? It's being built in Alaska. Almost finished at this point."

Hannah nodded around her first bite. "Piper mentioned it, yes."

It took him a deep breath to say the next part out loud. He'd told no one. "Last summer, around the time you and Piper showed up, Brendan asked me to take over as captain of the

Della Ray. So he could move to the new boat, focus on building a second crew so we can better compete during crab season."

He waited for the congratulations. Waited for her to gasp, come around the island, and hug him. Truthfully, he wouldn't have minded the hug.

Instead, she lowered the spoon and watched him solemnly, a wealth of thoughts dancing behind her eyes. "You don't want to be the captain of the *Della Ray*?"

"Of course I don't, Hannah." He laughed, a buzz saw turning against the back of his neck. "It's an honor to be asked. That boat—it's . . . a part of the history of this town. But, Jesus, I'm not interested in that level of responsibility. I don't want it. And he should know me well enough to realize that. You should know me well enough to realize it, too."

Hannah blinked. "I do know you well enough, Fox. The first conversation we ever had was about you being content to take orders and walk away whistling with a paycheck."

Why did he hate the first impression he'd given her when it was perfectly accurate? He was even perpetuating it now. Doubling down. Because it was the truth—he was content like this. Needed to be.

At eighteen, he'd had aspirations of being something other than a fisherman. He'd even formed a start-up with a college friend and fellow business major. Westport and his tomcat status were almost in the rearview when he realized he could never escape it. From thousands of miles away, his past and the expectations people had for him cast a shadow. Spoiled the business and partnership he'd tried to build. His reputation followed him, poisoning everything it touched. So, yeah, there was no sense trying to be something he wasn't.

Men didn't want a leader, a captain, they couldn't respect.

"That's right." He turned and took a beer out of the fridge, uncapping it with his teeth. "I'm fine right where I am. Not everyone has to strive for greatness. Sometimes getting by is just as rewarding."

"Okay." He faced Hannah again in time to see her nod, seeming like she wanted to stay silent but was unable to do it. "Have you let yourself visualize being captain, though?"

"Visualize it?" He raised an eyebrow. "You've never sounded more LA."

"If LA gets one thing right, Peacock, it's therapy."

"I don't need therapy, Hannah. And I don't need you to play the supporting actress, all right? That's not why I told you. So you could talk me through my problems."

She reared back, losing her grip on the spoon. It clattered onto the island, and she had to slap a hand down on it to stop the tinny noise. "You're right," she breathed. "That's exactly what I'm doing. I'm sorry."

Fox wished for quicksand to swallow him whole so he wouldn't have to see the dazed acceptance on her face. Had he really put it there? What the hell was wrong with him? "No, I'm sorry. That was a shitty thing for me to say. I'm sorry. I'm being . . . defensive."

Her mouth lifted at the corner, but her heart wasn't fully in the smile. "Being defensive? You've never sounded more LA."

God, he liked her.

"Look, I can't"—there was a pulsing squeeze in the dead center of his body, demanding he give her something, a pound of flesh, in exchange for snapping—"visualize it. Okay? When I visualize myself as the captain, I see an imposter. I'm not

Brendan. I don't take everything under the goddamn sun seriously. I'm just a good time, and everyone knows it."

He took a long sip of his beer, set it down with a clank. A few years back, Brendan had promoted him to relief skipper, and despite Fox's reservations, he'd grudgingly taken the position, knowing he'd seldom be required to take the wheel from steady-as-hell Brendan. Ever since then, the men liked to joke that Fox didn't mind sloppy seconds. When he took the wheel for a brief spell, they equated it to his one-night stands.

In and out. Just long enough to get your dick wet, right, man?

Fox laughed, pretended to let it roll off his back, but the comments dug under his skin, deeper each time. Especially since last summer. Now Brendan wanted him to be captain? To face even more skepticism and lack of respect? Not a fucking chance.

"Eventually he'd realize asking me was a mistake. I'm just trying to be considerate and save everyone some valuable time."

Hannah sat silent for a moment. "This is how you feel when I say I'm not a leading lady, I guess."

That gave him pause. The fact that she'd cast herself in some permanent benchwarmer role did drive him crazy. But no, they were coming from different places entirely. "The difference is, you want to be a leading lady. I don't want to be the hero of the story. I'm not interested."

She pressed her lips into a line.

Fox narrowed his eyes at her. "Are you doing that thing with your mouth because you're trying to trap all the psychological terms you want to throw at me?"

Her expression turned miserable. "Yes."

He forced a laugh. "I'm sorry to disappoint you, Freckles, but there's nothing here. Not everyone is fertile ground for fixing."

She lifted her shoulders and let them drop. "Okay, I won't try. If you tell me you don't want to be the captain, I'll believe you. I'll support that."

"Really?"

"Yes." A few seconds slid by. "After you visualize yourself being good at captaining. Put yourself in the wheelhouse and imagine yourself enjoying it. The crew thinks of you as a good time, but there is a time for fun and a time for responsibility. They see that you recognize the difference."

"Hannah . . ." Why was he panicking? He didn't want to visualize himself being taken seriously as Brendan's replacement. That would only lead to false hope. Didn't she realize that? Besides, it wasn't possible. Even if his imagination could conjure something so unlikely, he would never be able to realistically see himself in that leadership position. "I can't do it," he said, jerking a shoulder back. "I can't see it, Hannah, and I don't want to. All right? I appreciate you trying for me."

After a moment, she nodded. "Okay." A slow, playful smile. "I'm afraid our time together is up. We'll resume this discussion during next week's session."

"I'm sorry there weren't any breakthroughs."

She took her time enjoying another bite of chocolate ice cream, his suspicions rising when her mouth took on a cocky shape around the spoon. His bottle of beer remained poised an inch from his lips as he watched Hannah swagger around the counter, neatly placing her spoon in the dishwasher. "Oh, I think I sowed a few seeds."

And maybe she had.

Because when she looked up into his eyes, he pulled enough strength from her to visualize himself in the wheelhouse, just for the briefest moment. For the very first time since Brendan asked him to consider the job, he let himself grip the imaginary wheel, knowing he wouldn't have to give it up the second Brendan came back from taking a leak or fixing something in the engine room. He'd have it from the time they set sail, right up until docking again. He imagined hearing his voice over the radio, movement on the deck.

Returning home having done everything right, earning the respect of the crew—that's where he got stuck. He couldn't see that for the life of him.

Fox banished the image as quickly as possible, clearing his throat hard. "Good night, Freckles."

"Good night," Hannah said warmly, going up on her toes to kiss his cheek. "What kind of music day did you have?"

He let out a breath, happy to be back on familiar ground. "Coming home after four days on the water? Mmm. Something about home."

"'Home.' By Edward Sharpe and the Magnetic Zeros."

He barely kept his hand from lifting to brush back her hair. "I don't know that one," he managed.

"I'll text it to you before I go to sleep. It's perfect."

Fox nodded. "You?"

She waggled her eyebrows and backed away. "'Just One Kiss' by the Cure."

"Cute."

Watching her cross the apartment in her short red dress, smiling knowingly at him over her bare shoulder before disappearing into the guest room, Fox started to wonder if living with Hannah could be dangerous in more ways than one.

Put yourself in the wheelhouse and imagine yourself enjoying it. The crew thinks of you as a good time, but there is a time for fun and a time for responsibility. They see that you recognize the difference.

Hannah thought if she dug around a little, she'd find something interesting or worthwhile under his surface? She'd find his long-buried ambition?

Maybe he should show her exactly what he did best.

He could blur every thought in her beautiful head, leaving only the certainty that he lived up to the hype. That he was only good for one thing.

Fox pictured Hannah on the other side of the wall, that red dress slipping down to her ankles. How her skin would flush if he walked through the door.

Just one kiss, he'd say, exhaling against the nape of her neck. *Let's see about that.*

Don't. Don't fuck this up.

And he would. In a heartbeat. When the truth was . . . for the first time in a long, long time, he didn't want a girl thinking he was only good for one thing. Hannah was like a leaf blower aimed right at his undisturbed pile of possibilities, and damn, the hope felt kind of good. At the same time, he wanted them stuffed back under the tarp. Protected.

Fox took a step in the direction of her room, replaying that kiss, imagining the bump of the bed and her cries filling the apartment. It was only by the grace of God that he made it into his room without knocking on her door. But hell if he didn't spend the whole night thinking about it.

Chapter Eight

There was no filming on Saturday and most of the cast and crew headed to Seattle to take advantage of the time off. Hannah received a text from Christian at ten in the morning that read, **You coming to Seattle, yes or no? I don't care either way.** And while it was incredibly hard to pass up such a kind and generous invitation, Hannah was anxious to get some sister time with Piper. With Brendan back on terra firma to entertain his parents, the captain very wisely handed Piper his credit card, grunted at her to be careful, kissed her like the sky was falling, and nudged a dazed Piper toward Hannah, who waited in the driveway pretending to get sick over the public display of affection.

"Okay, but seriously," Hannah said, climbing into the passenger side of Brendan's truck, which they were borrowing for the day. "Does your vagina ever get tired?"

Piper snorted. "Sometimes I swear it is, but that's just my cue to hydrate." Hannah fell sideways onto the seat laughing, her sister ruffling her hair with an indulgent smile. "When he's doing it right, it never gets old." Piper checked her makeup in the rearview, smacked her lips together, and started the truck. "Someday you'll have a reason to agree."

Hannah didn't like where her mind went—and it went there immediately.

The way Fox stared at her last night as she'd walked into her bedroom.

He must not have expected her to glance back over her shoulder or he wouldn't have had that look in his eye. Honestly, the word "seductive" normally sounded ridiculous to her. A word that reminded her of old Sharon Stone movie trailers. Or maybe she'd hear it once in a while flipping through cable where the coffee commercials lived.

Seductive blends. Seductive aroma.

She'd never really considered the true meaning of the word until now. Fox was attractive. Like, insanely so. That was a given. But last night, that look in his eye had accidentally given her a peek behind the curtain, and it was like setting foot in a new country with a different currency and climate. She would even venture to call his expression smoldering. He'd been thinking about sex—no mistaking it. And while she'd be lying to say there wasn't always a current of physical tension running between them, she'd always assumed Fox just gave it off all by himself. It came with the territory of being in his vicinity.

Last night was different.

Last night, for that brief moment, all of that potent sexual energy had been concentrated on her, and she'd heated like an oven, the knobs on her awareness turned to the highest setting. Did he want to sleep with her? The fact that he'd given her advice on how to capture Sergei's attention made the possibility seem remote. But the mere thought of Fox wanting her was like skydiving. A free-falling, leave-her-stomach-in-the-air event.

At UCLA, she'd dated one of her fellow music history majors, that relationship lasting just over a year. It was serious enough to introduce him to her parents and take a vacation together in Maui. But her interest in him had mainly been based on convenience, since they had classes together, and he didn't make a fuss when Hannah retreated into her headphones. He'd just hop on the Xbox and zone out, too. After a while, the relationship turned into a competition of finding ways to ignore each other—definitely no reason to use the word "seductive."

Even while nursing her crush on Sergei, she'd dated. An extra she'd met on set, fresh from a farm in Illinois, following his dream in Los Angeles. A stunt coordinator who spent the entire date hitting her with classic movie trivia, which she didn't technically mind—they were social media friends now—but there'd been no viable connection.

In other words, she'd been playing in the minor leagues.

If that kiss at the party was any indication, Fox was in a major league all his own when it came to intimacy. Sure, she'd known that. In theory. He was a certified Casanova and didn't even bother trying to deny it. Experiencing those skills last night, putting that knowledge into practice, had been eye-opening to say the least.

She was pretty sure her brain and ovaries had briefly swapped locations during that kiss.

If he wanted to sleep with her—and come on, it was entirely possible she'd misread him—what would she do with all of that . . . seductive smolder? Why couldn't she stop thinking about it now? How he would move. How he would groan when the relief hit. What the fronts of his muscular thighs would feel like against the backs of hers.

He would do it right.

He'd dehydrate the shit out of her.

"Hannah."

"What?" she shouted.

Piper squeaked and swerved the truck, shooting Hannah a wide-eyed look. "I asked if you wanted to stop for coffee."

"Oh. Sorry." Was she sweating? "Of course I do."

Hannah shook herself, focused on counting the white lines painted in the middle of the road. Guilt settled into her stomach like sediment in a wineglass. No more thinking about Fox in those terms. Sex terms. The kiss, followed by that hungry look, had just thrown her for a loop. Now she needed to get back on track. Back to batting in the minors. Back to her harmless crush on the director. She'd probably misread Fox, anyway.

After they stopped for giant lattes smothered in caramel and whipped cream, Piper drove Hannah about forty minutes south to an outdoor shopping mall. They spent the day browsing racks but were too busy talking and catching up to buy much of anything, although Piper walked out of the lingerie store looking very superior with a little pink bag, and Hannah bought a new pair of round tortoiseshell sunglasses. They spent most of their time together lingering over lunch at a cozy French bistro, continuing to order more and more coffee so they wouldn't get kicked out.

The sky was darkening by the time they headed back to Westport, Hannah singing along to the radio, badly, but her sister was used to it.

"Hey," Piper said when the song had ended. "Brendan is bringing his parents into Cross and Daughters tonight. Come and meet them?"

"As if I would pass up a chance to meet those responsible for spawning the Mean One?" She tugged the phone out of her pocket. "Let me just text Fox."

Piper sniffed loudly.

"I'm staying with him. It's the polite thing to do." Hannah started to fire off a quick text, then hesitated. "Should I invite him?"

"It's Saturday night—he doesn't have"—her sister looked at her meaningfully—"plans?"

"Plans, like . . . oh." Her stomach had no right to drop. "I—I mean, he didn't mention anything. Like a date. But if I invite him, the worst he can say is no."

Why was she nervous he would turn her down? Tell her he was headed to Seattle for his usual recreational activities? What Fox did with his time was none of her business. Her fingers hovered over the screen for a few more seconds before she tapped out a text.

> **HANNAH (7:18 PM):** Heading to Cross & Daughters with Piper if you're interested.

A minute later, he answered.

> **FOX (7:19 PM):** See you there, Freckles.

Hannah let out a slow breath and tipped her head back against the seat. The speed with which her stomach calmed was alarming. But it did. Like a raging sea turning into a tranquil lake in the space of four words. What was *that* about? Did she simply covet the short length of time she had to spend with a friend? That was totally possible, right?

They walked into Cross and Daughters a little while later, the evening crowd only starting to trickle in. Hannah's heart squeezed the moment she stepped over the threshold, bombarded by images of her and Piper sanding the old, neglected bar, finding that photograph of Henry behind a piece of plywood, sprinting to the door with a flaming frying pan, getting ready for the grand opening. So many memories packed into such a small space. And there was a definite satisfaction that came from looking up and knowing she was the one who hung the gold, spray-painted fishing net from the ceiling.

Piper slipped behind the bar to consult with Anita and Benny, the newly hired waitress and bartender Piper had told her about over lunch. Her sister looked so confident, pointing out things on the drink menu, answering a question about how to operate the register. A year ago, Piper had never seen a checkbook, let alone balanced one. Now she owned and operated a successful bar.

God, Hannah was proud of her.

"You okay over there?"

She turned at the sound of Fox's deep drawl, finding him leaning back on a bar stool, one arm resting along the back of the seat, the other steadying a beer bottle in his lap. There was no help for the prickles that ran along her scalp, down her neck, and around to the front, hardening her nipples into points. It happened so fast, she didn't have time to think of something to counter the effect, like slugs or snot or foot fungus.

Fox watched it happen knowingly, too, the blue of his eyes deepening a shade as they dipped to her breasts, the beer bottle lifting to his sculpted lips for a long, hard pull.

Get yourself together, Hannah.

This was simply the effect Fox had on women. But she didn't have to be like everyone else and let it become A Thing. She could acknowledge his attractiveness and remain objective, right?

"Hey. Yes. I was just, um . . ." Begging herself to stop being an idiot, Hannah hopped onto the stool beside him. "I was just remembering all the work that went into this place."

He nodded. "You girls brought it back to life."

She nudged him with an elbow, sighing inwardly when his firm muscle didn't budge in the slightest. "You helped."

"I was just here for the company," he said quietly, holding her gaze long enough to turn her stomach into a jungle gym. Then, as if forcing himself to switch gears, he reached over and tapped her nose. "What do you want to drink?"

"Hmmm. No liquor. I filled my yearly quota last night. Beer, maybe?"

"Beer it is."

Fox nodded at Benny and ordered something vaguely German-sounding. A moment later, Hannah was sipping on a cold pint glass full of a golden substance, an orange wedge stuck on the rim. "This is good. This is beer?"

He grinned. "Uh-oh. Someone is going to fill their yearly beer quota, too."

"Oh no. Not me. I have to be on set in the morning."

"We'll see." Cockily, he crossed his arms. "You haven't been here in a while."

Hannah paused midway through a sip. "What's that supposed to mean?"

She never got her answer, because at that same moment, Piper poked her in the shoulder, presenting Brendan's parents with a flourish. "Hannah, this is Mr. and Mrs. Taggart. Michael and Louise, this is my sister, Hannah."

Oh, these were Brendan's parents, all right. No mistaking it. They were stiff shouldered and serious, not at all comfortable in the bar setting. But they were trying, even if their smiles were distracted. Without looking at Piper, Hannah could feel her sister's nerves over having her future mother- and father-in-law in the bar, so Hannah did what she did best. She called forth her inner hype girl.

Putting on a broad smile, Hannah slipped back off the stool and leaned in to kiss the cheeks of the older couple, squeezing their hands at the same time, drawing their full attention. "It's so lovely to meet you. Are you enjoying your time back in Westport?"

Louise's tension unlocked slightly. "Yes, we are. Not much has changed about the town and I find that quite comforting."

Like mother, like son, huh?

"Piper has been telling me all afternoon how incredible it has been to have you visiting them. You should be worried about her locking you in the house and not letting you go."

Louise chuffed a little, her cheeks tinting with pink. "Oh. Well, isn't that sweet."

Hannah nodded. "She even created a signature cocktail for your visit. The . . . Taggart-tini. Right, Pipes?" Her sister stared back at her unblinking, a smile frozen on her face. "What are you waiting for? Get back there and make them one."

Piper turned and circled around to the other side at the pace of a sloth.

Wanting to buy her sister some time to actually create the Taggart-tini, Hannah laid a hand on Fox's arm. "You must know Fox, right? He grew up with Brendan."

It was impossible to mistake the slight cooling in Louise's temperature. Very subtle, but Hannah detected it in the pinch around the corners of her mouth. "Yes, of course we do. Hello, Fox."

Fox turned slightly and nodded at the couple. "Good to see you, Mr. and Mrs. Taggart." His smile seemed forced. "Hope you're having a nice visit."

"We are, thank you," Michael said, equally stiff.

Hannah frowned inwardly at the exchange, itching to address it with Fox, but Piper chose that moment to slide two cloudy red martinis across the bar. "Here it is!" Piper sang through her teeth. "The Taggart-tini."

"Oh, well, I couldn't possibly . . ." Louise started, clutching her collar.

"Oh, but you will, won't you?" Hannah passed the drinks to the couple, helping them clink their rims together. "One sip won't hurt."

Twenty minutes later, Louise had Piper's face in her hands, her words ever-so-slightly slurred. "I have never seen my son so happy. You are an angel. An absolute angel, isn't she, Michael? Our son smiles now! It's almost disconcerting how often he smiles, and you—you are going to give me grandbabies, aren't you? Oh please. You angel. My son is a lucky man."

Piper looked over at Hannah, blinking back grateful tears.

Thank you, she mouthed.

Hannah let out a satisfied exhale and went back to her beer, which was unfortunately warm now, realizing after several moments that Fox was staring at her. "Damn, Hannah. That was nothing short of masterful."

She gave a subtle bow. "The power of alcohol, Peacock."

"Uh-uh." Adamantly, he shook his head. "That was all you."

"Piper was having a hard time relating to Louise. They just needed a little push, that's all. Who doesn't love Piper?" She looked back over her shoulder to where Louise was now attempting to slow dance with Piper to a power ballad. "Let's see if my sister is still grateful tomorrow when she's got a hungover future mother-in-law on her hands."

Fox chuckled. "Nothing some greasy potatoes can't cure. The important thing is, the ice is broken."

Don't bring up the weird exchange between Fox and Louise. Don't. Why do you always have to address every little thing? "Speaking of ice . . ." *Nice segue, Barbara Walters.* "Did I imagine a little awkwardness between you and Brendan's mother?"

He took his time answering. "Nah, you didn't imagine it." His laugh crackled as he shifted in the chair. "Nothing serious. They were just protective of Brendan growing up, and I was, you know, the bad influence on her otherwise perfect kid."

There was no bitterness in the way he said it. Just making a statement.

"Do you think you were a bad influence?"

"No," he said slowly, after several seconds had ticked by. "I was, uh . . . promiscuous before the other guys my age were ready. But I'd never put pressure on anyone else to do . . . what I did. What I do," he amended quickly. "God, no. I'd never do that."

It seemed like he wanted to say more. A lot more.

Hannah wanted to hear it. That explanation masked something deeper, but he was already restlessly ordering them both another beer, changing the subject to what she'd done that day. The obviously sore topic was forgotten, and soon they were laughing. Other members of the *Della Ray* crew steadily made their way through the door and joined the group, until they were all crowded around two stools, telling stories, Hannah getting reacquainted with the locals who'd come to mean so much to her last summer.

She didn't have this in LA. And she'd missed it. A lot.

Back home, she went to work and went home. Every once in a while, she'd go out for a drink with her coworkers at Storm Born, but she never got *this* feeling. The one that said she was in the right place. That she was home and would be accepted here, no questions asked. Every time. During a particularly long-winded story from Deke, Hannah felt Fox watching her and looked back, the alcohol thrumming along in her veins, sending goose bumps riding in a slow wave up her arms and neck.

Right, it's the alcohol.

In a daze, she watched as he wet his lower lip, rubbing the moisture together with the top one, leaving his mouth looking fresh and male. His heavy-lidded blue eyes never leaving her.

Seductive blends. Seductive aromas.

Sharon Stone.

Go home, you're drunk.

"It's time for quarters!" Benny called out behind the bar, ringing a bell that was mounted above the register. "Who are tonight's victims?"

Fox took Hannah's wrist and raised her hand before she knew what was happening.

"How about sister versus sister?" Brendan shouted from the back of the bar.

Hannah and Piper locked eyes through the crowd like two western gunslingers.

"It's on!" Hannah cried.

The bar erupted in cheers.

So much for going home.

Fox tipped back on his stool to get a better view of Hannah where she was holding court in the middle of the bar, competing against her sister in the silliest game of quarters he'd ever witnessed.

The game had one rule.

Bounce the quarter off the table. Land it in the pint glass.

But in Cross and Daughters, there was a twist. Every time a player landed a quarter in the glass, they had to tell the entire bar an embarrassing fact about themselves. The tradition started one night when a sunburned tourist decided to play quarters and was somehow convinced this rule was the norm. What started as a way to razz an out-of-towner had become standard game play.

Hannah hadn't even flinched at the rules, just nodding as if they made perfect sense. Not for the first time, he marveled over how easily she fit into this place, like she'd always been there. She'd come here last summer and gotten a part-time job at Disc N Dat, melding seamlessly with the younger generation slowly making their mark on this old fishermen's town. What would life here be like if the pair of Bellingers hadn't shown up? Brendan would still be wearing his wedding ring, years passing as he turned harder, more closed off. Fox . . .

Nothing would be different on his end, he thought hastily.

He'd be exactly the same.

So, all right. Maybe he wouldn't be standing on the edge of the crowd, with a smile on his face a mile wide, watching Hannah laugh so hard she could barely stand up. There was no helping it. She felt like the sunrise coming up over the water after a bad storm. And she was terrible at quarters. Her only saving grace was that Piper was worse.

Both of their quarter rolls had run out before getting a single one in the glass. Now they were scooping quarters off the floor into their pockets and getting back in position, trying to compete while doubled over in laughter. Fox wasn't the only one held in complete thrall, either. The locals were enamored with both sisters, but he couldn't for the life of him take his eyes off Hannah. The entire place surrounded the girls, cheering them on—and finally, finally, Hannah got a quarter in the glass, sending the customers into a frenzy.

"What's your embarrassing fact?" Fox shouted over the noise.

Hannah cringed. "I failed my driver's test because I kept changing the radio station." She held up some fingers. "Three times."

"What she lacks in concentration behind the wheel, she makes up for in driving me home from jail," Piper added, laying a kiss on Hannah's cheek. "Just kidding, Louise!" she called to her gaping mother-in-law, sending her and Hannah into a fit of hysterics. She almost lost her balance completely, and Fox figured that was his cue to take her home.

He set his half-empty beer down on the closest table and approached Hannah, acutely aware of everyone within earshot, including Piper and Brendan. They were already wary of Hannah staying in his spare room. Every word out of his mouth, every action was being scrutinized to gauge his interest and intentions. The last thing Fox wanted was another "talk" from Brendan. He'd had enough of those on the boat.

So he tried to sound as casual as possible when he stopped in front of Hannah, ducking down a little to her level until their eyes met. "Hey, I'm heading home if you want to walk with me." Briefly, he met Brendan's eyes. "Or stay and get a ride. It's up to you."

Without a doubt, if she went with option number two, Fox knew he'd sit in his room and wait until she was safely inside.

"I should definitely go now if I don't want to be a zombie on set tomorrow," she said, turning and throwing her arms around Brendan and Piper. "I love you guys. See you soon."

"We love you, too," Brendan said, patting her on the head and earning heart eyes from his wife. Not that he saw it, because he was busy giving Fox a death stare.

Right.

It was easy to see what his friend was trying to communicate to him.

Walking out of the bar with Hannah would send the wrong signal. A bad one. Get everyone's tongues wagging and ultimately make her look bad. God, that was the last thing he wanted. He needed to be more careful. As of now, they'd kept her temporary stay in his guest room pretty quiet, but leaving the bar together on a Saturday night would whip up any speculation that might already be brewing.

"I'll meet you outside," Fox said in a rush, turning and walking blindly through the crowd with a pit in his stomach. When he stepped out into the cool spring mist, he couldn't resist looking back through the window from where he'd just come, watching Hannah wave to everyone on the way out, getting caught up in long good-byes, until finally she joined him in the nighttime shadows.

Without a word, Hannah linked their arms together, laying her head against Fox's shoulder, the show of trust cementing right over the hole in his belly.

"Jesus, Freckles," Fox said, tracing the part running down the center of her head. "We need to work on your quarters game."

She gasped. "What do you mean? I won!"

"Ah, no. You were the least-worst loser."

Her laughter rang down the misty street. "What is the advantage of winning when you have to tell people something embarrassing about yourself? It's backward."

"Welcome to Westport."

She sighed, rubbed her cheek against his arm. "On nights like this, I think I could live here."

Fox's heart lurched so hard he had to wait a moment to speak. "Oh yeah?"

"Yeah. But then I remember what a crazy idea that is. I can't live in Westport and continue working in entertainment. And the bar . . ." She smiled. "The bar is Piper's."

Well, that's that. Right?

How the hell would he handle it if Hannah moved here, anyway? He'd see her constantly. Every Saturday night would be like this. Pretending to her and everyone watching that he didn't want to take her home. *Really* take her home. And once that happened, well. He'd be screwed. He'd have broken his own rule about not hooking up in Westport, fucked his relationship with Brendan, and potentially hurt Hannah's feelings. It was best for everyone if she stayed in LA.

But tell that to the disappointment so heavy that it almost dragged him down to the cobblestones.

They turned right on Westhaven and crossed the street, walking along the water without verbally agreeing to it. "Do you love the ocean as much as Brendan does?"

There she went, asking him questions that made him think. Questions that wouldn't allow him to skate by with a quip— and he didn't really like doing that with Hannah, anyway. He liked talking to her. Loved it, actually, even when it was hard. "I think we love it in different ways. He loves the tradition and structure of fishing. I love how wild nature can get. How it can be more than one thing. How it evolves. One year, the crabs are in one place, the next they're in another. No one can . . . define the ocean. It defines itself."

Hannah must have been holding her breath, because she blew it out in a rush. "Wow." She looked out over the water. "That's lovely."

He tried to ignore the satisfaction of being acknowledged and understood because of something that came out of his mouth. It wasn't often that happened to him. But he couldn't shrug it off, so he just let it settle in.

"Okay, I think you've convinced me. I want to hunt king crabs." Hannah nodded firmly. "I'm going to be your newest greentail."

He couldn't tell if she was joking or not.

She better be joking.

"A rookie is called a green*horn*—and that isn't happening, babe. You can't even keep your balance during quarters." An actual shiver blew through him thinking of Hannah on the deck, fifteen-story waves building in the background. "If you hear me screaming in the middle of the night, you're to blame for my nightmares."

"I can just be in charge of the music on the boat."

"No."

"You got me feeling all romantic about the ocean. It's your fault."

He looked down into her face and finally, thank God, was positive she was joking. And goddamn. In the moonlight, her amused features, her shining eyes . . . they were a masterpiece. His body thought so, too. It liked her mouth most of all, how she moistened the lush pillows of her lips, as if preparing for a kiss. Who wouldn't kiss this beautiful girl, so full of life, in the moonlight?

Fox lowered his head slightly. "Hannah . . ."

"Be careful of that one," someone shouted from across the street. "Run while you can, girl."

Laughter broke out, and Fox knew, before turning to look, that it would be the old-man regulars from Blow the Man Down, smoking outside in their usual spot. The same men he'd made jokes to hundreds of times about his exploits in Seattle. Because it was easier to give them what they wanted. Laugh with them, instead of being laughed at. Make the joke, instead of being the joke. And above all else, don't let them see how much it all bothered him.

Hannah blinked several times and stepped back from him, as if becoming aware of her surroundings and what had almost happened between them. They'd almost kissed. Or did he imagine that? It was hard to think with the warning signal going off in his head. Jesus, he didn't want Hannah to hear the kind of garbage that came out of these men's mouths.

"Who are those guys?" she asked, leaning slightly to look past him.

"No one." He took her wrist and started walking at a fast clip, glad she'd worn sneakers so she could easily keep up. "Just ignore them. They're drunk."

"Your mama didn't warn you about tomcats like this one? Make sure he shells out the cab fare—"

Hannah skidded to a stop beside Fox, yanking her arm free.

Before he could get ahold of her again, she'd marched halfway across the street.

"Hey, scumbag! How about you shut your mouth?" She jabbed a finger at the leader, and his cigarette froze on the way to his mouth. "Mamas don't bother warning girls about jerks like yourself, because no one would come within ten feet of you. Smelly old ball sac!"

"Now hold on. It's just a bit of fun," offered the man.

"At whose expense?" Hannah shouted, turning in a circle, searching the ground.

Fox, who'd been standing behind her completely dumbfounded, caught between awe and self-disgust, forced his throat to start working. "What are you doing?"

"Looking for something to throw at them," she explained patiently.

"Okay, how is Piper the one that ended up in jail?" He wrapped a forearm around her waist and shuttled her down the street toward his building, no idea what to say. None. He'd never had anyone stand up for him like that.

And he didn't want the breathless warmth winging its way into his chest. Would never be ready for the . . . dangerous hope that started to rise to the surface. Hope that if this girl believed he was worth a damn—enough to defend him in the street like this—maybe he was worth the effort?

No. Been there, done that whole dance with optimism. Wanted no part of it.

Right?

"Hannah, you didn't need to do that. In fact, I wish you hadn't." He really didn't enjoy the flash of hurt in her eyes. "They were way out of line."

"No, they weren't." He laughed, even though it felt like razor blades. "They know it's okay to make those jokes to me, because I make them about myself. It's fine."

"Yeah, it really sounds fine," she murmured, allowing Fox to pull her up the stairs of his building, standing silently as he unlocked the door. Part of him, honest to God, wanted to throw his arms around her and say thank you, but no. No, he didn't need a defender. He'd earned that ridicule, fair and square, hadn't he?

The last seven months were nothing but an anomaly.

Even if his celibacy, even if the constant of Hannah's friendship, had made him feel better about himself than he had in years.

They walked into the apartment, and Fox turned on the one and only lamp.

He wanted to shut himself in his bedroom, before the shame of Hannah witnessing that ridicule on the walk home seeped out through his pores and turned visible, but he couldn't let her hurt expression be the last thing he saw that night. So Fox did what he did best and made light of it. "Have to admit, I'm pretty impressed by your creative use of the term 'ball sac.' Ten out of ten."

Her lips crept up into a smile on one end. "Are we okay?" She wet her lips. "Are you?"

"Everything is fine, Freckles." He laughed, the empty apartment mocking him. "Get some sleep, huh? See you in the A.M."

After a moment, she nodded. And that's where he left her, staring after him thoughtfully, halfway between the kitchen and the front door.

As soon as Fox was alone in his bedroom, he dropped his forehead to the cool door, barely resisting the urge to bash his head against it. Obviously he hadn't fooled Hannah into thinking he didn't give a shit about anything. That life was just a series of pleasures and amusements for him. This girl, she saw through it. Worse, she wanted to reach him. But he couldn't let that happen.

And he knew exactly how to prevent her from looking too deeply.

Chapter Nine

$\mathcal{H}$annah woke up at six A.M. with mice using her brain as a trampoline.

Her hand slapped down on the side table, fingers closing around her AirPods, shoving them into her ears. Next came her phone, her thumb locating the music app and selecting Zella Day from her library, letting the notes drift through the fog and wake her up slowly. Today was Sunday. Not an ideal day for working, but it was her first day on set as slightly more than a production assistant—she was an observer now, ooh, ahh—and she needed to set the right tone. Calm but focused.

Hannah, you didn't need to do that. In fact, I wish you hadn't.

Fox's reprimand from the night before came rushing back, and the mice ceased bouncing on her brain, creeping off to go hide in a hole somewhere. Oh man, she'd really yelled at those old men from the middle of the street, hadn't she? Not a dream? Truthfully, she was fine owning that reaction. Even if she *had* thrown something at them, they would have deserved the resulting concussion.

They'd deserved it for treating him—anyone, really—with so little respect.

Why didn't Fox think so?

He'd seemed fine before bed. Maybe the alcohol had amplified a situation that was really no big deal? What if fishermen simply spoke to each other that way and she'd misread the intention behind it?

But none of it sat right, so she resolved to ask Fox about it later and forced herself to focus on the upcoming day at work. She ran through the scenes in her mind, searching for inspiration to enrich the score, but an hour passed without anything feeling exactly right. Which was concerning. She'd never gone so far as to think scoring movies was her calling. That would have been putting the cart way before the horse. But she'd always been confident in her ability to pull songs from memory to perfect the mood of any situation. What if she'd been *too* confident?

The scent of ginger distracted Hannah from her troubling thoughts.

It wasn't an unpleasant smell at all. Quite the opposite. It was almost . . . stimulating in its richness? And she'd smelled it in the apartment before, but never so strong. What was that?

Hannah tossed aside the covers and climbed out of bed, leaving her AirPods in on the way to the bathroom, where she brushed her teeth and used the toilet, grudgingly removing the earbuds to shower. Fox had no reason to be awake this early, so she tried to be as quiet as possible, wrapping a towel tightly around her body and tiptoeing toward the guest room.

When the door to his bedroom opened and he breezed out, mid-yawn, in nothing but black briefs, Hannah ran smack into the side of the couch, sending a jolt of pain through her hip. It sent her stumbling back a couple of feet, her ass bumping into a floor lamp. Seriously, leave it to her to find two of the only pieces of furniture in the extremely sparse apartment and hit them . . . and now she was staring. Of course she was staring. What else was she supposed to do?

Fox was coming toward her with a lopsided grin and barely any clothes.

Dimples out. Ready to film a razor commercial.

And whoa. Until that moment, she hadn't even been aware of his tattoos.

The outline of an actual fox stretching across his right hip, a giant squid wrapped around an anchor on the left side of his rib cage, a series of different-sized stars on his pec, plus other ones she didn't have the wherewithal to decipher because his muscles were demanding attention. Were muscles supposed to be so thick? Yes. Yes, because he hadn't bought these in a gym. He'd come by them hauling giant steel pots out of the water, pulling in nets of fish, from balancing on a deck during rough weather.

"Whoa there, Freckles," he said in a raspy morning voice, tipping his head toward the teetering lamp. "Still getting your sea legs?"

"Um . . ." Resolutely, she looked down at the floor. "I guess I'm more hungover than I realized. Better lay low tonight."

The closer he came, the stronger the scent of ginger. And the harder it became not to look at Fox in all his nearly naked glory. Listen, Hannah got horny with the best of them. Once in a while, at least. Mostly when listening to Prince. But the times she'd felt slightly wanting and uncomfortable were a far cry from this cinching of muscles, this filtering of warmth to her private areas.

Guilt invaded her middle. Not quite enough to scare off her lady boner, but enough to mentally berate herself for being a bad friend. How was Hannah any better than the girls who'd called dibs on Fox at the party on Friday night?

"I, um . . ." She tipped her head down so the wet hair would curtain her face. *Must resist the call of those chisel-cut hip abductors.* "There's an early call time. I need to hurry up and get down there."

"Where are you filming today?"

Was his voice closer than before? The goose bumps racing up her skin made her wish dearly for something more substantial than a towel to cover herself. "We're shooting on the harbor. A kissing scene, actually. The big finale. We should have the lighting we've been waiting for."

"Finale?" he echoed quickly. "You just started."

"We don't always shoot the scenes in order. Sometimes it depends on the availability of the locations . . ." He stepped in front of Hannah, giving her no choice but to look up at the ceiling, where she pretended to search for cracks. Otherwise she wouldn't trust herself not to stare straight into the eye of the storm.

Also known as his crotch.

"You can't look at me, can you?" Fox said, amused. "I'm not used to having someone else in the house. You want me to put on sweatpants next time?"

Jesus, no, screamed the pervert who had rented space in her head.

"Yes, please. And I'll . . . use my robe, too. I didn't think you'd be awake."

The heat of his chest warmed her exposed shoulders, and everything down there turned soft and wet. She became acutely aware of the sound of his hands settling on his hips, skin rasping on skin. His height and strength compared to her.

It was shameful to be reacting to her friend this way.

She obviously wasn't going to sleep with him. At this juncture in her life, she wasn't interested in casual sex. Especially with Fox. He didn't merely eschew long-term, he was all about *no* term. Having her around afterward would make him uncomfortable, he'd regret getting physical, and that would ruin their friendship.

I'm just a good time, and everyone knows it.

His statement from Friday night drifted into her thoughts, and for some reason, the memory made her want to look him in the eye. He was scrutinizing her kind of expectantly, as if waiting for her to expire from arousal or attempt to climb him. Was he . . . trying to throw her off-balance for some reason? Why?

She couldn't work through it when that smell was muddling her brain. What kind of nuclear pheromones was this guy giving off?

Very discreetly, she hoped, Hannah inhaled his scent.

"What is that?"

His brows drew together. "What is what?"

"That ginger smell. Is it like . . . lotion or aftershave or something?"

"No." He smirked. "None of those."

She waited for him to elaborate. He didn't. "What is it, then?"

He very briefly touched the tip of his tongue to the corner of his lips, his blue eyes twinkling. "Massage oil."

Of all the explanations, Hannah was not expecting that. "Massage oil." She laughed. "Were you, like, giving yourself a massage—" Flames climbed her face. "Oh. Wow. Walked right into that. I . . . Were you . . . d-doing that this morning?" She waved her hands frantically. "Never mind. Don't answer that."

His grin only widened. "Yeah, I was. First time I've had a chance since our last fishing trip. Had to blow off some steam. Should I have asked permission first?"

"No." Oh no. Now she was thinking about Fox asking for her permission to masturbate. It was like someone saying, "Don't think about pink elephants."

Except the pink elephant was Fox's penis.

"No, of course not. This is your apartment." And now she was reluctantly fascinated. "You use massage oil for that?"

He hummed in affirmation. "It doubles as a lubricant. You're welcome to borrow it." His attention dropped to the knot between her breasts, then lower, to the spot where the hem of the towel brushed her mid-thigh. "But only if you like to make yourself nice and sensitive first." He rubbed his knuckles over the breach of his belly button, through dark-blond hair and faded ink. "Kind of like foreplay with your own fingers."

A swallow got stuck in her throat.

A bead of sweat ran down the small of her back.

"I'll leave it in the bathroom cabinet." He winked at her as he backed away, eventually turning for his bedroom. "Orange bottle."

"Oo-kay," she said, tongue heavier than lead. "Thanks?"

Did friends share lube?

Maybe only people who were friends with *this* particular man?

"I'll be working on the boat all day," he said on his way into the bedroom, shutting the door behind him before calling through the crack, "See you down at the harbor, Freckles."

Oh.

Great.

She walked to her room in a daze.

Fox watched the film crew move like clockwork from his vantage point on the deck of the *Della Ray*. Three big white trailers were parked on the road, young people with headsets and clipboards scurrying around. Others congregated around a table of food and drinks. Large fluorescent-lamp-looking things surrounded two actors—a moody, skinny guy and a redhead who went from mooning over each other to checking their phones and not speaking in between takes.

For the last hour, he'd been replenishing supplies with Sanders and repairing the hydraulic launcher. They really only needed the piece of equipment for crab season, but apparently he was making every excuse to be out on deck.

Where he had a clear view of the film set.

Hopefully after this morning, Hannah wouldn't feel the need to defend his character anymore. She'd just disregard him with a knowing smirk, like everyone else, and he could get rid of this hope she inspired in him. He could stay where it was safe. Where his crewmates and fellow Westport residents chuckled and joked about him, but at least they weren't questioning his legitimacy as a leader.

Surely Hannah would laugh off a guy who had a favorite brand and scent of massage oil? Even though he'd never needed the shit until recently.

Usually, if he required relief and his hand was the only option, he just worked it out with a lathered palm in the shower. Now that he was seeing his five digits exclusively, he'd sprung for something with a little pizzazz. Sue him.

Brendan would kick his ass if he knew Fox had spoken to her like that. But he'd had to weigh the threat of his best friend's wrath against Hannah's growing expectations of him. Because he was definitely not a fucking captain. Not someone to be trusted with a valuable boat or the lives of five men. Definitely not someone Hannah offered her mouth to in the moonlight. Or berated strangers over.

Just a good time. Nothing more, nothing less.

Sanders walked out on deck beside Fox and greeted him with a grunt. He tossed down the wrench he'd been using to repair the oil pump and swiped a hand over his wealth of carrot-colored hair. "Fuck sake, it's hot down there. I'm thinking of installing a window in the hull. Do you think Brendan would mind?"

"If you sank the ship in hopes of a cross breeze? No, not at all," Fox answered drily, a stillness settling over him at the sight of Hannah and Sergei discussing something over a clipboard. His fingers gripped the rope he was coiling in his hand, letting the material bite into his skin, harder and harder until Hannah finally walked away. Was the director staring after her?

Yeah. He was.

That kiss the other night had worked its magic. Good.

Maybe she'd asked him to lift a heavy piece of filming equipment. Or employed some strategic lip biting. All thanks to his urgings.

It wouldn't be too long before they were both headed back to LA with a shiny new appreciation for each other.

Great.

Ignoring the acidic taste in his mouth, Fox went back to repairing the launcher and tried to focus. The sun beat down on the deck, unseasonably hot, until he and Sanders eventually gave up on shirts and shoes altogether.

Fox used to hate this kind of tedious work. He wanted to be out in the gale, warring with waves, battling their impact, witnessing nature at her angriest. Watching as she changed her mind in a matter of seconds. Maybe humans couldn't change, but nature could. Nature lived to change.

Lately, he hadn't minded the pedantic tasks as much. The repetition of bringing the *Della Ray* out to sea, docking it safely, and preparing it for the next run. Beneath his feet, the deck was warm, the vessel bobbing gently in the water, catching wakes from other boats taking tourists out to whale watch or on pleasure excursions. Salt flavored the air. Gulls floated on the breeze overhead.

In some other life, maybe, he would wrap his hands around the wheel of his own boat and greet nature on his own terms. Introduce himself as the one in charge, instead of the one who took orders and went home without the weight of responsibility. Growing up, occupying the wheelhouse had been the dream. A given. He'd learned to block it out, though. He'd blocked it so thoroughly, light couldn't even seep in around the edges.

A trill of notes in Fox's pocket had him swiping a forearm across his sweaty forehead and slipping out his cell.

Carmen.

He squinted an eye down at the name, trying to remember the face that belonged to it. No luck. Maybe the stewardess? If he answered the phone, her voice would probably jog a memory. Or he could ask for a reminder of her social media handle and figure it out that way. Most of the girls he met up with in Seattle didn't get bent out of shape over his blurry memory, anyway. They were just as interested in low commitment as Fox.

Staring down at the phone, he let it go to voicemail without answering, knowing damn well the box was full. He hadn't listened to the messages in months.

A minute after the phone stopped ringing, a text popped up on the screen.

Are you around tonight? —C

A vein started to throb in the middle of his forehead. Probably from the sun.

He tossed aside his phone, scrubbing at the itch on the back of his neck. He'd answer the message later. Or he wouldn't. There was something about the steady stream of hook-up calls that almost . . . panicked him lately. Had there always been so many?

Fox made no excuses for liking sex. The buildup and release of it. That race at the end when he didn't have to think, his body just doing the job.

Fox's phone dinged with another text message—not totally unusual for a Sunday, since his weekends were usually reserved for women, although his phone saw the most traffic on Friday nights. Lately he'd been going so far as to throw the goddamn thing into the refrigerator so he wouldn't have to hear or see any of the incoming messages. When was the last time he even answered one of them? Or left Westport to hook up?

You know exactly how long it has been.

After Hannah left last summer, he'd gone to Seattle. Once. Determined to rip out the twinge she'd left in his chest, the constant barrage of images of their days together.

He'd brought someone out for a drink, literally sweating over how shitty he'd felt the whole time, unable to focus on a single word she'd said or their surroundings. When the tab arrived, he'd dropped a fistful of cash on the bar, made an excuse, and bounced, the roiling in his stomach only settling when he'd pulled over to text Hannah.

Sanders cracked a can of Coke open to Fox's right.

"You going to answer those booty calls, man?" The deckhand took a gulping pull of his drink, balancing it on the edge of the boat. "How am I supposed to live vicariously through you if you're not even living?"

"Oh, I'm going to call them back." Fox flashed a smile that made the throb in his head worsen. "Maybe all of them at once."

Sanders's guffaw ran circles around the harbor.

On cue, Fox's phone started ringing again.

He yanked once, twice at the leather cuff around his wrist.

"Answer," Sanders said casually, tipping his head at the device. "We're almost done here."

In a high-pressure job full of ball-breaking adrenaline seekers, showing weakness was a bad idea, unless he wanted even more mockery. "You just want to listen in and steal my moves."

"You don't need moves, pretty boy. You just show up and take your pick. Me? I've got a face like a fucking walrus. I need moves." Sanders drained the rest of his soda in disgust. "I suffered through that live-action *Cats* movie last night trying to score points with the wife. One fart—one—and I lost all my progress."

Fox bit back a smile. "No luck, huh?"

"Had to sleep on the couch," grumbled the deckhand.

"Don't take it so hard, man." Fox shivered, despite the heat. "That movie could dry up the Pacific."

"I don't know, there's just something about Judi Dench . . ." Sanders mused.

Fox's phone beeped with another text, and he seriously considered throwing the damn thing in the ocean. He didn't even bother checking the name this time. He wouldn't be able to remember her face and that only made the taste in his mouth worse.

"What are you doing here? Playing hard to get?" Sanders chuckled, prodding Fox in the gut with an elbow. "That would be a first."

"Yeah." Fox laughed, his gaze straying back to where the movie was filming, finding Hannah in the group, surprised to find her looking back at him over her shoulder, her lip caught between her teeth. Thoughtful.

He saluted her.

She sent him back a half smile.

"Yeah . . ." Sanders was still going. "You've never been one to play hard to get. Remember senior year? Almost didn't graduate because you spent so much time getting busy in the parking lot."

Fox tore his eyes quickly off Hannah, feeling guilty for even looking at her while having this discussion. "Hey." He shrugged. "I still think it should have earned me extra credit toward my physical education grade."

Sanders laughed and went back to work.

So did Fox, but his movements weren't as fluid, cranks turning on either side of his forehead. Eventually he found himself braced on the edge of the boat, seeking out Hannah once again, watching as she talked to a sharp brunette. He could tell by Hannah's body language that something was off. Wrong.

Was that the soundtrack lady?

Had the songs come back for Hannah?

He could have asked her about it this morning instead of trying to divert her focus from his insecurities to something he was not insecure over in the slightest—sex. Too late for regrets now. Too late to worry about how his best friend would react if he knew Fox had talked to Piper's little sister about jacking off while he was wearing nothing but briefs and a smile.

Brendan was still clearly worried that Fox would make a move on Hannah. Despite the Talk. Despite common decency and the fact that touching her would almost definitely be unforgivable. But no one expected good behavior out of him. Not Brendan, not the people in town, the crew, anyone. Sanders had just neatly reminded Fox of that. Reminded him of it so well, he felt like a shower was in order.

No one trusted him. So the hell with it. Why try in the first place? A leopard couldn't change its spots.

A few minutes later when a visibly frustrated Hannah started speed walking to his apartment, Fox knew more than enough about women to recognize her problem. The flushed skin, the way she kept sneaking him covert looks. Lifting the hair off her neck to fan herself. She was turned on, frustrated. Horny. And that was one issue he damn well knew how to fix. What was the point of resisting?

Last night with the men outside Blow the Man Down, this morning with Sanders—hell, every day of his life—proved he couldn't outrun the notions about him. Giving in to his attraction to Hannah would serve him twofold. He could scratch this goddamn seven-month itch and cut off her bid to discover what really made him tick. One hookup with Hannah would bring everything back to surface level, where he was comfortable.

Hannah might still want the director. But hey, Fox's college girlfriend had used him as a hall pass—without his knowledge—for the better part of a year. No reason Hannah couldn't use him for the same purpose, right? Just a meaningless good time.

Despite the fact that he was breathing through the hole of a straw, Fox didn't even bother putting on his shirt before he followed Hannah to his apartment.

Chapter Ten

There was no formal plan in regard to how she would be observing Brinley. That meant it was up to Hannah to create her own opportunities, in between wrangling actors, instructing the extras, and making sure lunch deliveries were going to arrive exactly right. Pickles on this one, no pickles on the other. Why was it always pickles? It was right there in the name—they can be picked off.

Christian was extra grouchy this morning thanks to his boyfriend's visit to Westport getting delayed, and the mood appeared to be contagious. It was clear from the dark circles under everyone's eyes that most of the crew had overindulged on Saturday night, and of course, a seagull shat on Maxine's head, delaying production by an hour while it was cleaned out, the actress restyled.

Hannah decided to use the lost hour to her advantage.

The moment there was a lull in her responsibilities, Hannah approached the music coordinator where she sat in a chair beside Sergei's vacant one.

"Morning, Brinley," she said, smiling.

A cool once-over. "Oh, hey." She scanned the notes in her lap. "Hannah, right?"

"Yes."

For no other reason than the boat was visible right over Brinley's shoulder, Hannah's gaze strayed to the *Della Ray*, where it sat docked in the harbor. It was not the first time she'd looked since arriving on set. In fact, everyone and their mother was staring at Fox and his godlike body glistening in the sunshine. His physique was the only thing saving the cranky cast and crew from turning to cannibalism this fine Sunday morning. Moreover, he didn't seem aware of the distraction he created, just casually sucking up everyone's already limited concentration.

Even Brinley lowered her sunglasses and threw a glance or two toward the boat before refocusing on Hannah . . . who was definitely not thinking about the fact that she'd been in the same apartment while Fox cleared his pipes.

First time I've had a chance since our last fishing trip.

Had to blow off some steam.

What did that mean exactly? Obviously that he was . . . jonesing for release. Was it a hardship for Fox to last four or five days without pleasure? Did he, like, light candles, get completely naked, and stroke himself really slowly, adding more oil as he went along? Biting his lip? Teasing himself? Just making a meal out of the whole affair?

Now, that was a disruptive piece of imagery.

Hannah could go months before it dawned on her that, hey! She had a vagina with a whole bunch of complicated nerve endings and she really ought to explore it more often.

Well, she could really go for exploring it right about now.

She'd worn a loose tunic dress and cardigan, though the latter had been discarded thanks to the heat. Sensibly dressed, yet at the moment, she felt almost naked. Fire tickled the back of her neck, her nipples chafing uncomfortably in her bra. Her thoughts refused to stay organized.

And her roommate parading around in all his tattooed seducer-of-women glory wasn't helping. That orange bottle of massage oil was calling her name. At this point, she might rip off the cap with her teeth to get it open.

But first. Work.

This chance with Brinley was months, if not years, in the making, and Hannah couldn't just blow an opportunity this huge because her body was misbehaving—and it was. *So* misbehaving. She wasn't supposed to lust after her friend. The only thing keeping Hannah from all-out guilt was the strange intuition that he'd done this to her on purpose.

Realizing she'd allowed the silence to stretch too long, Hannah cleared her throat and determinedly tore her attention off the muscle-strapped fisherman. "Um . . ." She angled her body toward the set where Christian and Maxine would have their big kiss, the water stretching out behind them, a couple of anchored vessels outlined in the horizon. "I was wondering if you could share your plans for the scene?"

"Sure," Brinley said without looking up. "I'm not straying from the original vision. I know the setting has changed drastically from LA to Westport. But I think the industrial sound is even edgier, given the small-town vibe. It's an interesting contrast."

"Oh. Yeah." Hannah nodded enthusiastically.

Did she agree, though? Contrast *was* interesting. There was definitely something to be said for bringing a modern spin to period dramas with the music. Putting hip-hop to ballet. Playing opera during a murder scene. An oddity like that could make a moment stand out. Could ramp up the drama. Familiar music could help an audience relate to something unfamiliar. And in this case, Sergei's art house viewership would appreciate a kiss set to industrial, because God forbid it was *too* romantic.

What music would she use in this scene, instead?

Her mind drew a big old blank.

As if sensing a moment of weakness, Brinley turned to her with an expectant smile. "What do you think?"

Mentally, Hannah browsed her album collection back home in Bel-Air, but she couldn't see a single cover, couldn't read any of the names. What was wrong with her? "Well . . ." she started, searching her mind for something useful to say. Anything that would make her worthy of this chance. "I've been reading about this technique. Giving the actors small earpieces and playing the music while rolling so they can emote at the appropriate times. Essentially act in tandem with the music—"

"Do you really think Christian would go for that?" Brinley cut in, going back to sorting through her notes. "He complains when we mic him. He stopped a take this morning because the tag in his T-shirt was too itchy."

"I could talk to him—"

"Thanks, but I think we'll leave that idea for another day."

After a moment, Hannah nodded, pretending to be absorbed by her clipboard so no one would see her red face. Why would she suggest a new technique with her first breath? Before they'd even built a rapport? She should have just agreed with

Brinley's choice and waited for a better chance to give input. Once she'd proven herself as helpful. Instead, she'd established herself as an upstart who thought she knew better than the veteran.

Sergei trundled down from one of the trailers, smiling broadly at Hannah. "Hey there." Reaching their twosome, he put a brief hand on Hannah's shoulder, squeezing, before letting it drop away. And whoa. What? He'd definitely never done anything like that before. Not unless she was bleeding from a head wound. Actually, if she wasn't mistaken, he was giving her sidelong glances while conferring with Brinley about the scene structure.

Hannah really should have been listening. Observing. As she'd asked to do.

But that was a difficult feat when something very important was occurring to her. The director's hand on her shoulder had elicited not a single tingle. There was far less gravitational pull in Sergei's direction than there had been on Friday. Normally, standing this close to him would have made her pulse tick along a little faster. At the very least she would be hoping she didn't have coffee breath.

Right now, all she wanted to do was be alone.

With that stupid orange bottle. Why couldn't she stop thinking about it?

Against her will, Hannah's attention strayed to the *Della Ray* where Fox was lifting a metal trap with very little effort, his trapezius muscles flexing, along with a lot of other ones she couldn't name. Once it had been secured, he scrubbed a forearm over his dark-blond hair, leaving it haphazard and sweaty. Suddenly it was becoming difficult to swallow. Very difficult.

She hated herself a little bit in that moment. Was she this easy to distract? The man standing not a foot away was a visionary director. A genius. He treated her with respect, and he was exceptionally good-looking, in a tortured artist kind of way. Sergei was her type. She'd never been one to get distracted by the hot guy passing through. Ever.

Yet she'd never been more turned on in her life, and it had everything to do with the man who was lending her his guest room. She just needed to handle it. Purge the desire. She hadn't *appreciated* herself in a really long time, and she'd been over-stimulated this morning. Once she got control of her hormones, appeased them, she could focus on this potential new facet of her job. Maybe even decide if she truly wanted to make it a career. She could also go back to having an appropriate interest in Sergei. This long-standing crush who was finally starting to show interest in her.

Yes. That was the plan.

"Lunch is here," one of the interns called from the other side of the trailers.

Thank God.

"I think I'll grab mine to go," Hannah murmured to no one, turning to leave. Stealthily. Looking right and left, whistling under her breath. *No one is going to know you're on a masturbation break. Relax.*

Hannah made it a few steps before Sergei caught up with her. "Hey. Hannah."

Oh no. Her body was already doing that hot-anticipation thing it did when she decided the mood was right. Wheels were in motion. Could Sergei tell just by looking at her? That she had plans that included gingery massage oil?

"Yes?" she croaked.

He traced the path of his goatee where it ran around his mouth, frankly looking kind of . . . shy? "Where are you running off to?"

Oh, nowhere. Just have a quick errand to run in Orgasm Village.

"I left something . . . at the apartment." She pointed to her face. "Sunscreen. I'm going to end up looking like Rudolph without it."

"Oh. No, you could never."

Why wasn't she exploding over that compliment?

A few weeks ago, at the mere suggestion from Sergei that he found her attractive, she would have found a private place to blast "For Once in My Life" by Stevie Wonder and dance (terribly) in place. Now all she could do was search for an excuse to get away. This was when she needed to reach out and brush her fingers against his arm. Locate his bicep and test for firmness, like an avocado at the farmer's market. Or remind him of their physical differences, as Fox had suggested. *You man, me woman. Science says we should do it!* But she didn't have the slightest desire to flirt or try to snag his interest.

What is happening to me?

"I could walk with you," he suggested.

Again, nothing. Not a spark of joy to be had.

No, she *did* like Sergei. The sparks would return. She just needed to eradicate this . . . temporary physical spell she was under. "No, that's okay." She waved him off. "Go eat your sprouts and hummus on wheat. I'll be back before you know it."

He nodded, looking disappointed, and she didn't even have the room to feel bad. There was only the selfish hunger that raked invisible hands down the front of her body, teasing erogenous zones wherever they touched.

Orange bottle. Orange bottle.

Hannah already had the key out by the time she got to Fox's building, and she slid it into the lock now, entering the dark, empty apartment and closing the door behind her. She was panting. Panting. It was ridiculous! But she beelined for the bathroom anyway, snatching the almighty bottle off the bathroom shelf and carrying it to the guest room like a running back protecting a football.

"Oh my God," she muttered, closing the bedroom door and leaning her forehead up against it. "Calm down."

Easier said than done, though.

Her hands were almost too unsteady to remove the bottle cap. Especially when she thought of the way Fox uncapped beer with his teeth. Why was that so stupidly hot? His dentist must be appalled.

Finally, Hannah got the top off the bottle, and the aroma filled the air, sensual and rich and heavy with sex. No wonder she'd been so determined to figure out the source. She wedged the container between her knees and stripped the dress off over her head, letting it drift to the ground—

The apartment door opened and closed.

What the . . . ? she mouthed.

"Hannah," came Fox's voice from the other side of the bedroom door. Like the immediate other side. It sounded like he was speaking right against the wood. *Don't think of wood.* "Are you okay in there? Looked like something was wrong."

"I'm fine," she lied—not very successfully, since her voice sounded like it had been sanded raw. "I just needed a minute."

Too much silence passed.

Then: "I can smell the oil, Hannah."

Fire blazed up her neck and cheeks. "Oh my God," she said, dropping her forehead to the door again. "This is so embarrassing."

"Stop that, Hannah." His voice had fallen another octave. "I wasn't embarrassed this morning when I admitted to doing the same thing."

"You didn't do it during business hours."

His low laugh made the tiny hairs on the nape of her neck stand up. "If you're done berating yourself for having natural impulses, you can open the door."

"What?" she breathed, staring at the barrier in shock. "Why?"

A slow exhale. "Hannah."

That was all he said.

What did he mean by that?

Hannah.

Narrowing her eyes, she tried to read between the lines, and meanwhile, none of the heat tickling her belly had dissipated. In fact, God help her, standing in her bra and thong with Fox right on the other side of the door was exciting her more.

And it shouldn't be.

For a lot of reasons.

One, he was unavailable. *I'm not in the relationship race and I never will be.* After he'd made that statement, he'd backed it up by trying to help her win another man. Never mind she'd kissed him at that party because she couldn't seem to help it. She'd wanted to. Nothing to do with Sergei at all. But he'd made it clear he'd just been helping her out.

Right?

Another reason she shouldn't be considering throwing open the guest-room door? They were friends. She liked him. A lot. If she let him in and something happened, things would get awkward. Fox would probably regret hooking up with a houseguest immediately, because there would be no easy exit.

That brought her to the third reason she absolutely should not open the door.

The gut feeling that Fox had intentionally tried to put her off-balance this morning with his innate sexuality. That he'd wielded it like a weapon for some purpose she wasn't fully grasping.

So there she was, armed with her three reasons and gingery lube, when the knob of the bedroom turned, an inch of space appearing between the door and the jamb. And then another. Another. Until she was stepping back to allow it to swing open completely, her tummy muscles seizing at the sight of Fox outlined in the entrance to her room. Shirtless, filthy, rugged, and sweaty.

Uh-oh.

His gaze traveled down to the black triangle of her thong, a muscle popping in his jaw. "Don't move."

Frozen in place, she watched through the doorway as Fox crossed to the kitchen sink and washed his hands, drying them on a rag and tossing it away. And then he was prowling back in her direction through the unlit apartment, entering the room once more, and closing the door behind him. "Get over here, Hannah."

The rasped order almost made her moan. Did Fox washing his hands mean what she thought it did? That he was planning on . . . touching her? It was such a practical action. Like he was getting down to business. "I don't think that's a good idea."

"It's a great idea if you need to come." She took a step forward, and he caught her wrist, pulling her close, closer, until they were about to collide, then he moved at the last second and let her come up softly against the door, facing away from him. His fingers sunk into Hannah's hair, angling her head to the left, his breath fanning her neck, her vision doubling when he settled his hands on her waist and squeezed, his palms scraping slowly to the center of her belly, waking up a bunch of Jane Doe hormones, never before encountered and therefore never named. "Goddamn, Hannah. You are such a sexy little thing."

"Fox . . ."

"Uh-huh. Let's talk this out for a second," he said thickly against her neck, just grazing her skin with his teeth, his knuckles scrubbing side to side over her belly button. "You left the set like it was on fire to come over here and touch yourself."

She made an unintelligible noise that might have passed for a yes. Were they really discussing this out loud? Was this actually happening?

"I know it wasn't the director that made you need this." Ever so slightly, his fingertips brushed the waistband of her panties, the tip of his middle digit sneaking under, teasing right and left. "Maybe you'll go to him for stimulating conversation, but I'm where you come for the down and dirty."

What?

With an effort, Hannah tried to make sense of that. Not just the words coming out of his mouth, but the rebellion they provoked inside her. *Think.* Not so easy when slowly, so slowly, he crowded her closer to the door, and there . . . his erection met her bottom, his hips rolling as if he was doling out a treat. "Do you want my fingers between your legs?"

Yes.

Honestly, she almost screamed it.

There was something wrong with this picture, though. If her libido would stop wailing like a baby for a second, she'd be able to piece it together. "Fox . . ."

"This is what I do, Hannah. Let me do it." His tongue journeyed up the side of her neck with such blatant, animal sexuality, her eyes crossed. "It can just be a secret between friends in the dark."

Friends.

That word got through to her.

And then: *This is what I do.* A brag . . . but not. Because there was an edge just under the surface of his tone that didn't belong in a scenario like this. All day long, there had been a nettle under her skin regarding his behavior that morning, and now she understood what was happening. The why was still a mystery, but at least she had a starting point. "Fox, no."

His hands stilled immediately, lifted, and laid flat on the door. "No?"

It was painfully obvious he'd never heard that word before. Not from a woman. Hannah couldn't blame a single one of them, either. There was something about the way he spoke so frankly, touched with an aim toward arousing, moved so fluidly, that made inhibitions and insecurities seem irrelevant. They were only two people scratching an itch, and there was nothing wrong with that, right? He was a walking invitation to let loose.

But she wasn't falling for it.

Hannah didn't have a game plan. Couldn't formulate one when her brain and her vagina were at total odds. So she spoke honestly, without second-guessing herself.

"Okay . . ." She licked her lips, whispering into the dark. "Fine. You made me this way. You made me need to . . . do this. Talking about blowing off steam and . . . and the shirtlessness. Is that what you want to hear?"

"Yes," he growled beside her ear. "Let me finish you."

"No."

His hands curled into fists on the door, a humorless laugh pushing the hair at her temple around. "What are you worried about, Hannah? Making things weird between us? It won't. You know what is weird? The fact that I haven't fucked you. It's as easy as breathing for me."

"No, it's not."

As soon as she said it, the belief turned solid as concrete.

That was the edge she heard in his voice. That was why he'd seemed to almost be performing this morning. Acting. Over-compensating.

A pause ensued. "What?"

"It's not easy for you. Is it?" She turned between Fox and the door, looking up into his guarded expression, a heavy object tumbling end over end in her stomach. "Sex is what you do? Maybe. But it's not all you do. Stop trying to push that garbage on me. You did it this morning and you're doing it now."

His straight line of white teeth flashed in the darkness as he puffed a laugh. "Jesus, Hannah. Here we go with the psychology bullshit."

"Call it whatever you want."

All at once, his demeanor turned casually seductive. He dropped his mouth down, leaving it a millimeter away from hers. "You know," he rasped, his lips ghosting over hers. "I could talk you into it."

"You're welcome to try."

Okay, she really shouldn't have said that.

His ensuing smirk spelled disaster.

"Drop the oil, wet girl," he said. "We both know you don't need it."

God, that was such a cocky—and annoyingly true— statement. The line should have irked her. Not pushed her back toward that pinnacle of need, right where she'd been before she'd glimpsed the potential demons inside this man.

Her breath accelerated, heat licking at her buzzing nerve endings. She'd already admitted to Fox that he'd been the one to turn her on. But she needed to check the boxes of her own desire here. It couldn't be him that did it for her.

There was no denying that she wanted to share something with him, however. She'd called him out on using sex as a weapon, called his bluff on intimacy being so easy for him. His wall had come down briefly, unnerving him, and now Hannah wanted to be vulnerable in front of him. To give Fox a piece of herself in return.

An apology, maybe. Or an invitation to watch her be defenseless, as she'd seen him a few moments ago.

Exposure for exposure.

Hannah dropped the oil.

And he chuckled knowingly.

The sound cut off quickly when she slipped her fingers down the front of her panties, slowly parting her wet folds with her middle finger. Fox's innate sexuality allowed Hannah to keep eye contact while doing something so intimate. Something so out of character. Touching herself in front of a man, being the star of the show. She was stepping way outside her comfort zone to try to let him in.

The pad of her finger rode over her clit, nearly buckling her knees.

She made a sound, half moan, half stuttered breath.

"Hannah," he hissed between gritted teeth, those hands planted high above her head on the door, flexing thick laborer's muscles. Oh Lord. Having this man standing so close, exuding bucketloads of masculinity, smelling of sweat and massage oil, was going to end this pretty fast. "Let me take over."

All she could do was shake her head, a tightening sensation already beginning to occur deep in her core, some unreached place that she must only be tapping now. She would have remembered feeling this way before. This out of control and focused at the same time. Stroking herself to climax in front of this man was the ultimate rush, and yet, there was so much more happening. Communication passing between them that was way more important than physical relief.

Fox, obviously not giving up on throwing her off course, ran his nose up the slope of her neck, humming in her ear. "I was trying to keep this innocent, but maybe you're holding out for a better offer from me?" His breath filled her ear. "You want me to spread you out on the bed and use my tongue on that pussy, Hannah? Say the word and I'll do the rest. All you have to do is slide your fingers into my hair and hold on."

With that, Hannah lost the ability to breathe, her fingers moving faster on the sensitive pearl of flesh. It swelled along with the pressure inside her, and Fox's body heat, his scent, the way he watched her with salacious intention, his own breath turning shallow, made every inch of her more sensitive. Her hair follicles seemed to reach out to him, receiving an electrical charge in response, and she trembled, thighs squeezing tight around her hand. "You're enough when you're not touching me," she whispered, not even sure she said it out loud until Fox's expression went from lusting to dumbstruck, his chest starting to heave. "You're enough on your own."

She watched his face, watched the confusion give way to hunger and swing back again. "Hannah," he said raggedly, dropping his hands to rake them up and down her hips, twisting his fingers in the sides of her panties. "All right, I give in." The growl he let loose into her neck shook Hannah down to her toes. "You want to fuck, babe? Hop up here and let's get it done."

It was like he couldn't fathom a woman wanting nothing but his presence.

As if her turning him down only meant she wanted a different act.

A different favor from him.

Hannah didn't think there was a single thing under the sun that could turn her from hot to cold in that moment, but that glimpse past his exterior did it. The vulnerability shining through despite Fox's best efforts was like a desk fan blowing across her sweaty skin, turning it clammy. Something akin to indignation scaled the walls of her chest. Something was wrong here. Something was inside of Fox that shouldn't be, and she wanted to put a name to it.

Attempting to slow her breathing, Hannah removed her fingers from her underwear, letting them fall to her side. "Fox . . ."

He stepped back like he'd been shocked, nostrils flaring.

Opened his mouth to say something and snapped it shut again.

They stared at each other for long seconds. And then he reached for the doorknob, moving her gently but firmly out of the way so he could stride out, not stopping until he'd left the apartment.

Hannah stared at nothing, the opening riff of "Dazed and Confused" by Zeppelin playing in her head. What the heck just happened?

It wasn't totally clear, but suddenly she didn't feel so good about calling him Peacock—and in that moment, Hannah vowed she never would again.

Chapter Eleven

Fox would just pretend like it never happened.

That's all there was to it.

What had actually happened, anyway? Nothing.

Apart from seeing Hannah in a bra and panties, which was an image that would be burned into his brain for all eternity, he'd put his mouth on her neck, run his hands over her smooth skin. Dirty talked her a little bit. So what? Even though he'd almost slipped, no boundaries had been crossed.

There was nothing to be tense about.

No reason for this fissure in his gut.

Fox scrubbed a hand up and down the back of his neck forcefully, trying to rid himself of the tightness. He stood in the kitchen surrounded by ingredients for potato leek soup, vegetables finely chopped on the counter with no cutting board. He'd made a mess, and he could barely remember doing it. Or walking to the store to buy everything he needed. All he knew was that Hannah would be back from set any minute now, and he felt like he owed her an apology. She'd needed something from him, and he'd failed to give it.

He'd turned her off.

Not on. *Off.*

Hannah must like the director more than he thought. Otherwise she would have let Fox blow her mind, right? That had to be the reason she'd stopped before it was over. Couldn't be anything else. Couldn't be that Fox had exposed himself by accident, and she didn't like what she'd seen.

Could it?

He stirred a dash of thyme into the soup, watching cream swallow the green flecks, very aware of the pulse beating thickly in his throat. It wasn't as though rejection was a totally foreign concept to him. But after college, he'd kept himself out of situations where being denied was a possibility. He did his job well, went home. When he hooked up, the terms were already outlined with the woman ahead of time, no gray areas. No confusion about anyone's intentions. No chances were taken. No new horizons were embarked upon.

This thing with Hannah was nothing if not a new horizon.

It was friendship . . . and maybe that was another reason why he'd fucking pushed it earlier today. Because he didn't know how to be a friend. The possibility of failing at it, disappointing her, was daunting. Now, distracting her with sex? That was so much easier.

The sound of a key turning in the lock made Fox's insides seize up, but he stirred the soup casually, looking up with a quick smile when Hannah walked in. "Hey, Freckles. Hope you're hungry."

She visibly took his measure, hesitating before turning to close the door—and Fox couldn't help but take advantage of those few seconds she wasn't looking at him, absorbing as much as he could. The messy bun at the nape of her neck, strands of sandy-blond hair poking out on all sides. Classic Hannah. Her profile, especially her stubborn nose. The practical way she moved, pressing the door shut and locking it, her shoulder blades shifting beneath her T-shirt.

Jesus, she'd looked so hot in her underwear.

In street clothes, she was someone's little sister. The girl next door.

In a black bra-and-panties set, holding massage oil, eyes laden with lust, she was a certified sex kitten.

And she might have purred for him temporarily, but she wanted to get her claws into someone else. He needed to get on board with that. For real this time. Deep down, he'd believed that if he just put in a little effort, of a physical nature, she would fall at his feet and forget all about the director. Hadn't he? Well, he'd been mistaken. Hannah wasn't the type to genuinely like one man while hooking up with another, and it had been wrong, sickeningly wrong, to put her in that position.

Fox zipped his attention back to the stove when Hannah faced the kitchen once again. "That smells amazing." She stopped at the island behind him, and Fox could sense her working up to something. He should have known she couldn't just pretend this afternoon didn't happen. That wasn't her style. "About what happened today . . ."

"Hannah." He laughed, adding a forceful shake of pepper to the pot. "Nothing happened. It's not worth talking about."

"Okay." Without turning around, he knew she was chewing on her lip, trying to talk herself into dropping the subject. He also knew she wouldn't succeed. "I just wanted to say . . . I'm sorry. I should have stopped sooner. I—"

"No. I should have let you have your privacy." He tried to clear the pinch in his throat. "I assumed you would want me there, and I shouldn't have."

"It wasn't that I didn't want you there, Fox."

Christ. Now she was going to try to make him feel better over the rejection? He would rather turn the hot pot of soup upside down over his head than listen to her explain she was being true to her feelings for the director. "You know, it's totally possible to just eat this soup and talk about something else. I promise your urge to hash out every detail of what happened will pass."

"That's called suppression. It's very unhealthy."

"We'll survive just this once."

She moseyed around the far side of the island, dragging her finger along the surface. Then she reversed her course, filling one cheek with air and letting it seep out.

Man, it was wild that he could be frustrated with her inability to drop a sensitive subject while being grateful for it at the same time. He'd never met anyone in his life that gave a shit as hard as Hannah. For other people. She thought that compassion made her a supporting actress instead of a leading one, and didn't realize that her empathy, the fierce way she cared, made her something bigger. Hannah belonged in a category far more real than the credits of a movie. A category all her own.

And he wanted to give in to her. To rehash what happened in the bedroom earlier, his reaction to being made . . . useless. At least in that moment, he wanted to give in and let her sort through his shit, no matter how much this discussion scared him. Because every day that passed, she came a little closer to going back to LA, and Fox didn't know when he'd have her near him again. Maybe never. Not in his apartment. Not alone. This opportunity would be gone soon.

He used a ladle to fill two bowls with the thick soup, added spoons and slid one across the counter to Hannah. "Can we just work up to it a little?" he said gruffly, unable to look at her right away.

When he did, she was nodding slowly. "Of course." She visibly shook herself, picked up the spoon, and blew on a bite, inserting it between her lips in a way he couldn't help but watch hungrily, his abdomen knitting together and flexing beneath the island. "Should I distract us by telling you I had a terrible day? Not because of"—she jerked her head in the direction of the guest room—"not just because of that."

His vanity was in fucking shreds. "Okay. What else was terrible about it?"

"Well, we didn't get the shot we needed, because Christian wouldn't come out of his trailer after lunch. Might mean adding days to the schedule, if we're not careful." Fox shouldn't have been surprised when his pulse jumped happily at the possibility of Hannah staying longer, but he was.

How intensely did he feel for this girl and in what way? Everything, every feeling or non-feeling, was usually wrapped up in sex for him. Only sex. Even if the director wasn't in the picture, was he capable of going beyond that with Hannah?

"And I tried twice to approach Brinley, but she was pretty determined to blow me off. I'm not sure I'm going to get the experience I was hoping for and . . . don't tell anyone this part."

Fox raised an eyebrow. "Who am I going to tell?"

"Right." Her voice dropped to a whisper. "I don't love the direction she's going with the score on this film."

Containing his amusement was difficult. "Your shit-talking needs work."

"I'm not talking shit. I just . . . Sergei shifted gears by changing the location to Westport, and I don't think she shifted gears with him. There is grit in her choices. An LA club-scene vibe." He kept his smile in place when she mentioned the other man, but it took an effort. "The songs don't fit, but I can't make suggestions without looking like a know-it-all."

"What about talking to"—he tried to lick the acidic taste out of his mouth, gave up, took an extra-large bite of soup— "Sergei?"

"Go over her head?" Hannah drew an X onto the surface of her soup with the tip of her spoon. "No, I couldn't do that."

He scrutinized her for a second. "If you were in charge, what would you do differently?"

"That's the other terrible part of my day. I don't know. The songs aren't coming to me like they usually would. I guess . . . something that captured the timeless spirit of this place. The layers and generations . . ." She trailed off, quietly repeating that last word. "Generations."

When she didn't elaborate, Fox realized he was holding his breath, waiting to see what she said next. "Generations . . . ?"

"Yeah." She shook her head. "I was just remembering the sea shanties my grandmother gave me the other day. A whole folder of them she found. They were written by my father, apparently."

"Wow." He set down his spoon. Almost said, *Why didn't you tell me?* But thought it would sound presumptuous. "That's exciting, right?" He studied her features, noticing the tension around the corners of her mouth. "You're feeling some kind of way about the whole thing, yeah?"

She made a wishy-washy sound. "It's nothing."

"Oh no. Nope." He pushed his bowl aside, crossing his arms over his chest. "You want to bury my feet in cement and force me to talk about shit that makes me uncomfortable, Freckles, you're going to do the same."

"Uh, excuse me. Where do you get off being right?"

He cracked a smile, waved her on. "I'm waiting."

Glumly, she shoveled a final bite of soup into her mouth and made a whole show of mimicking him, pushing her bowl aside and crossing her arms. "Look. This is me stalling."

Why did he have to like her so fucking much, huh? "I can see that."

"This isn't going to distract me from the actual conversation we're going to have," she warned him.

His lips twitched. "Noted."

"Well. Fine." She dropped her hands and started to pace. "It's just that . . . you know, Piper, she really connected to the soul of Henry Cross. When we were here last summer? And me . . . I was kind of pretending to."

She stopped pacing to look at him, judging his expression, which he kept impassive. On the inside, he was curious as hell. "Okay. I get pretending."

Hannah studied his face thoughtfully before continuing. "I was two years old when we left Westport. I don't remember anything about Henry Cross or this place. No matter how much I dig, I can't . . . I can't feel anything for this . . . invisible past. Nothing but guilt, anyway."

"Why are you under pressure to feel something?"

"I'm not under pressure, really. It's just that I usually would. Feel something. I can watch a song play out in my head like a movie and bond with the words and sound, connect with something written about a situation I'm not even familiar with. I'm an emotional person, you know? But this . . . It's like zip. Like I've got a mental block on anything related to my father."

It was really bothering her. He could see that. And thus, it was bothering him. Not only that this lack of connection with Henry Cross was under her skin, but . . . what if he couldn't find the right words to make it better? Comforting women wasn't exactly his forte. "Do you want to forge some kind of bond with the past? With Henry?"

"I don't know."

"Why were you drawn back here?"

"I missed my sister. I missed this place. I even missed you a little," she said playfully, but sobered again quickly. "That's all."

"Is that all? Missing people? Or are you chewing on something you can't quite name?" Fox wished he had his shirt off, so he could feel less exposed. And what sense did that make? "Same way you came in here, poking at me until I gave in and agreed to have the damn talk . . . Maybe you're just doing the same with this place. Poking around until you find the way in. But you know what? If it doesn't happen, it doesn't make you guilty of anything, Hannah."

Slowly, gratitude spread across her features, and he let out a breath. "Thanks." She stared at something invisible in the distance. "Maybe you're right."

Desperate for some way to get the attention off himself, at least while he was attempting to dole out comfort, he coughed into his fist. "Want me to take a look at them? I might recognize one or two."

"Really? You still . . . sing shanties on the boat?"

"I mean, not very often. Sometimes Deke starts one off. Not joining in kind of makes you a dick. Case in point, Brendan never sings along."

That got a laugh out of her, and some weight left his shoulders. "Okay, I'll go grab them." She seemed nervous about the whole thing, so they might as well get comfortable. While Hannah was in the guest room, he put their bowls in the sink and moved to the living room, taking a spot on the couch. A minute later, she returned with a faded blue folder stuffed with papers and sat on the floor in front of the coffee table, pausing slightly before opening it. She ran a finger over a line of script, brows drawn in concentration, then handed him a stack.

Fox scanned a few lines on the first page, didn't recognize the lyrics, but the second one was very familiar. "Ah, yeah. I know this one well. The old-timers still sing it sometimes in Blow the Man Down." His chuckle betrayed his disbelief. "I didn't know Henry Cross wrote this. You always kind of assume these songs are a million years old."

Hannah shifted into a cross-legged position on the floor. "So you know that one. Can you sing it?"

"What? Like, right now?"

She gave him puppy-dog eyes, and his jugular stretched like the skin of a drum. *Sucker.* But knowing he could help, knowing he could do something to potentially make her happy? That was like holding the keys to a kingdom. Even if he had to sing to get to the other side. The desire to give Hannah what she needed had him adjusting the paper in his lap, clearing his throat.

There was a huge possibility this wouldn't mean much to her, either, but when she looked at him like that, he had to try. "I mean, if it means that much to you . . ."

In a voice that definitely wouldn't win him any contests, Fox started to sing "A Seafarer's Bounty."

Chapter Twelve

Born unto the fog
And ferried by the tide,
To the womb of his ship
Where he earns his pride,
A seafarer's bounty
Means coin in hand and no one at his side.

The hunt has no end.
It's a game, it's the fame.
A love to defend.
A treasure to claim.
Boots to the deck, men, come on now, let's ride.

Trade the glass
For my lass.
And the wild
For my child.
Trade the wind
For her.

Trade the mayhem
For them.
And it's anchors down. There's a life beyond the tide.

Treasure is not mere
Rubies and gold.
When a seafarer finds his warmth
From the cold.
No longer are the deep blue waves his only bride.

Home is the fortune,
Health is the prize.
To lie in her arms,
To look in their eyes,
By the laws of the land, a sailor will learn to abide.

Trade the glass
For my lass.
And the wild
For my child.
Trade the wind
For her.
Trade the mayhem
For them.
And it's anchors down. There's a life beyond the tide.

Soon, loves, soon.
Soon, loves, soon.
One last ride,
At the rise of the moon.

Then it's home to my bounty.
We'll write our family's tune.

Hannah was eleven when she got her first pair of headphones. She'd always sung along loudly to whatever played on satellite radio. Always had a knack for remembering the words, knowing exactly where the tempo picked up. But when she got those headphones, when she could be alone with the music, that's when her enjoyment of it soared.

Since they were a gift from her stepfather, of course they were completely over the top. Pink noise-canceling ones that were almost too heavy for her neck to hold up. So she'd spent hours upon hours in her room lying down, head supported by a pillow, playing the music her mother had loaded onto her phone. Billie Holiday had transported her to the smoky jazz rooms of the past. The Metallica she'd downloaded, despite lacking her mother's permission, made her want to rage and kick things. When she got a little older, Pink Floyd made her curious about instruments and method and artistic experimentation.

Music could cut her straight down the middle. Nothing else in her life had the power to do that. She often wondered if something was wrong with her that a real-life event could have less of an impact than a song written fifty years ago. But those two parallel lines—real life and art—had never collided like this. And for the second time since she'd met Fox, he was inside the experience with her. This experience she'd always, always had alone. *Wanted* to have alone. The first time had been at the record expo in Seattle when they'd shared a pair of AirPods in the middle of a busy aisle, the world ceasing to exist around them. The second time was now. In his living room.

Fox sang her father's words, filling the unadorned living room with an echo from the past that wrapped right around her throat and squeezed.

His singing voice was slightly deeper than his speaking one, low and husky, like a lover whispering to someone in the dark, and that fit him so well, the intimate quality of it. Like he was passing on a secret. It racked her with a warm shiver and circled her in a hug she desperately needed, because, oh God, it was a beautiful song. Not just any song, though . . . It was about her family.

She knew from the first refrain.

An intuition rippled in her fingertips until she had to grasp them together in her lap, and as more and more lyrics about a fisherman's growing dedication to his family passed Fox's lips, his image begun to blur. But she couldn't blink to rid herself of the moisture, could only let it pool there, as if any movement might swipe the melody from the air, rob her of the growing burn in the center of her chest.

So many times she'd tried to bridge the gap between herself and this man who'd fathered her, and never succeeded. Not when she'd gone to visit the brass statue in his honor up at the harbor, not in looking at dozens of photographs with Opal. She'd felt a tremor of nostalgia upon opening Cross and Daughters with Piper, but . . . there had been nothing like this. Hearing the song was almost like having a conversation with Henry Cross. It was the closest she would ever come. This explanation of his conflicting loves—the sea and his family.

At one point, at least while writing this song, he'd wanted to quit fishing. He'd wanted to stay home more. With them. It just didn't happen in time. Or he kept being pulled back to the ocean. Whatever the reason may be, with his confession, he finally became real.

"Hannah."

Fox's worried voice brought her head up, and she found him rising from the couch, coming toward her. He let the paper float down to rest on the table, and she watched it happen through damp eyes, her heart flapping in her throat.

"Sorry, I didn't expect that. I didn't expect . . ."

She let the sentence trail off when her voice started to crack. And then Fox was scooping her up off the floor into his arms. He seemed almost stunned that he'd done it, circling for a moment as if he didn't know what to do with her now that he had her, but he finally turned and carried her from the room. With her forehead tucked into his neck—when did it get there?—she watched as they stopped in front of the door to his bedroom, his muscles tensing around her. "Just . . . I'm not suggesting anything by bringing you in here, okay? I just thought you'd want to get away from it."

Did that make any sense? Not really. But to her, it did. And he was right. She wanted to be removed from the moment before it ate her alive, and he'd sensed it. Fox shouldered open the door and brought her into his cool, dark bedroom, sitting them on the edge of the unmade bed, Hannah curled in his lap, tears creating twin rivers down her face. "Christ," he said, ducking his head to meet her eyes. "I had no idea my singing was this bad."

A watery laugh burst out of her. "It's actually kind of perfect."

He looked skeptical, but relieved she'd laughed. "I didn't remember what the song was about until I was halfway through it. I'm sorry."

"No." She leaned her temple against his shoulder. "It's good to know I'm not made of stone, you know?"

His fingers hovered just above her face momentarily, before he used his thumbs to brush away her tears. "You're the furthest thing from that, Hannah."

Several moments ticked by while she replayed the lyrics in her head, content to be held in an embrace that was unrushed and sturdy. "I think maybe . . . up until I heard the song, there was part of me that didn't really believe Henry could be my dad. Like it was all some mistake and I've been going along with it."

"And now?"

"Now I feel like . . . he's found a way to reassure me." She turned her face into his chest and sighed. "You helped with that."

His forearm muscles twitched beneath her knees. "I . . . No."

"Yeah," she insisted softly. "Opal thought Henry might be where I got my love for music. It's weird to think it came from somewhere. Like a little boop of DNA makes my spine tingle during the opening notes of 'Smoke on the Water.'"

Fox's chest rumbled. "It's 'Thunderstruck' for me. AC/DC." A beat passed. "All right, I'm lying. It's 'Here Comes the Sun.'"

His warm T-shirt absorbed her laugh. "There's no way to hear it without smiling."

"There really isn't." He stroked his fingertips down her right arm, then seemed to pull back, as if he'd done it without thinking and realized it was too much. "I always wonder why you don't play an instrument."

"Oh, do I have a story for you." Her arm still tingled from where he'd touched it. They were sitting in the dark, speaking in hushed tones on his bed. She was in his lap and wrapped in his arms, and there was nothing uncomfortable about it. None of the awkwardness that would normally come from blubbering in front of someone who wasn't Piper. Although Hannah couldn't deny there was an underlying tension in Fox. Like electricity that he didn't know how to turn off but was clearly trying to. "I went through such an obnoxious hipster phase when I was thirteen. Like I thought I was truly discovering all these classic songs for the first time and no one understood or appreciated them like me. I was terrible. And I wanted to be different, so I asked for harmonica lessons." She tilted her head back, found his eyes in the dark. "Word to the wise, don't ever learn the harmonica while you have braces."

"Hannah. Oh God. No." His head fell back briefly, a laugh puffing out of him. "What happened?"

"Our parents were in the Mediterranean, so we walked to our neighbor's house and they were in France—"

"Ah, yes. Typical neighborhood problems."

She snorted. "So their landscaper offered to drive me and Piper—who had actually peed her pants laughing—in the back of his truck." She could barely keep her voice even, the need to giggle was so great. "We were driven to the closest hospital in the back of a pickup truck while the harmonica was stuck to my face. Every time I exhaled, the harmonica would play a few notes. People were honking . . ."

His whole body was shaking with laughter, and Hannah could tell he'd finally, fully relaxed. The sexual tension didn't leave completely, but he'd shelved it for now. "What did they say at the hospital?"

"They asked if I was taking requests."

He was laughing before, but now he fell backward, the sound booming and unrestrained. Hannah yelped as the mattress dipped, causing her to roll without warning on top of him. She ended up sprawled with her hip against his stomach, her upper half twisted so their chests were pressed together.

Fox's laughter died when he realized their position.

Their mouths were only an inch apart—and Hannah wanted to kiss him. Terribly. His darkening eyes said he wanted the same. If she was being honest, she wanted to straddle his hips and do a lot more than kiss. But she listened to her instincts, the same ones she'd heeded that afternoon, and held back, scooting away so they were no longer touching and her head was resting on his pillow. Fox watched her from under his hooded eyelids, his chest rising and falling, then carefully arranged himself across from her, his head on the other pillow. As if following her lead.

They stayed like that for a while, several minutes passing without either of them saying a word. Almost as if they were getting used to being in a bed together. Being this up close and personal without the weight of expectations. It was enough to simply lie there with him, and Hannah needed him to know that. She couldn't shake the feeling that it was important for him to know that nothing needed to happen between them for this time together to be worthwhile.

"All right . . ." he started, watching her steadily. "I guess we've worked up to it."

Hannah didn't move. Didn't even swallow.

Fox shifted on the bed, held out the wrist on which he wore a leather bracelet. "This belonged to my father. He worked down the coast a ways. A fisherman, too. He married my mother after she got pregnant with me, but the marriage didn't last beyond a few pretty miserable years." He twisted his wrist, making the leather turn a little. "I wear this to remind myself I'm exactly like him and that will never change."

The way he said it dared her to recoil. Or issue a denial.

But she only held his gaze and waited patiently, her fist curled into his pillow, eyes and mouth puffy from crying. Cute and compassionate and singular. One of a kind. And she was interested in this sob story?

What the hell was this, anyway? A heart-to-heart in the dark with a girl? His headboard should be cracking off the wall right now. She should be screaming into his shoulder, drawing blood on his back. The cornered animal inside him bayed, begging him to distract. To reach over and fist her dress, drag her across the bed and roll right on top of her, make her dizzy with his tongue in her mouth.

His weapon had been taken away, though. She'd disarmed him this afternoon.

No armor. Nothing to deflect with.

And part of him seriously hated the vulnerable state in which she'd left him. The railing of his ship had disappeared, no barrier to block him from toppling into the turbulent sea. He didn't want this kind of intimacy. Didn't want sympathy or pity or understanding. He was just fine continuing to guard the wound. Pretending it wasn't there. Who the hell was she to come and rip off the bandage?

She was Hannah. That's who.

This girl who didn't want to have sex with him—and yet was still interested. Lying there in his bed wanting to know more about him. No sign of judgment. No impatience. No movements at all. And as much as he resented the intrusion into his inner hell, Jesus, he fucking adored her, wanted to give her anything she wanted. So badly that it burned.

I wear this to remind myself I'm exactly like him and that will never change.

With his words hanging in the atmosphere, he stuffed his hand under the pillow, putting the bracelet out of sight. "I never made a conscious choice to be like him, I just was. Even before I'd ever been with a girl, it was like . . . everyone treated me like being . . . experienced was inevitable. There is something in my personality, the way I look, I guess. The parents of my schoolmates were always saying, *Look out for that one. He's got the devil in his eyes.* Or, *He's the one your mama warns you about.* It didn't make sense when I was younger, but as I got older and started to recognize my father's behavior with women, I figured it out. My sixth-grade teacher used to say, *He's going to be a heartbreaker.* Everyone laughed and agreed and . . . Look, I don't remember exactly when it started, only that I eventually embraced that image once I was in high school until there was a blur. Just a fucking blur of bodies and faces and hands."

He breathed in and out through his nose, locating the courage to keep going. To completely unwrap himself in front of this girl whose opinion mattered so much to him.

"When I was a senior, my mom sent me to visit my father for a weekend. He'd been trying to reach out, sending cards and whatnot. They didn't have a formal arrangement, she just thought he deserved a shot. And . . . after a couple of days at his place, I knew. I knew I didn't want to be like him, Hannah."

Some details he kept to himself.

Already he felt like this whole seedy explanation of his life-style was corrupting Hannah. This sweetheart with all the fucking promise in the world and a head full of songs didn't need his past taking up space in her mind. They were on opposite ends of the bed, like two sides of the moon—one dark, one light—so he wouldn't tell her about the revolving door of women he'd witnessed coming in and out of his father's apart-ment that weekend. Or the sounds he'd heard. The flirting and fighting and cloying smell of pot.

Fox swallowed hard, begging the pace of his pulse to slow. "Anyway."

A full minute passed while he tried to get it together. He wasn't sure he could explain the rest until Hannah slid her hand across the bed and threaded their fingers together. He flinched, but she held on.

"Anyway," he continued, trying not to acknowledge the warmth spreading up his arm. "I always had decent grades, believe it or not. Probably have Brendan to thank for that. He was always roping me into study groups and forcing me to do flash cards with him."

"Flash cards are so Brendan," she murmured. "I bet they were color-coded."

"And alphabetized." He couldn't help pressing the pad of his thumb to her pulse, rubbing the sensitive spot once before forcing his touch back to platonic. There was no distracting her with sex—she didn't want it. As much as that disappointed him, he was starting to find there was something freeing in not having to perform physically. In not having to fulfill an expectation. "Most of my friends stayed close for college, but I got out of here. I wanted to get rid of this image. This . . . label as the local stud. I'd earned it, fine, but I didn't want it anymore. So I left. I went to Minnesota and I found new people. I was a new person. The first two years of college, I dated occasionally, but nothing like what I was doing in high school. Not even close. And then I met Melinda. We didn't go to the same school, but she lived close by and . . . I thought it was serious. I'd never been in a real relationship before, but it felt like one. We went to the movies, out of town. I stopped seeing other people. It was like, shit . . . I can do this. I don't have to fit into the mold anymore."

A sharp object slid between his ribs, preparing to skewer.

"At the same time, I had this friend, right? Kirk. He was the one who introduced me to Melinda. As his family friend. Kirk and I shared a dorm room, both of us majoring in business. Sophomore year, we decided to work together on a start-up. We had this idea for an online stock footage company that would specialize in aerial shots. From drones." He shook his head. "There are companies now that do this. Your production company has probably used one. But back then, there wasn't anything like it. And we worked on it hard. We were going to be business partners. I was, like, a million fucking miles from who and what I'd been in Westport, you know?"

Was he really going to tell her the next part and humiliate himself on purpose? It was bad enough that he had to live with the embarrassment of what happened back then, let alone watch Hannah register it. But her grip was firm on his hand, her eyes unwavering, and he just kept going, like he'd been given an invisible push, no idea where he would land but knowing he couldn't stop now.

"One holiday weekend, Melinda was home visiting her parents. I'd lied, saying I was going home, too. I didn't, though. I never went home back then. I wanted to pretend Westport didn't even exist. No one knew who I'd been, and I wanted to keep it that way." He let out a long breath. "That weekend, I came back from finishing a paper in the library, and they were in our dorm. Together. Watching a movie in Kirk's bed." He tried to pull his hand free of Hannah's, because he was starting to feel dirty over what was coming and he didn't want that filthiness touching her, but she held on, tightening her hold. "So I confronted them. Explained that Melinda and I had been seeing each other for months. Kirk was livid, but Melinda . . . she just laughed."

Hannah frowned. Her first visible reaction to the whole sordid story. For some reason, he absorbed that reaction like a sponge. Yeah, it was confusing, right? Yeah. She thought so, too. That was something. He'd have to explain in a minute, and her confusion would clear up, but for now, that frown provided him the push he needed to finish.

"Turns out, I was her hall pass." The sharpness in his sternum pulled back and lanced forward. "She reminded Kirk that I was her free pass, they'd established it on day one, so he couldn't be mad she'd cheated. I was just the side-door guy. Not a serious boyfriend." He shrugged jerkily. "I didn't know they were dating because he never brought her around me. Because of this. Because he was jealous over her finding me attractive. And spoiler, she'd definitely called his bluff on the hall pass. He was not okay with it at all. He walked away from the start-up, moved out of the dorm. Never wanted to speak to me again—and I couldn't blame him. I'd done the exact type of shit everyone expected me to do since grade school. Brought sex with me everywhere I went, intentional or not. It didn't matter how much I tried to be someone else, this manwhore label is welded onto me. Melinda knew it without any information about my past. My business partner wouldn't even bring his girlfriend around me. It's just what they saw in me."

Fox realized he was breathing fast and took a moment to slow down.

"I dropped out after that. Didn't see a point in trying to convince people to believe I'm something I'm not. I've been working on the *Della Ray* ever since."

They stayed very still, very quiet for several moments.

Panic ensued when Hannah started to scoot closer, her expression somber.

"I'm a good time. I'm easy. I'm fine with that."

"No."

"Hannah."

When she reached his side of the bed to stroke his face, he pushed their foreheads together, teased her lips with a brush of his own. Hannah couldn't disguise her reaction. Or the soft shudder that worked through her limbs and belly. Slowly, he dragged her tight to his body, locking their mouths together. It was fight-or-flight. Go on the offensive or risk further exposure, no matter that he was fighting the exact thing giving him comfort.

Distract. Distract.

"Come on, babe," he breathed against her lips, groaning at the rapid swell between his legs, his fingers gathering the hem of her dress higher, higher. "I'll make it so good for you. I want to."

"No." She wrapped her arms around his neck and hugged him, her smaller chest heaving against his larger one. "We're okay just like this." She nudged his jaw with her nose and settled closer, as if letting him know she wasn't afraid. "Just like this."

Even after what he'd just told her?

Wasn't she paying attention?

She could resist him all she wanted, hold his hand and be his friend, but nothing would change him. His identity was set in stone. What did she want from him?

This, apparently. Just this.

Wanted whatever he was, a blend of faults and ugly truths, wanted him just to lie there with her.

It took him some time to wade through the disbelief, but he finally managed to slide one arm beneath Hannah, cradling the back of her head in one hand. Carefully, he drew her into his neck, his eyes closing over the balm she spread inside him. Not quite healing his wounds, but definitely dulling the pain for a while.

Just for a while. He'd just hold her . . . for a while.

Seconds later, Fox fell asleep in Hannah's arms.

Chapter Thirteen

Hannah opened her eyes on Monday morning and absorbed the sight of Fox across the pillow they shared, morning light beginning to peek through the blinds behind him, outlining his bedhead in burnished gold. With his mouth slightly parted, beard growth shadowing his jaw and upper lip, he was startlingly gorgeous. Seriously? At six A.M., he could be shooting an advertising campaign for Emporio Armani.

After last night, however . . . she couldn't look at him without seeing past the packaging to the uncut gem beneath. Smooth and glorious on the outside. But on the inside, his light hit a jagged peak and refracted in a thousand different directions.

A dull ache spread down the middle of her chest, deepening so quickly that she had to press a palm to the spot, rubbing to alleviate the pressure. The pain he'd revealed last night had walked across the bed and burrowed into her breast, refusing to vacate—and she didn't want it to leave. She didn't want him to carry it alone. He'd clearly been doing that a long time, letting the damage fester.

What did it mean for Hannah to help him shoulder the burden of his past? Was she being a good friend—and a friend only? Or did her determination to stand with Fox come from somewhere else entirely?

Somewhere . . . romantic?

Because that wouldn't be a good idea.

That wouldn't be a good idea *at all*.

After last night, she would never consider him a player again. By selling himself short and doubling down on his irreverent image, he was playing himself more than anything. But he was still Fox Thornton, confirmed bachelor and connoisseur of women. He didn't want a relationship, period. He'd told her that.

So no matter what sticky, reckless feelings might be bubbling to the surface, the supportive buddy position was the only one available to her, wasn't it?

Hannah's thoughts scattered like the head of a dandelion when Fox's blue eyes opened, spearing her from the other side of the pillow. They were warm, a little relieved. And then he blinked and up went his guard.

"Hey," he said slowly, studying her closely. "You slept here all night."

Words crammed into her chest. Phrases she'd learned from her therapists over the years. Things she wanted to say to Fox that would explain why he felt so terrible over what happened in college. Suggestions for adjusting his outlook, and assurances that none of it was his fault.

For once, all the fancy supportive language in the world felt inadequate, though. Somehow, over the course of the night, she'd entered the fray with Fox without making a conscious decision. She was in it, this battle for his soul. Now that she was here, however, it was beginning to seem unlikely that she could remain too long without . . . falling for him.

God. She was. Falling fast.

"Yeah," she murmured finally, sitting up and brushing some static-charged strands of hair out of her face. "Sorry, I must have really passed out."

He pushed up onto an elbow. "Wasn't looking for a sorry. It's fine."

Hannah nodded. She looked over at him and . . . oh boy, there it was. An overwhelming urge to touch him. To push him down onto the mattress, climb on top, and tell him in between kisses that he was way more than a hall pass. Way more than he gave himself credit for. But that went beyond supportive friend. Those were the actions of a supportive girlfriend—and she couldn't be that for him.

"I have to be at work early," Hannah managed.

"Right." He pushed a hand through his hair, visibly at a loss. "Huh."

"What?"

His big shoulder shrugged, the laughter not quite reaching his eyes. "It feels like I'm sending you off with nothing."

The chasm that had formed down the center of her heart last night widened, and she barely managed to swallow a sound of distress. And then the anger flooded in. How dare his teachers and full-grown adults sexualize him at such a young age? How could his father bring women over while his eighteen-year-old son was visiting? Who were those *monsters* he'd befriended in college? They probably worked for the IRS now. And yes, a fair bit of rage was directed squarely at herself, because she'd definitely called him a pretty-boy sidekick the first time they'd met. Peacock after that. She wanted to bang her head against the wall now for being like everyone else.

Before Hannah could stop herself, she'd turned and walked on her knees across the bed, wrapping her arms around Fox's neck, hugging him in a manner that was freakishly tight, but she couldn't seem to make herself stop. Especially when his arms crept up and surrounded her, pulling Hannah to his chest, his face dropping into the slope of her neck.

"You sang for me last night," she said. "You brought me as close as I'll ever get to Henry. That wasn't nothing."

"Hannah . . ."

"And after what you told me last night, I could sit here for hours and rant about toxic masculinity and undervaluing yourself, but I'm not going to do that. I'm just going to tell you that . . . I'll be back tonight and that you're really important to me."

His swallow was audible. "We sail for five nights on Wednesday. Two days from now. Kind of a longer trip than usual. I just . . . If you were curious or wanted to know when I'd be gone."

"Of course I want to know." She pressed her lips together. "That means you'll come home the day we wrap on *Glory Daze*."

They looked at each other hard, neither of them seeming to know what to do with that information. Timelines, schedules, leaving, coming back. How it related to them as two people who'd just slept in the same bed.

So she kissed his coarse cheek and gave him a final squeeze, trying not to notice the way his hips shifted, his mouth breathing hard against her neck. "Just this, Hannah?" His long fingers slid up into her hair to cradle the back of her head, subtly tilting it to the left and brushing his lips along her pulse. "Just hugging for us?"

With one word of encouragement, Hannah knew she would be flat on her back and would love every second. But maybe . . . maybe her mission here wasn't to be the supportive friend, but to prove to Fox that *he* could be one. That his presence and personality were enough without any of the physical trappings. "Just like this."

Was she asking a lot of Fox to try seeing himself in a new light? Wasn't she in the process of doing that herself—and not finding it very easy? Maybe if she wanted this man to believe he could captain a ship and rely on his wit and humor and spirit alone, then she had to believe in herself first. She couldn't ask him to reach for a higher summit if she wasn't willing to reach herself.

The opening notes of "I Say a Little Prayer" by Aretha Franklin tumbled through Hannah's head, and her eyes flew open, a grateful smile curving her lips. Hallelujah. The songs were back. Sure, the lyrics were a little alarming, considering she was lying in Fox's bed, but maybe the whole song didn't have to pertain to their relationship. Just some of it? Just the prayer parts, maybe?

Hannah swallowed. Why had the songs returned now? Had listening to Fox sing Henry's shanties last night shaken them loose? The beckoning of a new direction for her career? Or did the return of her music-minded thinking mean something else?

Reluctant to examine the possibilities too closely, Hannah allowed herself a long inhale of Fox's scent, then unwound her arms from his neck, refusing to acknowledge the low pulse between her legs or the flapping in her chest. Not today. Probably not ever.

She climbed off the bed, her back warmed by his attention, left the room, and went into the bathroom. Once she'd showered, dressed, and blown out her hair, she stopped in the living room, hesitating a moment before picking up the folder full of original sea shanties and holding them to her chest. With Fox nowhere in sight, she left the apartment, returning once for an umbrella due to the clouds moving in overhead. But instead of heading down to today's shooting site, she let the hook in her gut pull her toward the record store, instead.

Hannah sighed when Disc N Dat came into view, nondescript and lacking in any signage, the blue Christmas lights adorning the window the only indication that it was open for business.

Last summer, she'd taken a part-time job at the record store. Mainly to add enough money to their budget that Piper wouldn't have to cook anymore and potentially burn the building down. But she'd also needed a way to occupy herself so Piper wouldn't feel terrible about spending more time with Brendan. Throw in the fact that Hannah lived for records, and it had been the perfect short-term gig.

A sense of familiarity settled over Hannah when her hand curled around the bronze handle and pulled, the smell of incense and coffee wafting out and beckoning her into the musty haven. She was relieved, especially today, to see that nothing had changed. Disc N Dat was still reliably dated and welcoming, the same posters that had been there over the summer still pinned to the wall, row after row of Christmas lights twinkling on the ceiling, Lana Del Rey rasping quietly from the recessed speaker.

The owner, Shauna, walked out from the tiny back room, face buried in a coffee mug, appearing almost startled to have a customer. "Hannah!" She brightened, setting her cup down on a console table that displayed her beaded jewelry and dream catchers. "I was wondering when you'd finally stop by."

"Sorry it took me so long." They embraced in the center of the aisle—the kind of hug one gives the person who talked them through their first typhoon. "I really don't have any excuse." Hannah turned in a circle, absorbing her surroundings. "I think I was worried if I came back in here, I would quit my job on the spot and beg to get this one back."

"Well, I'll save you the trouble. We're not hiring, seeing as how we've only had two customers since the last time you were here."

Hannah blew out a laugh. "I hope they were quality, at least?"

"Those who manage to find us usually are," Shauna said, grinning. "So what's new with you?"

Oh, not much. Just in the process of realizing I have feelings for a man who is the definition of unavailable.

"Mmmm. Work, mostly." She walked her fingers along the plastic record sleeves of the *B* section. B.B. King, the Beatles, Ben Folds, Black Sabbath. But her head came up when Lana's voice faded out and a series of notes opened the next song—were those fiddles? Followed by the ominous pound of a drum. Then came the voice. The gravelly female call to attention that made the hair on Hannah's arms stand up.

"Who is this?"

Shauna pointed to the speaker questioningly, and Hannah nodded. "This is the Unreliables. My cousin's girlfriend is the lead singer."

"They're local?"

"Seattle."

Now *this* music would be perfect for *Glory Daze*. Replacing the industrial sound with the dramatic pound of the drum, the rush of emotion in the singer's voice, the folk element of the fiddles. It would bring the small-town story to life. Give the film more than just texture—this sound would give it character.

Only when Shauna came up beside Hannah did she realize she'd been staring into space. "What's in the folder?"

"Huh?" In confusion, she looked down to find Henry's collection of shanties beneath her arm. She'd brought them along to show Brinley, one music lover to another, hoping it might be a way to bond with the music coordinator. "Oh. These are, um . . . sea shanties. Original ones that were written by my father when he was still alive. Most of them are just words on the page. I'd have to go digging with the locals to learn the tunes, but I'm guessing it would sound something like this." She pointed at the ceiling. "Like the Unreliables . . ."

Hannah murmured that last part, because a light bulb had started flashing in her brain. She looked down at the folder, flipping it open and leafing through page after page of lyrics with no music. But what if . . . music could be added? The lyrics were deep and heartfelt and poetic. Compelling. They'd made Henry feel real to Hannah. What if she could take it one step further and bring his music to life?

Was that a crazy idea?

"Weird question for you," she said to Shauna. "How well do you know the Unreliables? Would they be willing to"—what did she even call this?—"collaborate? I have these songs from my father, and I'd love to add music like theirs, add a voice—and they would be perfect. I only have the words, obviously, so they'd have a lot of creative input . . ."

Oh boy.

Now that one light bulb had gone off, her whole head looked like Hollywood Boulevard at night. She'd gone days without inspiration, and now it was pouring in, all because of the faded blue folder in her hands.

Glory Daze took place in Westport.

Westport was Henry Cross.

How many times had she been told that?

Currently, the music soundtrack was made up of songs that already existed and that never felt right to Hannah. Music for another time and place that dulled the magic of this location. It dulled the impact of Westport as the backdrop. But what if the score was made up of songs written by the man who defined this place?

"You want to record them? Intriguing," Shauna said, pursing her lips. "So you'd want them to add their own spin to the shanties. Lay down some tracks . . ."

"Yes. I mean, if they're in Seattle, I could meet with them myself. Compensate them." If there was ever a time to give in and use the family money available to her, this was it. And wow. All of this felt like leading-lady moves. But they felt good, so she took them one step further. "I'd like to have some input as well."

Shauna nodded, seeming kind of impressed. "Let me reach out to my cousin to see if they're available. But don't count on them. It could be a dead end. They're not called the Unreliables for nothing."

"Right," Hannah said wryly, closing the folder and running her hand over the front cover, getting more and more caught up in the idea, something telling her this was it. This was big. She'd only had the idea a minute ago and already ached to get started. To dive into the process she'd always watched from the wings. She could be a part of it. With her father. "Thanks."

Shauna shuffled across the ancient floor and plopped herself down on a stool behind the counter. "Where have you been staying while you're in town? With Brendan and Piper?"

"Not this time. Brendan's parents are in town, so"—she swallowed, thinking about her temporary roommate's face relaxed in sleep—"I'm staying with Fox up on the harbor."

Shauna slapped her thigh. "Oh! Wait, I take back what I said about only having two customers. Fox has been in here a bunch, too, lately."

Hannah did a double take. "Has he?"

"Uh-huh." Shauna got distracted by a smudge on the front counter, scratching at it with her thumbnail. "Surprised me, too, the first time he walked in. You know, he was a senior at the high school when I was a freshman. *The* Fox Thornton." She shook her head. "You don't just expect that face to breeze in off the street. Took me a few minutes to stop babbling. But he has pretty good taste. Last thing he bought was Thin Lizzy. Live."

Confusion settled over Hannah. "But he doesn't even own a record player." She took a mental tally of the sparse apartment. "Unless it's invisible."

"Weird," Shauna commented.

"Yeah . . ." Deep in thought, Hannah backed toward the exit, needing to make one more stop before heading to set. She'd have to deconstruct the riddle of Fox's record-buying habits later. "Weird. See you soon?"

"I better."

Chapter Fourteen

Hannah shifted in her sneakers, curling and uncurling the blue folder in her hands, waiting for Brinley to finish talking on her cell.

There was a good possibility this wasn't going to go well. But the more Hannah turned over the idea of recording Henry's shanties, the more it felt right. Inevitable. At the very least, she needed to voice the concept. To try. For Henry. For herself. And maybe she needed to try for Fox, too. Not because he expected or required her to make leading-lady moves, but because she couldn't encourage him to reach beyond his capabilities if she wasn't willing to do the same.

Speaking of Fox, she had a serious itch to hear his voice. Right now, while her nerves were trying to get the better of her. Normally her go-to person would be Piper if she needed a verbal chill pill, but she found herself pulling up her miles-long text thread with Fox, instead, her stomach calming simply from seeing his name on the screen. Keeping Brinley in her sights, she punched out a message.

HANNAH (1:45 PM): Hey there.

FOX (1:46 PM): Hey Freckles. What's up?

H (1:46 PM): Not much. Just saying hey.

F (1:47 PM): If you miss me so much, tell them ur sick and come home. I'll take you shoe shopping with me.

H (1:48 PM): Play hooky with a fisherman? Sounds dangerous.

F (1:48 PM): You won't feel a thing.

H (1:49 PM): Lies. Back up. Shoe shopping? Did I accidentally text my sister?

F (1:50 PM): I need some new XTRATUFs. Rubber boots for the boat. At the risk of diminishing my insane sex appeal, mine are starting to reek.

H (1:52 PM): Sex appeal maintained. Unbelievable. 🙄

F (1:54 PM): It's a curse.

F (1:55 PM): I can see you from the window. Turn.

Hannah's upper half twisted to find Fox looking back at her from his upstairs apartment, and an involuntary smile spread across her face. She waved. He waved back. And a powerful yearning to spend the day with Fox caught her so off guard, her arm dropped, a king-sized knot forming in her throat.

H (1:58 PM): Is it weird I want to sniff your boots to judge exactly how bad they are?

F (1:59 PM): It's your funeral.

F (2:00 PM): You're one of a kind, Hannah.

H (2:01 PM): So they say. See you later. Thanks. 😗

F (2:02 PM): For what?

Hannah started to respond, but up ahead Brinley ended her phone call.

No guts, no glory. And her guts didn't feel quite as liquified after texting with Fox. It helped to see him there in the window, a reassuring presence, there when she needed him.

Putting some starch in her spine, Hannah picked her way through the set in the other woman's direction, doing her best not to look queasy. When she reached the music coordinator, the woman took a full minute to look up from the note she was writing on a legal pad. "Yes?"

"Hi, Brinley." Hannah rolled her lips inward, turning the folder over in her hands. "So I brought something I thought you might be interested in—"

"Is this going to be quick? I have to make a call."

"Yes." Hannah resisted the impulse to blow off the whole thing, tell Brinley it was nothing and walk away. "Actually, I don't know if this will be quick? But I definitely think it's worth carving out a few minutes." Hannah exhaled and flipped open the folder. "These are original sea shanties. Written by my father, actually. And they're good. Really good. A lot of them are about Westport and family and love. Loss. They capture the themes of the movie, and after speaking to my grandmother this morning, we have permission to use them. I think . . . well, I was hoping you would consider approaching Sergei about using these original songs? I know it would be some extra legwork getting them professionally recorded, but—"

"Exactly. How much are you planning to pile on top of this budget, Hannah?" Brinley's laugh was exasperated. "Your last suggestion dragged us to the Capital of Fish. And now you want to record an original soundtrack? Maybe you want to hold the premier in Abu Dhabi—"

"I'd like to see the songs, please," Sergei said briskly, stepping out from behind the trailer to Hannah's right, almost startling her into dropping the folder. His gaze was hard on Brinley, who'd gone a ghostly shade of white, but his demeanor softened when he reached out to take the folder from Hannah. "May I?"

This kind of upstaging scenario was the last place Hannah wanted to end up. Brinley was good at her job, and she respected the woman. She'd been prepared to hand over the songs and let Brinley claim the original score as her idea.

That wasn't going to happen now.

Hannah tried to communicate a silent apology to Brinley, but the coordinator's attention was focused on Sergei as he read through the first couple of shanties. "It's hard to get anything from just the words," he said, sounding disappointed. "There is no way to hear them set to music?"

Brinley shot triumphant daggers at her.

"Well . . ." Hannah started, once again experiencing the urge to take back the folder, laugh, apologize for the bad idea. Instead, she took a deep breath and kicked down the door of her comfort zone. "I'm in the process of doing that. I've already arranged to have them recorded. It's just a matter of whether Storm Born wants them for this project or not."

That's right. Hannah lied. Just a little.

She was planning on finding a way to record the shanties, wasn't she? Sure, that ball had been set in motion only a matter of hours ago. There was also a strong chance the Unreliables wouldn't be interested, or they would be unavailable when Shauna got in touch. If so, eventually she'd find somebody else. But bottom line, she was making it sound as though having the end product was imminent—and it wasn't.

Sergei had a severely short attention span, though. And she had him semi-hooked on this idea she believed in with her heart, her soul, her gut. If she didn't feed the director something real, something substantial, right now, it would blow out of his consciousness like white fuzzies from a dandelion.

And this was entertainment, baby. Fake it till you make it.

Sergei eyeballed her, right on the verge of interest. One more push.

How?

"I can . . . you know," she mumbled into her chest. "I can sing one of them—"

"Yes, let's do that," Brinley said, beaming, resting her chin on her wrist. "Hey!" She leaned sideways and called to a group of crew members. "Hannah is going to sing us a sea shanty."

The way everyone swarmed, she might as well have been Hailey Bieber walking out of LAX, suddenly the focus of rabid paparazzi. "Uhh." She cleared her throat, reaching out to take the folder back from Sergei. This song had reduced her to tears last night. Was she really going to sing it in front of all her coworkers? Not only was she worried about having the same response in public, but her love for music didn't exactly extend to sterling vocal abilities. "So . . . this is called 'A Seafarer's Bounty.'"

For once on the boisterous set, a pin could have been heard dropping.

Even Christian looked interested in the proceedings.

The first line of the song came out flat, kind of hushed. And then she happened to lift her eyes and see the *Della Ray* bobbing in the water just ahead in the harbor. Something moved inside her. Something deep and unknown, a little scary. A bridge to the past, to some other time. Her father had made his livelihood on that exact boat. He'd met his death on it. And she was singing one of his songs, so maybe she'd just better do it justice. She'd been handed all his words and thoughts. She'd never meet him, but in this small way, wasn't she bringing him back to life?

Hannah didn't realize how much her voice had risen until the song was nearly over and still no one spoke or moved. In no way did she fool herself into thinking her talent kept them as still as statues. God, no. Their inaction was probably due to the fact that she'd put more effort into the song than she'd put into anything before, except maybe creating the perfect playlist.

Her voice traveled across the harbor, the wind seeming to carry it out to the water. When the song was over, Sergei started clapping and everyone joined in. It was so unexpected, the crack of sound firing her back into the present, that she recoiled and almost fell on her ass, earning her an eye roll from Christian. But she didn't have a chance to thank everyone or hear Sergei's opinion about Henry's song before Brinley tossed down her legal pad. "Look, I have been working on synchronization rights to our songs for weeks. Our sound-mixing team has already approved the sequence and outline. I hope you're not taking this seriously, Sergei, because it would mean starting from scratch, and we're already over budget and behind schedule. It's a terrible idea. From a kid."

A chorus of ooohs went up behind Hannah.

Hannah's face flamed. With embarrassment, yes, but mostly indignation. There was nothing terrible about this idea. About Henry's songs. And it was that anger that drove Hannah to double down. Why be nice and try to keep things smooth sailing with Brinley? Obviously that wasn't going to happen, so she needed to fight for what was important. What she could control.

Hopefully.

Hannah did all the paperwork for Storm Born. She knew the numbers, had been reading through Brinley's cue sheets and sync contracts for years. She used that knowledge to her advantage now.

"No. Actually, using the shanties would put us back *under* budget. And the rights would be exclusive."

Sergei liked the word "exclusive." A lot. He looked back down at the folder, that creative vein worming around in his temple.

"We could provide a flat fee of twenty thousand to the artists for the recording session. Currently, we're spending more than that on the rights to one song. I'm not taking a broker fee, but my grandmother will take fifteen percent off the top of any profit from the soundtrack over the next ten years. We'd be saving the producers money this way and possibly putting an indie band on the charts." From the corner of her mouth, she whispered, "Exclusive," for good measure.

"But the time it would take—" Brinley argued.

"At the very least, I would like to hear a demo. These songs give the film historical value, they enrich the backstory." Sergei executed a dramatic walk through the silent crew, fanning a hand out over the water. "I'm picturing a fast-motion sunrise while the haunted voice of a sailor calls from beyond the horizon. We open with purpose. With gravity. The audience is pulled into the time and place with the voices of the people who live here. The men who trod these waters."

One couldn't technically tread on water, unless one was Jesus, but Hannah didn't think now was a good time to point it out. Sergei was in full inspiration mode; everyone held their breath, and Brinley looked about two seconds from stabbing Hannah with a Bic.

Sergei turned on a heel and faced the group. "Brinley, let's continue in the direction we've been heading. But I'd like to pursue Hannah's angle, as well. We are already behind schedule and over budget. Brinley is right about that." He stroked his chin thoughtfully, a move that used to make Hannah swoon but that she now observed objectively. *Please don't be because of a certain emotionally complicated relief skipper.* "Hannah, if you can really have these songs recorded and make them digital on a smaller budget, I'm going to take the change of direction under advisement."

"Let me make it simple for you," Brinley said sweetly. "If you do that, I quit."

A hiss of collective breath went up in the crowd, and some of it came from Hannah. This was definitely not how she'd envisioned this going down when she woke up this morning. Instead of bonding with Brinley over the discovered shanties, she'd now been pitted against a woman whose work she actually admired.

Sergei let the threat hang in the air for a few beats. "Well." He brushed a hand over his dark hair, unbothered, possibly even appreciative of the drama. "Let's hope you don't have to put your money where your mouth is." He strode through the parted sea of gaping crew members. "Hannah, could I speak to you privately?"

Oh Lord.

Was he trying to get her killed?

Hannah thought of asking if they could speak later, like when she wasn't under intense—in one case, homicidal—scrutiny, but didn't want to seem ungrateful for the opportunity he'd just given her. Although, the word "opportunity" might be pushing it. He wanted her to record Henry's songs. To possibly end up on the film score. God, she didn't even have contact with the Unreliables yet. For all she knew, they'd broken up. Faking it until she made it had seemed like a great idea in the moment. But the making it part was going to be a challenge.

Was she able to do it?

Hannah increased her pace to catch up with the director. "Hi," she said, drawing even with him on his brisk walk along the water. "What did you want to speak to me about?"

"You've been very assertive lately," he said, slowing to a stop, tugging on the sleeves of his turtleneck. "I confess, I was going to be selfish and keep you as a production assistant forever, but I've . . . had my eyes opened recently. I've been paying closer attention, and I can see you're taking on responsibilities far beyond your pay grade."

She scratched the back of her ear. "I can't argue with you there."

He laughed, his eyes crinkling at the corners.

Come on, hormones. Last chance to get excited.

They remained obstinately dormant.

"I'm curious to see if you can deliver on these additions to the score. I wasn't lying when I said they could bring a lot of character to the piece. That . . . final aspect that has been missing."

It was gratifying and kind of a relief to know she wasn't the only one who noticed the lack of magic. "Thanks. I won't let you down."

Sergei nodded, pulled on his sleeves again. "Separate from that. Completely separate . . . Look, I don't want you to think I'm giving you this chance because I . . . like you. Or expect something from you . . ."

Hannah almost asked him to repeat himself. Did he just say he liked her? It didn't sound as though he'd meant that in a platonic way, either. In fact, he couldn't seem to make eye contact with her. Was this for real? She dug frantically for excitement, for the former version of herself that pined for the moody director all hours of the day and night, but . . . if she was being honest, she couldn't remember the last time she'd doodled his name on a napkin or stalked his Instagram. "Yes?" she prompted him slowly.

"It's probably not a very professional question, but I find myself"—he blew out a puff of breath—"extremely curious to know if your relationship with the fisherman is serious. Are you two doing the long-distance thing or . . . will you be available to see other people when we're back in LA and not so . . . distracted?"

Was her relationship with Fox serious?

That was a really good question. Hannah guessed neither of them would know which answer to give. Yes or no. And yet all signs pointed to yes. They'd kept up a ritual of texting each other every night for seven months. They knew each other's deepest insecurities. They'd slept in each other's arms, and hey, they talked freely about masturbation. So there was that.

When she thought about Sergei, her brain made muffled *beep-boop* sounds. She liked his drive and his creativity and vision. His turtlenecks flattered his slim physique. They would have mutual interests if they ever really engaged in a personal discussion. Fine. It would be just . . . fine.

But when she thought about Fox, her stomach turned into a bouncy ball. So many emotions rolling around at once— longing, protectiveness, confusion, lust—and on top of those humdingers, she was infinitely more excited to see him at home tonight than go on a date with Sergei upon returning to LA.

It was entirely possible her interest in the director had started fading around seven months ago, when a certain Fleetwood Mac album showed up on the doorstep, and now it was completely null and void.

Still, as far as an answer to the question, was her relationship with Fox serious? She didn't know.

But she found herself taking a deep breath and saying, "Yes, it's serious."

And somehow, saying it out loud felt entirely right.

⚓

Later that afternoon, Hannah walked slowly to Fox's apartment.

She'd rushed back to Disc N Dat after filming to impress upon Shauna the urgency of getting in touch with the Unreliables and stood there while her friend placed the call. She left copies of the shanties for Shauna to pass on, along with the exciting (and hopefully enticing) news that Storm Born would be able to pay the band.

It would be pretty crushing if they didn't come through, since they had the perfect sound, but worst-case scenario, she'd start hunting down other options bright and early tomorrow morning.

Toward the end of filming, the clouds overhead had darkened, settling a gloomy mood over Westport. Rainstorms always made Hannah want to go crawl into bed with her headphones, but after turning down Sergei—by telling him she was serious about Fox—she needed a minute before coming face-to-face with the fisherman. Would he know just by looking at her that she'd voiced such an impossibility out loud?

But maybe it wasn't *completely* impossible.

She couldn't stop replaying what Shauna told her. She supposed it wasn't crazy unusual that Fox would stop into Disc N Dat. It was a small town. He'd been the one to introduce Hannah to the shop in the first place.

The fact that he'd been buying records, though . . .

To the casual observer, Fox's purchases wouldn't be a big deal. Only he knew what they would mean to Hannah. It made no sense to keep it from her, unless there was some important reason. On set this afternoon, she'd scrolled back through their text messages and found the one that had tickled her memory, made her pulse click in her ears.

> **F (6:40 PM):** Apart from being dark and dramatic . . . what makes a man your type? What is eventually going to make a man The One?

> **H (6:43 PM):** I think . . . if they can find a reason to laugh with me on the worst day.

> **F (6:44 PM):** That sounds like the opposite of your type.

> **H (6:45 PM):** It does, doesn't it? Must be the wine.

> **H (6:48 PM):** He'll need to have a cabinet full of records and something to play them on, of course.

> **F (6:51 PM):** Well obviously.

Record collecting wasn't an interest he'd enjoyed before they met last summer. Him buying albums now was pertinent information. Where was he keeping them? And if he was hiding them from her . . . what *else* was he hiding?

Either he didn't want Hannah reading too much into his new collection or there was a lot to read into it and he needed more time before admitting that.

Unless, of course, she was completely nuts and he was just a dude who'd forgotten about buying a few albums. But for a man who never purchased anything for his apartment, wouldn't they have stood out? Been remarked on by now?

Lube had been a main topic of interest, but not a stack of vinyls?

Let's say, hypothetically, he'd started collecting records because he had a low-key interest in being Hannah's type. Never mind that her knees trembled over that possibility. How far did his interest go? She didn't know. But the same intuition that had led to calling their relationship "serious" was buzzing now. Telling her to wait, to be patient, to stay the course with Fox.

That if he was hiding records, he was hiding a desire to be . . . more.

Despite his assurances of the opposite.

Deep in thought, Hannah carefully wedged the new albums she hadn't been able to resist under one arm and let herself into the apartment. When she walked inside, she was immediately greeted by the spicy scent of aftershave—and when Fox walked out of his bedroom in dark jeans and a slate-colored button-down, she knew.

He was going on a date.

Hannah's stomach plummeted to the floor.

Chapter Fifteen

Fox was going to see his mother.

He always found out on short notice when she was working in the vicinity of Westport. If Fox wasn't on the water, he always jumped, because he never knew when she'd be back again. He'd definitely been a little disappointed when Charlene called to say she'd be in Hoquiam for the night, because going to see his mother meant he wouldn't be home with Hannah.

Hannah, who had slept in his bed last night, her tight little butt in his lap for a good two hours somewhere in the middle of it all. She'd barely walked out his front door this morning before he rolled onto his back, gripped his cock, and came after six strokes. Six. It usually took him a good five minutes, at least. He'd thought of Hannah during every one of those six strokes. Same way he had every time since last summer. Only now, she wasn't just the girl he couldn't stop thinking about. She was the girl who flat-out refused to fuck him.

And goddammit. Now she walked into the apartment, clothes damp and clingy from the rain, and there he went, thinking about being inside her again. Picturing her bowed back, her mouth open on a cry of his name, the slap of flesh on flesh. *Stop it, you bastard.*

Until recently, Fox had never fantasized about anyone specific while beating off.

A body was just a body.

But in his fantasies with Hannah, their minds were in sync as well as their physical selves. They laughed as often as they moaned. Even thinking of their fingers gripped together, the trust in her eyes, added to the insane pleasure. Imagining himself inside Hannah felt great. *Better* than great. His orgasms were more satisfying by leaps and bounds.

And that scared the holy shit out of him.

Fox was distracted from his troubling thoughts when Hannah stopped short just inside the door, framed in the lazy rainstorm, her face going from thoughtful to dismayed. Sad, even? "Oh," she said, giving him a once-over. "Oh."

He tried valiantly to ignore the pounding in his chest. Jesus, it got louder and harder to manage every time they were in the same room. For the longest time, he'd thought if they just slept together, it would go away. This twisting, hot, melting, spearing sensation she inspired in him with a blink of her eyes. He'd feel shitty afterward for jeopardizing their friendship, but at least it would be over and he could stop obsessing about her so much. Now he was beginning to seriously doubt *anything* would work.

"Hello to you, too," he said, voice sounding strained.

"Sorry, I just didn't expect— I . . ." She dropped the bag she was holding underneath her arm, jolted, then stooped down to pick it up. "You're going on one."

Fox frowned. "Going on one what?"

"Going out." She stood slowly, holding the bag to her chest, eyes big and trained on him. "Going out on a date."

Understanding dawned.

And then he saw her demeanor for what it was. This assumption that he was going on a date had thrown her big-time. Honestly, part of him wanted to shake her and say, *Now you know how I feel sending you off to your director every morning.* But what would that argument make them? A couple?

They weren't. She lived in a different state and was actively pining for someone else. All he had to offer was a notched-up bedpost and the mockery that came along with it. Potentially for both of them. A relationship between them wasn't happening, despite her obvious disappointment that he could be going on a date. And so for a split second, Fox considered letting Hannah believe he *was* going to meet someone else. Maybe it would put an end to whatever was happening between them. They shouldn't be sleeping in the same bed, shouldn't be telling each other deep, dark secrets. Look where it led. Jealousy. Longing that made him want to carry her back into his bedroom, wrap himself in her goodness, and feel normal again. She was the only person who made him normal. Made him . . . okay.

In the end, Fox couldn't force himself to do it. He couldn't let her think for a second that he'd rather spend his time with anyone else. It would have haunted him. "My mother is in town," he said, relief coating his stomach when he saw hers. "Well, she's in Hoquiam—tonight only. About forty minutes from here. That's where I'm going. To see her."

Her shoulders relaxed. It took her a moment to respond. "Why tonight only?"

Fox's lips edged up into a half smile. "She's a traveling bingo caller. Goes up and down the coast running bingo nights at various churches and rest homes."

"Oh . . . wow. I did not expect you to say that." Amusement danced behind her features. "Are you going to play bingo?"

"Sometimes I do. But mostly I help with crowd control."

"You have to keep control of the bingo crowd?"

"Freckles, you have no idea."

Glancing down at the bag in her hand, her smile turned into a curious one, a line appearing between her brows. "Fox"—she seemed to scrutinize him—"do you have a record player?"

Too late, he recognized the brown paper bag stamped with the purple logo for Disc N Dat and his gut seized. Of course she'd gone there. Why wouldn't she visit at least once? It had been shortsighted of him to buy his records there when she could so easily find out he'd been to the shop. "Do I have a record player?"

Hannah raised an eyebrow. "That's what I just asked you."

"I heard."

Her chest rose and fell. "You do have one."

"I didn't say that."

"You don't have to."

"Hannah."

But she was already striding forward, on a mission, making panic sink like an anchor in his belly. Hiding the record player and albums from her had been selfish. He'd felt selfish so many times. But he'd bought the fucking thing for reasons he didn't know how to express out loud. A gut-born need to be what she wanted.

And Hannah . . . she would make him admit to it.

On her way past Fox, she set her paper bag down on the kitchen table and circled the room, her gaze finally landing on his locked cabinet. "Is she in there?"

Fox gulped. "Yes."

Hannah made a wounded sound, pressing a hand to the center of her chest.

This was it. No escaping what came next. With the discovery of the record player locked up in the cabinet, she was going to know how often he thought of her. She'd know the best parts of his days were her text messages before bed. She'd know his hands shook with the need to touch her when she was in the shower. That he could no longer look at other women, and his existence had become undeniably priestly. That all day long, her words from this morning had rung in his head, packing his chest tight with some unnamed emotion.

I'm just going to tell you that . . . I'll be back tonight and that you're really important to me.

Hannah remained silent so long, chewing on that full lower lip, he wondered if she was going to say anything at all. She seemed almost conflicted. What was she thinking?

"All this time, Fox? Really?" Her voice turned into a hushed whisper, and his pulse started to hammer against his eardrums. "I've been listening to music on my phone for no reason?"

Fox's breath released slowly, relief warring with . . . disappointment?

No. That couldn't be right.

Either she was letting him off the hook . . . or she didn't realize the significance of him buying the record player. To be close to her. To have a connection to that day they'd spent together in Seattle when he'd felt human and heard for the first time in as long as he could remember. To be the man she imagined herself with. "I was . . . saving it as a surprise," Fox said, reaching behind the cabinet for the leather pouch and removing the key, highly aware of how odd and telling it was that he'd hidden the damn thing. Beginning to sweat, he turned it in the lock. "Thought I'd break it out if you had a bad day at work, you know?"

His eyes closed when she hummed. From right behind him. She was so close he could almost feel the vibration on the back of his neck, his every hair follicle waking up. God, he wanted to touch and taste her so bad. Would get down on his knees if she batted her eyelashes. There was no denying the undercurrents between them—her distraught reaction to him going on a date spoke volumes. But he forced himself to accept what she was offering him, instead. Friendship.

Hannah knew it couldn't work between them. She knew it as well as he did, and she was saving them when he wasn't strong enough to do it. Maybe it would eventually get easier to keep his hands to himself. If he got friendship with Hannah out of the bargain, he had no choice but to be grateful.

Fox unlocked the cabinet and stepped back, absorbing her expression like a dry sponge dropped into the ocean.

When her face transformed with delight, he wanted to kick himself for not showing her sooner. "Oh. A Fluance." She ran her finger along the smooth edge. "Fox, she's beautiful. Are you taking good care of her?"

His lips twitched. "Yes, Hannah."

She stepped back and tilted her head, looking at it from a different angle. Released a happy sigh. "This is such a perfect choice for you, too. The wood chassis reminds me of the deck of a ship."

"That's exactly what I thought," he said, honestly. The validation she always seemed to give so effortlessly pushed him to open the cabinet beneath, revealing the neat row of records he'd collected over the last seven months. He laughed at her strangled gasp. "Go ahead. Play something."

She spoke with quiet reverence, bending forward to peruse the selection of everything from metal to blues to alternative. "Please. I'm going to be playing something all night while you're gone."

"No, you won't, because you're coming with me."

He didn't think there was anything that could compete with the records, but Hannah's eyes zipped to his with that pronouncement, and they stared at each other in the ensuing silence. Did he plan on inviting Hannah to come meet his mother? No. No, it shouldn't even have occurred to him. Introducing a girl to Charlene? Pigs must have been flying. But as soon as the words were out of his mouth, he couldn't imagine the night any other way. Of course she was coming with him. Of course.

"Who am I to turn down a bingo game so rowdy it needs crowd control?" she asked, breathless, her cheeks ever so slightly pink—and he had to restrain himself from kissing them. From tracing his lips down to her flushed neck and worshiping it until her panties were soaked. "Let me go change."

"Yeah," he said thickly, stuffing his fists into the pockets of his jeans.

Hannah was almost to her room when she stopped and jogged back to the turntable, pulling a Ray LaMontagne album out carefully and settling the needle on the first track, her lips curling happily at the first crackle. "For atmosphere," she explained, eyes twinkling.

Then she fluttered back to her room, leaving Fox staring after her with his heart clogging his throat.

Phew. That had been a close one.

Chapter Sixteen

Fox wasn't joking.

This bingo crowd came to win.

When they pulled into the church parking lot, there was already a line extending around the corner, and the (mostly) senior citizen players looked none too happy about being kept outside in a steady drizzle.

Fox turned off the engine and leaned back, tapping a finger in quick succession on the bottom of the steering wheel. Anxious. That's how he'd been on the second half of the ride, and although she didn't know why, she started to wonder if the jumpiness stemmed from seeing his mother.

Maybe she should be home searching for backup bands if the Unreliables didn't come through, but she didn't want to be anywhere else. The invitation to meet Fox's mother felt almost sacred. Like a glimpse behind the curtain. And she'd been unable to do anything but say yes.

Simply put, she wanted to be with him. Around him.

He'd bought a record player and hidden it.

She wasn't buying his excuse that he'd saved it for a rainy day. A surprise to pull out of the hat after a bad day on set. No, that was total baloney—and she was pretty sure both of them knew it. This man buying anything permanent for his bare-bones apartment had significance. And Hannah could admit to being a little scared to find out more. To peel back more layers and discover if her rapidly growing feelings for this man were returned. Because what then?

Apart from the obvious obstacle—they didn't live in the same state—a relationship between them would never work. Would it?

Fox claimed not to want a girlfriend or any commitments.

Hannah was the total opposite. When she decided to commit herself to someone or something, she went in one thousand percent. Loyalty to the people she cared about hummed in her blood. Loyalty made her Hannah.

She'd pretended the record player was cool. No big deal. A fun discovery. But her apparently self-destructive heart wanted to pounce all over the deeper meaning. Ignoring that desire burned, but she forced herself to focus on the here and now. Where Fox clearly needed a friend to distract him, to ground him, and that's who she'd be. Refusing to allow things between them to get physical had unlocked what felt like . . . trust between them. And it felt rare and precious, a lot like meeting his mother.

Hannah traced Fox's profile with her eyes, the strong planes of his face backlit by the rain-blurred driver's-side window. A line moved in his jaw, that finger still tapping away on the steering wheel. There was no denying she wanted to reach over, turn his head, and kiss him, finally let the fire burn out of

control between them, but . . . just this—being a true friend—
was more important.

"This is my favorite sound," she said, unhooking her seat
belt and getting more comfortable in the passenger seat. "It
doesn't rain very often in LA. When it does, I go driving just to
hear the drops land on the roof of the car."

"And what kind of music do you play?"

Hannah smiled, enjoying the fact that he knew her so well.
"The Doors, of course. 'Riders on the Storm.'" She sat forward
to fiddle with his satellite radio, searching for the classic rock
station. "It really lends itself to the whole main-character
moment."

"The main-character moment?"

"Yeah. You know, when you've got the perfect mood going,
soundtrack to match. And you're on a rainy road, feeling
dramatic. You're the star of your own movie. You're Rocky
training for the fight. Or Baby learning how to merengue
in *Dirty Dancing*. Or you're just crying over a lost love." She
turned slightly in the seat. "Everyone does it!"

Fox's expression was a mixture of amused and skeptical. "I
don't do it. I'm damn sure Brendan doesn't, either."

"You're never on the boat, hauling crab pots, and feel like
you're being watched by an audience?"

"Never."

"You're a filthy liar."

He tipped back his head and laughed. Quieted for a second.
"When I was a kid, I loved the movie *Jaws*. Watched it hundreds
of times." He shrugged a big shoulder. "Sometimes when our
crew is in the bunks talking, I think of that drinking scene
with Dreyfuss, Shaw, and Scheider."

Hannah smiled. "The part where they sing?"

"Yeah." He sent her a sideways squint. "I'm a total Scheider."

"Yeah, no, I have to disagree. You're definitely the shark."

His bark of laughter made Hannah turn more fully in the seat, leaning her cheek against the leather. Through the window, she could see the line of seniors eagerly moving inside, but Fox didn't seem in a rush to leave the car just yet, his tension still obvious in the lines of his body.

"What is your mom like?"

The subject change didn't seem to surprise him at all, and he reached for the leather bracelet resting in his lap, twisting it in a slow circle. "Loud. Loves an inappropriate joke. She's kind of a creature of habit. Always has her pack of cigarettes, her coffee, a story ready to go."

"Why are you nervous to see her?"

As if realizing he'd been transparent, his gaze zipped to her, then away, his Adam's apple lifting and falling slowly. "When she looks at me, she obviously sees my father. Right before she smiles, there's a little . . . I don't know, it's like a flinch."

A sharp-tipped spear traveled down her esophagus. "And you still come to see her. That's pretty brave."

He shrugged. "I should be used to it by now. One of these times I will be."

"No." Her voice was almost drowned out by the rain. "One of these times, she'll realize you're nothing like him and she'll stop flinching. That's more likely."

It was obvious that he didn't agree. In a clear effort to change the subject, he plowed his fingers through his dark-blond hair and shifted slightly to face her. "I didn't even ask you how filming went today."

Hannah blew out a breath, responsibility crashing down on her like a pile of bricks. "Oh, it was . . . interesting, I guess?"

His brow knit. "How?"

"Well." She dragged her bottom lip through her teeth, telling herself not to say the next part. It was selfish, wanting to see Fox's reaction. Secretly hoping it would give her some hint as to how he felt about her. What would she even do with that information? "Sergei hinted at wanting to go out. When we get back to LA."

An eye twitch was her only hint as to what was taking place in his head. "Oh yeah?" He cleared his throat hard, staring out through the windshield. "Great. That's . . . great, Hannah."

I turned him down.

I told him we were serious.

She wanted to make those confessions so badly, her stomach ached, but she could already see his incredulous expression. *I'm not in the relationship race and I never will be.* Fox might have been hiding a wealth of music and deeper meanings in a locked cabinet, but on the surface? Nothing about his confirmed bachelorhood status had changed in the space of a week, and if she pushed for too much too soon—or hinted at her deepening feelings—he could balk. And God, that would hurt.

"Um. But that's secondary to what else happened." She mentally regrouped, hemming in her disappointment. "It's kind of a long story, but bottom line? I have been tasked with recording a demo of Henry's sea shanties that could potentially replace the current movie score. And if that transpires, Brinley is threatening to quit, and the crew is taking bets on whether or not that day will come. Or if I can actually pull it off."

"Jesus," Fox muttered, visibly filling in the blanks. "How did that happen?"

She wet her lips. "Well, you know how the songs in my head went missing?" He nodded. "They came back this morning, with 'I Say a Little Prayer.' They started to flow back in. And then I was standing in Disc N Dat and it hit me: there are no better songs for the soundtrack than Henry's. It just makes sense. They were written about Westport." She paused. "Shauna is helping me get in contact with a Seattle band to maybe, possibly, record the shanties. I was going to get them recorded either way, but when I brought up the possibility of using them in the movie to Brinley—"

"She got her toes stepped on."

"I didn't mean to toe step," she groaned. "I was just going to float the option, but Sergei overheard the whole thing." Was she imagining the way every one of his muscles tightened at the mention of the director? "Anyway, it feels like a challenge has been issued. To show whether or not I'm ready for more responsibility with the company. Or maybe just . . . professionally. With myself."

"You are," he stated emphatically. Then: "Don't you think you're ready?"

Hannah turned her face into the seat and laughed. "My LA therapy-speak is beginning to rub off on you."

"Oh God. It is." He shook his head slowly, then went back to scrutinizing her. "That was a bold move, Freckles. Putting out feelers for a band. Approaching her with the songs. You don't want the challenge?"

"I don't know. I thought I wanted challenges. But now I'm just scared I won't deliver and I'll realize I was never meant to be a leading lady all along, you know? That feeling is just for driving alone in my car and listening to the Doors."

"Bullshit."

"I could say the same for your belief that you can't captain a ship," she pointed out quietly.

"The difference being I don't want to be a leader." There was far less conviction in his tone than the last time they'd spoken about him taking over the *Della Ray*, but he didn't appear to notice it. Hannah did, though. "You, Hannah? You can do this."

Gratitude welled in her chest, and she let him see it. Watched him absorb it with no small surprise. "Those songs would probably have remained meaningless in the folder if you hadn't sung for me." His chest rose and fell, but he could no longer look at her. "Thanks for that."

"Hey." He scrubbed his knuckles along the bristly shadow of his jaw. "Who am I to keep my minimal talent from the world?"

As if the cosmos had aligned perfectly, "You've Lost That Lovin' Feelin'" by the Righteous Brothers came on the radio and a blissful sigh escaped Hannah. "I'm glad you feel that way, because you're definitely singing this with me."

"Afraid not—"

She dropped her voice and sang the opening bars, making him laugh, the husky sound a low bass line in the rain-muffled car. For the second time that day, her lack of vocal skills made her want to stop, but when Fox glanced at the entrance to the church auditorium with renewed anxiousness, she turned up the volume and kept going, snatching a pen out of his cup holder to serve as a microphone. By the second verse, Fox shook his head and joined in. They sat in the rain, singing at the tops of their lungs, all the way until the final note.

When they finally walked into the church hall several minutes later, the stiffness was completely gone from Fox's shoulders.

Chapter Seventeen

Charlene Thornton was exactly as Fox described.

She wore big vintage eyeglasses with a rose tint, a long sweater wrapped around her slender body, and there were hints of gray springing out from her temples. The church hall was packed full of folding tables, and she walked through them, holding court, dropping witticisms on the bingo players as she passed, smoothing feathers that had been ruffled from their wait in the bad weather.

There was a pack of Marlboro Reds in her hand, though she didn't seem in a rush to do anything, let alone go outside and smoke one. She seemed more inclined to use the pack to gesture or possibly as a safety blanket.

Hannah wasn't prepared for the flinch Fox had warned her about, especially coming from his own mother. Or the fierce surge of protectiveness that permeated her, head to toe. It was so strong that she reached for Fox's hand and wound their fingers together without thinking, her heart leaping a little in her chest when he not only didn't pull away but tugged her closer to his side.

"Hey, Ma," he said, leaning down to kiss her cheek. "Good to see you. You look great."

"Likewise, of course." Before he could pull away, she caught his head in both hands, scanning him with a mother's eyes. "Would you look at these goddamn dimples on my son?" she called over her shoulder, turning several heads. "And who is this young lady? Isn't she just cute as hell?"

"Yeah, this is Hannah. She's pretty cute, but I wouldn't recommend messing with her." His lips jumped at one end. "I call her Freckles, but her other nickname is the Captain Killer. She's famous in Westport for going toe-to-toe with Brendan. And most recently for calling some of the locals ball sacs."

"Fox!" Hannah hissed.

Laughing, Charlene released her son's head and planted bent wrists on her hips. "Well, now, I'd say that deserves the best seat in the house." She turned and waved for them to follow. "Come on, come on. If I don't start soon, there is going to be a riot. Nice to meet you, Hannah. You're the first girl Fox has ever brought to meet me, but I don't have time to make a big deal out of it."

Dammit. Hannah liked her right away.

And she'd really wanted to hate her after that flinch.

Charlene pushed her and Fox toward some chairs at the top of the hall, right in front of the stage where her bingo equipment had been set up, pulling some bingo cards and blotters out of her apron and dropping them onto the table.

"Good luck, you two. Grand prize is a blender tonight."

"Thanks, Ma."

"Thanks, Mrs. Thornton," Hannah said grudgingly.

"Please! Let's not stand on ceremony." She squeezed Hannah's shoulders, guiding her into one of the metal chairs. "You'll call me Charlene and I'll hope my son has the good sense to bring you around again so you have the chance to call me any damn thing at all. How about that?"

Leaving that question hanging in the air, Charlene sailed off.

Fox exhaled, looking chagrined. "She's a character."

"I really wanted to be mad at her," Hannah said glumly.

"I know exactly how you feel, Freckles," he responded, the words almost swallowed up completely in the shuffle of chairs and buzz of excitement around them. Across from Fox and Hannah sat two women who had erected a portable barrier between each other, ten cards spread out in front of them both, a rainbow selection of blotters at the ready.

"Keep your eye on Eleanor," said the woman on the right, closest to the stage. "She's an unrepentant cheat."

"You just shut your mouth, Paula," hissed Eleanor over the barrier. "You're still bitter about me winning that Dutch oven two weeks ago. Well, you can shove that high-and-mighty attitude where the sun doesn't shine. I won fair and square."

"Sure," Paula muttered. "If fair and square means cheating."

"Is it even possible to cheat at bingo?" Hannah asked Fox out of the side of her mouth.

"Stay neutral. Don't get involved."

"But—"

"Be Switzerland, Hannah. Trust me."

They were still holding hands under the table. So when Eleanor leaned across the table and smiled sweetly—bitter accusations apparently forgotten—and asked how long

Hannah and Fox had been dating, Hannah's answer sounded somehow fabricated. "Oh. No, we're just"—her gaze locked with Fox's fleetingly—"friends."

Paula was openly skeptical. "Oh, friends, huh?"

"This is what they do now, this younger generation," Eleanor said, straightening her cards unnecessarily. "They don't do labels and no one goes steady. I see it with my grandkids. They don't even go on dates, they do something called a group hang. That way there is no pressure on anyone, because God forbid."

Now Paula just looked disgusted with the both of them. "Youth is wasted on the young." She prodded the table with a bony finger. "If I was fifty years younger, I'd be labeling the heck out of anything that walked upright."

"Paula," Eleanor scolded through the barrier. "We're in a church."

"The good Lord already knows my thoughts."

Hannah looked at Fox, both of them practically shaking with unreleased laughter, their hands squeezing the blood out of each other under the table. They were saved from any further commentary about the downfalls of their generation when Charlene turned on the microphone, sending a peal of feedback through the church hall. "All right, you old buzzards. Let's play bingo."

It wasn't a date (or a group hang).

They were just two friends playing bingo.

Just two friends occasionally holding hands under the table, his knuckle brushing the inside of her thigh here and there. At some point Fox decided the hall was too noisy to hear Hannah properly and he'd yanked her chair closer, pretending not to notice her questioning look. What the hell was he doing?

Was he one of those idiots who wanted something twice as much because he couldn't have it? The director had asked her out. Pretty soon, they would be back in LA, and Sergei would have all the access to Hannah he wanted, while Fox was in the Pacific Northwest, probably staring at his phone waiting for her daily text message. Which is exactly how it needed to be.

And yet.

Every time Fox thought of Sergei holding her hand instead of him, he wanted to swipe an arm across the bingo table and upset everyone's cards. Scatter them all over the floor. Then maybe kick over the church bulletin board for good measure. Who the hell did this motherfucker think he was to ask out Hannah Bellinger?

A better man than him, probably. One who hadn't been cheapening himself since approximately one day after his balls dropped. Like father, like son. Wasn't that why he wore the bracelet that was currently resting on Hannah's thigh?

"Sweet Caroline. This is so addictive," Hannah whispered to him. And he heard it easily, because he was sitting way too close, trying not to stare at those little curly wisps of hair that the rain had created around her face. Or the way she sucked in a breath every time she got to blot out a square. Or her mouth. Dammit, yes, her insanely lush mouth. Maybe he should just lean over and kiss it, the hell with the consequences. He hadn't tasted her since that night of the cast party, and the need for another hit was unbearable.

"Addictive," he rasped. "Yeah."

Hannah's eyes shot to his, then down to his mouth, and the thoughts that ran through his mind were not appropriate to have in front of his mother. Anyone's mother, really.

This need for Hannah never went away, but it was especially heavy right now. Having her there was more comforting than Fox could have predicted. He forced himself to go see his mother occasionally, not only because he cared about her, but because that involuntary flinch validated his existence as a responsibility-free hedonist.

But Hannah . . . she was starting to pull him the opposite way. Like a gravitational force. And right now, stuck between Hannah and the reminder of his past, going in her direction seemed almost possible. She was here with him, wasn't she? Playing bingo, singing with him in the car, talking. Decidedly not fucking. If Hannah liked him for more than his potential to give her an orgasm . . . if someone so smart and incredible believed he was more . . . couldn't it possibly be true?

As if reading his mind, Hannah rubbed her thumb over the back of his knuckles, turning slightly and resting her head on his shoulder. Trustingly.

Like a friend. Just a friend.

God. Why couldn't he breathe?

"Bingo!" crowed one of the women sitting across from them.

"Oh hell. Did I hear Eleanor call bingo down there?" Charlene said, whistling into the microphone and banging the mini gong she kept perched on her station. "Eleanor, you have been on fire these past couple of weeks."

"That's because she's a filthy cheat!" Paula spat.

"Now, Paula, be a good sport," Charlene scolded lightly. "We all get a lucky run once in a while. Eleanor? My handsome son is going to bring me your card so I can check it over, okay?"

Eleanor handed the card to Fox with a flourish, baring her teeth in a triumphant smile entirely for Paula's benefit. Fox scooted his chair back, wishing the round had gone on longer so Hannah's head could have rested on his shoulder for another few minutes. Maybe if he played his cards right, she'd sleep in his bed again tonight? The prospect of holding her while she slept, waking up beside her, made him eager to get home and see how he could maneuver it . . .

Christ. Who am I anymore?

He was trying to come up with a way to get Hannah into bed so they could have an entirely platonic sleepover. Did he even own a dick anymore?

She'd probably be dreaming of another man the entire time.

Counting the minutes until she went back to LA.

Fox handed the card to his mother, realizing he'd nearly mangled the damn thing in his fist.

"Thank you, Fox," Charlene sang, leaning forward to cover the microphone. "You serious about that girl, son?"

He was caught off guard by the question. Probably because he'd never spoken to his mother about girls before. Not since he'd turned fourteen and she'd made him watch an online tutorial on how to apply a condom. After which she'd put an empty coffee can in the pantry and kept it full of singles and fives at all times. She'd told him it was there, pointedly, without explaining the exact purpose. But he'd known she was supplying him with condom money. Before he'd ever had sex, she'd predicted his behavior.

Or maybe he'd behaved a certain way because it had been expected.

Fox had never really considered that possibility. But over the course of the last week, there'd been a sense of emerging from a fog. Looking around and wondering how the hell he'd gotten to that exact spot. Empty hookups, no responsibilities, no roots digging into the earth. Had he been living this way too long to consider stopping?

You have stopped, idiot.

Temporarily.

Right.

With his mother's question still hanging in the air, Fox glanced back at Hannah. God, every cell in his body rebelled at the idea of meeting another woman—not Hannah—in Seattle. But he'd tried to escape himself before and it blew up in his fucking face. It left scars and taught him a painful lesson about the impression he gave people simply by existing. And he wasn't going to try it again, was he? For this girl who could decimate him by choosing someone else? In a sense, she *had* chosen someone else already.

"No," he finally answered his mother, sounding choked. "No, we're friends. That's it." He flashed her a grin that almost hurt. "You know how I am."

"I know you came home from school every day since freshman year smelling like Bath and Body Works." She chuckled. "Well, be careful with her, will you? There's something about her. Almost like she's protective of you even though she barely reaches your chin."

He caught the urge to tell Charlene that, yeah, that's exactly how she made him feel. Protected. Wanted. For reasons he couldn't have fathomed before meeting her. She liked him. Liked spending time with him.

"I'll be careful with her." His voice almost shook. "Of course I will."

"Good." She switched hands covering the microphone so she could reach up and cradle the side of his face. "My darling heartbreaker."

"I've never broken anyone's heart."

That was true. He'd never been close enough to anyone for that to be a possibility. Not even Melinda. He might have given his college girlfriend more of himself than anyone who came before, but they'd been nowhere near as close as Fox and Hannah.

Did he want to get even closer to Hannah?

If Sergei was out of the picture, what would closer look like?

A relationship? Hannah moving to Westport? Him moving to LA? What?

It all sounded completely ridiculous in the context of Fox's life.

"And, Jesus, I'm not going to start now," he added, shooting his mother a wink. "You want me to drop the blender off to Eleanor?"

Her smile dimmed slowly. "Are you sure?"

"I think I can handle it."

Charlene hesitated slightly before hefting up the small appliance, clearance sticker still attached to one side, handing it to her son. Fox stepped down off the stage and made his way back to the table. Everyone turned to watch him go by—or look at the blender, rather—like vipers in the grass. He set it down in front of Eleanor, pretending he didn't notice the tension at the table. Maybe if he ignored it, they would follow his lead.

Wishful thinking.

As soon as he set the blender down in front of Eleanor, Paula pounced.

Her bony fingers dug into the top of the box, but Eleanor was no rookie. She'd anticipated the move and started stabbing at Paula's hands with her blotter, leaving blue marks on the woman's skin. A hubbub ensued, bingo players shuffling around to get a better look at the action. Confident he could defuse the stressful situation—he was a king crab fisherman, after all—Fox inserted himself in between the women, giving them his best smile, in turn.

"Ladies. Let's end the night friends, huh? Let me get you both a soda from the snack bar and—"

Eleanor swung the blotter and got him right in the center of the forehead.

Hannah gasped, her hands flying up to cover her mouth.

And then her shoulders started to shake.

Could he really blame her for giggling? There was a giant blue dot in the middle of his forehead. He was a human bingo card. Weirdly, he was enjoying her happiness, even though it was at his expense. "Really, Hannah?" he drawled.

She dissolved into laughter, no longer trying to hide it. "Does anyone have a tissue?" she asked through her tears. "Or a wet wipe?"

"That's going to take some scrubbing," called someone from the cheap seats.

On her way around the table, someone pressed a pack of tissues into Hannah's hand, and she continued toward him, almost stumbling she was laughing so hard. And before Fox knew it, he was allowing Hannah to take his hand and pull him out the side door into the cool, misty night.

The rain had stopped, but moisture lingered in the air along with the distant smell of the ocean. Streetlamps cast yellow beams on puddles, turning them into pools of wavy, wind-blown light. Traffic moved in a hush on the nearby highway, the occasional big rig letting out a long-winded honk. It was a setting that, over the last seven months, might have made him feel lonely and exasperated with himself for missing Hannah. But there wasn't any loneliness now. There was only her. Opening the pack of tissues with her teeth, taking one of them out, and bringing the soft sheet to his forehead, her body still racked by laughter.

"Oh my God, Fox," she said, moving the tissue in circles. "Oh my God."

"What? You've never seen a geriatric hit job before?"

Her peal of renewed mirth rang through the quiet parking lot and shot his heart up into his mouth. "You tried to tell me bingo needed crowd control, but I didn't believe you. Lesson learned." She was giggling so hard, she could barely keep her arm up, the appendage repeatedly dropping to her side. "You were so confident, the way you stepped in between them." She dropped her voice to mimic him. "Ladies, ladies. Please."

"Yeah," he muttered. "Apparently you're not the only one who's immune to me, huh?"

He didn't mean to say it out loud, but it was too late to trap the words.

They were out there, and Hannah wasn't laughing anymore.

Wind blew through the scant space between them, whispering and damp in the silence, making more of those perfect curls at the sides of her forehead. And Fox realized he was holding his breath. Waiting for her to let him down gently.

He forced a chuckle. "Sorry, I meant—"

"I'm not immune," she breathed. "I'm far from immune to you."

The soft admission made his knees feel like fucking jelly, but right on the heels of that, he went hard. Everywhere. Each one of his muscles pulled taut, his cock turning thick in his briefs. "How far?"

Sandbags weighing down her eyelids, she let him see the answer. Her thirst for him. And in response, her name caught in his throat, his tone one of surprise. Relief.

Slowly, Hannah moved more thoroughly into the shadow of the building, turning and leaning back against the wall, reversing their positions in a deliberate dance, taking her time tracing the planes of his face. Wrecking him with her simple, perfect touch. The way she curled her fingertips into the collar of his shirt and drew him down, down, so they could exhale roughly against each other's mouths.

"Kiss me and find out."

He made a halting sound and moved, unable to stop himself now that he'd been given permission, catching her hips in his hands and gradually pinning her to the brick barrier, molding their lower bodies together until she whimpered.

"You're sure."

"Yes."

"Thank you, Jesus."

Where the hell to start? If he kissed her mouth first, he swore he might eat her whole, so he zeroed in on her neck, fisting her ponytail and tugging left, giving himself a clear path up to her ear and breathing a trail up that incredible softness, finishing his exhale just beneath her lobe. He savored her cry greedily, rejoicing in the way she went limp between him and the brick wall, her fingers twisting in the front of his shirt for purchase.

Still—still—worried he might implode if he actually allowed himself the singular flavor of Hannah's mouth, he nonetheless attacked those parted, waiting lips, groaning brokenly as her taste sank into his bones, made him light-headed.

God. Oh God.

He wrapped his tongue around hers and pulled hard, once, twice. He sensed her awareness, her anticipation, her hips squirming where he kept them stationary on the wall. Her movements rubbed against his erection, working him the hell up. So intensely worked up, so eager to fuck, he recognized immediately that he'd never, not once, wanted anyone like this.

Hannah was good. Hannah was right.

Being inside her would be a celebration, not merely part of a routine.

There was nothing typical about this. Or practiced. It was a spontaneous combustion of the urges he'd been suppressing where Hannah was concerned, both physical and emotional, and that implosion bred an urgency in him.

Now. He needed her now.

Fox dropped his hips down and lifted her slightly, creating friction against her sex, and her eyes rolled back, hands pulling him closer. Their mouths moved in a frantic rhythm, tongues meeting in long strokes, his hands traveling down her hips and up the valley of her sides, sensitizing the smooth skin beneath her shirt. Making her wet and pliant. He knew that truth like he knew the sea.

"You a virgin, Hannah?" Fox rasped, lightly scraping his teeth up her throat.

"No," she whispered, eyes dazed.

"Thank God," he growled, growing impossibly harder. Hungrier. "Once I'm good and deep, I don't think I'll be able to slow down."

He surged up with his hips again, watching her face closely, memorizing her tiny gasps of air, relishing the way her tits dragged up and down on his chest, nipples erect. God, this sweet, horny girl. He couldn't wait to get her out of that bra and panties. Get her splayed out, nothing in the way of his tongue, his fingers, his cock. She'd be screaming down the mother-fucking building tonight—

A shrill sound splintered his thoughts apart.

A phone ringing.

No. No, phones had no place here. Phones didn't matter.

They were part of reality, and this . . . this was way better than any reality he'd ever known. One where he didn't feel like an actor phoning in his part. But the sound kept up, over and over, vibrating where their hips met until, finally, they broke apart, foreheads pressing together as they looked down at the source of the noise. "M-my phone," Hannah stuttered, breathing hard.

"No."

"Fox . . ."

"No. God, I love your fucking mouth."

Their lips clashed again, battling to get the best taste, before she pulled her mouth away, neck losing power, eyes glazed over. "We can't just . . . here. We c-can't." She visibly struggled to form coherent thoughts, and Christ, could he relate. His head was overflowing, taking every particle of common sense with it. "Your mother is inside and there are things, like talking things, we have to do. I think?"

"Talking things," he exhaled gruffly, holding her chin steady, tipping it up so he could look at her beautiful face. "I talk to you more than I've ever talked to anyone, Hannah."

She blinked. Softened. "I want you to. I love that you do."

"Yeah?"

"Yeah. But . . ."

Her phone rang again, and he gritted his teeth, needing to hear what was going on in her head. Maybe it would help him figure out what was happening in his own. Because as far as he could tell, he was getting really damn close to either ruining his friendship with Hannah or being turned down again.

He loathed both of those options.

Sleeping together would mean potentially hurting her feelings when he couldn't give her any more than sex. And it would be a cold day in hell before he asked this girl to be friends with benefits. If another man suggested that to her, he would deck the asshole. How could he do the same?

Or she might not be immune, but didn't want him like this. Not enough, anyway. The lust might be there, but her willpower was strong enough to overcome it. Because ultimately she wanted someone else.

His chest lurched, a nerve starting to jump behind his eye.

"Go ahead and answer it," he rasped, easing her against the wall and backing off, turning to shove a handful of fingers through his hair.

Better to have her take the call than deliver him *that* blow, right?

"Shauna," Hannah said a second later into the phone, her breath still a touch labored. "Please tell me you have good news."

A long pause.

She sucked in a breath and turned in a circle, patting her pockets as if looking for a pen somewhere on the rain-soaked ground. Fox opened the notes application on his phone and handed it to her, nodding when she gave him a grateful look. Hannah stopped moving abruptly, both devices lighting up her face. "Tomorrow?" She shook her head. "No way they could pull that off. No way I can pull that off. Right?"

What? Fox mouthed.

She held up a finger. "Okay, could you send me their contact info and the address of the recording studio? Thank you! Thank you so much, Shauna. I owe you."

Hannah dropped the phone to her side, looking almost as dazed as when they were kissing. "What's happening, Freckles?"

"The band I want for Henry's shanties? They're leaving on tour in two days. For six months. They're going to be in the studio tomorrow recording some reels for Instagram and—"

"Reels. You lost me."

"It's not important." She waved the phones. "They like the material I sent and can work through the night on arrangements. Lay down a demo of the tracks tomorrow. The money I offered is a lot for an indie band to pass up. So is the opportunity to be on a film soundtrack. If Sergei likes what they do, they'll make time on tour to come back and record for real." A few seconds went by. "I mean, I could wait and try to find an LA band. But I know the way Sergei works and he'll lose interest in the whole idea if I don't move fast."

Hannah swiped her thumb over the screen of her phone, tapping. She closed her eyes when a woman's throaty growl filled the air outside the church hall, accompanied by twin fiddles and a snare drum—hand slowly lifting to her throat, the mouth he'd so recently kissed curling into a smile.

"This is them," she said. "I'm definitely going to Seattle."

Fox realized he was smiling back at her, because his heart wouldn't let him do anything else when she was happy. "No, Freckles. We're going to Seattle."

She brightened. Actually brightened at the news he'd be coming along. Did she really think he'd let her travel alone? "But your fishing trip . . ."

"Not until Wednesday morning. That gives us the entire day tomorrow."

"Okay," she breathed, shifting, then reaching out a hand for him to take. Leaving it there for a long moment, her expression vulnerable until he grabbed on, his throat in a manacle. Hannah hesitated to move back toward the bingo hall right away, and Fox sensed their earlier discussion was far from over. The same way a red sky meant rain was coming, Hannah needed every loose end tied together. And in this case, the loose ends were inside him. She wasn't going to stop digging until she found and identified them one by one.

Part of Fox was relieved as hell that she cared enough to try. But the rest of him, the man who guarded his wounds like a junkyard dog, had his back bunched up beneath the collar. She was either going to pour salt into those wounds by rejecting him . . . or force him to suture himself. Was he even close to prepared for either one?

No.

Since college, his defense mechanism had been to bail out before he could be patronized or reminded he was only good for one thing. But bailing wasn't going to be possible with Hannah. Not in the way he usually did it—by pulling a disappearing act. God no. He didn't _want_ to disappear on her. But he could put a stop to this snowballing expectation of sex between them. Now. He could do that before she pulled the rug out from under his feet. Because with Hannah? He wouldn't survive the landing.

Chapter Eighteen

The ride home was quiet.

They returned to the church hall to say a quick good-bye to Charlene, and then Fox held Hannah's hand all the way to his car. He opened the door for her like they were on a proper date, a muscle flexing nonstop in his cheek. Charged silence followed as he got them back onto the highway. What was he thinking?

What was *she* thinking?

Her thoughts were in disarray, like a tornado had blown through.

That kiss.

Holy hell.

The one they'd shared at the cast party was the gentle opening notes of "The Great Gig in the Sky." But the one against the church wall was that wailing solo three-quarters of the way through the song. The one that never failed to make her want to wax poetic about the complexity of women and their turbulent hearts.

And speaking of turbulence, there was no better description for what Fox's skilled mouth had done to her. Her body had responded like a flower finally being given sunlight, desperate and starved. Even now, she could still feel the zap of electricity in her fingertips, the dampness on the seam of her jeans.

Once I'm good and deep, I don't think I'll be able to slow down.

At the memory of that blunt pronouncement, Hannah turned her head and moaned soundlessly into her shoulder, the intimate muscles below her waist catching and releasing. Were they going home to have sex? Was that what she wanted?

Yes.

Obviously.

There was little doubt that sex with Fox would be mind-blowing. She'd known that since meeting him last summer. But if he thought they didn't have a reason to talk first? To solve some things? He was out of his ever-loving mind. Their relationship was a complicated riddle that got more confusing every day. They were good friends, highly attracted to each other. They'd behaved like a couple tonight, no denying that. No denying how much she'd liked it, too. Holding his hand under the table, sharing private jokes with their eyes, no words necessary.

Her feelings for Fox were growing at an exponential rate, with no signs of slowing down, and she could only liken it to heading for a steep waterfall in a kayak. Hannah might mean more to Fox than the average girl, but that didn't mean he wanted to be more than friends.

Charlene's flinch popped into Hannah's head, and she traced her eyes over Fox's stiff jaw, his hair made messy by his own fingers. And not for the first time, she saw someone who was scared. His expression reminded her of the afternoon she'd turned him down in the guest room, stripped him of his sensual power. She saw that same trepidation now. Like maybe . . . maybe he did want to be the man who held her hand at bingo and drove her to Seattle, but flinches and leather bracelets and hang-ups from the past got in his way. Made him doubt he could do it.

Was she reaching?

Hannah dragged her eyes off his perfect profile, watching the windshield wipers move in their rhythmic pattern on the glass, catching the obscuring rain and smoothing out the view, making it clear so they could move ahead. Doing it over and over again until the rain finally stopped.

What if she could do the same with Fox?

Stay steady, unwavering until his view cleared?

Was she strong enough for that?

Forget strong. Trying to lure this man out of bachelorhood was flat-out self-destructive, and it could end with her heart in tatters. Although walking away, going back to Los Angeles, as if Fox wasn't claiming more and more acreage in her heart, seemed infinitely worse than trying.

Oh boy. A sign for Westport passed on the side of the road, but it might as well have said Trouble Ahead.

Hannah swallowed hard. "So, um"—she clutched the nylon of the seat belt—"are you sure about driving me to Seattle in the morning? I have no idea what to expect when I get to the studio. Could be a lot of waiting."

"I'm sure, Hannah." He cut her a sidelong glance. "Now ask me what you really want to ask me."

Her stomach flopped over at the continual proof that he knew her so well. "Okay." The pulse at the base of her neck sped up. "You, um . . . we . . . um . . . You know, that was definitely kind of foreplay back there, right? Like, you asked if I'm a virgin and that seems like, yeah, you were checking for a reason. A reason like sex."

His long fingers stretched on the steering wheel, then gripped it seemingly tighter. "That's accurate enough. Keep talking."

"Well. I guess I'm wondering what would happen after. After we did that. If we did that."

He rolled a shoulder. "Wait for me to get hard again. Hit a different position."

"Fox."

"Hannah. I can't answer what I don't know," he said through stiff lips. "What do you want me to say? Do I want to fuck you? Yes. Oh my God, I"—his eyes closed briefly, those fisherman's hands flexing on the steering wheel—"I want you underneath me so bad that I can't lie in bed without already feeling you there. I've never even had you, and your body haunts mine."

That took the breath right out of her lungs, leaving her winded. Thank God he kept going, because there was no chance of her speaking with that statement hanging in the air. *Your body haunts mine.*

"Look"—his chest rose and fell hard—"it's better if we don't. You wouldn't believe how much it kills me to say that. But the fact that you're already asking me what happens afterward is a good sign it's a bad idea. Because what happens afterward, Freckles, is I usually call a cab and get the hell out."

"Why?"

"I guess . . . so I can own the fact that I'm just about sex . . . before they do. All right?" he said in a burst. "I'd rather leave instead of seeing that look on anyone's face ever again. Almost like . . . *Wow, how cute. The pretty boy thought this was more than a quick fuck.* Owning who I am is easier than getting hit with the proof that I've been used. No one gets to make me feel shitty. And it's not just the women making me feel like a joke. It's . . ."

"Keeping talking," she said, forcing herself to take in the hard confession, to keep treading water for him so he could let it all out. "Who else makes you feel that way?"

It took him a moment to continue, his gaze pinned straight ahead on the road. "When I get a text or a phone call in front of the crew, if I even hint that I might not be interested in whatever empty hookup is being thrown into my lap, they treat me like something is wrong with me. It's always been like that. The male pressure to live up to this expectation—and I don't even know when the hell it was set."

Heat pressed in behind her eyes. This was not okay. None of it was okay. But she wanted, needed, to know the name of every ugly truth swimming around inside him. "It's wrong every time someone makes assumptions about what you feel or want. You set your own expectations for yourself and there's nothing . . . less masculine about saying no, if that's what they're putting on you. Jesus. Of course there isn't."

His throat worked long and hard. So long she wasn't sure he was going to respond. "If I'd met *you* in college, Hannah, I could have excused the shit I did before. Chalked it up to wild oats or something—and been your man. Through and through. But now I've just been doing this so damn *long*. I've . . . paved over whatever chance I had at a clean slate. I've become what people seemed to want me to be. I've earned my reputation, and as good as you are, as sweet and fucking wonderful as you are, Hannah, I don't want to be the one thing you fail at. Or the choice you question." He cursed under his breath, pushed restless fingers along the back of his neck. "I won't kiss you again. I shouldn't have done it tonight. I know better. If we weren't interrupted . . ."

When he threw the car into park, she realized they were already outside his building, the ocean whitecaps appearing and disappearing across the road.

Silence dropped like a knife in the car, nothing to fill it except the lap of waves on the rocks and their accelerated breathing.

"Even if we weren't interrupted tonight, we'd still be having this conversation," Hannah said.

He was already shaking his head. "Why? What are you trying to get out of this little chat?" His mouth twisted, and she saw something in his face she'd never seen before. Something she couldn't quite name. "Anyway, you've obviously got the director hooked now." His swallow was loud enough to drown out the waves. "Maybe . . . maybe you should focus on that. Him."

"I turned him down," Hannah said. "When he asked if we could go out once we're back in LA, I said no."

It was blatantly obvious how hard he tried to hide his relief, but she saw it. She saw it blare through him like a siren, tension melting from his muscles, his eyes, his jaw. And she knew that unnamed emotion she'd seen before had been jealousy. "Well," he said, stiffly, after a few seconds had ticked by. "Maybe you shouldn't have done that. Sex is the only satisfaction you can get from me."

"No. It's not." Her voice shook. "I get satisfaction from holding your hand. Hearing you sing. Being your friend—"

"Being my friend?" He scoffed. "Then it's a good thing we're not going to fuck, because you'd just be another hookup to me afterward."

Hannah recoiled like she'd been slapped, shock and hurt punching a hole in her throat. Blindly, she reached for the passenger-side door handle and pulled, throwing herself out of the car. Ignoring his panicked call of her name, she took the outside stairs leading to his second-floor apartment two at a time, accelerating when she heard his steps pounding behind her.

She reached his door, her hands shaking as she tried to locate the apartment key in her pocket. She found it but never got the chance to slide it into the lock, because Fox was behind her, wrapping her tightly in his arms, drawing her back against his chest. Hard. "I didn't mean that," he said into her hair, pressing his lips to the crown of her head. "Please, Freckles. You need to know I didn't mean that."

Thing was, she did know.

There was the pink Himalayan salt lamp, hidden record player, introducing her to his mother, singing the shanty for her, offering to drive her to Seattle. The Fleetwood Mac record. Seven months' worth of texts. Even the way he was holding her now, his breath racing in and out, like he'd break down if she stayed mad. She knew he didn't mean the hurtful thing he'd said. She knew. But that didn't mean his dismissive words didn't sting.

Hannah realized in that moment that she could run away from the potential hurt that would come from fighting for Fox. Or she could hold her ground. Refuse to back down. Which would it be?

Fight. Like a leading lady.

He was worth it.

Even if a relationship between them wasn't possible or couldn't work out, she wasn't going to let the hideous beliefs inside him fester forever. She refused.

There wasn't a label for what they were to each other. Friends who burned to sleep together didn't quite communicate the gravity of what existed between them, waiting to be unearthed. But she knew this wasn't about curing him or being the best supporting actress. She wasn't falling into a pattern. Being supportive, as she'd done so many times in the past, was easy. So easy. As was being on the periphery and not an active part of the narrative. But this time, the consequences of her actions in *this* story could determine her future. Not a friend's and not her sister's.

Hers. And Fox's.

Did they continue their story together or apart?

She couldn't imagine the latter. Not for the life of her. Unfortunately, that didn't mean he felt the same. Even if he did, a relationship could be too much to hope for at this stage. They could end up friends *only*—that was a real possibility. One that made her stomach sink to the floor. Making the decision to be the one who pushed for a future together was scary. Terrifying. It made failure and rejection a possibility. He was worth fighting for, though. If anything forced Hannah to dig in and remain strong, it was the need to prove that to Fox. To *make* him believe in himself.

Even if it benefitted some other girl someday—and not her. She was unselfish enough to show him what was possible. That letting someone else in didn't have to be scary. She could do that, couldn't she?

Hannah took a deep breath for courage and turned in Fox's arms. She only caught a fleeting glimpse of his tortured eyes before lifting up on her toes and molding their lips together. Kissing him.

Momentarily surprised, it took him a few seconds to participate, but when he did, it was with gusto. He let out a broken, surrendering moan into her mouth, stumbling forward and pressing Hannah against the door, his hands lifting to frame her face, their mouths moving together feverishly in promise and apology.

Breaking away before it went too far might have been the hardest thing Hannah had ever done in her life, but she managed it, ending the kiss and rubbing her forehead against Fox's, shaken by the throb of energy between them.

"I'll see you in the morning," she whispered against his mouth.

Turning from his dazed expression, she let herself into the apartment and beelined for the guest room. She closed herself inside and slid down the back of the door, ending in a pool of hormones and resolve on the floor.

Better get some sleep. Fox and his deeply rooted doubts would still be there when the sun came up. Maybe if she had more time in Westport, she could chisel away at them little by little. Hope he'd eventually realize he was capable of a healthy commitment. She was running short on time, though. Her only option was to work with the days she had remaining.

Tonight he'd told her his modus operandi was to leave before any woman could demean him. Well, Hannah wasn't going to allow that. She could show up after their argument, after the hurtful words and revelations, and prove their relationship was resilient. That he could be part of something stronger than the pull of the past. That she could look him in the eye and respect him and care. She could show up, period. That was what she'd been doing all along, perhaps subconsciously, and she wasn't getting off course now. Hopefully she would leave Fox with the belief, the possibility, of more.

The courage and confidence to try again.

Hannah's eyes landed on the folder of sea shanties resting on her bed.

Yes, tomorrow she'd fight, in more ways than one.

Chapter Nineteen

Fox stood at the stove, spatula in hand, his gaze fastened to the door of the guest room, every cell in his body on high alert. Who was going to walk out that door? Or, more importantly, what was her game?

He'd barely slept at all last night, replaying the drive home. Every word she'd said, the meaning behind that kiss outside the apartment. What the hell was she playing at? He'd told her, plain as day, that they weren't going to bed together. That she should stick with her director, because nothing more than friendship could come from this thing between them.

Why did all those statements seem so empty now?

Probably because if she walked out of the guest room at this moment and kissed him, he would drop to his knees and weep with gratitude.

I'm wrapped around her little finger.

He needed to unwrap himself. Fast.

Didn't he?

Here he was, making her pancakes, more apologies for the inexcusable thing he'd said to her last night crammed up tight behind his windpipe. *Then it's a good thing we're not going to fuck, because you'd just be another hookup to me afterward.*

Christ, he didn't deserve to live after lying like that.

Or better yet, he *did* deserve to live with the expression on her face afterward and the knowledge that he'd put it there. Scumbag. How dare he? How dare he say poisonous shit like that to this girl who, perhaps unwisely, gave a damn about him?

He'd spent a long time trying to avoid the belittling expression on a woman's face when she implied he was a hall pass or a meaningless diversion. The one Melinda had all those years ago while lying in bed with his best friend. He'd never thought about seeing that look on Hannah's face—not until last night. Not until he'd confessed everything to her and his past had nearly crowded him out of the car.

If Hannah ever looked at him like that, she might as well slice the heart right out of his chest. Melinda's betrayal would be laughable compared to what Hannah's disappointment or dismissal would do to him. Even the possibility had caused him to strike first. To say something to push her away and protect himself in the process.

God. He'd *hurt* her.

And she might have expressed that pain, but . . . she'd forgiven him with that kiss.

That purposeful, no-holding-back kiss.

Which brought him back to his current worry. Who would walk out of the guest-room door? His best girl Hannah? Or Hannah with a plan? Because that kiss last night, the one that turned his dick into a stone monument, had resolve behind it. She'd stroked his tongue without any hesitation. Like she wanted him to know she meant it. She was all in. And that terrified him as much as it . . .

Teased hope to life in his chest.

Dangerous, stupid hope that made him ask questions like *What if?*

What if he just put his head down and dealt with the lack of respect from his crew? Took on some of the responsibilities he tried so hard to avoid?

Because someone worthy of Hannah would need to be responsible. Not him. Right? Just . . . someone. Whoever it was. He couldn't have an apartment totally lacking in character or comforts. He would need to have upward mobility in his job. Like going from a relief skipper to the captain. But that was just an example, because he wasn't referring to himself.

He wasn't.

Fox nodded firmly and flipped the pancake on the griddle, approximately 4.8 seconds passing before his attention snuck back to the door to watch the shadows move underneath. How ridiculous to miss someone he'd only seen the night before. Starting tomorrow, he'd be on the boat for five days. If he missed her after one night apart, 120 hours were going to be pretty damn inconvenient. Maybe he should practice blocking the emotion now.

You don't miss her.

He examined the churning in his chest.

Well, that hadn't worked.

"Hannah," he called, his voice sounding unnatural. "Breakfast."

The shadows stopped moving briefly, started again. "Coming in a sec."

Fox let out a breath.

Great. They were going to pretend like last night never happened. They were going to act like he hadn't spilled the insecurities he'd harbored for the majority of his life. Like he never revealed the seemingly well-natured ridicule he received from the crew. They'd kissed before and gotten over it.

This would be no different.

Why was the churn in his chest getting worse?

Maybe . . . he didn't want them to get over it.

When Hannah walked out of the bedroom, Fox's spatula paused in midair and he sucked up the sight of her like a vacuum cleaner.

No bun today. Her hair was down. Smooth, like she'd used one of those irons on it. And she wore a short, loose olive-green dress instead of her usual jeans. Earrings. Suede black boots that reached all the way up to her knees, making those hints of visible thighs look like dessert.

I should have jacked off.

It was hard enough to be around Hannah ordinarily. Spending the day with her in Seattle dressed for easy access? Torture. He wouldn't be able to blink without seeing the ankles of those boots crossed at the small of his back.

The smell of burning blasted him back to the present. Great. He'd decimated the pancake. Turned it almost totally black while ogling the girl who was making him consider buying some throw pillows and window treatments.

"Hey," she said, tugging on one of her earrings.

"Hey," he returned, picking up the burned pancake with his fingers and throwing it in the trash, pouring fresh batter onto the pan. "You look nice."

And I'd like to throw you down on the couch and devour you.

"Thank you."

Fox hated the tension hanging between them. It didn't belong. So he searched for a way to dispel it. "How late did you stay up making a road-trip playlist?"

"Too late," she answered without hesitation, wincing. "You can't really blame me, though. We're going to a recording studio in the grunge capital of the world. I'm overstimulated." She slid onto one of the stools in front of the kitchen island and propped her chin on a fist. "Sorry, babe. You're going to be sick to death of Nirvana and Pearl Jam by this afternoon."

That "babe" hung in the air like napalm, and he almost burned a second pancake. She proceeded to scroll through her phone, as if the endearment had never left her mouth, while it kicked him in the stomach over and over again. He'd called her "babe" before, too, but never like this. Never just . . . across the kitchen island in the broad daylight with the smell of warm syrup in the air. It was homey. It made him feel like one half of a couple.

Was this her plan? To walk out here after his ugly behavior last night and . . . stay? Not just in his apartment, but *with* him. Their bond intact. Unwavering. Because the fact that she knew every part of him, inside and out, and she was still sitting there . . . it was having an effect. The relief and gratitude that hit him was huge. Welcoming. And it was causing him physical pain not to hold her right now. Call her "babe," too, and give her a good-morning snuggle. Ask to hear about her dreams. Last night at bingo, he'd slipped into the role of boy-friend, and it was kind of scary how good it had felt. To hold her hand and laugh and let his guard down.

The more he thought of that final kiss last night, the more it felt like a promise. That she wasn't giving up on him? Or . . . the possibility of them?

Had he actually said the words "I won't kiss you again"?

Like actually said them?

That promise sounded absolutely ridiculous to him in the light of day. Especially when she took a bite of the pancake he'd made, making a husky little sound of pleasure at the taste, her finger dragging a path through the syrup on her plate and dip-ping into her mouth. Sucking on it greedily.

Was it hazardous to operate a motor vehicle with a dick this hard?

"I see what you're doing, Hannah."

She glanced up, startled, the picture of innocence. "What do you mean?"

"The dress. Calling me 'babe.' The finger sucking. You're trying to seduce me into thinking . . . this kind of morning thing could be normal for me."

"Is it working?" she asked, eyes momentarily serious as she took another bite.

He couldn't answer. Couldn't do anything but picture Hannah sitting there every single morning. Indefinitely. Knowing she'd be there. Knowing she *wanted* to be there.

With him.

"Might be, yeah," he admitted hoarsely.

Obviously startled by his confession, she paused mid-chew, swallowing with visible difficulty. Taking a moment to recover while they stared at each other over the counter. "That's okay," she said quietly. "That's good."

He had the sudden, overwhelming urge to go lay his head down in her lap. To surrender his will, which was thinning by the moment, and let her do with him what she would. He'd woken up with the intention of staying strong, committed to remembering all the reasons that being one half of a couple with Hannah was not in the cards. They'd almost escaped this visit unscathed. Hannah, most importantly. Less than a week to go—and he would be fishing for most of it. Giving her false hope now could lead to her being hurt and he would rather tie an anchor to his foot and jump overboard.

His resolve was already weakening, though.

The what-ifs were becoming more and more frequent.

There was still a stubborn voice in the back of Fox's head, telling him she deserved better than some responsibility-free tramp who had been bed hopping since he was in high school. But it was growing more and more subdued in the face of her . . . commitment to him. Is that what it was? All his cards were on the table. He'd taken off a layer of skin last night and exposed himself. Yet here she sat, not budging. Just being there. Right alongside of him. Permanent. And he was starting to realize the commitment already ran both ways. He'd formed it long before now. For Hannah, hadn't he? Somewhere along the line, he'd started thinking of Hannah as *his*. Not just his friend or girlfriend or sexual fantasy. His . . . everything.

And as soon as he admitted that to himself he . . . burned another pancake. But most importantly, the sense that she belonged to him—that they belonged to *each other*—took root.

Which explained why, a few hours later when they walked into the recording studio and several band members looked Hannah over with interest, Fox wrapped an arm around her shoulders and almost growled, *Back off, she's taken.*

This man was fully overboard.

Hannah's girl-crush on Alana Wilder was instantaneous.

The lead singer of the Unreliables was in the recording booth when they entered Reflection Studio, the sound of her throaty purr electrifying the air and holding Hannah in thrall. She approached the glass as if hypnotized, skin prickling with excitement, already imagining Henry's words belted out to the masses from the curvy redhead's throat.

Before she could lift a hand to the glass, as if to touch the music, Fox's warmth surrounded her, his palm rubbing up and down her bare arm. Tingles speared down to her toes, hair follicles sighing in contentment. Oh dear. She'd been wrong before. Traveling to grunge heaven to record a demo wasn't overstimulating.

This was.

With awareness coiling in her belly, Hannah tilted her head back to look at Fox questioningly and found his irritated gaze focused on something besides the woman belting out lyrics like she was born into magic.

Hannah followed his line of sight and found a couch occupied by three musicians, one holding a guitar, the second with a bass resting sideways in his lap, the third with a fiddle that looked like it had seen better days.

"Are you the girl from the production company?" asked the fiddle player.

"Yes." She extended a hand and walked toward the trio, finding herself moving in tandem with Fox, whose touch now rested on the small of her back. "Er . . . I'm Hannah Bellinger. Nice to meet you."

She shook hands with the guitar and bass players, noting they looked kind of amused by the fact that Fox was towering behind her like a bodyguard.

"Wow," Hannah breathed, tipping her head at the recording booth. "She's incredible."

"Isn't she?" This from the bass player, whose voice held a hint of the Caribbean. "We're just here for decoration."

"Oh, I'm sure that's not true." She laughed.

"We'll lose that job, too, now that you're here." The fiddle player stood, taking her hand and kissing her knuckles. "You're definitely easier on the eyes than us ugly bastards."

Fox's comically forced laughter lasted five seconds longer than the rest of theirs.

Hannah turned and raised an eyebrow at him over her shoulder.

What is wrong with you?

Seeming to realize the spectacle he was making of himself, he coughed into a fist and crossed his arms, but remained close. Was he jealous?

If she wasn't so shocked, she might have been . . . thrilled? Last night, she'd done a lot more than work on the grunge playlist to end all grunge playlists. While selecting songs, her determination to fight to change Fox's mind about himself had only built. She wasn't going back to Los Angeles without him knowing he could be more than some beautiful joke. A man who everyone expected to fulfill some bullshit destiny simply because he could. Not happening.

And maybe the fact that he could feel jealous was an indirect sign of progress? Maybe being jealous over her would prove to him he could want to get serious with . . . someone else someday?

If, for instance, he and Hannah weren't meant to be.

Hannah ignored the horrible burning in her breast and turned back around. "Have you had a chance to look at the songs I sent over last night?"

"We have. Been burning the midnight oil working on arrangements."

"You'll be happy with them," the bass player said, definitively, a musician's arrogance on full display. "No question."

The fiddle player gave her a look that was half chagrin, half apology for his bandmate. "Soon as Alana is done in there, we'll run through the shanties, make sure it all works for you."

She smiled. "That would be great, thank you."

The trio went back to their conversation, and Hannah returned to the glass to watch Alana, Fox coming up beside her. "What was that?" she whispered at him.

"What was what?"

"You're being weird."

"I'm being helpful. They were looking at you like a ten-tier birthday cake just walked in the door." He wasn't quite succeeding in pulling off a casual tone, an agitated hand lifting to scrub at the bristle on his jaw. "Musicians are bad news—everyone knows that. Now they'll leave you alone. You're welcome."

Hannah nodded, pretending to take him seriously. "I see." A few seconds of silence passed. "Thanks for the consideration, but no thanks. I don't need you running interference. If one of them is interested, I'll deal with it myself."

Now his eye ticced. "Deal with it how?"

"By deciding yes or no. I'm capable of doing that on my own."

Fox studied her as if through a microscope. "Why are you doing this to me?"

Hannah exhaled a laugh. "Doing what? Calling your bluff?" His jaw looked ready to shatter, his eyes revealing a hint of misery. "If you're jealous, Fox," she said quietly, "just say you're jealous."

Conflicting emotions waged a war on his face. Caution. Frustration. And then he visibly gave up the battle, standing in front of her naked with honesty. "I'm jealous as fuck." He seemed to be having a hard time getting breath into his lungs. "You're . . . *my* Hannah, you know?"

She tried very hard not to tremble or make a show of what was happening inside her. But there was a Ferris wheel turning at max speed in her stomach. Did he really just say that out loud? Now that he had, now that it was out there, she couldn't disagree. She'd been his for months. *Don't freak out and put him back on guard.*

Instead, she went up on her toes. "Yeah. I know," she whispered against his mouth.

Fox let out a relieved breath, his color returning gradually. He looked like he was right on the edge of making another admission, saying even more, his chest rising and falling. He wet his lips, his gaze raking over her face. But before he could say a word, the door of the booth was kicked open and out came Alana, stomping into the lounge area. "All right, folks." She clapped her hands twice. "Let's talk shanties before these two start making out, yeah?"

Dealing with her imposter syndrome on the heels of Fox's admission was no small task. Hannah felt pulled in several directions, acutely aware of the man stationed like a pillar at her side, his exposed energy vibrating like a raw nerve, while also determined to watch her artistic vision come to life.

Who was she to give an opinion on musical arrangements?

But after the third take, there was something not working about the refrain in "A Seafarer's Bounty." It fell horizontal in the middle, and as a listener, her interest flatlined, too, when it should have been absorbed. The band seemed satisfied with their angle, and, man, they were *so good*. Way better than she should have expected on short notice. Why not just be grateful and move on?

She stood beside Fox in the corner of the control room, listening to the song's playback over the speaker, while on the other side of the glass, the band was visibly preparing to start the next song. Running through the lines individually.

Could she just interrupt the process with an opinion that might be totally wrong?

"Just tell them what's bothering you," Fox whispered in her ear, laying a lingering kiss on her temple. "You'll regret it if you don't."

"How can you tell something is bothering me?"

He studied her face, almost seeming like he was battling the weight of his affection, nearly making Hannah's legs liquify. "You get this expression on your face when you listen to music, like you're trying to climb inside it. Right now, it looks like the door is locked and you can't get in."

"Yeah," she whispered, an ache moving in her breast. Unable to say more.

Fox nodded at her, his own voice strained when he said, "Kick it down, Hannah."

Adrenaline rippled up through her fingertips, along with a white-capped wave of gratitude. Urgency rushed in and she didn't hesitate a second longer. Approaching the microphone that extended up from the mixing desk, she pressed the button to talk. "Alana. Guys. The refrain on 'A Seafarer's Bounty.' When we get to 'trade the wind for her,' can we pause and embellish a little? How do you feel about drawing out the word 'wind' on a four-part harmony?"

"Make it sound like the wind," Alana called back, forehead wrinkling in thought. "I like that. Let's run through it."

Hannah let go of the talk button and exhaled in a rush, exhilaration coasting down from the crown of her head, down to her feet. When she leaned back, she knew she would land against Fox's warm chest, their fingers weaving together just like the music, rivaling the thrill of the band's next version of "A Seafarer's Bounty."

She'd been right. That one addition and it soared.

After that, the day was nothing short of a fairy tale.

In no way did the Unreliables live up to their name. In Hannah's head, they would henceforth be called the Reliables, but she sensed they'd be offended if she legitimized them, so she kept it to herself.

Sitting beside Fox on an old love seat, she listened to the band sing her father's songs about the ocean, tradition, sailing, home. At one point, Fox left and came back with tissues and only then did she realize her eyes had gone misty.

It sounded like a cliché, but they brought the words to life, made them curl and dance on top of the page, infusing them with sorrow and optimism and strife.

Alana seemed to feel every note, as if she'd known Henry personally, and lived through the triumphs and tragedies of his songs with him. Her band anticipated her and adjusted on the fly, boosting her, supporting her as she wove. Magic. That was how it felt to take part in the creative process. As an obsessive listener of music, Hannah had benefitted from that kind of inventiveness since she could remember, tucked away in the worlds turning inside her headphones, but she'd always taken it for granted. She couldn't see herself doing that ever again.

They ordered lunch in to the studio, the band members telling Hannah and Fox stories from the road. At least until they found out Fox was a king crab fisherman and then all they wanted were his stories. And he delivered. Brushing his thumb up and down the base of Hannah's spine, he recounted the close calls, the worst storm he'd ever seen, and the pranks the crew played on each other.

On the next take, there was even more flavor to Alana's vocals. Hannah and Fox watched it happen from outside the booth, his arm settling around her shoulders and pulling her close. He performed the action as if testing it, testing them both, and then one corner of his mouth edged up, his hold tightening with more confidence.

"Your stories did that," Hannah managed, nodding at Alana, then looking up at Fox to find him staring back down at her. "Do you hear that note of danger in her voice? You inspired her. The song is richer now because of you."

Fox stared back at her stunned, then moved in slowly to lay a kiss on her lips. With the sides of their bodies pressed together, they let the music wash over them.

Hannah wanted to stay and listen to them record the entire demo, but Fox had to leave in the morning, so they parted ways with a round of hugs, well-wishes on their tour, and a promise to have the digital recording files to Hannah the next day. She didn't realize her fingers were intertwined with Fox's until they were halfway to his car. Overhead, clouds were beginning to thicken in the early evening sky, as they were wont to do in Seattle, passersby on the sidewalks carrying umbrellas in preparation for the moisture collecting in the atmosphere.

Their earlier conversation came back to her in stark clarity, and the thoughtful expression on Fox's face suggested he was thinking about it as well. Would they pick up where they left off?

Doubtful. He would pretend it never happened. Kind of like this morning when he'd tried to gloss over the gravity of the prior evening by making pancakes and greeting her oh-so-casually.

Fox hit the button on his key ring to unlock the car door, opening the passenger side for Hannah. Before she could let go of his hand and climb in, he held fast, keeping her upright.

"If you're up for a detour . . ." he said, twisting one of her flyaways around his fingers and tucking it behind her ear. "There's somewhere I want to bring you."

His face was so close, his eyes so breathtakingly blue, her body so attuned to his size and warmth and masculine scent, that if he asked her to swim to Russia with him, she'd have vowed to give it the old college try. "Okay," she murmured, trusting him a hundred percent. "Let's go."

Chapter Twenty

Fox had always prided himself on not taking anything seriously.

The memory of his failed reinvention burned in the center of his chest like a cattle brand, so he'd spent years doubling down, leaning into an identity that perhaps burned him even worse, but at least he could be good at it. It was what everyone expected, and there wouldn't be any more painful surprises.

And now he was going to open up wide, expose himself to all manner of outcomes he couldn't control. Because he was in love with Hannah. Stupid, hot-under-the-collar, pulse-tripping love that crowded his chest and throbbed in his fingertips. Might as well face it, he'd started stumbling last summer, and now? Now he was flat on his ass with canaries taking laps around his head.

He loved her humor, her tenacity and bravery, the way she defended the people she loved like a soldier in battle. He loved the fact that she didn't shy away from the tough subjects, even though they scared him in the moment. Her iron will, the way she closed her eyes and mouthed song lyrics like they were baptizing her. Her face, her body, her scent. She'd infiltrated him, become a part of him before he'd realized what was happening, and now . . .

He didn't want her out. He wanted to stay locked in her goodness.

And Jesus Christ, he might as well be walking on a tightrope across the Grand Canyon. In his experience, the only thing that came from reaching past his capabilities was failure. Getting slapped down and sent back to the beginning. But as they'd sat in the recording studio, Hannah leaning into his side, as if she belonged to him—it had felt so damn good—he'd started to wonder again . . . what if. What if.

She was set to return to LA soon, so he needed to answer that question. Or he was going to wake up one morning and put her on a bus out of his life, and the very idea of that covered his skin in ice.

Driving up to the security gate and handing a twenty-dollar bill to the guard, he still didn't have an ending to the what-if question. But he did have absolute faith in Hannah's ability to draw it out of him, if he let her. If he truly dropped the last of his defenses, she'd guide him there. Because she was the most extraordinary, loving, intelligent being on earth, and he cared about her so much it sometimes stole his ability to think straight.

"Where are you taking me?" She split a look between him and the windshield, the greenery rolling past on either side, draped in twilight. "I love surprises. Piper threw me a surprise party when I turned twenty-one and I had to lock myself in the bathroom because my nonstop tears of joy were embarrassing everyone."

Fox, having an easy time picturing that, smiled. "What is it that you love so much about them?"

She tugged the hem of her dress down, drawing his eye. "The fact that someone thought about me, I guess. Wanted me to feel special." She bit her lip and glanced over at him from the corner of her eye. "I bet you hate them, don't you?"

"No." Normally he might have left it at that, but he wasn't being charming or elusive or easy tonight. He was taking the words in the back of his mind and letting them out of his mouth. Starting now. And every time he balked, he'd think of putting Hannah on a bus. He might not have a solution in mind, since keeping her in Westport—just for him?—seemed like a stretch, but when he let Hannah know his thoughts, he always felt closer to her afterward, always felt better, so he couldn't go wrong with that. "You're a surprise, Hannah. How could I hate them?" He cleared his throat hard. "Even familiar . . . you're a constant surprise."

Silence ticked by slowly. "That's a beautiful thing to say."

More words were pressing up against the inside of his throat, wanting to get out, but the actual surprise was coming into view up ahead and he wanted to see her reaction. "Anyway. We'll see if we can keep the crying to a minimum tonight." He put the car into park several yards from the art installation, circling around the back bumper to open her door, offering his hand. "Come on, Freckles."

Her smooth fingers slipped into his, a furrow forming between her brows as she took in the giant steel towers, Lake Washington spread out behind them. At this time of day, they were the only ones there, giving the attraction kind of a lonely, abandoned feeling. Ironic since he'd never felt less lonely in his life. Least of all while holding her hand. "What is this place?"

"It's the Sound Garden," said Fox, guiding her toward the water. "The towers were designed so that when the wind hits them, they play music."

Fox studied Hannah's face, watched it transform with wonder when she heard the first howling note travel through the towers, the haunting melody that somehow softened the air, thickening it like they were inside a snow globe, their surroundings moving slowly. The whitecaps, the clouds, even the shift of her hair all seemed to travel at a different, more languid pace.

Unlike Fox's heart, which was beating out of his chest.

"Oh my God." A fine sheen formed in her eyes. "I can't believe this is just . . . here. And I knew nothing about it? Fox, it's . . . incredible." A loud whistle of sound whipped in the air, and she closed her eyes, laughing. "Thank you. Wow."

He stared down at their linked fingers, and it gave him the strength he needed to leap. "I wanted to bring you here last summer. That weekend we went to the record convention. But I was afraid to suggest it."

She opened her eyes and studied him. "Afraid? Why?"

Fox shrugged a shoulder. "You'd come to Westport for your sister. Such a selfless thing to do, working on the bar and living in that dusty little apartment and . . . you deserved a day just for you. I'd already spent so much time searching for that convention, finding something you might enjoy, though. I got worried that showing you the Sound Garden on top of the expo might make how I felt obvious. Might tip my hand."

There was never a sight more beautiful than Hannah standing on the shore with the sunset making her glow, the wind teasing strands of hair across her mouth. "'Tip your hand,'" she repeated with a blink.

Keep going. Confess every last word.

Think of Hannah getting on a bus back to LA.

"I had it bad for you. If the convention didn't make it obvious, I thought for sure the Fleetwood Mac album would do it." His voice stumbled. "I've got it so bad for you, Hannah. Really"—he blew out a breath—"really bad. I tried to keep you out of here." He knocked his free fist against his chest. "But you won't go. You're never going to go. You just won't."

"Fox . . ." she murmured haltingly, her tone weaving in seamlessly with the howling of the towers. "Why is it bad?"

"God, Hannah. What if I'm not what you need? What if everyone knows it but you? What if you realize it's true and I have you . . . *then* lose you? That would fucking kill me. I don't know what to do—"

"I've got it really, really bad for you, too."

The oxygen in his lungs evacuated in a rush, leaving his thundering heart in its wake. "If you'd gone out with Sergei, I would have fucking lost it, Freckles. You know that? I'd have begged you on my hands and knees not to go anywhere with him. I've been going crazy waiting for you to call my bluff—"

"I wouldn't have gone." Her hold tightened on his hand. "It was only a meaningless crush, but even that . . . even that went away. And I just hung on to the idea of it, so I wouldn't have to admit that I knew. I knew exactly why you left that album for me."

His body almost buckled under the relief, but he clung to his caution. "And what it meant scared you. It should. I should scare you, Hannah. I don't know how to do this." He dug through the cobwebs in his chest to find the truth for her. "I've gotten used to the way everyone thinks of me as this . . . this fucking reprobate. Someone who lives to get their rocks off. A good time and nothing more. But if . . . Hannah, I swear to God, I can't handle them doubting my character when it comes to you. It would break me. Do you understand? To have people waiting and wondering when I'm going to screw it all up. That I couldn't handle. To have your name spoken with sympathy because you're with me. I can already hear them. *She's out of her mind. He'll never settle down. He's not a one-woman man.* I'll want to die hearing them say that shit. It's the one form of ridicule I can't take. When it's attached to *you*."

Her chest rose and fell like she'd just swum eight miles. "Fox, if we were together, my trust would be the only trust that matters. And you would have it. I know who you are. If other people haven't looked closely enough, that's their flaw. Their dilemma. Not ours."

He swallowed a fist-sized obstruction. "You'd trust me?"

"Yes."

The fact that she looked pissed at him for even asking made his throat close up, flooded him with so much adoration, he almost choked on it. "I don't know what trying looks like for us. I just know that I want to."

"Oh, Fox," she whispered, bringing them chest to chest and pressing close, laying a cool palm against his cheek. "We've been trying this whole time."

There was no way to keep himself from kissing her after that.

With his heart rupturing and repairing on repeat in his rib cage, Fox dropped his mouth down on top of hers and begged her with his tongue and lips to save him from the middle of the ocean where he'd been existing without her for so long.

Fox came on like a storm.

Hannah still hadn't quite managed to catch her breath after all that was said, and she definitely wasn't going to get the chance now. His lid was off, there was nothing left between them, and, God, she was so glad she'd forced herself to wait until the right time to let the dam break.

Their kiss was honest and raw and unquenchable, as real as the rain starting to fall around them, soaking into the earth, wind howling through the garden structures, trapping them in the center of a force field.

Fox's hands were in her hair, tunneling through, as if desperate to touch every single strand while his mouth quite simply fucked hers. He'd been holding himself at bay or maybe presenting his playboy facade to seem unaffected. But that was gone now, dropped like a veil, and his hunger was brutally naked. And she matched him, clinging to his dampening, sinewy shoulders, plying herself on strokes of his tongue. His hands raked down her spine, where they gathered the hem of her dress, exposing her in degrees.

The kiss slowed momentarily, his eyes communicating the question.

Can I?

Hannah was already nodding, skin enflamed, positive if he didn't touch her, all of her, that very second, she was going to melt into the ground along with the rain. But Fox didn't give that a chance to happen, his big, capable hands plunging down the rear of her panties, taking hold of her bottom, claiming ownership with a rough squeeze. "Been dying to do this for months," he ground out against her lips, molding her buns in his hands. "Been wanting it in my hands, bent over in my lap . . ."

"Now seems like the ideal time," she gasped.

"Nah . . ." He proceeded to walk her backward, toward the car, his voice seductive, hypnotic. "Want to look at your beautiful face the first time I take you." He caught her mouth in a hard, wet kiss. "Am I going to take you now, Hannah?" Her back met the side of the car, and she moaned at the rough press of his muscular body, the drag of his hand around the curve of her hip where it wedged between their bodies, his fingertips on the verge of sinking down the front of her underwear now. "Are you going to let me touch it this time or tell me no again?" Those fingers pressed down on the swell of her mons. "If you want to say no, we'll stop. I've gotten pretty fucking good at waiting for you." His open mouth dipped to her throat, exhaling heat into the hollow. "Waiting for you is the best I've ever had."

"I don't want to wait. N-no. No waiting."

He chuckled, licked a path up to her ear, and bit down, almost buckling her knees. Were those her teeth chattering? She didn't have the chance to find out or be embarrassed, because Fox's mouth trapped her once again in a cyclone of sensation, those long, knowing fingers slowly, slowly traveling downward on her sex. Stopping right when they reached the good part and teasing with light side-to-side brushes that sent heat flaring down to her toes. When she was right on the verge of begging him to touch lower, Fox eased back from the kiss to watch her face, his middle finger parting her flesh, gently petting her clitoris. "Ah, babe." He dragged his bottom lip through his teeth. "This sweet little thing wet for me?"

"Yes," she managed, mentally coining a new phrase.

Death by Fox.

Hannah would never define him by his innate sexuality, but pretending he wasn't insanely skilled would be futile. Because God almighty. He wielded his abilities like a sword. He knew where to touch her, how to speak, understood the virtues of pacing, and her body appreciated that like nobody's business. Her intimate flesh grew damp so rapidly, she was actually shaking between Fox and the car. And he knew it. The knowledge was there in the total and utter confidence of the finger rubbing her clit, a second one joining it and pressing just that much harder, causing her head to fall back, a whimper racking her entire frame. "Oh . . . my God," she hiccupped.

He looked her square in the eye and ripped off her panties in one twist. "Haven't even started, Hannah." His knees landed on the soft earth in front of her, rain dripping off the ends of his dark-blond hair, moisture trickling down his cheeks. And he seemed to sense that she was about to float away on a cloud of never-before-encountered lust, because he barred his forearm across her hips, pinning her roughly to the car, and buried his mouth between her thighs, sinking, pushing, pulling his tongue through the split of her femininity.

Watching her the whole time. Observing her reaction to that first perfect, deliberate drag of friction. Fox groaned, his pupils dilating, forearm flexing against her belly.

That absolute, unabashed carnality gave her permission to palm her breasts through the bodice of the dress, chafing the heels of her hands over stiff nipples, enjoying the way he watched her through darkening eyes. She arched her back, allowing him to settle the instep of her foot on his shoulder and go deeper with every stroke of his eager tongue, his lips closing around her sensitive bud, sucking lightly, rhythmically until her muscles began to quicken, pulsing, her vision turning hazy, her head thrashing side to side on the car. "Oh my God. I'm already . . ." She panted, the sound ending on a moan, her fingers twisting in his wet hair. "It's already . . . I'm going to. It's coming. I'm coming."

As if he wasn't already doing enough, doing the most, he chose the moment of her confession to press his middle and index fingers inside her. Deep. Until he executed that move, she'd loved the light finesse of his touch, but unbeknownst to her, she'd been starving for that rough push. But Fox knew. He knew everything about everything, and God, oh God, he delivered it, standing halfway through her orgasm to thrust his fingers into her clenching heat. In and out, fast. No gentleness in sight. Just his open mouth groaning on top of hers, her moisture spreading down his thick fingers, the sky weeping around them.

"Fox," she gasped, holding on to his shoulders, almost alarmed by the intensity with which her legs trembled, her flesh constricting, releasing, his fingers entering and leaving her slowly, slowly with the ebbing of her orgasm.

And it wasn't enough, somehow. The best climax of her existence wasn't enough. Nothing physical would ever be enough without him—all of him—ever again. That unchangeable

knowledge concreted itself inside her as their mouths connected, demolished, her fingers racing down his stomach to
unfasten his belt.

"Need you. Need you."

He caught Hannah's wrist, dragging her palm up and
down his erection, his teeth catching her bottom lip, pulling. "I'm ready for you. Been aching so long." He yanked
down his zipper and planted both hands on the top of the
car. "Touch me. Please. Get a fist around it and stroke me hard.
Fuck me up."

How?

How was she continuing to get wet? She'd already hit the
peak of all peaks.

The way he looked at her, that's how. The bald honesty of
his words, the crude thrust of his hips when she circled him
with a hand and pumped. Firmly, like he'd asked. Her breath
growing choppy when his arousal swelled and stiffened more,
impossibly, giving her fist even more ground to cover. "Oh.
Jesus . . ." she exhaled before she could stop herself.

A glimmer of familiar cockiness in his eyes made her heart
spin crazily. "Ah, come on, babe." He wet his lips, a groan
building and breaking from his mouth, his attention fastened
on the treatment of her hand, the way she choked him up
and down, massaging him intimately. "You knew it had to
be huge."

She breathed a laugh, and he did, too, though the husky
sound quickly turned into hot, panting breaths against her
forehead, gasped instructions for her to go faster. Faster,
faster . . . until his breath began to labor, and he reached for the
door handle leading to the backseat.

"In," he rasped, not waiting for her to comply, just ripping the door open, wrapping an arm around the small of Hannah's back and dragging her inside, not stopping until her back was flat on the seat, the crown of her head almost reaching the opposite door.

His body came down on top of her, their mouths connecting frantically, her fingertips searching for the hem of his T-shirt, ripping it off so she could feel his chest, touch it, kiss his bare skin. Levering up so he could do the same to her dress, her bra, all their clothes save his pants ending up on the floor in a matter of seconds, his remaining jeans pushed down to his knees by two pairs of eager hands, their mouths ravenous.

"I have to get a condom on or we're going to be in trouble," he said in between kisses, his hips moving between her thighs, mouth traveling up and down her neck. "For the record, I didn't plan on this happening in the backseat of my car."

"Oh, you just thought you'd bring me to the most romantic place in the world to someone like me and I wouldn't want to rip your clothes off?"

He panted a laugh and fumbled the wallet he'd just fished out of his jeans pocket. "I didn't think past telling you how I feel and hoping like hell it would mean something to you." He picked the wallet back up and ripped credit cards out one by one, his shaking hands dropping them everywhere. "Swear to God, the one time it counts and I can't be smooth to save my life."

Hannah had a playlist consisting of 308 love songs and not one of them could describe this moment accurately. Not even close. Realizing she loved this man while he ripped his wallet apart looking for protection, his hair falling into his eyes, muscles heaving under ink and a light layer of sweat. Sunset lit the car in a deep orange, and she felt that rich color spread inside her chest, too, where her heart battled to keep up with the love that bloomed freely and wildly, a lot like the spring storm creating warm, white noise around the car.

I love him. I love him.

But then. Fox ripped the condom wrapper open with his teeth and rolled it down his abundant length, forearms flexing in the golden glow of sunset, his jaw going slack while looking at the place between her legs with anticipation—and lust came roaring back to the forefront. As soon as he was covered, they dove for each other once more, not a hint of restraint in their kisses. They were skin to skin, weathered man of the sea pressing down on her softness, one hand separating them briefly to bring the thick head of his sex to the entrance of Hannah's.

And then he pushed inside her in one slow, smooth motion, rocking home.

Hannah hissed out a breath and dug her fingernails into his hips, blindsided by the ripple of unequaled pleasure that sped through her and pulled taut.

"Yes," she whimpered. "More."

As if the feel of her was unexpected, Fox heaved a curse and slapped his hand down on the rapidly fogging window above her head. "Jesus Christ, so hot and tight." He reared his hips back and punched forward, making a low sound of misery, a shudder passing through his frame. "No. Dammit." His body flexed with tension on top of her. "Stay still. Stay still. Wasn't kidding when I said I can't be smooth with you. Then you have to go and feel so fucking perfect . . ."

"You feel pretty smooth to me," she said on a jagged exhale, bearing down around him with her inner walls. Milking his thickness with her femininity. "Mmmm. Please. Fox."

"Please stop, Hannah, stop . . ." As if he couldn't control it, his lower body ebbed back and rolled forward sinuously, filling her slowly, touching all different spots along the way, and she cried out, drawing blood on his hips. "I've just needed you so fucking long," he gritted out.

"You don't think I love that?" She trailed her touch inward and gripped his flexed buttocks, slowly rocked him deeper, lifting her hips at the same time, earning a long, hoarse sound from his throat. "You don't think I love feeling the proof of how bad you need me?"

"You want it, I'll give it to you," he rasped, rolling their foreheads together, kissing her roughly, tangling their tongues. "You want anything, I'll give it to you."

"Show me how badly I make you need to come."

His nostrils flared, his eyes closing—and when he opened them back up, there was a trace of the devil in them. And she loved being trapped in the eye of that male determination. She loved the way his upper lip curled, his forearms crowding close on either side of her head, his mouth dropping to an inch above hers. "Knees up, Hannah." He pulsed inside her, pupils blocking out the blue of his eyes. "Let's see how deep I can get it before you scream."

Spoiler: it didn't take very long.

Dutifully, eagerly, she brought her knees up, grazing them along his rib cage and locking them high on his torso. His next thrust made her eyes roll back in her head, the second one making her squirm out of pure confusion. How and what was he reaching inside her that seemed to unlock some undiscovered force? Pressure rode low and threaded through her core, knitting her together so tightly, she couldn't think or breathe, the roof of the car looking more and more like the gates to heaven. With his open, grunting mouth on her neck, he rode her roughly, yet somehow cherishingly at the same time, his tongue and lips continuously worshiping her throat, his mouth finding hers to swallow her screams. Yes, she was screaming his name, and he was, indeed, as deep as possible, scooping her hips off the seat with hard drives that quickened, roughened, going faster and faster. His body flattened her, using the flesh between her legs in the most deliciously frantic way, as if desperate for her to acknowledge his desire—and she did.

She had her proof. She had it and then some.

"Fox," she wailed between her teeth.

"I know you're close. I can feel it."

"Yes. Yes."

"Loving that cock, aren't you?" His teeth scraped her lobe and bit down. "Been craving it the way I've been craving this hot-ass pussy, day and night. On land and off. Now give it up, girl. Show me you love being on that back for me."

Her orgasm wound tight, tighter, and she dug her heels into his bucking ass, her mouth wide and gasping against his shoulder, her sex squeezing in one never-ending pulsation. "Ohhh God. Oh God."

He broke, moaning in fits and starts, the tempo of his drives stuttering, his mouth latching on to hers and holding, air rattling from his nose, his hands fisting in her hair. "Hannah." A rough, desperate kiss, another one, robbing the soul straight out of her body. "Hannah. Hannah."

The hard body that had just propelled her to a height of bliss she never knew existed collapsed on top of her, gathering her close and breathing heavily, his heart galloping against hers. Her legs were still locked around his waist, their bodies slick with sweat, and she didn't see herself moving in the foreseeable future. Maybe ever. Apparently being boneless *was* a thing.

"You make me feel like I'm in the exact right place." He exhaled into her neck, kissing it reverently. "Nothing to run or hide from. Nothing I want to avoid."

She turned her head and their mouths melted together. "It's okay to trust that feeling. I have it, too."

Fox studied her face with such intensity in his blue eyes, she didn't dare draw a breath. Then he swallowed heavily and turned them onto their sides, facing each other, his arm keeping her close. And they stayed there, breathing in the scent of each other's skin, until the storm stopped.

Chapter Twenty-One

$\mathcal{F}$ox cracked open an eye that felt like it had been welded shut.

When he saw the explosion of sandy-blond hair draped across his chest, a smile spread across his face, his heart lifting into his throat like an elevator and lodging behind his jugular. Hannah.

He didn't move a muscle. Yes, because he didn't want to disturb her. But mainly because he wanted to savor every little detail, soak them into his memory bank. Like the slope of her bare back, the dusting of tiny freckles that popped up along that smooth column, like stars in the sky over the ocean. He'd look at those stars completely different now. He'd revere them.

Very slightly, he lifted his head so his gaze could traverse her spine, lower to the sexy backside she'd definitely begged him to spank last night in the middle of the third . . . fourth round? They'd barely made it in the door before he'd stripped her down and carried her over his shoulder to the bedroom, kicking the door shut behind them. And there they'd stayed, only emerging once for chocolate ice cream and a sleeve of graham crackers.

To call it the best night of his life would be an inexcusable understatement. He'd been right to tell her everything. Because if he thought she was perfection on legs before, she'd completely unlocked now. Gone was the hesitation in her eyes. Apparently, opening up meant getting more in return. Considering he'd never get enough of Hannah, being honest was definitely the way to go.

What else could he give her, though?

Permanence, whispered a voice in the back of his head.

A sharp object materialized in his gut, prodding, digging in.

This morning he left for five days on the water. When he came back, the movie would be wrapped. Sweat broke out on his skin when he thought of her boarding that bus, but what the hell could he do about it? Ask her to move in? He'd just gotten over the hurdle of admitting his feelings—and not even the extent of them. Not the part about being in love with her. Not yet.

She had a job back in LA. The career she wanted as a music coordinator would almost definitely have to be based there. So what was the plan? Ask her to move to his empty-walled bachelor pad and spend three to five days out of every week without him? Or did they do the long-distance thing?

That second option gave him fucking hives.

His cute, perfect, freckle-faced girlfriend running around LA being cute, perfect, and freckle-faced without him? He'd want to bang his head against the wall nonstop. It wasn't that he didn't trust her; it was the possibility of her finding a better, more local option. A long-distance relationship between them would incite the critics, too, no doubt. They didn't know he'd been faithful to Hannah. They wouldn't even believe it if he told them how easy it had been. How he couldn't fathom wanting anyone else. Like he'd told Hannah yesterday, having their ridicule connected to her? Whether it be the implications that he'd break her heart, use her, or turn out just like his father and cheat?

That he couldn't live with.

But what other option did he have but long-distance? For now, at least. Until they'd spent at least five seconds as boyfriend and girlfriend, right? Until she was positive that Fox was good for her. What she wanted. In a way, he'd been in a long-distance relationship with Hannah since last summer. Now that feelings had been acknowledged, being separated would be a lot harder, but he would do it. He'd get down to LA as much as possible and lure her to Westport any damn way he could.

And eventually, when they were both ready, there would be no luring necessary.

One of them would simply leave their life behind.

If Hannah was the one to do that, would she regret it, though? What would he need to do to ensure that didn't happen?

Hannah yawned into his chest and smiled up at him sleepily, sending his pulse sprinting in dizzying circles. And he should have known. He should have known that the second she was awake, looking at him, everything would be all right.

I'll just talk to her.

Problem solved.

"Morning," came her muffled greeting against his skin.

"Morning." He trailed his fingertips up and down her spine, eliciting a purr of appreciation. "How's your tush?" He cupped the buns in question. "Sore, I bet."

Her laughter vibrated through them both. "I knew you were going to bring up the spanking thing." She lightly wormed a finger between his ribs. "I'm never going to ask again."

"You won't have to." He grinned. "I know what you like now, freaky girl."

"I was caught up in the moment."

"Good. That's exactly where I want you." Fox caught Hannah under the arms and flipped her over, rolling on top of her, fitting their curves together with a groan and staring down at the most incredible sight imaginable. Hannah, naked. Tits decorated in love marks from his mouth. Blushing and giggling in his bed. How the hell was he supposed to leave for five days? Who could expect that of a man? "You're so damn beautiful, Hannah."

Her amusement died down. "Happiness does that to a person." *Talk to her. It always, always works.*

She intertwined their fingers on the pillow, like she already knew. Of course she did. This was Hannah. The first and last girl he'd ever love.

"Your time here went so fast," he said thickly, looking her in the eye.

Her nod was slow. Understanding. "Now we're under the gun to figure it out."

The pressure of shouldering the worry alone dissipated like it was never there. Just like that. *The truth will set you free.* Apparently that wasn't just a generic phrase uttered by some politician three hundred years ago. "Yes."

"I know." She leaned up and kissed his chin. "It's going to be okay."

"How, Hannah?"

She wet her lips. "Do you . . . want me to be here when you get back?"

Pressure came spilling back in, caking his organs in cement. He scrutinized her eyes, finding nothing but earnest hope. "Was that . . ." He choked on the words. "Was it even a possibility that you wouldn't be here? Jesus Christ. Yes, I want you here." He swallowed a handful of spikes. "You better be here."

"I will. Okay, I will. I just wasn't sure if this was . . . if you expected me to know this was a one-time thing. Or casual, maybe. Like we could spend time together whenever I come to visit Piper . . ."

"It's not casual." Fuck. His throat had lit itself on fire. "How are you even asking me that?"

She inhaled and exhaled beneath him, seeming to mull something over.

"What's going on in your head?" he asked, getting right up close, pressing their foreheads together, as if he could extract her thoughts. "Talk to me."

"Well . . ." Her skin turned clammy against him. "It's just, you know, Seattle isn't far, and there are opportunities for me, for what I want to do . . . there. It's a creative job, not a nine to five. I probably wouldn't have to commute constantly. Just occasionally. I could think about relocating. To be closer to you."

The first emotion he experienced was utter relief. Euphoria, even.

They wouldn't have to do long-distance and he could see her every day.

The second was complete awe that he could make this girl want to uproot herself to be near him. How the hell had he managed to pull that off?

But the panic crept in, little by little, blanketing his awe.

She was talking about moving closer.

Now.

Living with him, really. Because that's what it would be, wouldn't it? When someone relocated to be closer to their boyfriend, they didn't live in separate apartments. Was she sure about him? *That* sure? Look how many times he'd come close to messing up this entire thing with Hannah already. Pushing her toward another man. Trying to sexualize himself so she'd do the convenient thing and disregard him as a player like everyone else. What hope did he have of giving her a reliable future?

They would laugh at her, too. Behind her back.

They'd think she was out of her goddamn mind, moving all the way north for a man who'd never been serious about a plate of fries, let alone a woman. He'd never even nurtured a houseplant. Would he be able to nurture an up-close-and-personal relationship with a live-in girlfriend? In a way that was worthy of Hannah? He refused to take the helm of the *Della Ray*. He was a walking innuendo among his friends and family. Now he had the audacity to believe he could be the right one for this girl?

Maybe she needed the long-distance time to be sure. He wouldn't be able to stand it if she dropped her life, her career for him, and then realized she'd acted impulsively.

"Hannah . . ."

"No, I know. I know. That was, like, really jumping the gun." She sounded winded. So was he. She reached for her phone on his side table, lighting it up. "What time does the boat leave this morning?"

"Seven," he responded hoarsely.

That was it? The conversation was over?

He'd had fifteen seconds to make a decision that would determine her future?

With an exaggerated wince, Hannah turned the screen so he could read it: 6:48.

"Christ," he groaned, forcing himself to roll off her deliciously bare body, dragging the duffel bag out from beneath his bed without taking his eyes off her once. He hated the indecision on her face, like she was suddenly feeling out of place in his bed, but hell if he knew what to do about it. What could he say? *Yes, move here. Yes, change your life for me—a man who just got the bravery to admit his feelings less than twenty-four hours ago.* A really huge part of him wanted to say those things. Felt ready for anything and everything with this girl. But that remaining niggle of doubt kept his mouth shut. "Hannah, please be here when I get back."

She sat up, shielding her body with the sheet. "I said I would. I will."

Talk to her.

Fox stood and crossed to his dresser, ripping out boxers, socks, thermals, shoving them into the bag. Heart in his throat, he stopped to look at her, cataloguing her patient features one by one. "I don't have enough confidence in myself to ask you to . . . change your life, Hannah. Not this fast."

"I have confidence in you," she whispered. "I have faith."

"Great. Would you mind sharing it?" God, why was he speaking to her so angrily, when all he wanted was to crawl back in the bed and bury his face in her neck? Thank her for having that faith, reward her for it with strokes of his body until she was delirious? "I'm sorry. I shouldn't be talking to you like that when you've done nothing wrong." He gestured between her and the duffel bag. "You think you could fit in here so I could bring you with me? Because an hour from now, I'm probably going to be sick over leaving like this."

"Then don't leave like this." She came up on her knees and shuffled to the edge of the bed, still clutching the sheet between her breasts. "Kiss me. I'll be here when you get back. We'll leave it at that."

Fox lunged for her like a dying man, dragging her body up against his and fusing their mouths together. Tunneling his fingers through her unbrushed hair, tilting her head, slanting his open mouth over hers, rubbing their tongues together until she moaned, her body sagging into him. He'd be leaving the harbor with a hard dick, but so be it. She was well worth the discomfort.

His fingers curled around the top of the sheet with the intention of ripping it off, giving her one more orgasm just to hear her call his name in that husky way of hers, and Fox knew he had no choice but to go. He'd never leave otherwise. He'd stay inside her all day, wrapped up in her scent, the sound of her laughter, the drag of skin on skin. And it would be the best. It would feed his fucking soul. But it didn't feel right to make love to her when he couldn't even commit to a course of action. Be confident in where they were headed, the way she was prepared to be.

He couldn't do that. Not to Hannah.

Fox broke the kiss with a curse, shoveling unsteady fingers through his hair. He held her tight for too-short seconds until, regretfully, he pressed her back into the pillows and tilted her chin up. Making eye contact but already missing her like hell. "Sleep here while I'm gone?"

After a second, she nodded, her expression unreadable.

"Be careful out there."

Her concern was like standing in front of a radiator, taking away the chill like only she could. "I will, Freckles."

Leaving her there, he dressed quickly, pulling on a long-sleeved thermal shirt, jeans, and a sweatshirt. Tugging thick socks onto his feet and shoving them into his boots. Fitting a cap onto his head. Restless now, he took one last look at her and walked out of the room.

Outside, morning mist enveloped him so that he couldn't see his building after a few hundred yards, and the pit in his stomach grew with every step he took toward the docks.

Go back.

Tell her to move here.

That seeing her on a daily basis would be your version of heaven.

God knew it was the truth. A few minutes away from her arms and he was already back to being cold.

He stopped halfway across the street, purpose beginning to settle over him. What if he *could* make her happy? What if they could prove everyone wrong? What if she just stayed and stayed and stayed, so he could wake up every morning and feel fucking substantial and alive, the way he'd done today? He would do everything in his power to give her that same feeling, so she'd never regret leaving LA—

"Fox!"

Brendan's voice beckoned him through the fog, and he took a few reluctant steps forward, the mist moving out of his way to reveal the harbor, the *Della Ray* in her usual slip in the distance. He nodded at his friend. They pounded fists.

Guilt he didn't want to feel tripped and fell in his belly.

He'd been so consumed with Hannah and the separate reality they'd created together that he'd all but forgotten Brendan's request that Fox keep his hands off his future sister-in-law. Realistically, nothing could have stopped him. His feelings for Hannah were too powerful to heed any kind of warning. That was obvious now. But the guilt wouldn't be pushed aside. Not when Fox knew Brendan's concern was warranted. After all, they'd been friends for a long time. While Brendan had been studying, learning the fishing business, Fox had been participating in very different extracurricular activities.

"What's up?" Fox asked, shouldering his duffel bag.

Brendan's gaze was unusually elusive. The captain was the type to look someone in the eye when speaking, impressing upon them his Very Important Words. "Something came up and I need to drive my parents home."

Fox processed that. "They're not flying?"

"No. There was some flooding in their basement while they were gone. Figured I'd drive them home and get it straightened out."

"All right," Fox said slowly. What was going on here? Brendan had never missed a job. Not once since Fox had known him. And surely if this was going to be the first time, he would have called and saved everyone the hassle of packing and hauling their asses down to the harbor. "So . . . the trip is canceled?"

The utter joy that blared through Fox almost knocked him over.

Five added days with Hannah.

He was going to be back inside her warmth in two minutes flat. And tonight he was going to take her to dinner. Wherever she wanted to go. A concert. She'd love a concert—

"No, it's not canceled. I'm just handing over the captain duties for the trip." Before Fox could react, Brendan was dropping the keys to the *Della Ray* into his palm. "She's all yours."

Fox's relief screeched to a halt. Brendan was now busy folding back the sleeve of his shirt with jerky movements. His friend had never been very good at deception, had he? Yeah, he'd even showed up at school on senior ditch day while everyone else had gone to the beach. This was a man who'd stayed faithful to his deceased wife for seven damn years. He was as honest as the ocean glimmering with the sunrise behind him, and there was no way he'd forgo a fishing trip for a flooded basement. His responsibilities and his customs were stitched into his very fabric.

For the first time, Fox was envious of that.

Even while annoyance nagged at the back of his neck.

Brendan had absolute conviction when it came to making decisions and sticking to them. He knew exactly what he wanted the future to look like, and he executed the steps to make it happen. Proposing to Piper. Commissioning a second boat to expand the business. The only place Brendan seemed to fall short was the absurd belief that Fox belonged in a wheelhouse. Believed it so much that he'd stand there and lie.

Fox nodded stiffly, flipping the keys over once in his hand. "Did you really think you could pull this off?"

Brendan squared up, firming his jaw. "Pull what off?"

"This. Lying to me about some imaginary flood so I'd be forced to captain the boat. What did you think? If I did it once, I'd realize it's meant to be?"

Brendan thought about holding on to his story, but visibly gave up after 2.8 seconds. "I hoped you'd realize the responsibility is nothing to be scared of." He shook his head. "You don't think you've earned the right? The trust that comes with it?"

"Oh, you trust me now? You trust me to captain the boat, but not with Hannah. Right?" His bitter laughter burned a path up his chest. "I'm all good to take the lives of five people in my hands. But I better keep my filthy hands off your future sister-in-law. I'll break her heart. I'll go behind her back. Which is it, Brendan? Do you trust me or not? Or is your trust just selective?"

Until Fox asked the question out loud, his voice absorbed by the mist around them, he didn't realize how heavy the weight of that worry, that distinction had been. Just perched on his shoulders like twin stacks of bibles.

For once, Brendan seemed at a total loss, some of the color leaving his face. "I don't . . . I never would have thought of it that way. I didn't realize how much it bothered you. The whole Hannah thing."

"The whole Hannah thing." He snorted. What a paltry description for being so in love with her, he didn't know what to do with himself. "Yeah, well. Maybe if you paid a little closer attention, you'd realize I haven't been to Seattle since last summer. There's been no one else. There will never be anyone else." He pointed back at his apartment. "I've been sitting there for months, thinking about her, buying records, and texting her like a lovesick asshole."

He closed his fist around the keys until they dug into his palm.

Was this what it would be like if he was with Hannah?

Constantly trying to convince everyone he wasn't the careless tramp he'd once been? Even the people who were supposed to love him—Brendan, Kirk and Melinda, his own mother—had looked at him and seen a character beyond repair.

Hannah has faith in you. Hannah believes in you.

Fox was caught off guard by the hesitant vote of confidence that came from within, but it made him think maybe . . . just maybe there was a chance he wasn't a lost cause.

Still, he allowed the thought to germinate. To grow.

If he could be a worthwhile friend to Hannah, if he could make *that* tremendous girl stick around and value him, his opinion and company, maybe he could do this, too. Be a leader. Captain a boat. Inspire the respect and consideration of the crew. After all, he had changed. He'd changed for the girl who was lying drowsy in his bed. In the beginning, she'd made some of the same assumptions about him that other people did. But he'd shifted her opinion, hadn't he?

Could he do it with the crew? Could he be the *more* that Hannah deserved?

He'd never know unless he tried.

And when he thought of Hannah in the recording studio the day before, bravely voicing her opinion—taking chances and succeeding—he found the courage to reach down and tap into an undiscovered reserve of strength. Strength he'd gotten from her.

Fox forced a patient smile onto his face, even though his insides had the consistency of jelly. "All right, Cap. You win. I guess . . . I've got the wheel on this trip."

Chapter Twenty-Two

$\mathcal{H}$annah stood outside Opal's apartment, waiting for her grandmother to reach the door. The last time she was here, just over a week ago, she'd been filled with dread over going inside. Talking about her father. Feeling totally disconnected from Opal and Piper in the process. Now, though, her shoulders were firm instead of slumped. She didn't feel like an imposter or like she was faking it until she made it. She belonged here.

She was Opal's granddaughter.

Finally the main character of her own life.

Youngest daughter of Henry Cross.

They'd come to an understanding through his music. Once, a long time ago, he'd loved her. He'd held her in his arms in a hospital room, taught her how to toddle, and gotten up with her in the middle of the night. He'd gone off to sea thinking he would see her again. And Hannah liked to think, maybe in a way that only she could understand, they'd had a nice, long visit through his songs, given each other a sense of closure. It was quite possible she'd even been given some fatherly advice in a roundabout way, because she'd woken up on Monday morning, the final day of shooting, with an idea. A place to go from here.

A place that would mean continuing to work in music . . . and be near Fox.

If that's what he wanted.

A knot that had grown familiar over the last five days grew taut in her belly, agitating the coffee she'd drunk this morning. If she went back to LA as originally planned, it would be with a heart broken beyond repair. Being without Fox since he'd left only cemented that belief. She missed him so much she ached with it. Missed the way he frowned and parted his lips slightly when she talked, like he was concentrating hard on what she was saying. She missed the way he tucked both hands under his armpits in the cold. Missed his devilish laugh, the stroke of his palm down her hair, the halting way he spoke when he was about to drop some honesty.

The fact that he'd learned how to be honest with her at all times.

Every time she closed her eyes, she envisioned him striding down the dock in her direction, opening his arms, the decision to put in the work, to build a relationship with Hannah right there on his face.

What if it wasn't, though? What if five days on the water made him realize it was too much too soon? Or too much work, period?

Maybe she'd been impulsive to suggest leaving LA to be closer to Fox. Maybe she should have just gone back home and tried to do the long-distance thing for a while. But she couldn't see herself being happy with that. Not now. Not when she knew how right it felt to have him at her side. At her back. All around her. Didn't he feel the same?

Yes. He did—and she'd have faith in his actions. She'd have faith in them.

The door opened and there stood Opal, a row of curlers down the center of her head. "Oh! Hannah. I was just in the middle of taking these rollers out and now you've caught me looking a fright. Come in, come in. It's just us girls. Who cares!"

Hannah entered on a laugh, tucking a finger into her jeans pocket to make sure the envelope was still there, as she'd done a hundred times on the walk from set to Opal's building.

"What brings you by, my dear? Not that you need a reason!"

She followed Opal into the bathroom and started helping her remove the final row of pink foam curlers. "I would have called first, but I was too excited." She wet her lips. "You remember when I asked for permission to use Henry's songs in the movie we're filming?"

"I surely do. But you said it was a long shot." Opal's hands dropped to the sink. "Don't tell me it's really going to happen, Hannah." She scrutinized Hannah's expression, and her own transformed with awe. "I don't believe it. I . . . How? How? They're not even recorded properly. They're just words on a page."

"Not anymore," Hannah murmured, relaying the events of the last week. "Come on, I have one cued up on my phone ready to play." She hooked an arm through Opal's, leading her from the bathroom to the couch. Once they were settled, she snuck out her phone and opened the sound file, exhaling roughly as the music filled the room. The opening dance of the fiddle and bass, followed by the purr of Alana Wilder's vocals, the muffled beat of the drum added in postproduction.

Hannah thought of the moment on set when she'd approached Sergei and wordlessly handed him a set of AirPods, hitting play and watching his eyes go wide, his fingers tapping on his knees. That sense of accomplishment. No matter what he decided, she'd created something magical. She'd moved the dials until it all came together and overcome the doubt to get it done.

Her first leading-lady move—and definitely not her last.

Opal covered her mouth with both hands, her knuckles going white. "Oh, Hannah. Oh, this does my soul good. It's the closest I've come to speaking with him in twenty-four years. It's extraordinary."

Warmth spread in her chest. "There are more. Three total. And I'm working on recording the rest." She took the envelope out of her pocket and handed it to Opal, her pulse beginning to tick faster. "In the meantime, the songs have been copyrighted in your name, Opal. You'll be getting a percentage of the income generated by the soundtrack, but I managed to negotiate a signing bonus, too. For the use of Henry's songs in *Glory Daze*. It doesn't include whatever the production company will have to pay you if they use the songs in advertisements—"

"Hannah!" Opal gaped at the check she'd pulled out of the envelope. The one Sergei had handed her this morning. "I get to keep this?"

"That's right."

"Oh, I couldn't," she said, flustered, trying to hand back the check.

Hannah pressed it back against her grandmother's chest. "You will. Henry would have wanted it." She swallowed around the sharp object in her throat. "I feel confident saying that now. Before . . . I wouldn't have. But his songs helped me know him, understand him better . . . and family was his life." She smiled. "This is a good thing, Opal."

Her grandmother sighed, and the last bit of resistance left her. "He would have been so damn proud of you."

"I hope so," Hannah said, pressing a wrist to her burning nose. "Now let's get the rest of those curlers out. You've got some cash to burn through."

Half an hour later, Hannah was back on set, still hugged by the warm glow.

She wrapped her arms around her trusty clipboard, enjoying the feel of it against her chest, knowing today would be her last day as a production assistant. She'd been right to start at the bottom and learn the ropes, but that time was coming to a definitive close. Propping other people up was something she'd always do naturally, because she loved being supportive. But career-wise? It was time to support herself, too, and go after what she wanted next. To chase the high she'd gotten by creating art on her own terms.

The entire crew crowded into one half of Cross and Daughters. On the other side of the bar Hannah had renovated with Piper, lights beat down on Christian and Maxine, capturing their final scene in the movie. One that Sergei, true to form, had written into the script at the last second, wanting to maximize the new soundtrack. There had been no plan to shoot at Cross and Daughters, but thankfully, Hannah technically owned half the bar. She'd called Piper for permission, either way, and her sister would be stopping by shortly to serve drinks to the celebrating crew.

In the scene building to a crescendo in front of Hannah, Christian and Maxine were dancing palm to palm, happiness and hope slowly transforming their features. Their movements grew more joyful. Less restrained. It would be in slow motion, Hannah knew, and it would be a perfect way to leave the audience.

After two more takes, Sergei yelled, "Cut!" He hopped out of his director's chair and high-fived the closest boom mic guy. "That's a wrap."

Everyone cheered.

Christian dropped character faster than a speeding bullet. "Who has my coffee? Hannah?"

She waved at him. Waited until he looked relieved, then gave him the finger.

His laughter filled the bar.

Still, she was in the process of taking pity on the actor and delivering his cold brew once more for old time's sake when Sergei stepped into her path. "Hannah. Hey." Did he seem almost . . . nervous? "I just wanted to say again how much grain the new score is adding to the film. It wouldn't have been the same without the songs. Or this place." He laughed. "You almost had as much to do with the movie as I did—and I'm the one who wrote and directed it."

A nostalgic fondness for the director made her smile. "And you did a great job, Sergei. It's going to be your best work yet."

"Yes, thank you." He hesitated. "You've already given notice, and I respect that. It's obvious you're ready for bigger and better things, but I'll regret not asking one more time if you'll accept a higher position. Since Brinley appears to be keeping her word about quitting, someone has to step in as music coordinator."

A month ago, she would have had to pinch herself, thinking she'd been hit by a bus and was approaching the pearly gates. A huge part of her was thrilled beyond belief that she'd proven herself enough to warrant this kind of offer. She just couldn't take it. Not only because she wanted to make things work with Fox, but because she'd loved working for herself. Discovering a band, being part of the process, coming up with a vision, and seeing it through. She planned to continue in her newfound leading-lady role.

"Thank you, but this is going to be my last project," she said. "I don't think I would have discovered what I really wanted to do without Storm Born. The experience has been invaluable, but I'm moving on."

"And moving out of LA, too, I'm guessing." His chagrin turned down the corners of his mouth. "For the fisherman."

"Yes." Once again, she had to suppress the scary doubt that marched into her stomach like stormtroopers. "Yes, for Fox."

Sergei made an unhappy sound. "You'll let me know if anything changes. Career-wise or personally?"

She wouldn't.

Even if the worst happened and things didn't work out with Fox, she knew what it felt like to love someone now. In that wild, brutal way that couldn't be fenced in or reasoned with. The crush she'd had on the director seemed like a sad, wet noodle in comparison. "Of course," she said, squeezing his arm.

"Okay, beauties. Who is ready to party?"

Hannah snorted at the sound of Piper's voice and the resulting gasps as everyone recognized her. Hannah turned around just in time to receive a smacking kiss on her cheek—which definitely left a Piper-sized lipstick mark—and watched everyone marvel as the former party princess of Los Angeles neatly stowed her purse behind the bar and smiled at the closest crew member. "Get you a drink?"

Christian came up beside Hannah, jaw in the vicinity of his knees. "Is that . . . Piper Bellinger?"

"The very one," Hannah answered, love rushing through her veins. "She moved here last summer after she fell in love with a sea captain. Isn't that romantic?"

"I guess. How do you know her?"

"She's my sister. We own this place." She tipped her head in the direction of the bar. "How about something a little stiffer than coffee?"

His mouth opened and closed until eventually he sputtered, "Yeah, I think I need it."

Hannah and Christian had just managed to wade through the buzzing crew to the bar when Hannah stopped dead in her tracks. Outlined in the door of Cross and Daughters was Brendan. But . . . it was only late afternoon. The *Della Ray* wasn't scheduled to be back in the harbor until tonight. Did they get back early? Nerves and anticipation warred in her stomach at the possibility of seeing Fox earlier than expected. But something in Brendan's expression caused the nerves to win.

"Hey," she murmured when her future brother-in-law reached her. "Aren't you supposed to be out on the boat right now? Are you back early?"

Brendan doffed his beanie and turned it over in his hands. "Not back early. I put Fox in charge of this run."

Hannah started, replaying that explanation six times in her head, some unwanted trepidation turning over in her gut. "You did? Was that a last-minute decision?"

"It was. Didn't want to give him a chance to back out." Brendan hesitated, trading a glance with Piper. "It seemed like a good idea. And it might work out exactly like I hoped it would. The man has great instincts, knowledge, and respect for the ocean—he just needs to believe in himself." He cleared his throat. "It didn't occur to me until after the boat left that it might have been bad timing. With everything . . . going on between you two. He was game for the challenge, but it's a lot at once."

"Wait . . ." Hannah swallowed a robin's-egg-sized lump, pleasure and shock turning her very still. "He told you about us?"

"Some."

Hannah made an exasperated sound. "What does that mean?"

"He told Brendan he hasn't been to Seattle since last summer," Piper supplied, leaning forward on the bar to join the conversation. "He's been waiting for you, Hanns. Like a 'lovesick asshole'—and that's a direct quote."

She barely had time to process the immense weight of that revelation when she noticed Brendan still looked nervous. And she knew there was more.

"I put the rest together without him telling me. I figured with him feeling like that, and you two in close quarters, something was . . . probably happening. Even though I went and spoke to him before you arrived. Asked him to keep things platonic—"

"You did *what*?"

"And," Brendan continued, "I may have reminded him to keep things friendly a couple of times since." He cleared his throat. "A couple . . . dozen."

"I take partial blame," Piper called, wincing. "We were trying to look out for you. But I think maybe . . . No, I *know* we underestimated him in the process. We've been doing it for a long time."

"Yeah. He had every right to throw that back in my face before he left." Brendan replaced the beanie on his head and accepted the pint Piper placed on the bar in front of him, drinking from it deeply as if the whole conversation had made him thirsty. When he set it down again, he took his time looking at Hannah. "I kept crowing about how much I trust him, wanting him to take my spot behind the wheel, but I didn't put my money where my mouth is. I regret that."

Heat tingled in the tip of Hannah's nose. Fox had told her his worst fear was someone questioning his intentions toward her, but it had already happened. His own best friend had done it. Had he been hurting over it all this time?

God, she was so proud of him for taking the keys to the boat. For trying.

She couldn't help but worry, though. Brendan was right. It was a lot at once.

They were right on the verge of carving out a unique place for themselves. A place to try to be together. To build on what was already a treasured friendship and make it into so much more. But a lot of Fox's insecurities were wrapped up in how people saw him. The town. The crew. What if his turn as captain didn't go as planned? What if he came home too discouraged to pick up where they'd left off?

It wasn't that she didn't believe in him. She did. But they'd left things unsettled, and this unexpected change of plans might have thrown off the balance even more.

Two weeks ago, she'd wanted to be a leading lady. For the sake of her career, not her love life. But tonight she'd have to gather up her newfound sense of self-purpose and be prepared to go to war if necessary, wouldn't she? Because she was no longer the type to watch from the sidelines or live vicariously through others, bolstering them when required. No, this was her story line, and she had to write it herself. Scary, sure. But if she'd learned anything since coming to Westport a second time, it was that she was capable of so much more than she realized.

Hannah signaled Piper for a drink. "Some liquid courage, please."

"Coming right up." A moment later, Piper shook something in a metal tumbler and poured it into a martini glass, sliding it in front of her sister. "You know"—Piper twisted an earring—"alcohol doesn't hurt, but I find some ice-pick heels and great hair lend the most courage of all."

"Let's do it." Hannah tossed back the drink. "I'm slightly ticked at both of you for warning Fox away from me, a capable adult human, but I need all the help I can get."

"That's fair," Brendan rumbled.

"Totally fair. I'm about to make it up to you." Piper threw back her shoulders with a sense of purpose. "Brendan, watch the bar. We have work to do."

Fox checked the final item off his clipboard and hung it back on the nail, letting out the breath he'd been holding for the last five days. He took the hat off his head and dropped into the captain's chair, staring out at the harbor. Letting the tension seep out.

Below, on the deck of the *Della Ray*, he watched the last of the haul get loaded by Deke, Sanders, and the rest of the crew. Normally he would be down there helping them, but he'd been on the phone with the market, preparing them for the arrival of fresh swordfish. He'd been inspecting the boat from top to bottom, making sure everything in the engine room was running properly, the equipment sound, the numbers recorded.

He'd done it.

A successful five-day trip.

He'd given orders and they'd been followed. It helped that he'd been insulated by the wheelhouse, instead of down on the deck where most of the ball breaking took place. Moreover, when the men retired to their bunks at night, exhausted, Fox had stayed up late mapping their course for the following morning, refusing to disappoint Brendan.

Or Hannah.

There hadn't been much of a chance to determine how the men felt about him taking over—and maybe that was for the best. Maybe if he kept his head down and completed a few more jobs without incident, he could ease back into the group slowly, having built the beginnings of a new reputation. Hard to believe such a thing was possible after years of the lifestyle he'd been living. Then again, he never thought he'd give up sex for half a year in exchange for witty text messages and record collecting. But here he was.

Dying. Fucking *dying* to get home to his girl.

He missed her so much, he was full of cracks.

She'd fill all of them in. And he was starting to think . . .

Yeah. That he could eventually do the same for her.

"Hey, man," Deke said, slapping the side of the wheelhouse and ducking his head in. "All set. I'm leaving for the market."

"Great," Fox said, fitting his hat back on. "Call me when you have a number." At the market, an attendant would test the fish for a grade of quality and decide on the price paid for each one. The process was important, because it determined the amount of everyone's paycheck. "I'll pass it on to Brendan, and he can contact them for payment."

"Sounds good." Deke nodded at him, followed by a playful look of disgust. "Look at you in the captain's chair. All large and in charge and making extra bank. Like you needed any help getting laid, huh?"

Sanders swung into the wheelhouse beside Deke, elbowing his friend. "Right? Why don't we just roll out a red carpet to the end of the dock? Make it even easier for the ladies to find you."

Fox was frozen to the seat.

Jesus. Really?

He hadn't expected their attitudes toward him to change overnight, but there wasn't even a hint of respect in how they spoke to him. Not even the slightest change in their demeanors or judgment of him. If they spoke to Brendan like that, they would have been fired before they finished a sentence.

Fox felt like he'd been hollowed out by a shovel, but he summoned a half smile, knowing better than to let his annoyance show. Or the ribbing would probably only get worse. "Seriously, I'm flattered by how obsessed you are with my sex life. Spend a little more time thinking of yours and we wouldn't have this problem." He pushed to his feet and faced them, his next words coming out involuntarily. They just sailed right past his better judgment, because his mind was occupied with thoughts of one person. "Anyway, I'm not going to Seattle. Or anywhere else. I'm going to see Hannah."

Their twin expressions of disbelief made his gut bubble with dread.

"Hannah," Sanders repeated slowly. "The little sister? Are you *serious*?"

Sensing he'd made a huge mistake bringing her up like this—it was *way* too soon, when he'd clearly earned none of the esteem that a man should have in order to be Hannah's boyfriend—Fox brushed past them out of the wheelhouse, seeing nothing in his path. But they followed. "Heard a rumor about you two at Blow the Man Down, but even I didn't think you were *that* much of a dog," Sanders said, some of his amusement fading. "Come on, man. She's a sweetheart. What are you thinking?"

"Yeah," Deke chimed in, crossing his arms. "You couldn't pick one of the thousand other women at your beck and call?"

"That ain't right, Fox." Sanders's expression was transforming to disgust. "You're supposed to wife a girl like that—you don't chew her up and spit her out."

"You don't think I *know* that?" Fox growled, taking a lunging step in their direction, his sanity going up in flames, along with the stupid, shortsighted hope that had been building. "You don't think I know she deserves the best of fucking everything? It's *all* I think about."

I kiss the ground she walks on.

I love her.

They were momentarily shocked into silence by his outburst, studying him with subdued curiosity, but instead of asking Fox about his intentions, Deke said, "Does Brendan know about this?"

And Fox could only turn and walk away laughing, the sound painfully humorless.

God, the way they'd looked at him. None of the respect afforded to the captain of a boat. He'd been an idiot to think they could ever see him in a new light. They'd treated him like the scum of the earth for even breathing the same air as Hannah, let alone being in a relationship with her. Fox could only imagine Hannah getting the same talk from her sister, their mutual friends, everyone in her life—and the idea made him nauseous, a dagger slipping through his ribs and twisting.

His worst nightmare was coming to fruition. Even earlier than expected.

But he could stop it now. Before it got worse for Hannah. Before she moved all the way to Westport and realized what a mistake she'd made.

Before *she* was forced to make this hard decision.

No, he'd make it for them both, even if it killed him.

There was an invisible match in his hand, lit and ready. He didn't seem to have much choice but to douse the best thing in his life in kerosene and toss the matchstick right on top.

Chapter Twenty-Three

An hour later, Fox stood in the shadows, leaning against the fish-and-chips shop across the street from Cross and Daughters. He should have stayed home. He shouldn't be out here trying to catch a glimpse of Hannah through the front window, his very existence seeming to hinge on just *seeing* her. At least one more time before he explained that he'd been wrong. Wrong to even consider that he could be good for her.

Someone walked out of the bar to light up a smoke, and in that brief second the door was open, Hannah's laughter drifted out through the opening. His body jolted off the wall, muscles tightening like bolts.

All right, look, he was still responsible for her safety until she went back to Los Angeles, so he'd just . . . make sure she got home okay.

Was he insane? If he had one ounce of self-preservation running in his blood, he'd have gone back to his apartment and changed the locks. Drunk a fifth of whiskey, blacked out, and woken up when she'd gone.

What had he done instead?

With the words of Sanders and Deke ringing in his head, he'd gone through the motions of a shower. Put on cologne. She was in town, and there was no earthly way he could stay away. Him needing to be near Hannah was just a fact of life. But once he saw her, he had to do the right thing.

Get your head in the game.

You are breaking it off with her.

A screwdriver slid into his gut at the thought of that. Breaking it off. It sounded so harsh, when his actions were the opposite of harsh. He was preventing her from making a mistake by wasting her time on him. Signing herself up for the same lack of respect that had become a normal part of his life. He couldn't let her move a thousand miles to be with someone who people— people who *knew* him—assumed would *chew her up and spit her out.* If his own crew thought so little of him, what would the whole town think? Her family?

So go in there and tell her.

He would . . . soon.

He'd gotten on the boat Wednesday morning on an upswing of hope. During the trip, the captain's wheel felt good sliding through his hands, the grain rasping against his palms. For a brief moment in time, the dreams of his youth had reappeared and sunk their hooks in, but that feeling was long gone right now. With Hannah believing in him, Fox thought he could earn the same honor from the men of the *Della Ray*, but that obviously wasn't going to happen. He was stuck in this place of no forward movement, boxed in by his reputation, and he wouldn't get her caught there alongside him. No fucking way.

Fox paced a few steps on the sidewalk, still unable to see Hannah through the window. Maybe he'd go to Blow the Man

Down, have a drink to settle his nerves, and come back. He started walking in that direction—and that's when he saw her.

Standing at the bar inside Cross and Daughters.

First, he saw her face, and his heart dropped into his stomach, a ripe tomato hurtling down a hundred-foot well and splattering at the bottom. God. God, she was beautiful. Hair down, curling in places he'd never seen it curled before.

He knew that expression on her face well, that mixture of earnestness and distraction, because she probably couldn't help listening to the music, repeating the lyrics in her head, the words derailing the course of whatever conversation she was having. In this case, a conversation with a man.

Not Sergei, but an attractive, actor-looking type.

Fox ran his tongue along the front of his teeth, his throat drying up.

Don't you dare be jealous when you're about to end things. She'd be back in LA soon talking to millions of men. There would probably be a whole herd of them waiting on the highway off-ramp, full of the right words and good intentions and—

And that's when he noticed the little turquoise dress.

"Ah, Jesus," he muttered, changing directions again. Moving at a much quicker pace this time. Even before he walked through the door of the bar, Fox wanted a lot more than a closer look. He'd spent five lonely nights on the ship with a hard-on, his dick stiff and aching for Hannah and Hannah only. So when he started to weave through the crowd, focused solely on her, his hands were already itching, and that was not a good sign. If this hard discussion was going to be successful, those hands needed to stay off her.

Be strong.

She turned, and their eyes met—and thank God the music was loud, because he made a sound midway between agony and relief. There she was. Safe and alive. Gorgeous and all-knowing and merciful and perfect. Any man with half a brain in his head would get down on his knees and crawl toward her, but he . . . couldn't be that man. It was especially hard to acknowledge that when her face brightened, the hazel color of her eyes deepening to a mossy copper, that heart-shaped mouth spreading into a smile.

"Fox. You're back."

"Yeah," he managed, sounding like a garrote was tightening around his throat. And it was a good thing Piper was behind the bar, or he might have kissed Hannah then and there. Two seconds in her presence, and he almost ruined his plans. Would have been worth it, though. "How . . . are you?"

A glimmer of sadness ran a lap around her face—because he hadn't kissed her?—and she set her drink down on the bar. "Good. I'm fine." Why did she seem to be measuring her breaths so carefully? Was something wrong? "Fox, this is Christian." She gestured to the man to his right. "He's the lead actor in the film. He's an absolute nightmare."

"She speaks the truth," purred the actor through his teeth, holding out a hand to Fox. "And you must be the one taking her away from us."

Just when Fox thought his stomach couldn't knot any tighter, it twisted into a pretzel. She'd already made plans. She'd made plans that would make it easier for them to be together. With Hannah standing in front of him, so familiar and sweet and soft, the word "plans" didn't sound quite as daunting. It was when they were apart that he started to doubt his ability to execute any kind of plan. It was the doubt of *others* that shook him.

The leather cuff around his wrist turned into molten metal, branding his skin.

"Oh. No," Hannah rushed to say, her face rapidly turning pink. "I mean, I . . . I'm leaving the production company. But that's a decision that I made . . . for me. Separate from Fox. Or anything."

Until that news came out of her mouth, Fox hadn't truly processed the weight of it. What it meant for her. "You quit your job?"

She nodded. Breathed, "They're going to use the songs. In the film."

"Aw, Hannah." His voice sounded like sandpaper, and he had to rub at the center of his sternum, the rush of feeling there was so intense. "Damn. Damn, that's amazing. You did it."

Her eyes sparkled up at him, communicating a million things. Her nerves, her excitement, her pleasure to be sharing the news with him. Fox sucked it down like a glass of cool water placed in front of a thirsty man.

"Yes . . ." Christian swirled his drink lazily, his attention moving back and forth between Hannah and Fox with unabashed interest. "Now she's off to go discover more new bands and plug them into indie soundtracks. Hannah Bellinger, music broker. She's going to be too good for me soon."

She placed a solemn hand on the actor's shoulder. "I'm already too good for you."

The guy tossed back his head and laughed.

The caveman part of Fox's brain relaxed.

There was nothing to be jealous over here. Hannah and Christian were obviously just friends. But there was still a lot to worry about. It couldn't be a coincidence that Hannah quit her job on the heels of them discussing potential logistics of a relationship, right? Had she made the move in anticipation of them trying?

Despite his worry over that, he wanted to hear more about this new job. Music broker. What did that mean exactly? Would she be traveling a lot? Was it Seattle-based? How excited was she on a scale from one to ten?

"You've definitely made a lot of decisions since I left," he said, keeping his questions to himself. Very soon, they wouldn't be any of his business.

Hannah studied his face. "Looks like you've made a lot of decisions, too."

"Lord, the undercurrents are a-flowing," Christian muttered, regarding them. "I'm going to go make fun of the interns. You folks have fun working this out."

Silence landed hard as soon as they were alone.

His brain repeated the speech he'd practiced on the walk through town. *I'm sorry. You are amazing. My best friend. But I can't ask you to move here. I can't make this work.*

His mouth said, "You look incredible."

"Thanks." She forced a smile, a fake one, and he wanted to kiss it right off her mouth. *You don't fake anything with me.* "Are you going to break up with me here or somewhere a little more private?"

"Hannah." Shock made her name sound ravaged, and he tuned his face away, unable to look at her. "Don't say 'break up.' I don't like how that sounds."

"Why?"

"It sounds like I'm . . ."

Pushing you away. Severing our connection.

Oh God, he couldn't do that. Might as well ram an ice pick into his heart.

"Can we mutually agree on this, please?" Fox asked, his lower body coiling tight when someone in the crowd nudged her closer, bringing the tips of her breasts up against his chest. Momentarily, he lost his train of thought. Was she even wearing a bra with that dress?

What had he been saying?

"If we both agree on this"—he swallowed the word "breakup"—"change of status, then we can stay friends. I need to stay friends with you, Hannah."

"Mmmm." The hurt she was trying so desperately to hide—chin lifted, gaze unwavering—gutted him slowly. "So when I come to Westport for a visit, we'll hang out like nothing ever happened. Maybe listen to my Fleetwood Mac album?"

It took him a moment to speak. To form a response. Because what could he say to that? He'd confessed the truth to her at the Sound Garden.

I had it bad for you. If the convention didn't make it obvious, I thought for sure the Fleetwood Mac album would do it. I've got it so bad for you, Hannah.

Really . . . really bad.

Was she remembering those words, too? Is that why she raised her chin another notch and delivered yet another blow to his resolve? "Look, I'm not going to fight you on this, Fox." She rolled a delicate shoulder. "You're ending whatever this was developing into and that's fine. It's your right."

He watched helplessly and miserably as she wet her lips.

What happened now? They just walked away from each other?

Was he really strong enough to do that?

"Could you do one last thing for me?" she asked, brushing their fingertips together ever so slightly.

"Yes," he said hoarsely, his temples beginning to pound.

Hannah tilted her head, and he eagerly memorized the curve of her neck.

"I want a good-bye kiss."

Fox's eyes flew to Hannah's, lust racking him, along with . . . panic. Flat-out panic. No way he could kiss her and leave it at that. Was she aware of how difficult that would be? How impossible? Was that her game? Her expression was so innocent, it didn't seem possible. Nor was it possible to deny her request. To deny her anything.

He'd kiss her here. In public, where it was safe.

Right.

Like anything about touching her was safe when he was on the verge of breaking. Shattering into a thousand tiny pieces.

Fox licked his lips and stepped closer to Hannah, his hand settling on her hip as if magnetized. His thumb encountered a very slight shape, almost like a . . . tiny strap, and he looked down, watching his fingers feel it out. "What panties are these?"

"I don't see how that matters. This is just a kiss."

It's a G-string. I know it's a fucking G-string.

Jesus, she'd look so hot in it.

"Right." He exhaled, pulse hammering at the base of his neck. "A good-bye kiss."

"That's right." She blinked at him slowly. "For closure."

Closure.

Case closed.

That was what he'd decided. That was what needed to happen.

She'd thank him someday.

Her mouth was so soft-looking, lips parted just a touch, waiting for him to place his own on top of them. One kiss. No tongue. No tasting or he'd be a goner, because no one on the planet had her perfect flavor, and he needed the memory of it to fade, not grow stronger.

Nice try.

The memory of her is never, ever going to fade.

Fox, apparently self-destructive, lowered his head anyway, desperate to get his fill of her one last time—

A bell started ringing behind the bar, Piper yelling, "Last call. Pay up and hit the bricks, kiddies."

Hannah tugged out of his arms, shrugging. "Oh well."

His mind struggled to play catch-up, the fly of his jeans infinitely tighter than it had been upon walking into the bar. "Wait. What?"

Despite her flushed complexion, her tone was casual. "Bad timing, I guess."

"Hannah," he growled, stepping into her space, twisting his hands in the sides of her dress. "You're getting the kiss."

She made a wishy-washy sound. "I mean, I guess I need to grab my bag from your apartment, anyway. The bus leaves at seven in the morning."

His head swam, stomach bottoming out, crashing straight down through the floorboards of Cross and Daughters. He'd known the bus would eventually depart, but somehow he'd blocked out that information. No staving it off now. She was going. Leaving. Her decision had been hinging on him, and they both knew he'd made it.

You're doing the right thing.

"I'm going to change out of this dress, too," she muttered, half to herself.

Oh, but he heard it. And definitely pictured her stepping out of the turquoise material in nothing but a G-string and heels. Definitely imagined his mouth on her skin and, Christ, that utterly perfect coming-home feeling only Hannah gave him.

Piper rang the bell again, and the bar lights flashed.

"I guess we better go," Hannah said, breezing past him.

Worried he might very well be walking to his doom, Fox was helpless to do anything but follow.

Chapter Twenty-Four

Hannah's heart was breaking.

He'd done it. He'd really done it.

She'd been concerned, of course. That Fox would return from his trip, having been duped by his best friend, and strain under the pressure of simultaneous shifts in his career and personal life. But she'd hung on to her faith, positive he wouldn't be able to look her in the eye and put a stop-work order on what they were building together. He'd done it, though. He'd really, actually done it, and as she clipped up the stairs to his apartment, her heart bumped along behind her, bruised and bloody.

God. The disobedient organ had almost burst free from her chest when he walked into Cross and Daughters, she'd been so happy to see him.

Stupid. So naive and stupid.

Get your bag and leave.

Just go.

Kissing him would only make the pain ten times worse, anyway. She'd kept the good-bye kiss in her back pocket as a last resort, knowing it would break down any defenses he'd built up over the last five days, but now . . . now she didn't want to fall back on last resorts. She wanted to find a dark place to crawl into and cry.

Part of her knew that wasn't fair. If Fox didn't want to be in a relationship, she should respect that, be a big girl, and wish him well. After all, she'd known about his cemented bachelor status since the beginning. This wasn't breaking news. But tell that to her heart.

Hannah unlocked the door and went inside, heels clicking as she traversed the apartment, Fox entering slowly behind her. The scent of his shower still hung in the air, and she breathed it in, making her way to the bedroom, where she'd left her suitcase packed and ready to go, some sixth sense telling her being prepared was wise. She'd hoped to unpack it again tomorrow, however. To stay in Westport. That he wouldn't let her leave without figuring out where they stood.

As was her routine, she tapped on the pink Himalayan salt lamp, forgoing the overhead light, casting the dark room in a blushing glow. Heaving the case up onto the bed and unzipping it, she took out a pair of cotton panties, jeans, and a Johnny Cash T-shirt. Laid the outfit on the bed and went to close the guest-room door so she could change. But she drew up short when she found Fox standing in the doorway, outlined in pink, watching her with a forearm propped high on the jamb, expression torn and tortured.

"I need to change."

He didn't move.

Frustrated with him, with everything, she marched over and shoved at the center of his chest to try to get him out of the room, her annoyance only increasing when his sturdy fisherman frame didn't budge an inch. "Let me change so I can go."

"I don't want you to leave like this."

"We don't always get what we want."

Still, he stayed put, grinding glass with that square jaw.

And she'd had enough.

Hannah couldn't remember a single time in her life she'd wanted to lash out so badly. By nature, she was not a lasher. She was a helper. A mediator. A solver. He didn't want her to stay but wouldn't let her change so she could leave, either? Who the hell did he think he was? Her hands itched to push him again. Harder. She had a more effective weapon, though, and she'd learned from the best how to use it. She'd be hurting herself in the process, sure, but at least she'd have her pride.

Show him what he'll be missing.

On her way back to the bed, she stripped the turquoise dress over her head, getting an immense amount of satisfaction from his shaky hiss of breath. Slowly, she folded the borrowed garment, bending forward slightly to tuck it into her suitcase, and Fox's guttural curse filled the room.

"Christ, Hannah. You look hot as fuck."

Every last one of her nerve endings popped like champagne corks as his warmth materialized behind her. When she straightened and her bare back landed flush against his heaving chest, she could only compare it to that breathless moment on a Ferris wheel when you hit the top the first time and the world spreads out in front of you, huge and wondrous. Hot shivers traveled up her arms, starting at her fingertips, her nipples tingling and tightening—and he hadn't even touched her yet.

A notch in Hannah's throat made her want to turn around, press her face into his chest, and beg him not to walk away from them. She almost did it. Until he placed his open mouth beneath her ear and murmured, "Time for that good-bye kiss yet?"

And her determination to show him what he was giving up renewed itself.

Not only that, but she wanted to take a sledgehammer to his walls and walk away while the rubble smoked. Those desires belonged to a stranger. Then again, so did the love and heartbreak she'd experienced with this man. None of it was familiar and all of it hurt, so she'd indulge her impulses and deal with the fallout later. It was going to be painful no matter what, right?

Hannah turned, the smooth movement of her hands climbing his chest derailed by the tortured look on his face. She recovered quickly, however, taking tight hold of his collar and turning them, urging Fox into a sitting position on the edge of the bed. His eager blue eyes landed everywhere, her pouting breasts, her mouth, the place between her legs, his hands raking up and down the thighs of his jeans, throat muscles working roughly.

"Just one kiss," Hannah whispered against his mouth. "Our last."

He made a jagged sound that shifted a spike inside her. Made her want to hold him, but the hurt urged her on. Overrode the impulse.

Slowly, she straddled his lap and sat down, scooting until she met the proof of what he really wanted, the stiffness, the generous length of it. And she pressed down with her hips, letting her tongue tease into his mouth at the same time, soft lips writhing gently on top of hard ones, his stubble grazing her chin. Just as the pace started to pick up, his hands closing around her butt cheeks to draw her closer, closer, Hannah pulled her mouth away, both of them breathing erratically.

Fox's fist wound in her hair, his hips shifting beneath her. "You didn't strip for me just to be kissed, Hannah."

He yanked her lower body tighter against his lap, dragging the valley of her sex over the ridge of his erection, rocking her once, twice, making her whimper loudly. "What else were y-you thinking?"

Fox huffed a pained laugh. "Whatever act you're putting on, please knock it off," he growled, grinding their foreheads together. "Just be my Hannah."

The spike in her chest dug deeper. "I'm not your Hannah."

A possessive light came on in his eyes, though conflicted. As if he knew he'd forfeited the right to call her that but wasn't ready to relinquish the claim on his novelty just yet. Because that's what she'd been to him, right? A novelty. A temporary diversion. As badly as she'd wanted to be different, she'd gotten the same outcome as everyone else.

Not special.

"Maybe I planted a seed at least?" she half whispered. "Maybe one day you'll meet someone and this won't be as scary."

His eyes widened as she spoke. "*Meet* someone? Someone . . . else? Are you serious? You think this could happen *twice*?"

Hurt struck her. He wasn't hiding his feelings. He wanted her, needed her, but was still choosing to send her away? Goddamn him. Hannah tried to climb off his lap, but Fox—looking panicked—surged forward and caught her mouth in a kiss. A soul sucker that put every cell in her body on high alert. Warned them they were being invaded. She struggled to keep her thoughts clear, to remember her plan to make him regret sending her away, but there was only the magic of his mouth, his strong, welcoming body, and the hedonistic rock of their hips.

Her own barriers came crashing down, releasing a sob in her throat, her hands coming up to frame his face, holding him, running her fingers through his hair as they kissed desperately, so very aware it was the last time. It soon became obvious they weren't going to stop at kissing. A significant part of Hannah had known that when she took off the turquoise dress. His middle finger traveled down the crack of her backside to pet her flesh from behind, making sex that much more inevitable, because God, she was so wet. Instantly.

Their mouths moved at a frenzied pace, only breaking apart briefly to whip off Fox's shirt and then dive back in, her palms climbing over muscle and tangling back into his hair. He added a second finger against her dampening panties, then a third, massaging her from the back, his tongue sinking in and out of her mouth. Oh God, oh God, she wasn't in control anymore. Her body begged, pleaded for that full sensation, that stretch of him inside her . . . and she was fumbling with the button and zipper of his jeans before she'd even made up her mind to do so, ruled simply by need, need, need.

Time stopped when she drew him out through the opening, stroking him up and down in a loving fist. The kiss suspended itself, but their mouths remained right on top of each other, breaths firing in and out.

"Go on, babe, slip it in," he rasped, his eyes glazed with hunger and something else, something deeper she couldn't name. "It missed you. I . . . fuck. I missed you. I missed you so much. Hannah, please."

He'd struck her down, hurt her, made her vulnerable, so she closed her eyes and didn't respond in kind, though the words ached to escape her throat. *I missed you, too. I love you.* Instead, she guided his shaft between her thighs, Fox grunting and tugging the G-string to the side, allowing her to position his tip just inside her entrance and slowly, slowly, take him deep, both of them watching it happen, voyeurs of their own lust.

"Shit, shit, shit," Fox ground out, his head falling back. "No condom. I didn't put on a condom, Hannah."

He groped blindly for his wallet, but he gave up quickly, gasping and clutching Hannah's hips when she bucked involuntarily, moaning on his lap, digging her nails into his shoulders. "I . . . don't. I can't."

A shudder racked him. "You can't what? Stop?"

Was she nodding or shaking her head? She had no idea. The deep press of his hardness robbed her of rational thought, sensation rushing to her core, quickening those intimate muscles, turning them into throbbing little pulse points.

"Hannah," Fox said, forcing her to look him in the eye, his breath pelting her lips. "Are you on something?"

"Yes," she sobbed, the importance of the conversation finally making it through the sex static in her brain. "Yes, I get the shot. I get it."

She rode him with a circle of her hips, and his eyes rolled back in his head. "Oh. Jesus. That feels so fucking good." He visibly struggled to remain coherent. "I'm clean. Got checked last time you were here."

That confession made her quake. "And there's been no one since, has there."

It wasn't a question. She already knew the answer.

Eyes clenching shut, he shook his head. "No," he whispered. "God no, Freckles. I only want to be touched by you."

His mouth was back on hers, kissing her into a state of desperation, his hands holding her buttocks tight to rake her up and back in his lap, his thickness entering and leaving her in smooth strokes that rubbed that place, oh Lord, that spot. Right there. It was already swollen from his fingers, and now he exploited it, moving just right. Exactly how she needed, delivering friction that engulfed her entire body in heat. Made her feel sexual and powerful and feminine and uninhibited. So much so that she broke the kiss to lean back, offering her breasts to his mouth with unsteady hands, whining his name when he sucked her nipples eagerly, hungrily, left then right, their flesh now beginning to smack wetly.

And then Fox brought a hand down, roughly slapping her bottom, his teeth capturing the lobe of her ear. "Touch your clit." He spanked her again. Harder. Twice. "Help me get you there, Hannah. Now. Jesus, you've got me so fucking thick, I don't even know when the end is coming. I just know if I touch you there, it's over. Play with it."

Breath rattling in and out of her parted lips, Hannah dragged her shaking right hand downward from his shoulder and found that sensitive bud, biting her lip as she rubbed it up and down, up and down, switching to quick, quick circles, her moan mingling with Fox's as he jerked her up and back, faster, faster.

"Look at me while you do it." A bead of sweat rolled down the side of his head. "Look at me while we get you off."

"Not just me," she managed on an exhale.

He shook his head, the movement jerky. "Inside this tight thing without a rubber watching you ride dick like you've never had it so good?" He leaned back on his elbows and started to upthrust, abdomen flexing, bouncing her on his lap, breaking the dam of her pleasure wide open. "Nothing in this world could stop me getting off."

Hannah crested, lungs seizing, muscles locking tight as the orgasm took control, keeping her body prisoner while it wreaked havoc, clenching her sex around Fox and taking him past the breaking point, too. They ground out the pleasure, hips pushing down and pressing up, fingers digging into skin, teeth scraping flesh, loud groans rending the air of the glowing pink bedroom, his moisture streaking down her inner thighs, his dirty speech echoing in her head, prolonging the pleasure.

Inside this tight thing without a rubber . . .

Watching you ride dick . . .

Fox went flat on his back, taking Hannah with him, both of them spent but remaining locked together, her head resting on his shoulder. Their harsh inhales and exhales filled the room, his fingertips stroking up and down her back through the cooling sweat, mouth moving in her hair. A priceless embrace that was everything right in the world. Everything honest and perfect. And . . .

She wasn't giving this up.

God help her, she'd ridden the tide of more emotions tonight than she'd ever experienced in her life. Hopefulness, denial, devastation, anger. When he'd walked into Cross and Daughters obviously determined to break up with her, she'd lost her courage. Her resolve. The heartache had been so immense, there'd been no room for positivity. There was only survival. But before he'd returned from the ocean, she'd decided to fight, hadn't she? And now here she was, at the final round, weaving on her feet, closing in on unconsciousness, ready to quit just to mitigate the pain. Isn't this when she needed to be at her strongest?

Isn't this when being a leading lady really counted? When she wanted to quit?

And after what she'd accomplished over the last two weeks, she didn't have any excuses. She could do anything. She could be brave. Lying in the fetal position with a pint of ice cream wasn't going to salvage a relationship she knew damn well could be amazing and lasting. Fox needed her to believe in him right now, when his self-doubt was blinding him—and she needed to believe in herself, too.

Hannah kissed Fox's shoulder and rolled to the side, climbing off the bed.

Outwardly, she appeared calm, but on the inside her pulse was going a thousand miles an hour, a trench digging itself in her stomach. Fox sat up and watched her through bloodshot eyes as she dressed in jeans and her Johnny Cash T-shirt, eventually dropping his head into his hands, fingers tearing at his hair.

She zipped her suitcase again and stood in front of him, working to keep her voice even, though the effort didn't quite pay off. "I'm not giving up on us."

His head came up fast, eyes searching her face. With what? Hope? Shock?

"Yeah, um"—she swallowed, gathered her courage—"I'm not. Giving up on you. On us. You're just going to have to deal with it, all right?"

He was a man afraid to swim toward a life raft. She could see it.

"What happened since you left me?" she whispered, fighting the urge to stroke his face. His beautiful face that looked torn and haggard for once.

Fox pressed his lips together, looked away. Spoke in a raw voice. "It didn't matter. It was never going to matter how qualified I am for the captain's chair. How well I can manage the boat under pressure. No matter what I do, I'll just be someone they mock and doubt and criticize. Someone they can't respect or take seriously. A hall pass. The backdoor guy. And that will extend to you, Hannah. Your waters are clear and I'll muddy them." He massaged the center of his forehead. "You should have heard how horrified they were. Over us. I knew it would happen eventually, but goddamn, it was worse."

With every fiber of her being, she wanted to cradle his head to her breast and be gentle. Be supportive. If he'd been pushed into breaking up with her, whatever his crewmates said must have been bad. Really bad. But he didn't need sweet and cautious encouragement right now.

He needed a good, hard wake-up call.

"Fox, listen to me. I don't care how many different beds you've been in. I know you belong in mine. And I belong in yours, and *that's* what matters. You're taking something that happened in college out on us. You're taking the stupidity and shortsightedness of others out on us. The hurt they caused you . . . it's valid. It's meaningful. But you can't take the bad lessons you learned and apply them to every good thing that comes your way. Because there's nothing bad about what we have. It's really, really good." Her voice grew choppy. "You're wonderful, and I love you. Okay, you stupid idiot? So when you've done some thinking and pulled your head out of your stubborn ass, come and find me. You're worth the wait."

Eyes heavy with moisture, chest thundering up and down, Fox stood and tried to wrap his arms around her, but she moved out of his reach. "Hannah. Come here, please. Let me hold you. Let's talk about this—"

"No." Her body ached from the touch she denied herself, but she could be strong. She could do what needed to be done. "I meant what I said. Take some time and think. Because next time you tell me good-bye, I'll believe you."

On unsteady legs, she turned and wheeled her suitcase out of the apartment, leaving a ravaged Fox in her wake.

Chapter Twenty-Five

Fox had never been overboard, but that possibility struck fear in the heart of every fisherman. The chances of being sucked down into the icy cold drink, the air drawn straight out of his lungs, the hull of the ship becoming smaller and smaller above, land a distant memory. Yet he knew with dead certainty that meeting his demise at the bottom of the ocean would be favorable compared to watching Hannah walk out his front door, her shoulders shaking with silent tears.

He'd been so sure he was doing the right thing.

But how could the right thing make that sweet girl cry?

Oh Jesus, he'd made her cry. And she loved him.

She fucking loved him?

His feet wouldn't move, his eyes burned, his body ached. He should go after her, but he knew Hannah. None of the words in his head right now were the correct ones, and she wasn't going to accept anything less. Christ, he couldn't help but be proud of the way she'd looked him in the eye and read him the riot act, even as she tore the heart clean out of his chest. That was some real leading-lady shit.

I love you more than life. Don't go.

Those were the words he wanted to shout at her retreating back. They wouldn't penetrate, though. He could see that. She didn't want impulsive, emotional statements from him. She wanted him to . . . pull his head out of his stubborn ass.

The door clicked shut behind Hannah, and his knees gave out, dropping him down to the bed, not a stitch of clothing on. With his pounding head clutched in his hands, he shouted a vile curse into the silent room that smelled like her, a fishhook impaling his gullet and ripping downward, all the way to his belly. He needed her back in his arms so badly, his entire body shook in bereavement.

But as terribly as he wanted her back, Fox didn't know how to do it the right way. He had no earthly clue how to make his head healthy for her. For them.

He only knew one thing. The answers weren't in this empty apartment, and the lack of Hannah's presence mocked him everywhere. In his bedroom where they'd spent nights wrapped around each other, the kitchen where he'd fed her soup and ice cream, the living room where she'd cried over her father. As quickly as he could, he dragged his jeans and T-shirt back on, grabbed his car keys, and left.

The change of scenery didn't help.

It wasn't the apartment Hannah was haunting so beautifully.

It was him.

Didn't matter how hard he applied the gas pedal, she came with him, as if her mussed dirty-blond head was resting on his shoulder, her fingers lazily playing with the radio. The image struck so deep, he had to breathe through it.

Fox had no idea where he was going. No clue at all.

Not until he pulled up outside his mother's apartment.

He cut the engine and sat there dumbfounded. Why here?

And had he really been driving a full two hours?

Charlene had sold his childhood home a long time ago and bought a condo in what amounted to a retirement complex. His mother grew up next door to the old folks' home where her parents worked, and she'd always been most comfortable around the blue-haired crowd, hence her living situation and job as a bingo caller. Fox's father had always made fun of her for that, telling her she would get old before her time, but Fox didn't see it that way. Charlene just stuck to what she knew.

Fox stared through the windshield at the complex, the empty pool visible through the side gate. He could count on one hand the number of times he'd been here. A birthday or two. Christmas morning. He'd have come more often if he didn't know it was difficult for his mother to look at him.

On top of tonight's catastrophe, did he really want to see his mother and encounter the flinch? Maybe he did. Maybe he'd come here to punish himself for hurting Hannah. For making her cry. For failing to be the man she stubbornly believed him to be.

Take some time and think.

Because next time you tell me good-bye, I'll believe you.

Did that mean she didn't believe him tonight?

Did she know he wouldn't have made it a day without text-ing her? Did she know he'd melt at the sight of her for the rest of his life, every single time she visited Westport? Did she suspect he'd fly to LA and beg for forgiveness?

He probably would have done all those things.

But he'd still be the same person, with all the same hang-ups.

And he didn't want them anymore.

Admitting that to himself untangled the fishing line in his gut, gave him the impetus to climb out of the car. All the apartments were identical, so he had to double-check his mother's address in his phone contacts. Then he was standing in front of her door, fist poised to knock, when Charlene opened it.

Winced at the sight of him.

Fox took it on the chin, like he always did. Smiled. Leaned in and kissed her cheek. "Hey, Ma."

She folded her arms behind his neck, squeezing him tight. "Well! Caroline from 1A called and said there was a handsome man lurking in the parking lot, and I was going to inspect. Turns out it was my son!"

Fox attempted a chuckle, but his throat only sounded like a garbage disposal. God, he felt like he'd been run over, the aches and pains stemming from the middle of his chest. "Next time, don't go check it out yourself. Call the police."

"Oh, I was just going to look through Caroline's binoculars and have a gab about it. Don't worry about me, boy. I'm indestructible." She stepped back and looked at him. "Not sure I can say the same for you. Never seen you look so green around the gills."

"Yeah." Finally, she took his elbow and ushered him inside, pointing him toward the small dining-room table, where he took a seat. The round piece of furniture was painted powder blue, covered in knickknacks, but the misshapen frog ashtray was what caught his attention. "Did I make this?"

"Sure did. Ceramics class your sophomore year of high school. Coffee?"

"No, thanks."

Charlene sat down across from him with a steaming mug in her hand. "Well, go on." She paused to take a sip. "Tell me what happened with Hannah."

Fox's chest wanted to cave in just hearing her name. "How did you know?"

"It's like I always say, a man doesn't bring a woman to bingo unless he's serious about her." She tapped a nail against her mug. "Nah. But in truth, I could tell by the way you looked at her, she was something real special."

"How did I look at her?" He was afraid to find out.

"Ah, son. Like a summer day showing up after a hundred years of winter."

Fox couldn't speak for long moments. Could only stare down at the table, trying to get rid of the painful squeeze in his throat, seventeen incarnations of Hannah's smile playing in his head. "Yeah, well. I told her it was over tonight. She disagreed."

Charlene had to set her coffee down, she was laughing so hard. "Hold on to that one." She used her wrist to swipe at her eyes. "She's a keeper."

"You don't really think I could, though." He twisted the ceramic frog on the table. "Hold on to her. Hold on to anyone."

His mother's laughter cut off abruptly. "And why not?"

"You know why."

"I surely do not."

Fox laughed without humor. "You know, Ma. The way I kept Dad's legacy alive. The way I've carried on more than half my life now. That's what I know. That's what I'm used to. It's no use trying to be something I'm not. And, Jesus, I'm definitely not one half of a couple."

Charlene fell silent, looking almost pained. Proof that she agreed. Maybe she didn't want to say it out loud, but she knew he spoke the truth.

It was too hard to witness her disappointment, but when Fox stood to leave, Charlene spoke and he lowered back into the seat.

"You never had the chance to try . . . to be anything else. 'He's going to be a heartbreaker, just like his father.' That's what everyone used to say, and I laughed. I laughed, but it stuck. And then . . ."

"What?"

"This is hard to talk about," she said quietly, standing to top off her coffee, eventually sitting back down and visibly gathering her poise. "I'd spent years of my life trying to change your father. Make him a home, make him happy with me and me alone. Us alone. Well, you know how that worked out. He came home smelling like a perfume factory five nights out of seven." She paused to huff a breath. "When you got older and started looking like him, I guess . . . I guess I was too scared to try. To teach you how to be different from him and have my heart broken all over again if you resisted. So I just . . . I didn't resist. In fact, I joined in with the chorus and encouraged you to break hearts and . . . and the coffee tin . . ." She covered her face with her hands. "I want to die just thinking about it."

On reflex, Fox glanced at the cabinet, as if he might find it there, stuffed full of condom money. Even though he wouldn't. Even though it wasn't the same house. "It's okay, Ma."

"No, it's not." She shook her head. "I needed to explain to you, Fox, that you're nothing like him. To correct the damaging things you believed about yourself. These misconceptions. But you'd already started doing exactly what we encouraged you to do from the start. When you came back from college, you'd retreated into a hard shell. There was no talking to you then. And here we are now, years later. Here we are."

Fox ran back through everything she'd said, his deepest insecurities exposed like a raw nerve, but so what. Nothing hurt like Hannah leaving hurt. Not even this. "If you don't think I'm anything like him, why do you flinch every time you see me?"

Charlene paled. "I'm sorry. I didn't realize I was doing that." A beat passed. "Some of the time, I can live with the guilt of failing you. When I see you, though, that guilt hits me like a backhand to the cheek. That flinch is for me, not you."

An unexpected burn started behind his eyes.

Something hard began to erode in the vicinity of his heart.

"I remember some of the things he said to you, all the way back to fourth grade, fifth grade. Which one in the class was your girlfriend? When were you going to start going on dates? Boy, you'll have your pick of the litter! And I thought it was funny. I even said those things myself once in a while." She reached for her pack of cigarettes, tapped one out and lit it, blowing the smoke out of the side of her mouth. "Should have been encouraging you to do well in class. Or join clubs. Instead, we made life about . . . intimacy for you. From the damn jump. And I don't have any excuse except to say, your father's life was women. By default, so was mine. The affairs surrounded us at the time, took up all the air. We let it hurt our son, too. Let it turn into a shadow to follow you around. That's the real tragedy. Not the marriage."

Fox had to stand up. Had to move.

He remembered his parents saying those things to him. Of course he did. However, all the way up until this moment, it never once occurred to him that *all* parents weren't saying those things to their kids. Never occurred to him that he'd effectively been brainwashed into believing his identity was the sum of his success with women. And . . .

And his mother didn't wince when she saw him because he reminded her of his father. It was guilt. Fox didn't like that, either. He owned his actions and didn't want his mother claiming responsibility for them, because that would be cowardly. But, God, it was a relief. To know his mother didn't dread seeing his face. To know he wasn't broken, but maybe, just maybe, he'd been wedged into a category before he even knew what was happening.

More than anything in that moment, he wished for Hannah.

He wished to burrow his face into her neck and tell her everything Charlene had said, so she could sum it up perfectly for him in her Hannah way. So she could kiss the salt from his skin and save him. But Hannah wasn't there. She'd gone. He'd sent her away. So he had to rescue himself. Had to work this out for himself.

"People will think she's crazy to take a chance on me. People will assume I'm going to do to her what Dad did to you."

When no response was forthcoming, Fox looked back over his shoulder to find Charlene aggressively stubbing out her cigarette. "Let me tell you a story. Earl and Georgette have been coming to bingo for over a decade, sitting on opposite sides of the hall. As far away from each other as they can get. They might look like sweet little seniors, but let me tell you, they are stubborn as shit." Charlene lit another cigarette, comfortable in the middle of her storytelling. "Earl used to be married to Georgette's sister, right up until she passed. Young. Maybe in her fifties. And, well, through comforting each other, Earl and Georgette got to falling in love, right? Both of them worried about people judging them, so they stopped seeing each other. Cut each other right off. But hell if they didn't stare at each other across the bingo hall like two lovesick puppies for years."

"What happened?"

"I'm going to tell you, aren't I?" She puffed her smoke. "Then Georgette got sick. Same illness as her sister. And there was Earl, not only left to realize he'd missed out on creating a life with the woman he loved, but having no right to help her through the rough time. No right to care for her. Did it matter what other people thought at that point? No. It did not."

"Christ, Ma. You couldn't have picked something a little more uplifting?"

"I haven't finished yet," she said patiently, enjoying herself. "Earl professed his love to Georgette and moved in, nursed her back to health. Now they sit in the front row every time I host bingo in Aberdeen. Can't pry them apart with a butter knife. And you know what? Everyone is happy for them. You can't live life worrying about what people will think. You'll wake up one day, look at a calendar, and count the days you could have spent being happy. With her. And no one else, especially the ones wagging their tongues, are going to be there to console you."

Fox thought of waking up in fifteen years and having spent none of it with Hannah, and he got dizzy, his mother's kitchen spinning around him, his lungs on fire. Crossing to the living room, he fell back on the couch and counted off his breaths, trying to fight through the sudden nausea.

Exhaustion crashed down on him unexpectedly, and he wasn't sure why. Maybe it was having his long-standing issues unraveled, explained, and the subsequent weightless feeling in his stomach. Maybe it was the emotional excess or the utter depression of losing Hannah and making her cry, plus knowing his mother didn't secretly hate him. All of it wrapping around his head like a thick, fuzzy bandage, blurring his thoughts until they were nothing more than a fading echo. His head dropped back against the cushion, and his roundabout worries eventually sent him into a deep sleep. The last thing he remembered was his mother laying a blanket over him and the promise he made to himself. As soon as he woke up, he'd go get her.

Hang on. I'll be right there, Freckles.

Fox woke up in the sunlight to the chatter of voices.

He sat up and looked around, piecing together the night before, trying to clear the cobwebs that clung harder than usual. Tchotchkes on every surface, the lingering smell of Marlboro Reds. This was his mother's living room. He knew that much. And then their conversation came back in precise detail, followed by a sinking feeling in his stomach.

It was morning. Eight in the morning.

The bus . . . the bus back to LA left at seven.

"No." Fox almost got sick. "No, no, no."

He was off the couch like a shot, his stomach pitching violently. Several pairs of eyes stared back at him from the kitchen, belonging to the senior ladies who'd apparently congregated in Charlene's kitchen for coffee and donuts.

"Morning, honey," his mother sang from the table, in the same place she'd sat last night. Same mug in her hands. "Got a bear claw over here with your name on it. Come meet the lady gang."

"I can't. I . . . She's leaving. She's . . . left?" He patted the pocket of his jeans and found his phone, the battery at 6 percent, and quickly tapped Hannah's number, raking a hand through his hair and pacing while it rang. No way. No way he let her get on a bus back to California. He didn't have a plan yet, didn't have a strategy for keeping Hannah. He only knew that the fear of God was rattling his bones. That—the reality of her actually being gone—along with what his mother had said to him last night, had damn well put Fox's priorities in order.

My head is out of my ass, Hannah. Answer the phone.

Voicemail.

Of course it was the opening bars to "Me and Bobby McGee," followed by the husky efficiency of her greeting.

Fox stopped pacing, the sound of her voice against his ear washing over him like warmth from a fireplace. Oh God, oh

God, he'd been such a jackass. This girl, this one-in-a-billion angel of a girl, loved him. He loved her back in a wild, desperate, uncontrollable way. And he didn't know how to build a home with her, but they would figure it out together. That he was positive about.

Hannah gave him faith. She *was* his faith.

The beep sounded in his ear. "Hannah, it's me. Please, please, get off the bus. I'm coming home right now. I'm . . ." His voice lost power. "Just get off the bus somewhere safe and wait for me, all right? I fucking love you. I love you. And I'm sorry you fell in love with an idiot. I'm . . ." *Find the words. Find the right words.* "Remember in Seattle, you said we've been trying this whole time. Since last summer. To be in a relationship. I didn't fully understand at the time, but I do now. There was never going to be a life away from you, because, Jesus, that's no life at all. You, Hannah. Are my life. I love you and I'm coming home, so please, babe. Please. Will you just wait for me? I'm sorry."

Fox stopped and listened, as if she might somehow answer and reassure him like she always did, then hung up with dread curdling in his stomach. Looked up to find the women in various states of crying, from dabbing away tears to openly weeping.

"I have to go."

No one tried to stop Fox as he ran out the door and sprinted to his truck, throwing himself into the driver's seat and peeling out. He hit a stoplight on the way to the highway and cursed, slamming on the brakes. Restless without being in motion, he took out his phone again and called Brendan.

"Fox," the captain said, answering on the first ring. "I've been meaning to call you, actually. I want to apologize again—"

"Good. Do it another time, though." The light turned green, and he floored it, merging onto the highway, thanking God there didn't seem to be any rush hour traffic. "Is Hannah with you guys? Did she stay there last night?"

A brief pause. "No. She didn't stay with you?"

"No." Knowing he could have spent the night with Hannah—and didn't—was a bitter pill to swallow. It was a world that didn't make sense, and he never wanted to live in it again. Where would she have gone? There were a couple of inns in Westport, but she wouldn't check in somewhere, would she? Maybe she'd gone to the house where the crew was staying. All of them would have gotten on the bus an hour ago. She went with them. *She's gone.* "No, she's not with me," he rasped, misery washing over him. "Look. It's complicated. Predictably, I fucked everything up. I need a chance to fix it."

"Hey. Whatever you did, I'm sure you can repair it."

No accusations. No knowing sighs or disappointment.

Just faith.

Fox ached just above his collarbone. Maybe, like the ocean, he could evolve.

Maybe the crew would realize they were wrong about him after some time passed. After all, they were just following his lead, treating him like he asked them to. Like the cheap version of himself he'd presented. Demanding respect from Brendan one time was all it took to change his best friend's tune. What if that was all it took to do the same with everyone else?

And if it didn't work? The hell with them. His relationship with Hannah belonged to him and her. No one else.

Either way, he was going to do everything in his power to keep Hannah.

That was a given.

Imagining a future without her had his hands shaking on the wheel.

For the first time since he'd left for college, he was eager to find out how far his potential could reach. He was ready to take chances again. Maybe because he now knew, after speaking frankly with Charlene, that he'd been guided incorrectly. Or maybe because he was no longer so afraid of being judged. He was driving blindly, pretty sure Hannah had gone back to LA. *This* was pain. This was self-loathing. Losing the love of his life—his future—because he'd let the past win. He could endure and overcome anything but this.

Cradling the phone between his cheek and shoulder, he ripped off the leather bracelet and threw it out the window of his car. "I want the boat, Brendan."

Even without seeing his best friend's face, he could imagine the raised eyebrow, the thoughtful stroking of his jaw. "You sure?"

"Positive. And I'm putting in a new chair. Your ass grooves are in the old one." He waited for his friend to stop chuckling. "Is Piper there? Has she spoken to Hannah?"

"She's out on her run. I can call her—"

Fox's phone died.

The breath hissed out of him, and he threw the device onto the dashboard, heart slamming in his ears as he wove in and out of traffic. She couldn't be gone. All right, they hadn't agreed on a timeline for him to come and find her. Perhaps she thought she'd go back to LA and he'd take a few weeks or even months to figure out he'd die without her? Maybe he should have assumed she would leave this morning? Well, he hadn't.

He'd been thinking about it for weeks, and when the moment finally came, his heart had blocked the painful possibility.

Too late. He was too late.

God, she could have changed her mind. Maybe she wasn't giving him time to pull his head out of his stubborn ass at all. That would explain why she wasn't answering her phone. She'd deemed Fox more trouble than he was worth. If that was the case, it wouldn't matter if he flew to LA. Or drove like a bat out of hell and caught up with the bus. If she was done with him . . .

No.

No, please. He couldn't think like that.

With his skin somehow icy and sweating at the same time, Fox took the exit to Westport an hour and a half later, searching the streets for members of the cast or crew. Would he even recognize any of them? At that moment, he would have been grateful to see the fucking director and his yuppie turtleneck. None of the people waving as he passed were non-locals, though. None of them. No bus idling on the harbor.

Gone.

"No, Hannah," he said hoarsely. "No."

He parked haphazardly outside his apartment, prepared to go inside and pack a bag. He'd get on the highway and catch up with the bus. Wait for it to stop and beg her to listen. If he couldn't find the bus, he'd get on a plane. Bottom line, he wasn't coming back here until they were unequivocally committed. With a plan.

A plan.

He might have laughed if he wasn't on the verge of splitting straight down the middle. Suddenly, he could think of a million plans. Because he was capable of anything. They were. Together.

As long as she hadn't given up on him—

Fox walked into his apartment and stopped dead in his tracks.

Hannah sat cross-legged on the floor in front of his record player, giant can headphones over her ears, humming along to the music.

If she'd heard him or turned around in that moment, she would have seen him slump back against the door, shaking. Seen him use the hem of his T-shirt to wipe the scalding moisture from his eyes. Would have seen the prayers he mouthed at the ceiling. But, oblivious, she didn't turn. Didn't witness him devouring the tilt of her neck with his gaze, the line of her shoulders. Inhaling the breathiness of her voice singing along to Soundgarden.

As soon as he could walk straight, he went toward her, picking up her phone where it rested on the counter, his voicemail not yet played.

He dug for the right words.

Ones that could possibly express how much he loved her.

But in the end, all he had to do was listen to his heart and trust himself.

He came to a stop beside her, and she jolted and looked up at him.

They stared for long moments, searching each other for answers.

He gave her one by changing the record. Putting on "Let's Stay Together" by Al Green. Watching her expression soften with each word. Lyrics that couldn't have been more appropriate. When tears started to fill her beautiful eyes, Fox pulled Hannah to her feet and they slow danced to the music in her ears and the music in his heart, the headphones only coming off when the song ended.

"I love you," Fox said thickly, still rocking her side to side. Holding on to her like a life preserver in the middle of the Bering. "Oh my God, I love you so much, Hannah." He burrowed his face into her hair, starved for closeness to her, this incredible person who somehow loved him. "I thought you left," he said, lifting her off the floor and walking toward the bedroom. "I thought you left."

"No. I couldn't. I wouldn't." Her arms tightened around his neck. "I love you too much."

As he laid her down on the bed, tears leaked from his eyes, and Hannah reached up, wiped them away, along with her own. "What happened to you giving me time to pull my head out of my ass?"

"Six hours seemed like more than enough," she whispered up at him.

Happiness rushed in, crowding him from all sides. And he let it. Let himself accept it and think of all the ways he could give happiness to her in return. For the rest of his life. Every hour, every day.

Fox covered her with his body, both of them groaning against each other's mouth, sliding and writhing muscle on curves. "We can find a place in between here and Seattle. That way if you get a job in the city, we cut the commute in half for us both." He unfastened her jeans and pushed a hand inside, watching her eyes go blind when his fingers tucked into her panties and found her. There. Pressing between her seam of flesh and rubbing with increasing pressure. "Does that work for you?"

"Yes," she gasped when he slowly worked his middle finger inside, drawing it in and out. "Mmmm. I like that idea. W-we can find out who we'll become together. Without everyone around all the t-time."

Fox nodded, took his time tugging off her jeans and panties, eventually rendering her naked while he remained fully clothed on top of her, pressing her down into the bedclothes. "Whoever we become together, Hannah," he said, mouth roaming over hers, fingers reaching down to lower his zipper. "I'm yours and you're mine. So it's always going to be right." His throat started to close as he pushed inside her, those thighs of hers jerking up into the perfect position. "I didn't know what right felt like until you," he choked out. "I'm holding on to the good you give me. I'm holding on to you."

"I'm hanging on to you, too, Fox Thornton," she murmured unevenly, her body propelled up the bed on his first drive, eyes glazing. "Never letting go."

"I'm in for the good, bad, and everything in between, Hannah." He pressed his open mouth to the side of her neck and pushed deeper, deep enough, close enough to feel her breathe, and rejoiced in it. "Decades. A lifetime. I'm in."

Epilogue

Ten Years Later

The smooth voice of Nat King Cole filled the interior of Hannah's Jeep as it bumped along the snowy road. Her headlights caught the falling flakes, twilight giving the sky a purplish-gray glow, towering pines creating a now-familiar pathway on either side of her—a pathway home to her family.

After ten years of residing in Puyallup, it was hard to believe she'd ever lived in sunny Los Angeles at all. And she wouldn't trade it for all the records in Washington.

Her eyes drifted to the rearview mirror, where she could see shopping bags filled to overflowing with elaborately wrapped presents in the backseat, and contentment swept through her chest, so intense it brought tears to her eyes. There would never be anything better than this. Coming home to her family on Christmas Eve after four days on the road. She missed them so terribly, it cost her quite an effort to drive slowly, carefully on the winter road.

When her house came into view a minute later and her tires crunched to a stop in the driveway, her heart started to beat faster. Smoke curled lazily from the chimney of their log-cabin-style home, sleds—man-sized and child-sized—leaned up against the wall by the front entrance. A Christmas tree twinkled in one of the many windows. And when her husband walked into view with one of their daughters slung casually over his brawny shoulder, a laugh filled with yearning and love and gratitude puffed out of her in the quiet car.

They'd more than made it work, hadn't they? They'd made a life happier and filled with more joy than either of them could have expected.

A decade earlier, Fox and Hannah went to Bel-Air to pack her things. She could still remember the zero-gravity feeling of that trip. The lack of restraint that came with their commitment to each other, every touch, every whisper heightened, given new meaning. And yet, on the verge of what felt like true adulthood, they'd both been scared. But they'd been scared together, honest with each other every step of the way, and they'd become a formidable team.

Initially, they'd signed an apartment lease in town, this midway point between Westport and Seattle. She still missed that apartment sometimes, itched to walk the creaky floor and remember all the lessons they'd learned within those walls. How fiercely they'd loved, how loudly they'd fought and made up, the music they'd danced to, how Fox had gotten down on one knee on a night just like this and asked Hannah to be his wife, how they'd panicked when she got pregnant a year later. How they'd sat on the floor and eaten cake straight out of the box with forks—Fox in a suit, her in a dress—on the morning they bought this house.

Since then, they'd made a million memories, each day with a different soundtrack, and she cherished every single one.

Unable to wait another second to see Fox and the girls, Hannah opened the driver's-side door, careful not to slip on the driveway in her fancy wedge boots. Not practical in this weather, but she'd gone straight to LAX after her final client meeting. Thank God she wouldn't have to see the inside of another airport until mid-January, well after the holidays. Her travel schedule had definitely lightened over the years, the process more streamlined and virtual, but every once in a while, she discovered a band worth seeing in person, as she'd done this week.

Garden of Sound Inc. had started as Hannah's baby, a way of connecting up-and-coming bands with film production companies seeking fresh voices for their scores—and years later, she'd found herself a staple in the industry. After *Glory Daze* released and the Unreliables blew up, her name got passed around more and more. She'd built a reputation for giving films their signature sound, adding an entirely new layer of creativity to the process, and she couldn't imagine doing anything else.

Hannah opened the back door of the Jeep and considered calling Fox to help her carry the bags, but decided she'd rather walk through the front door and surprise the three of them. And she'd better get her butt moving, because Piper, Brendan, and their two kids would be arriving soon to stay through New Year's. Not to mention, Charlene—aka Grams—would be here in the morning.

Draping a heavy bag over each arm, Hannah bumped the car door shut with a hip and headed up the path, her cheeks already aching from smiling. She set down the presents just outside the front door and dug in her coat pocket for her keys. They jingled only slightly, but that was all it took to set off their pair of yellow labs barking.

Shaking her head and laughing, distracted by trying to get the key into the lock, Hannah almost didn't see the moose. But when the giant shadow moved in her periphery, she froze, slowly turning her head, mouth falling open in shock as the granddaddy of all moose moseyed toward her like they were going to have a casual chat in the supermarket. Moose were not especially dangerous animals, but they'd lived in this area long enough to hear about attacks. Usually the animals only reacted poorly when provoked, but she wasn't taking any chances. That thing could mow her down like a semitruck.

"Fox . . ." Hannah called, way too quietly to be detected by human ears. And then she dropped her keys in the snow. Come on. No way she was bending down to pick those up. She'd have to take her eyes off the beast. Abandoning the presents and sidestepping off the porch slowly, she backed in the direction of the car. The moose watched from its height of at least thirteen, maybe twenty-nine feet while Hannah slipped the cell from her pocket and dialed HOME.

"You must be outside, since the dogs are acting like maniacs," Fox answered, voice warm in her ear. "Thank God, babe. I missed you like hell. You need some help carrying in your suitcase? I'll be right—"

"Moose," she said in a strangled whisper. "There's a moose right outside the door. Keep the girls inside. It's eight hundred feet tall, I'm not even kidding."

"A moose?" Concern hardened his voice. "Hannah, get inside."

"I dropped my keys." She turned and ran, squealing in her throat the whole way. "I'm hiding behind the car."

He was breathing hard. "I'm coming."

No less than ten seconds later, her husband skidded out onto the porch, barefoot in sweatpants and a hoodie, banging pots together and shouting obscenities at the moose, backing the animal up several paces. In the front window of the house, their girls—six-year-old Abigail and four-year-old Stevie— screamed bloody murder, their little palms slapping against the window hard enough to rattle it. The dogs howled. And crouching down behind the back bumper of the Jeep, Hannah absolutely lost it. She laughed hard enough to slip on the driveway and land on her backside, which only made her laugh harder. By the time she got control of herself, she was looking up at Fox through tears of mirth.

Oh, but then, there was just . . . a long, wobbly sigh of appreciation for the man holding out his rope-worn hand to help her up. Age had done him so good. Now forty-one, the *Della Ray*'s captain had a full beard and dark blond hair, just beginning to show threads of gray, that almost reached his shoulders. He'd cut it once, last year, and the girls cried when they saw the shorter length, so he vowed to keep it long forever. They had their father wrapped around their pinkie fingers, and he would admit it to anyone who listened. Hannah estimated the devotion to his daughters made him around 400 percent more attractive.

And as always, his devotion to Hannah shone in his blue eyes, which were twinkling over the chaos, just like hers.

"He's gone," Fox said gruffly, wrapping their fingers together. "Come inside now and make up for scaring ten years off my life."

"Should be easy since I brought presents—"

She lost her balance, slipping on the ice, and Fox, his balance normally perfect thanks to his profession, went down with his wife. He tried to cushion her fall, but they just ended up sprawled on their asses in the driveway, snow falling around them, their howls of laughter bringing their daughters running from the house in flannel nightgowns and hastily shoved-on boots. While Abby and Stevie started an impromptu snowball fight, Fox pulled Hannah into his arms, tipping up her chin so he could look at her face, his heart knocking heavily against her shoulder.

"Jesus, Hannah," he whispered in a rough voice. "Do you ever get so happy, you can barely stand it?"

"Yes." She reached up and cradled his jaw. "With you? All the time."

He made a sound in his throat, brushed some snowflakes from her cheek. "Doesn't feel like enough to say I love you at this point."

"Our love is always enough. It's always more than enough."

Throat flexing, he nodded. Looked into her eyes for long moments, before lowering his lips and kissing her slowly, sweeping his tongue through her mouth enough times and with enough promise to make her squirm, breathless. One kiss only ignited their appetite, and with the dogs happily chasing the girls through the front yard, they were in no rush to stop. Not until minutes later when another car pulled up and Piper's giggle sailed out into the evening air, followed by Brendan's exasperated sigh.

"Hey, Aunt Hannah and Uncle Fox!" their nine-year-old nephew, Henry, called. "Get a room."

"We've got a whole house of them," Fox said, finally standing and pulling Hannah to her feet, tucking her against his side. "We've got everything we could ever want," he added, for her ears alone. And together, aunts, uncles, cousins, and dogs walked up the path to share Christmas Eve, same as they would every single Christmas, forever and always.

Have you read Piper's story? Find out how she

hooked a surly, sexy sea captain in . . .

IT HAPPENED ONE SUMMER

Available now!

Read on for a peek at the first few chapters.

Chapter One

The unthinkable was happening.

Her longest relationship on record . . . over in the blink of an eye.

Three weeks of her life *wasted*.

Piper Bellinger looked down at her lipstick-red, one-shoulder Valentino cocktail dress and tried to find the flaw but came up with nothing. Her tastefully tanned legs were polished to such a shine, she'd checked her teeth in them earlier. Nothing appeared amiss up top, either. She'd swiped the tape holding up her boobs while backstage at a runway show in Milan during fashion week—we're talking the holy grail of tit tape—and those puppies were on point. Big enough to draw a man's eye, small enough to achieve an athletic vibe in every fourth Instagram post. Versatility kept people interested.

Satisfied that nothing concerning her appearance was glaringly out of place, Piper trailed her gaze up the pleated leg of Adrian's classic Tom Ford suit made of the finest sharkskin wool, unable to quell a sigh over the luxurious peak lapels and monogrammed buttons. The way her boyfriend impatiently checked his Chopard watch and scanned the crowd over her shoulder only added to the bored-playboy effect.

Hadn't his cold unattainability attracted her to him in the first place?

God, the night of their first meeting seemed like a hundred years ago. She'd had at least two facials since then, right? What *was* time anymore? Piper could remember their introduction like it was yesterday. Adrian had saved her from stepping in vomit at Rumer Willis's birthday party. As she'd stared up at his chiseled chin from her place in his arms, she'd been transported to Old Hollywood. A time of smoking jackets and women traipsing around in long, feathered robes. It was the beginning of her own classic love story.

And now the credits were rolling.

"I can't believe you're throwing it all away like this," Piper whispered, pressing her champagne flute between her breasts. Maybe drawing his attention there would change his mind? "We've been through so much."

"Yeah, tons, right?"

Adrian waved at someone across the rooftop, his expression letting whoever it was know that he'd be right with them. They'd come to the black, white, and red party together. A minor soiree to raise money for an indie movie project called *Lifestyles of the Oppressed and Famous*. The writer-director was a friend of Adrian's, meaning most of the people at this gathering of Los Angeles elite were his acquaintances. Her girls weren't even there to console her or facilitate a graceful exit.

Adrian's attention settled back on her reluctantly. "Wait, what were you saying?"

Piper's smile felt brittle, so she turned it up another watt, careful to keep it one crucial notch below manic. *Chin up, woman.* This wasn't her first breakup, right? She'd done a lot of the dumping, often unexpectedly. This was a town of whims, after all.

She'd never really noticed the pace of how things changed. Not until lately.

At twenty-eight, Piper was not old. But she *was* one of the oldest women at this party. At every party she'd been to recently, come to think of it. Leaning on the glass railing that overlooked Melrose was an up-and-coming pop star who couldn't be a day older than nineteen. She didn't need tape from Milan to hold up her tits. They were light and springy with nipples that reminded Piper of the bottom of an ice cream cone.

The host himself was twenty-two and embarking on a film career.

This was Piper's career. Partying. Being seen. Holding up the occasional teeth-whitening product and getting a few dollars for it.

Not that she needed the money. At least, she didn't think so. Everything she owned came from the swipe of a credit card, and it was a mystery what happened after that. She assumed the bill went to her stepfather's email or something? Hopefully he wouldn't be weird about the crotchless panties she'd ordered from Paris.

"Piper? *Hello?*" Adrian swiped a hand in front of her face, and she realized how long she'd been staring at the pop star. Long enough that the songstress was glaring back.

Piper smiled and waved at the girl, pointing sheepishly to her glass of champagne, before tuning back in to the conversation with Adrian. "Is this because I casually brought you up to my therapist? We didn't go in depth or anything, I promise. Most of the time we just nap during my appointments."

He stared at her for several seconds. Honestly, it was kind of nice. It was the most attention she'd gotten from him since almost slipping in puke. "I've dated some airheads, Piper." He sighed. "But you put them all to shame."

She kept her smile in place, though it took more determination than usual. People were watching. At that very moment, she was in the background of at least five selfies being captured around the roof, including one of Ansel Elgort. It would be a disaster if she let her sinking heart show on her face, especially when news of the breakup got out. "I don't understand," she said with a laugh, sweeping rose-gold hair over her shoulder.

"Shocking," he returned drily. "Look, babe. It was a fun three weeks. You're a smoke show in a bikini." He shrugged an elegant Tom Ford–clad shoulder. "I'm just trying to end this before it gets boring, you know?"

Boring. Getting older. Not a director or a pop star.

Just a pretty girl with a millionaire stepfather.

Piper couldn't think about that now, though. She just wanted to exit the party as inconspicuously as possible and go have a good cry. After she popped a Xanax and posted an inspirational quote on her IG feed, of course. It would confirm the breakup, but also allow her to control the narrative. Something about growth and loving herself, maybe?

Her sister, Hannah, would have the perfect song lyric to include. She was always sitting around in a pile of vinyls, those giant, ugly headphones wrapped around her head. Damn, she wished she'd put more stock in Hannah's opinion of Adrian.

What had she said? Oh yeah.

He's like if someone drew eyes on a turnip.

Once again, Piper had zoned out, and Adrian checked his watch for the second time. "Are we done here? I have to mingle."

"Oh. *Yeah*," she rushed to say, her voice horrifyingly unnatural. "You couldn't be more right about breaking things off before the boring blues strike. I didn't think about it like that." She clinked her champagne glass against his. "We're consciously uncoupling. *Très* mature."

"Right. Call it whatever you want." Adrian forced a wan smile. "Thanks for everything."

"No, thank *you*." She pursed her lips, trying to appear as non-airhead-like as possible. "I've learned a lot about myself over the last three weeks."

"Come on, Piper." Adrian laughed, scrutinizing her head to toe. "You play dress-up and spend your daddy's money. You don't have a reason to learn anything."

"Do I need a reason?" she asked lightly, lips still tilted at the corners.

Annoyed at being waylaid, Adrian huffed a breath. "I guess not. But you definitely need a brain that functions beyond how many likes you can get on a picture of your rack. There's more to life than that, Piper."

"Yes, I know," she said, prodded by irritation—and more than a little bit of reluctant shame. "Life is what I'm documenting through photos. I—"

"God." He half groaned, half laughed. "Why are you *forcing* me to be an asshole?" Someone called his name from inside the penthouse, and he held up a finger, keeping his gaze locked on Piper. "There's just nothing to you, okay? There are thousands of Piper Bellingers in this city. You're just a way to pass the time." He shrugged. "And your time has passed."

It was a miracle Piper kept her winning smile intact as Adrian sailed away, already calling out to his friends. Everyone on the roof deck was staring at her, whispering behind their hands, feeling sorry for her—of all the horrors. She saluted them with her glass, then realized it was empty. Setting it down on the tray of a passing waiter, she collected her Bottega Veneta satin knot clutch with all the dignity she could muster and glided through the throng of onlookers, blinking back the moisture in her eyes to bring the elevator call button into focus.

When the doors finally hid her from view, she slumped back against the metal wall, taking deep breaths in through her nose, out through her mouth. Already the news that she'd been dumped by Adrian would be blasted across all the socials, maybe even with video included. Not even C-list celebrities would invite her to parties after this.

She had a reputation as a good time. Someone to covet. An "it girl."

If she didn't have her social status, what *did* she have?

Piper pulled her phone out of her clutch and absently requested a luxury Uber, connecting her with a driver who was only five minutes away. Then she closed the app and pulled up her favorites list. Her thumb hovered over the name "Hannah" momentarily, but landed on "Kirby," instead. Her friend answered on the first ring.

"Oh my God, is it true you begged Adrian not to break up with you in front of Ansel Elgort?"

It was worse than she thought. How many people had already tipped off TMZ? Tomorrow night at six thirty, they would be tossing her name around the newsroom while Harvey sipped from his reusable cup. "I didn't beg Adrian to keep me. Come on, Kirby, you know me better than that."

"Bitch, I do. But I'm not everyone else. You need to do damage control. Do you have a publicist on retainer?"

"Not anymore. Daniel said me going shopping doesn't need a press release."

Kirby snorted. "Okay, boomer."

"But you're right. I do need damage control." The elevator doors opened, and Piper stepped off, clicking through the lobby in her red-soled pumps, eventually stepping out onto Wilshire, the warm July air drying the dampness in her eyes. The tall buildings of downtown Los Angeles reached up into the smoggy summer night sky, and she craned her neck to find the tops. "How late is the rooftop pool open at the Mondrian?"

"You're asking about hours of operation at a time like this?" Kirby griped, followed by the sound of her vape crackling in the background. "I don't know, but it's past midnight. If it's not already closed, it will be soon."

A black Lincoln pulled up along the curb. After double-checking the license plate number, Piper climbed inside and shut the door. "Wouldn't breaking into the pool and having the time of our lives be, like, *the* best way to fight fire with fire? Adrian would be the guy who broke up with a legend."

"Oh shit," Kirby breathed. "You're resurrecting Piper twenty fourteen."

This was the answer, wasn't it? There was no better time in her life than the year she turned twenty-one and ran absolutely buck wild through Los Angeles, making herself famous for being famous in the process. She was just in a rut, that was all. Maybe it was time to reclaim her crown. Maybe then she wouldn't hear Adrian's words looping over and over again in the back of her head, forcing her to consider that he might be right.

Am I just one of thousands?

Or am I the girl who breaks into a pool for a swim at one o'clock in the morning?

Piper nodded resolutely and leaned forward. "Can you take me to the Mondrian, instead, please?"

Kirby hooted down the line. "I'll meet you there."

"I've got a better idea." Piper crossed her legs and fell back in the leather seat. "How about we have *everyone* meet us there?"

Chapter Two

Jail was a cold, dark place.

Piper stood in the very center of the cell shivering and hugging her elbows so she wouldn't accidentally touch anything that might require a tetanus shot. Until this moment, the word "torture" had only been a vague description of something she'd never understand. But trying to *not pee* in the moldy toilet after roughly six mixed drinks was a torment no woman should ever know. The late-night Coachella bathroom situation had nothing on this grimy metal throne that mocked her from the corner of the cell.

"Excuse me?" Piper called, wobbling to the bars in her heels. There were no guards in sight, but she could hear the distinctive sounds of *Candy Crush* coming from nearby. "Hi, it's me, Piper. Is there another bathroom I could use?"

"No, princess," a woman's voice called back, sounding very bored. "There isn't."

She bounced side to side, her bladder demanding to be evacuated. "Where do *you* go to the bathroom?"

A snort. "Where the *other* non-criminals go."

Piper whined in her throat, although the lady guard went up a notch in her book for delivering such a savage response without hesitation. "I'm not a criminal," Piper tried again. "This is all a misunderstanding."

A trill of laughter echoed down the drab hallway of the police station. How many times had she passed the station on North Wilcox? Now she was an inmate.

But seriously, it had been one hell of a party.

The guard slowly appeared in front of Piper's cell, fingers tucked into her beige uniform pants. *Beige.* Whoever was at the helm of law enforcement fashion should be sentenced for cruel and unusual punishment. "You call two hundred people breaking into a hotel pool after hours a misunderstanding?"

Piper crossed her legs and sucked in a breath through her nose. If she peed herself in Valentino, she would voluntarily remain in jail. "Would you believe the pool hours weren't prominently posted?"

"Is that the argument your expensive lawyer is going to use?" The guard shook her head, visibly amused. "Someone had to shatter the glass door to get inside and let all the other rich kids in. Who did that? The invisible man?"

"I don't know, but I'm going to find out," Piper vowed solemnly.

The guard sighed through a smile. "It's too late for that, sweetheart. Your friend with the purple tips already named you as the ringleader."

Kirby.

Had to be.

No one else at the party had purple tips. At least, Piper didn't think so. Somewhere between the chicken fights in the pool and the illegal firecrackers being set off, she'd kind of lost track of the incoming guests. She should have known better than to trust Kirby, though. She and Piper were friends, but not good enough for her to lie to the police. The foundation of their relationship was commenting on each other's social media posts and enabling each other to make ridiculous purchases, like a four-thousand-dollar purse shaped like a tube of lipstick. Most times, those kinds of surface-level friendships were valuable, but not tonight.

That's why her one phone call had gone to Hannah.

Speaking of whom, where *was* her little sister? She'd made that call an hour ago.

Piper hopped side to side, dangerously close to using her hands to keep the urine contained. "Who is forcing you to wear beige pants?" she gasped. "Why aren't they in here with me?"

"Fine." The guard flashed a palm. "On this we can agree."

"Literally any other color would be better. *No* pants would be better." Trying to distract herself from the Chernobyl happening in her lower body, she rambled, as she was wont to do in uncomfortable situations. "You have a really cute figure, Officer, but it's, like, a commandment that no one shall pull off nude khaki."

The other woman's eyebrow arched. "You could."

"You're right," Piper sobbed. "I totally could."

The guard's laugh faded into a sigh. "What were you thinking, inciting that chaos tonight?"

Piper slumped a little. "My boyfriend dumped me. And he . . . didn't even look me in the eye the whole time. I guess I just wanted to be seen. Acknowledged. Celebrated instead of . . . disregarded. You know?"

"Scorned and acting like a fool. Can't say I haven't been there."

"Really?" Piper asked hopefully.

"Sure. Who hasn't put all their boyfriend's clothes in the bathtub and poured bleach on top?"

Piper thought of the Tom Ford suit turning splotchy, and shivered. "That's cold," she whispered. "Maybe I should have just slashed his tires. At least that's legal."

"That's . . . not legal."

"Oh." Piper sent the guard an exaggerated wink. "*Riiiight.*"

The woman shook her head, glancing up and down the hallway. "All right, look. It's a quiet night. If you don't give me any trouble, I'll let you use the slightly less shitty bathroom."

"Oh, thank you, thank you, thank you."

With her keys poised over the keyhole, the guard hit her with serious eyes. "I have a Taser."

Piper followed her savior down the hall to the bathroom, where she meticulously gathered the skirt of her Valentino and eased the unholy pressure in her bladder, moaning until the final drop fell. As she washed her hands in the small sink, her attention caught on the reflection in the mirror. Raccoon eyes looked back at her. Smeared lipstick, limp hair. Definitely a long way from where she'd begun the evening, but she couldn't help but feel like a soldier returning from battle. She'd set out to divert attention from her breakup, hadn't she?

An LAPD helicopter circling overhead while she led a conga line had definitely reaffirmed her status as the reigning party queen of Los Angeles. Probably. They'd confiscated her phone during the whole mug shot/fingerprint thing, so she didn't know what was happening on the internet. Her fingers were itching to tap some apps, and that's exactly what she would do as soon as Hannah arrived to bail her out.

She looked at her reflection, surprised to find the prospect of breaking the internet didn't set her heart into a thrilling pitter-patter the way it did before. Was she broken?

Piper snorted and pushed away from the sink, using an elbow to pull down the door handle upon leaving. Obviously the night had taken its toll—after all, it was nearly five o'clock in the morning. As soon as she got some sleep, she'd spend the day reveling in congratulatory texts and an inundation of new followers. All would be well.

The guard cuffed Piper again and started to walk her back to the cell, just as another guard called down to them from the opposite end. "Yo, Lina. Bellinger made bail. Bring her down to processing."

Her arms flew up in victory. *"Yes!"*

Lina laughed. "Come on, beauty queen."

Vigor restored, Piper skipped alongside the other woman. "Lina, huh? I owe you big-time." She clutched her hands beneath her chin and gave her a winning pout. "Thank you for being so nice to me."

"Don't read too much into it," drawled the guard, though her expression was pleased. "I just wasn't in the mood to clean up piss."

Piper laughed, allowing Lina to unlock the door at the end of the gray hallway. And there was Hannah in the processing area, wearing pajamas and a ball cap, filling out paperwork with her eyes half closed.

Warmth wiggled into Piper's chest at the sight of her younger sister. They were nothing alike, had even less in common, but there was no one else Piper would call in a pinch. Of the two sisters, Hannah was the dependable one, even though she had a lazy hippie side.

Where Piper was taller, Hannah had been called a shrimp growing up and never quite hit the middle school growth spurt. At the moment, she kept her petite figure buried under a UCLA sweatshirt, her sandy-blond hair poking out around the blank red hat.

"She clear?" Lina asked a thin-lipped man hunched behind the desk.

He waved a hand without looking up. "Money solves everything."

Lina unlocked her cuffs once again, and she shot forward. "*Hannnnns*," Piper whimpered, throwing her arms around her sister. "I'll pay you back for this. I'll do your chores for a week."

"We don't have chores, you radish." Hannah yawned, grinding a fist into her eye. "Why do you smell like incense?"

"Oh." Piper sniffed her shoulder. "I think the fortune-teller lit some." Straightening, she squinted her eyes. "Not sure how she found out about the party."

Hannah gaped, seeming to awaken at least marginally, her hazel eyes a total contrast to Piper's baby blues. "Did she happen to tell you there's an angry stepfather in your future?"

Piper winced. "Oof. I had a feeling I couldn't avoid the wrath of Daniel Q. Bellinger." She craned her neck to see if there was anyone retrieving her phone. "How did he find out?"

"The news, Pipes. The news."

"Right." She sighed, smoothing her hands down the rumpled skirt of her dress. "Nothing the lawyers can't handle, right?

Hopefully he'll let me get in a shower and some sleep before one of his famous lectures. I'm a walking *after* photo."

"Shut up, you look great," Hannah said, her lips twitching as she completed the paperwork with a flourish of her signature. "You always look great."

Piper did a little shimmy.

"Bye, Lina!" Piper called on the way out of the station, her beloved phone cradled in her arms like a newborn, fingers vibrating with the need to swipe. She'd been directed to the back exit where Hannah could pull the car around. *Protocol*, they'd said.

She took one step out the door and was surrounded by photographers. "Piper! Over here!"

Her vanity screeched like a pterodactyl.

Nerves swerved right and left in her belly, but she flashed them a quick smile and put her head down, clicking as fast as she could toward Hannah's waiting Jeep.

"Piper Bellinger!" one of the paparazzi shouted. "How was your night in jail?"

"Do you regret wasting taxpayer money?"

The toe of her high heel caught in a crack, and she almost sprawled face-first onto the asphalt but caught the edge of the door Hannah had pushed open, throwing herself into the passenger side. Closing the door helped cut off the shouted questions, but the last one she'd heard continued to blare in her mind.

Wasting taxpayer money? She'd just thrown a party, right?

Fine, it had taken a considerable amount of police officers to break it up, but like, this was Los Angeles. Weren't the police just waiting around for stuff like this to happen?

Okay, that sounded privileged and bratty even to her own ears.

Suddenly she wasn't so eager to check her social media.

She wiped her sweating palms on her dress. "I wasn't trying to put anyone out or waste money. I wasn't thinking that far ahead," Piper said quietly, twisting to face her sister as much as she could in a seat belt. "Is this bad, Hanns?"

Hannah's teeth were sunk into her lower lip, her hands on the wheel slowly navigating her way through the people frantically snapping Piper's picture. "It's not good," she answered after a pause. "But hey, you used to pull stunts like this all the time, remember? The lawyers always find a way to spin it, and tomorrow they'll be onto something else." She reached out and tapped the touch screen, and a low melody flooded the car. "Check it out. I have the perfect song cued up for this moment."

The somber notes of "Prison Women" by REO Speedwagon floated out from the speakers.

Piper's skull thudded against the headrest. "Very funny." She tapped her phone against her knee for a few seconds, before snapping her spine straight and opening Instagram.

There it was. The picture she'd posted early this morning, at 2:42, accused the time stamp. Kirby, the traitorous wench, had snapped it using Piper's phone. In the shot, Piper was perched on the shoulders of a man whose name she couldn't recall—though she had a vague recollection of him claiming to play second string for the Lakers?—stripped down to panties and boob tape, but like, in an artistic way. Her Valentino dress was draped over a lounge chair in the background. Firecrackers went off around her like the Fourth of July, swathing Piper in sparkles and smoke. She looked like a goddess rising from an electric mist—and the picture was nearing a million likes.

Telling herself not to, Piper tapped the highlighted section that would show her exactly *who* had liked the picture. Adrian wasn't one of them.

Which was fine. A million other people had, right?

But they hadn't spent three weeks with her.

To them, she was just a two-dimensional image. If they spent more than three weeks with Piper, would they scroll past, too? Letting her sink into the blur of the thousand other girls just like her?

"Hey," Hannah said, pausing the song. "It's going to be all right."

Piper's laugh sounded forced, so she cut it short. "I know. It always turns out all right." She pressed her lips together. "Want to hear about the wet boxers competition?"

Chapter Three

$\mathcal{I}$t was *not* all right, as it turned out.

Nothing was.

Not according to their stepfather, Daniel Bellinger, revered Academy Award–winning movie producer, philanthropist, and competitive yachtsman.

Piper and Hannah had attempted to creep in through the catering entrance of their Bel-Air mansion. They'd moved in when Piper was four and Hannah two, after their mother married Daniel, and neither of them could remember living anywhere else. Every once in a while, when Piper caught a whiff of the ocean, her memory sent up a signal through the fog, reminding her of the Pacific Northwest town where she'd been born, but there was nothing substantial to cling to and it always drifted away before she could grasp on.

Now, her stepfather's wrath? She could fully grasp that.

It was etched into the tanned lines of his famous face, in the disappointed headshakes he gave the sisters as they sat, side by side, on a couch in his home office. Behind him, awards gleamed on shelves, framed movie posters hung on walls, and the phone on his L-shaped desk lit up every two seconds, although he'd silenced it for the upcoming lecture. Their mother was at Pilates, and out of everything? *That* made Piper the most nervous. Maureen tended to have a calming effect on her husband—and he was anything but calm right now.

"Um, Daniel?" Piper chanced brightly, tucking a piece of wilted hair behind her ear. "None of this is Hannah's fault. Is it okay if she heads to bed?"

"She stays." He pinned Hannah with a stern look. "You were forbidden to bail her out and did it anyway."

Piper turned her astonishment on her sister. "You did what?"

"What was I supposed to do?" Hannah whipped off her hat and wrung it between her knees. "Leave you there, Pipes?"

"Yeah," Piper said slowly, facing her stepfather with mounting horror. "What did you want her to do? *Leave* me there?"

Agitated, Daniel shoved his fingers through his hair. "I thought you learned your lesson a long time ago, Piper. Or *lessons*, plural, rather. You were still flitting around to every goddamn party between here and the Valley, but you weren't costing me money or making me look like a fucking idiot in the process."

"Ouch." Piper sunk back into the couch cushions. "You don't have to be mean."

"I don't have to be—" Daniel made an exasperated sound and pinched the bridge of his nose. "You are twenty-eight years old, Piper, and you have done nothing with your life. *Nothing.* You've been afforded every opportunity, given anything your little heart could ask for, and all you have to show for it is a . . . a digital existence. It means *nothing.*"

If that's true, then I mean nothing, too.

Piper snagged a pillow and held it over her roiling stomach, giving Hannah a grateful look when she reached over to rub her knee. "Daniel, I'm sorry. I had a bad breakup last night and I acted out. I won't do anything like that ever again."

Daniel seemed to deflate a little, retreating to his desk to lean on the edge. "No one handed me anything in this business. I started as a page on the Paramount lot. Filling sandwich orders, fetching coffee. I was an errand boy while I worked my way through film school." Piper nodded, doing her best to appear deeply interested, even though Daniel told this story at every dinner party and charity event. "I stayed ready, armed with knowledge and drive, just waiting for my opportunity, so I could seize it"—he snapped his fist closed—"and never look back."

"That's when you were asked to run lines with Corbin Kidder," Piper recited from memory.

"Yes." Her stepfather inclined his head, momentarily pleased to find out she'd been paying attention. "As the director looked on, I not only delivered the lines with passion and zeal, but I *improved* the tired text. Added my own flair."

"And you were brought on as a writer's assistant." Hannah sighed, winding her finger for him to wrap up the oft-repeated story. "For Kubrick himself."

He exhaled through his nose. "That's right. And it brings me back to my original point." A finger was wagged. "Piper, you're too comfortable. At least Hannah earned a degree and is gainfully employed. Even if I called in favors to get her the location scout gig, at least she's productive." Hannah hunched her shoulders but said nothing. "Would you even care if opportunity came knocking on your door, Piper? You have no drive to go anywhere. Or do anything. Why would you when this life I've provided you is always here, rewarding your lack of ambition with comfort and an excuse to remain blissfully stagnant?"

Piper stared up at the man she thought of as a father, stunned to find out he'd been seeing her in such a negative light. She'd grown up in Bel-Air. Vacationing and throwing pool parties and rubbing elbows with famous actors. This was the only life she knew. None of her friends worked. Only a handful of them had bothered with college. What was the point of a degree? To make money? They already had tons of it.

If Daniel or her mother had ever encouraged her to do something else, she couldn't remember any such conversation. Was motivation a thing that other people were simply born with? And when the time came to make their way in the world, they simply acted? Should she have been looking for a purpose this whole time?

Weirdly, none of the inspirational quotes she'd posted in the past held the answer.

"I love your mother very much," Daniel continued, as if reading her mind. "Or I don't think I would have been this patient for so long. But, Piper . . . you went too far this time."

Her eyes shot to his, her knees beginning to tremble. Had he ever used that resigned tone with her before? If so, she didn't recall. "I did?" she whispered.

Beside her, Hannah shifted, a sign she was picking up on the gravity of the moment, too.

Daniel bobbed his head. "The owner of the Mondrian is financing my next film." That news landed like a grenade in the center of the office. "He's not happy about last night, to put it quite mildly. You made his hotel seem like it lacks security. You made it a laughingstock. And worse, you could have burned the goddamn place down." He stared at her with hard eyes, letting it all sink in. "He's threatened to pull the budget, Piper. It's a very considerable amount. The movie will not get made without his contribution. At least not until I find another backer—and it could take me years in this economy."

"I'm sorry," Piper breathed, the magnitude of what she'd done sinking her even farther into the couch cushions. Had she really blown a business deal for Daniel in the name of posting a revenge snap that would make her triumphant in a breakup? Was she that frivolous and stupid?

Had Adrian been right?

"I didn't know. I . . . I had no idea who owned the hotel."

"No, of course not. Who cares who your actions affect, right, Piper?"

"All right." Hannah sat forward with a frown. "You don't have to be so hard on her. She obviously realizes she made a mistake."

Daniel remained unfazed. "Well, it's a mistake she's going to answer for."

Piper and Hannah traded a glance. "What do you mean by"— Piper wiggled her fingers in the shape of air quotes—"'answer for'?"

Their stepfather took his time rounding his desk and opening the bottom filing drawer, hesitating only a moment before removing a manila folder. He tapped it steadily on his desk calendar, considering the nervous sisters through narrowed eyes. "We don't talk a lot about your past. The time before I married your mother. I'll admit that's mostly because I'm selfish and I didn't want reminders that she loved someone before me."

"Awww," Piper said automatically.

He ignored her. "As you know, your father was a fisherman. He lived in Westport, Washington, the same town where your mother was born. Quaint little place."

Piper started at the mention of her birth father. A king crab fisherman named Henry who'd died a young man, sucked down into the icy depths of the Bering Sea. Her eyes drifted to the window, to the world beyond, trying to remember what came *before* this swanky life to which she'd grown so accustomed. The landscape and color of the first four years of her life were elusive, but she could remember the outline of her father's head. Could remember his cracking laugh, the smell of salt water on his skin.

Could remember her mother's laughter echoing in kind, warm and sweet.

There was no way to wrap her head around that other time and place—how different it was from her current situation—and she'd tried many times. If Maureen hadn't moved to Los Angeles as a grieving widow, armed with nothing more than good looks and being a dab hand at sewing, she never would have landed a job working in wardrobe on Daniel's first film. He wouldn't have fallen in love with her, and this lavish lifestyle of theirs would be nothing more than a dream, while Maureen existed in some other, unimaginable timeline.

"Westport," Hannah repeated, as if testing the word on her tongue. "Mom never told us the name."

"Yes, well. I can imagine everything that happened was painful for her." He sniffed, tapping the edge of the folder again. "Obviously she's fine now. Better than fine." A beat passed. "The men in Westport . . . they head to the Bering Sea during king crab season, in search of their annual payday. But it's not always reliable. Sometimes they catch very little and have to split a minor sum among a large crew. Because of this, your father also owned a small bar."

Piper's lips edged up into a smile. This was the most anyone had ever spoken to her about their birth father, and the details . . . they were like coins dropping into an empty jar inside of her, slowly filling it up. She wanted more. She wanted to know everything about this man whom she could only remember for his boisterous laugh.

Hannah cleared her throat, her thigh pressing against Piper's. "Why are you telling us all of this now?" She chewed her lip. "What's in the folder?"

"The deed to the bar. He left the building to you girls in his will." He set the folder down on his desk and flipped it open. "A long time ago, I put a custodian in place, to make sure it didn't fall into disrepair, but truthfully, I'd forgotten all about it until now."

"Oh my God . . ." Hannah said under her breath, obviously predicting some outcome to this conversation that Piper was not yet grasping. "A-are you . . . ?"

Daniel sighed in the wake of Hannah's trailed-off question. "My investor is demanding a show of contrition for what you did, Piper. He's a self-made man like me and would like nothing more than to stick it to me over my spoiled, rich-kid daughter." Piper flinched, but he didn't see it because he was scanning the contents of the file. "Normally I would tell anyone who demanded something from me to fuck off . . . but I can't ignore my gut feeling that you need to learn to fend for yourself for a while."

"What do you mean by"—Piper did air quotes again—"'fend'?"

"I *mean* you're getting out of your comfort zone. I *mean* you're going to Westport."

Hannah's mouth dropped open.

Piper shot forward. "Wait. What? For how long? What am I supposed to do there?" She turned her panicked gaze on Hannah. "Does Mom know about this?"

"Yes," Maureen said from the office doorway. "She knows."

Piper whimpered into her wrist.

"Three months, Pipes. You can make it that long. And I hope you would do it without hesitation, considering I'll maintain my film budget by making these amends." Daniel came around the desk and dropped the manila folder into Piper's lap. She stared at it like one might a scuttling cockroach. "There is a small apartment above the bar. I've called ahead to make sure it's cleaned. I'm setting up a debit account to get you started, but after that . . ." Oh, he looked way too pleased. "You're on your own."

Mentally listing all of the galas and fashion shows that would happen over the course of three whole months, Piper got to her feet and sent her mother a pleading look. "Mom, you're really going to let him send me away?" She was reeling. "What am I supposed to do? Like, fish for a living? I don't even know how to make toast."

"I'm confident you'll figure it out," Maureen said softly, her expression sympathetic but firm. "This will be good for you. You'll see. You might even learn something about yourself."

"No." Piper shook her head. Didn't last night yield the revelation that she was good for nothing but partying and looking hot? She didn't have the survival skills for a life outside of these gates. But she could cope with that as long as everything stayed familiar. Out there, her ineptitude, her uselessness, would be *glaring*. "I—I'm not going."

"Then I'm not paying your legal fees," Daniel said reluctantly.

"I'm shaking," Piper whispered, holding up a flat, quaking hand. "Look at me."

Hannah threw an arm around her sister. "I'm going with her."

Daniel did a double take. "What about your job? I pulled strings with Sergei to get you a coveted spot with the production company."

At the mention of Sergei, Hannah's long-standing crush, Piper felt her sister's split second of indecision. For the last year, the youngest Bellinger had been pining for the broody Hollywood upstart whose debut film, *Nobody's Baby*, had taken the Palme d'Or at Cannes. Most of the ballads constantly blaring from Hannah's room could be attributed to her deep infatuation.

Her sister's solidarity made Piper's throat feel tight, but there was no way she'd allow her sins to banish her favorite person to Westport, too. Piper herself wasn't even resigned to going yet. "Daniel will change his mind," she whispered out of the side of her mouth to Hannah. "It'll be fine."

"I will not," Daniel boomed, looking offended. "You leave at the end of July."

Piper did a mental count. "That's, like, only a few weeks from now!"

"I'd tell you to use the time to tie up your affairs, but you don't have any."

Maureen made a sound. "I think that's enough, Daniel." With a face full of censure, she corralled the stunned sisters out of the room. "Come on. Let's take some time to process."

The three Bellinger women ascended the stairs together, climbing up to the third floor where Hannah's and Piper's bedrooms waited on opposite sides of the carpeted hall. They drifted into Piper's room, settling her on the edge of the bed, and then stepped back to observe her as if they were medical students being asked to make a diagnosis.

Hands on knees, Hannah analyzed her face. "How are you doing, Piper?"

"Can you really not get him to change his mind, Mom?" Piper croaked.

Maureen shook her head. "I'm sorry, sweetie." Her mother fell onto the bed beside her, taking her limp hand. For long moments, she was quiet, clearly gearing up for something. "I think part of the reason I didn't fight Daniel very hard on sending you to Westport is . . . well, I have a lot of guilt for keeping so much of your real father to myself. I was in so much pain for a long time. Bitter, too. And I bottled it all up, neglecting his memory in the process. That wasn't right of me." Her eyelids drifted down. "To go to Westport . . . is to meet your father, Piper. He *is* Westport. There's so much more history . . . still living in that town than you know. That's why I couldn't stay after he died. He was surrounding me . . . and I was just so angry over the unfairness of it all. Not even my parents could get through to me."

"How long did they stay in Westport after you left?" Hannah asked, referring to the grandparents who visited them on occasion, though the visits had grown few and far between as the sisters got older. When Daniel officially adopted Piper and Hannah, their grandparents hadn't seemed comfortable with the whole process, and the contact between them and Maureen had faded in degrees, even if they still spoke on holidays and birthdays.

"Not long. They bought the ranch in Utah shortly after. Far from the water." Maureen looked down at her hands. "The magic had gone out of the town for all of us, I think."

Piper could understand her mother's reasoning. Could sympathize with the guilt. But her entire life was being uprooted for a man she didn't know. Twenty-four years had gone by without a single word about Henry Cross. Her mother couldn't expect her to jump all over the opportunity now because she'd decided it was time to dump the guilt.

"This isn't fair," Piper groaned, falling backward on her bed, upsetting her ecru Millesimo bedsheets. Hannah sprawled out beside her, throwing an arm over Piper's stomach.

"It's only three months," Maureen said, rising and floating from the room. Just before she walked out, she turned back, hand poised on the doorframe. "Word to the wise, Piper. The men in Westport . . . they're not what you're used to. They're unpolished and direct. Capable in a way the men of your acquaintance . . . aren't." Her gaze grew distant. "Their job is dangerous and they don't care how much it scares you, they go back to the sea every time. They'll always choose it over a woman. And they'd rather die doing what they love than be safe at home."

The uncharacteristic gravity in Maureen's tone glued Piper to the bed. "Why are you telling me this?"

Her mother lifted a delicate shoulder. "That danger in a man can be exciting to a woman. Until it's not anymore. Then it's shattering. Just keep that in mind if you feel . . . drawn in."

Maureen seemed like she wanted to say more, but she tapped the doorframe twice and went, leaving the two sisters staring after her.

Piper reached back for a pillow and handed it to Hannah. "Smother me with this. Please. It's the humane thing to do."

"I'm coming with you to Westport."

"No. What about your job? And Sergei?" Piper exhaled. "You have good things happening here, Hanns. I'll find a way to cope." She gave Hannah a mock serious face. "They must have sugar daddies in Westport, right?"

"I'm definitely going with you."

Nisha Ver Halen

ABOUT THE AUTHOR

New York Times bestselling author Tessa Bailey aspires to three things: writing hot and unforgettable character-driven romance, being a good mother, and eventually sneaking onto the judging panel of a reality-show baking competition. She lives on Long Island, New York, with her husband and daughter, writing all day and rewarding herself with a cheese plate and Netflix binge in the evening. If you want sexy, heartfelt, humorous romance with a guaranteed happy ending, you've come to the right place.

MORE ROM-COMS BY TESSA BAILEY

Fix Her Up

A bad-boy professional baseball player falls for the girl next door . . . who also happens to be his best friend's little sister.

Love Her or Lose Her

A young married couple signs up for relationship boot camp in order to rehab their rocky romance and finds a second chance at love!

Tools of Engagement

Two enemies team up to flip a house . . . and the sparks between them might burn the place down or ignite a passion that neither can ignore!

It Happened One Summer

The *Schitt's Creek*-inspired TikTok sensation about a Hollywood "It Girl" who's cut off from her wealthy family and exiled to a small Pacific Northwest beach town . . . where she butts heads with a surly, sexy local who thinks she doesn't belong.